THE PARIS LIBRARY

JANET SKESLIEN CHARLES

ISIS
LARGE
PRINT

First published in Great Britain 2020
by
Two Roads
an imprint of John Murray Press

First Isis Edition
published 2021
by arrangement with
John Murray Press
An Hachette UK Company

A catalogue record for this book is available
from the British Library.

ISBN 978–1–78541–947–8

Published by
Ulverscroft Limited
Anstey, Leicestershire

Set by Words & Graphics Ltd.
Anstey, Leicestershire
Printed and bound in Great Britain by
T J Books Ltd., Padstow, Cornwall

For my parents

CHAPTER ONE

ODILE

Paris, February 1939

Numbers floated round my head like stars. 823. The numbers were the key to a new life. 822. Constellations of hope. 841. In my bedroom late at night, in the morning on the way to get croissants, series after series — 810, 840, 890 — formed in front of my eyes. They represented freedom, the future. Along with the numbers, I'd studied the history of libraries, going back to the 1500s. In England, while Henry VIII was busy chopping off his wives' heads, our King François was modernising his library, which he opened to scholars. His royal collection was the beginning of the Bibliothèque Nationale. Now, at the desk in my bedroom, I prepared for my job interview at the American Library, reviewing my notes one last time: founded in 1920; the first in Paris to let the public into the stacks; subscribers from over thirty countries, a quarter of them from France. I held fast to these facts and figures, hoping they'd make me appear qualified to the Directress.

I strode from my family's apartment on the sooty rue de Rome, across from the Saint-Lazare train station,

1

where locomotives coughed up smoke. The wind whipped my hair, and I tucked tendrils under my tam hat. In the distance, I could see the dome of Saint-Augustin Church. Religion, 200. Old Testament, 221. And the New Testament? I waited, but the number wouldn't come. I was so nervous that I forgot simple facts. I drew my notebook from my handbag. Ah, yes, 225. I knew that.

My favourite part of library school had been the Dewey Decimal System. Conceived in 1873 by the American librarian Melvil Dewey, it used ten classes to organise library books on shelves based on subject. There was a number for everything, allowing any reader to find any book in any library. For example, Maman took pride in her 648 (housekeeping). Papa wouldn't admit it, but he really did enjoy 785 (chamber music). My twin brother was more of a 636.8 person, while I preferred 636.7. (Cats and dogs, respectively.)

I arrived on *le grand boulevard* where, in the space of a block, the city shrugged off her working-class mantle and donned a mink coat. The coarse smell of coal dissipated, replaced by the honeyed jasmine of Joy, worn by women delighting in the window display of Nina Ricci's dresses and Kislav green leather gloves. Further along, I wound around musicians leaving the shop that sold wrinkled sheet music, past the baroque building with the blue door, and turned the corner, on to a narrow side street. I knew the way by heart.

I loved Paris, a city with secrets. Like book covers, some leather, some cloth, each Parisian door led to an unexpected world. A courtyard could contain a knot of

2

bicycles or a plump concierge armed with a broom. In the case of the Library, the massive wooden door opened to a secret garden. Bordered by petunias on one side, lawn on the other, the white pebbled path led to the brick and stone mansion. I crossed the threshold, beneath French and American flags fluttering side by side, and hung my jacket on the rickety coat-rack. Breathing in the best smell in the world — a *mélange* of the mossy scent of musty books and crisp newspaper pages — I felt as if I'd come home.

A few minutes early for the interview, I skirted the circulation desk, where the always debonair librarian listened to subscribers ("Where can a fella find a decent steak in Paris?" asked a newcomer in cowboy boots. "Why should I pay the fine when I didn't even finish the book?" demanded cantankerous Madame Simon), and entered the quiet of the cosy reading room.

At a table near the French windows, Professor Cohen read the paper, a jaunty peacock feather tucked in her chignon; Mr Pryce-Jones pondered *Time* as he puffed on his pipe. Ordinarily, I would have said hello, but, nervous about my interview, I sought refuge in my favourite section of the stacks. I loved being surrounded by stories, some as old as time, others published just last month.

I thought I might borrow a novel for my brother. More and more now, at all hours of the night, I would wake to the sound of him typing his tracts. If Rémy wasn't writing articles about how France should help the refugees driven out of Spain by the civil war, he was insisting that Hitler would take over Europe the way he'd taken a chunk of Czechoslovakia. The only thing that made Rémy forget his worries — which was to say the worries of others — was a good book.

I ran my fingers along the spines. Choosing one, I opened to a random passage. I never judged a book by its beginning. It felt like the first and last date I'd once had, both of us smiling too brightly. No, I opened to a page in the middle, where the author wasn't trying to impress me. "There are darknesses in life and there are lights," I read. "You are one of the lights, the light of all light." *Oui Merci*, Mr Stoker. This is what I would say to Rémy if I could.

Now I was late. I hurried to the circulation desk, where I signed the card and slid *Dracula* into my handbag. The Directress was waiting. As always, her chestnut hair was swept up in a bun, a silver pen poised in her hand.

Everyone knew of Miss Reeder. She wrote articles for newspapers and dazzled on the radio, inviting all to the Library — students, teachers, soldiers, foreigners, and French. She was adamant that there was a place here for everyone.

"I'm Odile Souchet. Sorry to be late. I was early, and I opened a book . . ."

"Reading is dangerous," Miss Reeder said with a knowing smile. "Let's go to my office."

I followed her through the reading room, where subscribers in smart suits lowered their newspapers to get a better look at the famous Directress, up the spiral staircase and down a corridor in the sacred "Employees

Only" wing to her office, which smelled of espresso. On the wall hung a large aerial photo of a city, its blocks like a chessboard, so different from Paris's winding streets.

Noting my interest, she said, "That's Washington, DC. I used to work at the Library of Congress." She gestured for me to be seated and sat at her desk, which was covered by papers — some trying to sneak out of the tray, others held in place by a hole-puncher. In the corner was a shiny black phone. Beside Miss Reeder, a chair held a batch of books. I spied novels by Isak Dinesen and Edith Wharton. A bookmark — a bright ribbon, really — beckoned from each, inviting the Directress to return.

What kind of reader was Miss Reeder? Unlike me, she'd never leave books open-faced for a lack of a *marque-page*. She'd never leave them piled under her bed. She would have four or five going at once. A book tucked in her handbag for bus rides across the city. One that a dear friend had asked her opinion about. Another that no one would ever know about, a secret pleasure for a rainy Sunday afternoon —

"Who's your favourite author?" Miss Reeder asked.

Who's your favourite author? An impossible question. How could a person choose only one? In fact, my Aunt Caro and I had created categories — dead authors, living ones, foreign, French, etc. — to avoid having to decide. I considered the books in the reading room I'd touched just a moment ago, books that had touched me. I admired Ralph Waldo Emerson's way of thinking: *I am not solitary whilst I read and write,*

5

though nobody is with me, as well as Jane Austen's. Though the authoress wrote in the nineteenth century, the situation for many of today's women remained the same: futures determined by whom they married. Three months ago, when I'd informed my parents that I didn't need a husband, Papa snorted and began bringing a different work subordinate to every Sunday lunch. Like the turkey Maman trussed and sprinkled with parsley, Papa presented each one on a platter: "Marc has never missed a day of work, not even when he had the flu!"

"You do read, don't you?"

Papa often complained that my mouth worked faster than my mind. In a flash of frustration, I responded to Miss Reeder's first question.

"My favourite dead author is Dostoevsky, because I like his character Raskolnikov. He's not the only one who wants to hit someone over the head."

Silence.

Why hadn't I given a normal answer — for example, Zora Neale Hurston, my favourite living author?

"It was an honour to meet you." I moved to the door, knowing the interview was over.

As my fingers reached for the porcelain knob, I heard Miss Reeder say, " 'Fling yourself straight into life, without deliberation; don't be afraid — the flood will bear you to the bank and set you safe on your feet again.' "

My favourite line from *Crime and Punishment* 891.73. I turned around.

"Most candidates say their favourite is Shakespeare," she said.

"The only author with his own Dewey Decimal call number."

"A few mention *Jane Eyre*."

That would have been a normal response. Why hadn't I said Charlotte Brontë, or any Brontë for that matter? "I love Jane, too. The Brontë sisters share the same call number — 823."

"But I liked your answer."

"You did?"

"You said what you felt, not what you thought I wanted to hear."

That was true.

"Don't be afraid to be different," Miss Reeder leaned forward. Her gaze — intelligent, steady — met mine. "Why do you want to work here?"

I couldn't give her the real reason. It would sound terrible. "I memorised the Dewey Decimal System and got straight As at library school."

She glanced at my application. "You have an impressive transcript. But you haven't answered my question."

"I'm a subscriber here. I love English —"

"I can see that," she said, a dab of disappointment in her tone. "Thank you for your time. We'll let you know either way in a few weeks' time. I'll see you out."

Back in the courtyard, I sighed in frustration. Perhaps I should have admitted why I wanted the job.

"What's wrong, Odile?" asked Professor Cohen. I loved her standing-room-only lecture series, "English Literature at the American Library". In her signature purple shawl, she made daunting books like *Beowulf* accessible, and her lectures were lively, with a soupçon of sly humour. Clouds of a scandalous past wafted in her wake like the lilac notes of her *parfum*. They said Madame le Professeur was originally from Milan. A prima ballerina who gave up star status (and her stodgy husband) in order to follow a lover to Brazzaville. When she returned to Paris — alone — she studied at the Sorbonne, where, like Simone de Beauvoir, she'd passed *l'agrégation*, the nearly impossible state exam, to be able to teach at the highest level.

"Odile?"

"I made a fool of myself at my job interview."

"A smart young woman like you? Did you tell Miss Reeder that you don't miss a single one of my lectures? I wish my students were as faithful!"

"I didn't think to mention it."

"Include everything you want to tell her in a thank-you note."

"She won't choose me."

"Life's a brawl. You must fight for what you want."

"I'm not sure . . ."

"Well, I am," Professor Cohen said. "Think the old-fashioned men at the Sorbonne hired me just like that? I worked damned hard to convince them that a woman could teach university courses."

I looked up. Before, I'd only noticed the Professor's purple shawl. Now I saw her steely eyes.

"Being persistent isn't a bad thing," she continued, "though my father complained I always had to have the last word."

"Mine, too. He calls me 'unrelenting'."

"Put that quality to use."

She was right. In my favourite books, the heroines never gave up. Professor Cohen had a point about putting my thoughts in a letter. Writing was easier than speaking face-to-face. I could cross things out and start again, a hundred times if I needed to.

"You're right . . ." I told her.

"Of course I am! I'll inform the Directress that you always ask the best questions at my lectures, and you be sure to follow through." With a swish of her shawl, she strode into the Library.

It never mattered how low I felt, someone at the Library always managed to scoop me up and put me on an even keel. The Library was more than bricks and books; its mortar was people who cared. I'd spent time in other libraries, with their hard wooden chairs and their polite, "*Bonjour, mademoiselle. Au revoir, mademoiselle.*" There was nothing wrong with these *bibliothèques*, they simply lacked the camaraderie of real community. The Library felt like home.

"Odile! Wait!" It was Mr Pryce-Jones, the retired English diplomat in his paisley bow tie, followed by the cataloguer Mrs Turnbull, with her crooked blue-grey fringe. Professor Cohen must have told them I was feeling discouraged.

"Nothing is ever lost." He patted my back awkwardly. "You'll win the Directress over. Just write a list of your arguments, like any diplomat worth his salt and pepper would."

9

"Quit mollycoddling the girl!" Mrs Turnbull told him. Turning to me, she said, "In my native Winnipeg, we're used to adversity. Makes us who we are. Winters with temperatures of minus forty degrees, and you won't hear us complain, unlike Americans . . ." Remembering the reason she'd stepped outside — an opportunity to boss someone — she stuck a bony finger in my face. "Buck up, and don't take no for an answer!"

With a smile, I realised that home was a place where there were no secrets. But I was smiling. That was already something.

Back in my bedroom, no longer nervous, I wrote:

Dear Miss Reeder,
Thank you for discussing the job with me. I
was thrilled to be interviewed. This Library
means more to me than any place in Paris.
When I was little, my Aunt Caroline took
me to Story Hour. It's thanks to her that I
studied English and fell in love with the
Library. Though my aunt is no longer with
us, I continue to seek her at the ALP. I
open books and turn to their pockets in the
back, hoping to see her name on the card.
Reading the same novels as she did makes
me feel as if we're still close.
The Library is my haven. I can always
find a corner of the stacks to call my own,
to read and dream. I want to make sure
everyone has that chance, most especially

*the people who feel different and need a
place to call home.*

I signed my name, finishing the interview.

CHAPTER
TWO

LILY

Froid, Montana, September 1983

Her name was Mrs Gustafson, and she lived next door. Behind her back, folks called her the War Bride, but she didn't look like a bride to me. First of all, she never wore white. And she was old. Way older than my parents. Everyone knows a bride needs a groom, but her husband was long dead. Though she spoke two languages fluently, for the most part she didn't talk to anyone. She'd lived here since 1945, but would always be considered the woman who came from somewhere else.

She was the only war bride in Froid, much like Dr Stanchfield was the only doctor. I sometimes peeked into her living room, where even her tables and chairs were foreign — dainty like dollhouse furniture with sculpted walnut legs. I snooped in her mailbox, where letters from as far away as Chicago were addressed to Madame Odile Gustafson. Compared to the names I knew, like Tricia and Tiffany, "Odile" seemed exotic. Folks said she came from France. Wanting to know more about her, I studied the encyclopaedia entries on

Paris. I discovered the grey gargoyles of Notre-Dame and Napoleon's Arc de Triomphe. Yet nothing I read could answer my question: what made Mrs Gustafson so different?

She wasn't like the other ladies in Froid. They were plump like wrens, and their lumpy sweaters and boring shoes came in downy greys. The other ladies wore curlers to the grocery store, but Mrs Gustafson donned her Sunday best — a pleated skirt and high heels — just to take out the trash. A red belt showed off her waist. Always. She wore bright lipstick, even in church. "That one certainly thinks highly of herself," the other ladies said as she strode to her pew near the front, eyes hidden by her cloche hat. No one else wore a hat. And most parishioners sat in the back, not wanting to call themselves to God's attention. Or the priest's.

That morning, Iron-Collar Maloney asked us to pray for the 269 passengers of a Boeing 747 that had been shot down from the sky by Soviet K-8 missiles. On television, President Reagan had told us about the attack on the plane flying from Anchorage to Seoul. As the church bell pealed, his words rang in my ears: "Grief, shock, anger . . . the Soviet Union violated every concept of human rights . . . we shouldn't be surprised by such inhuman brutality . . ." The Russians would murder anyone, he seemed to be saying, even children.

Even in Montana, the Cold War made us shiver. Uncle Walt, who worked at Malmstrom Air Force Base, said a thousand Minuteman nuclear missiles had been planted like potatoes across our plains. Under round, cement crypts, the nuclear heads waited patiently for kingdom come. He bragged that the Minutemen were more powerful than the bombs that had destroyed Hiroshima. He said that missiles seek missiles, so Soviet weapons would bypass Washington and aim for us. In response, our Minutemen would soar, hitting Moscow in less time than it took me to get ready for school.

After Mass, the congregation lumbered across the street to the hall for coffee, doughnuts and the fellowship of gossip. Mom and I stood in line for pastries; at the pulpit of the percolator, Dad and the other men gathered around Mr Ivers, the president of the bank. Dad worked six days a week in hopes of becoming his vice-president.

"Soviets won't let anyone search for the bodies. Godless bastards."

"When Kennedy was President, defence spending was seventy per cent more than it is today."

"We're sitting ducks."

I listened without listening — in the endless wariness of the Cold War, these grim conversations were the soundtrack of our Sundays. Busy piling doughnut holes on my plate, it took me a minute to realise that Mom was wheezing. Usually when she had a spell, she had a reason: "The farmers are harvesting, and the dust in the air brings on my asthma," or "Father Maloney waves that incense around like he's trying to fumigate." But this time she clasped my upper arm, offering none. I steered her towards the closest table, to seats next to Mrs Gustafson. Mom sank on to the metal chair, pulling me down beside her.

I tried to catch Dad's attention.

14

"I'm fine. Don't make a fuss," Mom said in a tone that meant business.

"Tragic, what happened to those people in the plane," Mrs Ivers said from across the table.

"That's why I stay put," Mrs Murdoch said, "Gallivanting about gets you in trouble."

"Lots of innocent people died," I said, "President Reagan said a congressman was killed."

"One less freeloader." Mrs Murdoch shoved the last of her doughnut between her brown teeth.

"That's a rotten thing to say. Folks have a right to take a plane without getting shot down," I said.

Mrs Gustafson's eyes met mine. She nodded, like what I thought mattered. Though I'd made a hobby of observing her, this was the first time she'd noticed me.

"It's brave of you to take a stand," she said.

I shrugged. "People shouldn't be mean."

"I couldn't agree more," she said.

Before I could respond, Mr Ivers bellowed, "The Cold War's gone on for nearly forty years. We'll never win."

Heads bobbed in agreement. "They're cold-blooded killers," he continued.

"Have you ever met a Russian?" Mrs Gustafson asked him. "Worked with one? Well, I have, and can tell you they're no different from you or me."

The whole hall went quiet. Where had she met the enemy, and how had she "worked" with one?

In Froid, we knew everything about everyone. We knew who drank too much and why, we knew who cheated on their taxes and who cheated on their wives, we knew who was living in sin with some man in Minot. The only secret was Mrs Gustafson. No one knew what her parents' names were, or what her father did for a living. No one knew how she met Buck Gustafson during the war, or how she convinced him to jilt his high-school sweetheart and marry her instead. Rumours swirled around her but didn't stick. There was sorrow in her eyes, but was it loss or regret? And after living in Paris, how could she settle for this dull dot on the plains?

I was a "front row, raise your hand" student. Mary Louise sat behind me and doodled on the desk. Today at the blackboard, Miss Hanson tried her best to interest our seventh-grade class in *Ivanhoe*. Mary Louise muttered, "Ivan-no." Across the aisle, Robby's tanned fingers curved around a pencil. His hair — brown like mine — was feathered. He could already drive, since he had to help his folks haul grain. He brought the pencil to his mouth, the pink eraser brushing his bottom lip, I could stare at the corner of his mouth for ever.

French kiss. French toast. French fries. All the good things were French. For all I knew, French green beans tasted better than American ones. French songs had to be better than the country music that played on the only radio station in town. "My life done broke down when that cud-smackin' cow left me for a younger bull." The French probably knew more about love, too.

I wanted to sail down the runway of an airport, of a fashion show. I wanted to perform on Broadway, to peek behind the Iron Curtain. I wanted to know how French words would feel in my mouth. Only one person I knew had experienced the world beyond Froid — Mrs Gustafson.

Though we were neighbours, it was like she lived light years away. Each Halloween, Mom had warned, "The War Bride's porch light is off. That means she doesn't want you kids banging on her door." When Mary Louise and I sold Girl Scout cookies, her mom said, "The old broad's on a budget, so don't hit her up."

My encounter with Mrs Gustafson made me bold. All I needed was the right school assignment, and I could interview her.

As expected, Miss H. assigned a book report on *Ivanhoe*. After class, I approached her desk and asked if I could write about a country instead.

"Just this once," she said. "I look forward to reading your report on France."

I was so distracted with my plan that when I went to the bathroom, I forgot to check under the stalls and lock the main door. Sure enough, when I finished, Tiffany Ivers and her herd skulked near the sinks, where she teased her wheat-gold hair in front of the mirror.

"The flush didn't work," she said. "Here comes a turd."

Hardly sophisticated but when I studied my reflection, all I saw was turd-brown hair. I remained near the stalls, knowing that if I washed my hands, Tiffany would shove me into the faucet and I'd get drenched. If I didn't, they'd tell the school. They did that to Maisie — no one would sit by "Pee Hands" for a month. Arms crossed, the bathroom quartet waited.

The hinges of the door squeaked, and Miss H. peeked in. "Are you in here again, Tiffany? You must have bladder problems."

The girls strode out, eyes on me as if to say, *this isn't over*. That I knew.

Mom, the guerrilla optimist, would tell me to look on the bright side. At least old man Ivers had just one spawn. And it was Friday.

Usually on Fridays, my parents hosted dinner club (Mom roasted spare ribs, Kay brought a salad, and Sue Bob baked an upside-down pineapple cake), so I spent the night at Mary Louise's. Tonight, though, I stayed in my room and came up with questions for Mrs Gustafson. As the adults ate, laughter spilled out of the dining room. When it got quiet, I knew that like lords and ladies in England, the women took themselves off so the men could settle into their chairs and say the things they couldn't with their wives there.

While the women washed dishes, I listened to Mom's other voice, the one she used with her friends. With them she seemed happier. Funny how the same person could be different people. This made me think that there were things about Mom I didn't know, though she wasn't mysterious like Mrs Gustafson.

At my desk, I wrote down the questions as they came — When was the last time the guillotine sliced off someone's head? Does France have Jehovah's Witnesses, too? Why do folks say you stole your husband?

18

Now that he's dead, why do you stay? — concentrating so hard that I didn't know Mom was behind me until I felt her hand warm my shoulder.

"You didn't want to spend the night at Mary Louise's?"

"I'm doing my homework."

"On a Friday," she said, unconvinced. "Rough day at school?"

Most days were rough. But I didn't feel like talking about Tiffany Ivers. Mom pulled a present the size of a shoe box from behind her back. "I made you something."

"Thanks!" I tore open the wrapping paper and found a crocheted sweater.

I pulled it on over my T-shirt, and Mom tugged at the waist, happy with the sizing. "You're beautiful. The green brings out the flecks in your eyes."

A glance in the mirror confirmed that I looked like a dork. If I wore the sweater to school. Tiffany Ivers would eat me alive.

"It's . . . nice," I told Mom, too late.

She smiled to hide her hurt. "So what are you working on?"

I explained that I had to do a report on France and that I needed to interview Mrs Gustafson.

"Oh, hon, I'm not sure we should bother her."

"I only have a few questions. Can't we invite her over?"

"I suppose . . . What would you want to ask?"

I pointed to my paper.

Glancing at the list, Mom exhaled loudly. "You know, there might be a reason she's never gone back."

On Saturday afternoon, I hurried past Mrs Gustafson's old Chevy, up the rickety porch steps, and rang the doorbell. Ding-dang-dong. No answer. I rang the bell again. No one answered, so I tried the front door. It creaked open. "Hello?" I said and walked in.

Silence.

"Anyone home?" I asked.

In the stillness of the living room, books covered the walls. Ferns lined a stand under the picture window. The stereo, the size of a deep freezer, could fit a body. I flipped through her record collection: Tchaikovsky, Bach, more Tchaikovsky.

Mrs Gustafson shuffled down the hall as if she'd awoken from a nap. Even alone at home, she wore a dress with her red belt. In her stockinged feet, she seemed vulnerable. It occurred to me that I'd never seen a friend's car in front of her house, never known her to host family. She was the definition of solitude.

Stopping a few feet from me, she glared like I was a robber come to steal her recording of *Swan Lake*. "What do you want?"

You know things, and I want to know them, too.

She crossed her arms. "Well?"

"I'm writing a report on you. I mean, on your country. Maybe you could come over so I can interview you."

The edges of her mouth turned down. She didn't respond.

The silence made me nervous. "It looks like a library in here." I gestured to her shelves, which were full of names I didn't know — Madame de Staël, *Madame Bovary*, Simone de Beauvoir.

Maybe this was a bad idea. I turned to go.

"When?" she asked.

I looked back. "How about now?"

"I was in the middle of something." She spoke the words briskly, as if she were president and needed to get back to running the domain of her bedroom.

"I'm writing a report," I reminded her, since school came right after God, country and football.

Mrs Gustafson slipped into her high heels and grabbed her keys. I followed her on to the porch, where she locked the door. She was the only person in Froid who did.

"Do you always barge into people's homes?" she asked as we crossed the lawn.

I shrugged. "They usually answer the door."

In our dining room, she clasped her hands, then let them go limp at her side. Her eyes flitted to the carpet, the window seat, the family photos on the wall. Her mouth moved to say something, possibly, "Isn't this nice?" like the other ladies would, then her jaw clamped shut.

"Welcome," Mom said as she set a plate of chocolate chip cookies on the table.

I gestured for our neighbour to take a seat. Mom set mugs in front of her own plate and mine; in front of Mrs Gustafson's, she placed her teacup. I knew its story by heart. Years ago, when Mrs Ivers had gone on a "castle tour" of England, Dad gave her money to buy a fancy tea set for Mom. But porcelain is pricey, and Mrs Ivers returned with just one cup and saucer. Terrified the china would break, she kept it on her lap the entire transatlantic flight. In my mind, the slender cup covered in dainty blue flowers came from somewhere better. Finer. Like Mrs Gustafson.

Mom served the tea; I broke the silence. "What's the best thing about Paris? Is it really the most beautiful city in the world? What was it like growing up there?"

Mrs Gustafson didn't answer right away,

"I hope we're not bothering you," Mom told her.

"The last time I was interviewed like this was for a job back in France."

"Were you nervous?" I asked.

"Yes, but I'd memorised entire books to prepare."

"Did it help?"

She smiled ruefully. "There are always questions one is unprepared to answer."

"Lily won't be asking those kinds of questions." Mom addressed Mrs Gustafson, but her warning was meant for me.

"The best thing about Paris? It's a city of readers," our neighbour said.

She said that in friends' homes, books were as important as the furniture. She spent her summers reading in the city's lush parks, then, like the potted palmettos in the Tuileries Garden, sent to the greenhouse at the first sign of frost, she spent winters at the Library, curled up near the window with a book in her lap.

"You like to read?" For me, the classics assigned in English were a chore.

"I live to read," she replied. "Mostly books on history and current events."

That sounded about as fun as watching snow melt. "What about when you were my age?"

"I loved novels like *The Secret Garden*. My twin brother was the one interested in the news."

A twin. I wanted to ask what his name was, but she'd moved on. Parisians revel in food almost as much as in literature, she said. It had been many years, but she still remembered the pastry that her father brought her after her first day of work, a cake called a *financier*. Closing her eyes, she said the buttery almond powder made her mouth feel like heaven. Her mother adored *opéras*, swathes of deep, dark chocolate enveloped in layers of cake soaked in coffee . . . Fee-nahn-see-yay. Oh-pay-rah. I tasted the words and loved how they felt on my tongue.

Paris is a place that talks to you, she continued. A city that hums along to its own song. In the summer Parisians keep their windows open, and one hears the tinkling of a neighbour's piano, the snap of playing cards being shuffled, static as someone fiddles with the radio knob. There's always a child laughing, someone arguing, a clarinettist playing in the square.

"It sounds wonderful," Mom said dreamily.

Usually, on Sundays after church, Mrs Gustafson's shoulders slumped, and her eyes were like the neon sign of the Oasis bar on Monday — unplugged. But now, her eyes were bright. As she spoke of Paris, the angular lines of her face softened, and so did her voice. I wondered why she'd ever left.

Mom surprised me by asking a question. "What was life like during the war?"

"Hard." Mrs Gustafson's fingers tightened around the teacup. When air-raid sirens screeched, her family hid in the cellar. With food rationing, each person received one egg per month. Everyone grew skinnier until she thought they'd just disappear. On the streets, Nazis forced them through random check-points. Like wolves, they stayed in packs. People were arrested for no reason. Or small reasons, like staying out past curfew.

Weren't curfews for teenagers? Mary Louise's sister Angel had one.

"What do you miss most about Paris?" I asked.

"Family and friends," Mrs Gustafson's brown eyes grew wistful. "People who understand me. I miss speaking French. Feeling like I'm home."

I didn't know what to say. Silence seeped into the room. It made Mom and me fidgety, but didn't seem to bother our neighbour, who sipped the last of her tea.

Noticing Mrs Gustafson's empty cup, Mom jumped up. "I'll put the kettle on."

Halfway to the kitchen, Mom stopped suddenly. She teetered, and one hand shot out, grasping for the cupboard. Before I even thought to move, Mrs Gustafson leaped to her feet and slipped her arm around Moms waist to guide her back to the chair. I crouched beside Mom. Her cheeks were flushed, and she breathed in a slow and shallow way, like the air didn't want to go into her lungs.

"I'll be fine," she said. "I stood too quickly. I know better."

"Has this happened before?" Mrs Gustafson asked.

Mom looked at me, so I returned to my chair and pretended to brush away some crumbs.

"A few times," she admitted.

Mrs Gustafson called Dr Stanchfield. In Froid, adults all said the same thing: "In the city, you call a doctor, and he won't come, no matter how sick you get. Here, the secretary answers by the second ring, and Stanch is at your house in ten minutes flat." He delivered babies in three counties — the first person to hold many of us in his warm, speckled hands.

He knocked on the door and walked in with his black leather bag.

"You needn't have come," Mom said, flustered. She took me to see Stanch if I so much as sneezed, but had never made an appointment for her asthma.

"You let me be the judge of that." He gently moved her hair aside and held his stethoscope to her back. "Take a deep breath."

She inhaled.

"If that's a deep breath . . ." As Stanch took her blood pressure, he frowned. He said the numbers were high, and prescribed some pills.

Maybe Mom had been wrong when she said it was asthma.

After dinner, Mary Louise and I sprawled on my carpet to do our reports. "What'd Mrs Gustafson say?" she asked.

"That the war was dangerous."

"Dangerous? Like how?"

"The enemy everywhere." I imagined Mrs Gustafson on her way to work, the streets full of mangy wolves. Some would growl, some would nip at her high heels. And she kept going. Maybe she never went the same way twice.

"So she had to sneak around?"

"I guess."

"Wouldn't it be cool if she was a secret agent?"

"Totally." I imagined her delivering messages in musty books.

"Speaking of secrets . . ." She put down her pencil. "I smoked one of Angel's cigarettes."

"You smoked by yourself? Did not."

She didn't say anything.

"Did not," I repeated.

"With Tiffany."

Her words hit me hard. "If you smoke, I'll never talk to you again," I said. And held my breath.

We were both twelve, but Mary Louise knew everything first. Because of her sister Angel, Mary Louise heard about rubbers and keggers. My parents didn't let me wear make-up, so Mary Louise loaned me hers. She was stronger and faster than me, and I felt her sprinting away.

"Didn't like it that much anyways," she said.

26

In the coming weeks, Mom lost her appetite, and her clothes hung loose. Her medicine wasn't working. Dad took her to see a specialist, who said it was just stress. She was too tired to cook, so Dad made sandwiches. On Thanksgiving, he and I ate our grilled cheese at the kitchen counter. We glanced at the doorway, hoping Mom would feel well enough to join us.

He cleared his throat. "How is school going?"

I had straight As and no boyfriend, and Tiffany Ivers was trying to steal Mary Louise from me. "Fine."

"Fine?"

"All the other girls get to wear make-up. Why can't I?"

"A pretty girl like you doesn't need all that gunk on your face."

Most of what Dad said didn't register. I didn't hear his concern, didn't hear him say I was pretty. All I heard was the unequivocal no.

"But Dad —"

"I hope you don't nag your mother like this."

For the thousandth time, we both looked at the bedroom door.

Backpacks slung over our shoulders, Mary Louise and I trudged home from school. We stopped on First Street to pet Smokey the German shepherd, continued past the Fleschs', who had forty-seven ceramic gnomes scattered around their yard, one for each year they'd been married. On the corner lot, old Mrs Murdoch brushed back her lace curtains. If we cut across her lawn instead of taking the sidewalk, she called our parents.

In Froid, we all shopped at the same grocery store, we drank from the same well. We shared the same past, we repeated the same stories. Mrs Murdoch wasn't as mean before her husband keeled over shovelling snow. Buck Gustafson was never the same after the war. We read the same newspaper, we depended on the same doctor. On our way to here or there, we drove down dirt roads, we watched combines roll round the fields, their headers snatching up the wheat. The air smelled clean. Honest. Our mouths and nostrils filled with the tender taste of hay, and the dust of harvest pumped through our blood.

"Let's move to a big city," Mary Louise glowered at Mrs Murdoch. "Where no one knows our business."

"Where we can do anything," I added. "Like scream in church."

"Or not even go to church."

We paused at this, an idea so enormous it took time to sink in, and walked the last block to my house in silence. From the street, I could see Mom at the window. The reflection on the glass made her seem pale like a ghost.

Mary Louise headed home; I continued to the mailbox and held on to the weathered post, not ready to go inside. Mom used to make cookies and chat with friends at the kitchen counter. Sometimes, she'd pick me up from school and we'd drive to the Medicine Lake Refuge, her favourite place for bird-watching. In the station wagon, Mom and I faced the same direction; the road stretched before us, rich with possibilities. It was easy to confide in her about a run-in with Tiffany Ivers or a bad grade on a test. I could tell her the good things, too, like the time in PE class when Robby was team captain and he chose me first, even before he picked any of the boys. Each time I struck out, they complained bitterly, but he stayed at my side and told me, "You'll get 'em next time."

Mom knew everything about me.

At Medicine Lake, there were 270 species of birds. We moved through the knee-high needle-and-thread grass. Binoculars hung from the strap around Mom's neck. "Maybe hawks are more majestic," she said, "and piping plovers have the best name. Still, I like robins best."

I teased her for driving all this way to observe birds that we could find on our front lawn.

"Robins are elegant," she told me, "a good omen, a reminder of the special things we have right in front of us." She hugged me tight.

But now, she stayed home alone and rarely had the energy to talk, even to me.

Just then, Mrs Gustafson went to her mailbox, and I crossed the brown strip of grass that separated us. She held a letter to her chest.

"Who's it from?"

"My friend Lucienne in Chicago. We've written to each other for decades. She and I came over on the ship together — three unforgettable weeks from Normandy to New York." She regarded me. "Is everything all right?"

"I'm fine." Everyone knew the rules: don't draw attention to yourself, no one likes a show-off. Don't turn around in church, even if a bomb goes off behind you. When someone asks how you are, say, "Fine," even if you're sad and scared.

"Would you like to come over?" she asked.

I plunked my backpack in front of her shelves. There were books up and down, but only three photos, small as Polaroids, At my house, we had more pictures than books (the Bible, Mom's field guides and an encyclopaedia set that we'd found at a garage sale).

The first photo was of a young Marine. He had Mrs Gustafson's eyes.

She moved to my side. "My son, Marc. He was killed in Vietnam."

Once, when I was handing out bulletins at church, a flock of ladies landed near the basin of holy water. Just as Mrs Gustafson entered, Mrs Ivers whispered, "Tomorrow's the anniversary of Marc's death."

Shaking her head, old Mrs Murdoch replied, "Losing a child, nothing worse. We should send flowers or —"

"You should stop gossiping," Mrs Gustafson snapped, "at least at Mass."

The ladies dipped trembling fingers into the holy water, quickly made the sign of the cross, and slunk to their pews.

Running my hand over the top of the picture frame, I said, "I'm sorry."

"As am I."

The sorrow in her voice made me uneasy. No one ever came to visit her. Not her in-laws, not her French family. What if everyone she'd ever loved was dead? She probably didn't want me here, dredging up her losses. I moved to pick up my backpack.

"Would you like a biscuit?" she asked.

In the kitchen, I grabbed the biggest two on the plate and gobbled them down before she touched hers. Thin and crunchy, the sugar cookies were wrapped in the shape of a miniature spyglass.

She'd just finished the first batch, so over the next hour I helped roll out the rest. I appreciated that she didn't say anything about Mom. Not, "We miss your mother at the PTA, tell her everyone has to pull their weight." Or, "Nothing wrong with her that a pork roast couldn't fix." Silence had never felt so good.

"What are these cookies called?" I asked as I grabbed another.

"*Cigarettes russes.* Russian cigarettes."

Communist cookies? I put it back on the plate. "Who taught you to make them?"

"I got the recipe from a friend, who served them when I delivered books."

"Why couldn't she get her own books?"

"She wasn't allowed in libraries during the war."

Before I could ask why not, there was a pounding at the door. "Mrs Gustafson?"

It was Dad, which meant it was six o'clock — dinner time, and I was in trouble. Wiping the crumbs from my mouth, I prepared my case. Time slipped by, I had to stay to help finish . . .

Mrs Gustafson opened the door, and I expected hurricane Dad to rain down.

His eyes were wide, his tie crooked. "I'm taking Brenda to the hospital," he said to Mrs Gustafson. "Can you look after Lily?"

I wanted to say I was sorry, but he rushed off, not waiting for a response.

CHAPTER
THREE

ODILE

Paris, February 1939

The shadow of Saint-Eustache Church loomed over Maman, Rémy and me as we set forth from yet another dull Sunday service. Released from the oppressive grasp of incense, I sucked in icy gales of air, relieved to be away from the priest and his gloomy sermon. Maman prodded us along the pavement, past Rémy's second-favourite bookshop, past the *boulangerie* with the broken-hearted baker who burned the bread, through the entrance to our building.

"Which one is it today, Pierre or Paul?" she fretted. "Whoever he is, he'll be here any minute. Odile, don't you dare scowl. Of course, Papa wants to get to know these men; not all of them work at his precinct. One might be a perfect suitor for you."

Another lunch with an unsuspecting policeman. It was awkward when a man showed an interest in me, mortifying when he showed none.

"And change into your blouse! I can't believe you wore that faded smock to church. What will people think?" she said as she rushed to the kitchen to check on the roast.

In the hall, at the mirror with the chipped gilding, I re-braided my auburn hair; Rémy ran a dab of barber cream through his unruly curls. In French families, Sunday lunch was a ritual every bit as sacred as Mass, and Maman insisted that we look our best.

"How would Dewey classify this lunch?" Rémy asked.

"That's easy — 841. *A Season in Hell*."

He laughed.

"How many underlings has Papa invited so far?"

"Fourteen," he said. "I bet they're afraid to tell him 'no'."

"Why don't you have to go through this torture?"

"Because no one cares when men get married." With an impish grin, he snatched my scarf and pulled the scratchy wool over his head, knotting it under his chin the way our mother did. "*Ma fille*, women have a short shelf life."

I giggled. He always knew how to cheer me up.

"The way you're going," he continued in Maman's shrill manner, "you'll be on the shelf for ever!"

"A library shelf, if I get the job."

"*When* you get the job."

"I'm not sure . . ."

Rémy slipped off the scarf. "You have a library degree, you speak English fluently, and you got high marks at your internship. I have faith in you; have faith in yourself."

A knock at the door. We opened it to find a blond policeman in a peacoat. I braced myself — last week's

34

protégé had greeted me by rubbing his greasy jowls against my face.

"I'm Paul," this one said. He barely touched his cheeks to mine.

"Pleasure to meet you both," he said as he shook Rémy's hand, "I've heard good things about you."

He seemed sincere, but I had trouble believing Papa had said anything remotely positive about either of us. All we heard about were Rémy's dismal grades (yet he was best debater in his law class!) and my lacklustre housekeeping ("How can you sleep on a bed that has books all over it?").

"I've looked forward to today all week," the protégé told Maman.

"A home-cooked meal will do you good," she said. "We're glad you're here."

Papa thrust his guest into the armchair near the fireplace, then served the aperitif (vermouth for the men, sherry for the women). While Maman flitted from the seat near her beloved ferns to the kitchen, making sure the maid carried out her instructions, Papa presided from his Louis XV-style chair, his broom-shaped moustache sweeping assertions from his mouth. "Who needs these *chômeurs intellectuels?* I say let the 'intellectual unemployed' compose their prose while working in the mines. What other country distinguishes between smart loafers and dim ones? My tax money at work!" Each Sunday, the suitor changed; Papa's long-winded lecture never did.

Once again, I explained, "No one's forcing you to support artists and writers. You can choose ordinary postage stamps or those with a small surtax."

35

Next to me on the divan, Rémy crossed his arms. I could read his mind: *why do you bother?*

"I've never heard of that programme," Papa's protégé said. "When I write home, I'll ask for those stamps."

Perhaps this one wasn't as bad as the rest.

Papa turned to Paul. "Our colleagues are having a hell of a time with the detention camps near the border. All these refugees pouring in — soon there'll be more Spaniards in France than in Spain."

"There's a civil war," Rémy said. "They need help."

"They're helping themselves to our country!"

"What are innocent civilians to do?" Paul asked Papa. "Remain home and be butchered?"

For once, my father didn't have a reply. I considered our guest. Not the short hair that stuck straight up, nor the blue eyes that matched his uniform, but his strength of character and serene fearlessness in standing up for his beliefs.

"With all the political upheaval," Rémy said, "one thing's sure. War is coming."

"Nonsense!" Papa said. "Millions have been invested in security. With the Maginot Line, France is completely safe."

I imagined the line as an immense ditch on France's borders with Italy, Switzerland and Germany, where armies who tried to attack would be swallowed whole.

"Must we discuss war?" Maman asked. "All this grim talk on a Sunday! Rémy, why don't you tell us about your classes?"

"My son wants to drop out of law school," Papa said to Paul. "I have it on good authority that he skips class."

I racked my mind to find something to say.

Paul spoke before I could. Turning to Rémy, he said, "What would you like to do instead?"

It was a question I wished Papa would ask.

"Run for office," Rémy answered, "try to change things."

Papa rolled his eyes.

"Or become a park ranger and escape this corrupt world," Rémy said.

"You and I keep people and businesses safe," Papa said to Paul. "He'll protect pine cones and bear scat."

"Our forests are as important as the Louvre," Paul said.

Another answer that brooked no response from Papa. I looked to Rémy, to see what he made of Paul, but he'd turned towards the window and taken himself to a faraway place, as we often did during interminable Sunday lunches. This time, I decided to stay. I wanted to hear what Paul had to say.

"Lunch smells delicious!" I hoped to steer Papa's attention from Rémy.

"Yes," Paul added gamely. "I haven't had a home-cooked meal in months."

"How will you help your refugees if you quit law school?" Papa continued. "You need to stick to something."

"The soup must be ready . . ." Maman picked nervously at the dried fronds of her ferns.

Wordlessly, Rémy skirted past her to the dining room.

"You don't want to work," Papa called out, "but you're always the first at the table for meals!"

He couldn't stop, not even in front of a guest.

As usual, we ate leek and potato soup. Paul complimented her on the creamy soup, and she murmured something about it being a good recipe. The scrape of Papa's spoon on the porcelain signalled the end of the first course. Maman's mouth opened slightly, as if she wanted to tell him to be gentle. But she would never reproach Papa.

The maid brought out the rosemary mashed potatoes and roast pork. I squinted at the mantle clock. Usually, lunch dragged on, but I was surprised to see that it was already 2 p.m.

"Are you a student as well?" Paul asked me.

"No, I've finished studying, I've just applied for a job at the American Library."

A smile touched his lips. "I wouldn't mind working in a nice peaceful place like that."

Papa's black eyes gleamed with interest. "Paul, if you're not content in the eighth district, why not transfer to my precinct? There's a sergeant's position for the right man."

"Thank you, sir, but I'm happy where I am." Paul's gaze never left my face. "Extremely happy."

Suddenly, it felt as if it were just the two of us. *As he now leaned back in his chair, and lent his deep-set eyes upon her in his turn, perhaps he might have seen one wavering moment in her, when she was impelled to*

38

throw herself upon his breast, and give him the pent-up confidences of her heart.

"Girls working," Papa scoffed. "Couldn't you have at least applied to a French library?"

Regretfully, I left the tender scene with Paul, and with Dickens. "Papa, the Americans don't just alphabetise, they use numbers called the Dewey Decimal System —"

"Numbers to classify letters? You can bet some capitalist came up with that idea — they care more about figures than letters! What's wrong with the way we do things?"

"Miss Reeder says it's all right to be different."

"Foreigners! God knows who else you'll have to deal with!"

"Give people a chance, you might be surprised —"

"You're the one who's in for a surprise." He pointed his fork at me. "Working with the public is damn hard. Why, yesterday I was called in because a senator had been arrested for breaking and entering. A little old lady found him passed out on her floor. When the reprobate came to, he didn't stop shouting obscenities until he started vomiting. Had to hose him down before we could get the story out of him. He'd thought he was at his mistress's building, but that his key didn't work, so he crept up the trellis and into the window. Believe me, you don't want anything to do with people, and don't get me started on the scum running this country into the ground."

There he went again, complaining about foreigners, politicians and uppity women. I groaned, and Rémy tucked his stockinged foot over mine. Comforted by

39

this small touch, I felt the tension in my shoulders soften. We'd invented this secret show of support when we were little. Faced with our father's wrath — "Twice this week you've had to wear the dunce cap at school, Rémy! I should staple the damn thing to your head" — I'd known better than to console my brother with a kind word. The last time I had, Papa said, "Taking his side? I should thrash you both."

"They'll hire an American, not you," Papa concluded.

I wished I could prove the all-knowing *commissaire* wrong. I wished he would respect my choices, instead of telling me what I should want.

"A quarter of the Library's subscribers are Parisian," I countered. "They need French-speaking staff."

"What will people think?" Maman fretted. "They'll say Papa isn't providing for you."

"Many girls have jobs these days," Rémy said.

"Odile doesn't need to work," Papa said.

"But she wants to," I said softly.

"Let's not argue." Maman scooped the *mousse au chocolat* into small crystal bowls. The dessert, rich and dreamy, demanded our attention and allowed us to agree on something — Maman made the best mousse.

At 3p.m. Paul rose. "Thank you for lunch. I'm sorry I must go, but my shift starts soon."

We followed him to the door. Papa shook his hand and said, "Consider my offer."

I wanted to thank Paul for standing up for Rémy, and for me, but with Papa there, I remained silent. Paul moved closer, until he was just before me. I held my breath.

"I hope you get the job," he whispered.

When he kissed me goodbye, his lips were soft on my cheek, making me curious to know how his mouth would feel on mine. Imagining our kiss, my heart beat faster, like it did the first time I read *A Room with a View*. I tore through scenes, waiting for George and Lucy — who were so right for each other — to confess their unbridled love and embrace in a deserted piazza. I wished I could flip the pages of my life faster, to know if I'd see Paul again.

I moved to the window and watched him hurry down the street.

Behind me, I heard the glug-glug-glug of Papa pouring a digestif. Sunday lunch was the one time each week that he and Maman indulged themselves in the dark memories of the Great War. After a few sips, she reverently recited names of neighbours who'd been killed, as if each were a bead on her rosary. To Papa, the battles his regiment won seemed like defeats because so many of his fellow soldiers had died.

Rémy joined me at the window, where he picked at Maman's fern. "We scared off another suitor," he said.

"You mean Papa did."

"He drives me mad. He's so narrow-minded. He has no clue about what's happening."

I always sided with Rémy, but this once, I hoped that Papa was right. "Did you mean what you said . . . about war?"

"I'm afraid so," he said. "Hard times are coming."

Hard Times. 823. British fiction.

"Civilians are dying in Spain. Jews are being persecuted in Germany," he continued, frowning at the frond held between his fingers, "and I'm stuck in classes."

"You're publishing articles that raise awareness about the plight of refugees. You organised a clothing drive for them, and got the whole family involved. I'm proud of you."

"It's not enough."

"Right now, you need to focus on your classes. You were at the top of your class, now you'll be lucky to graduate."

"I'm sick of studying theoretical court cases. People need help *now*. Politicians aren't acting. I can't just sit at home. Someone has to do something."

"You need to graduate."

"A degree won't make a difference."

"Papa's not entirely wrong," I said gently. "You should finish what you start."

"I'm trying to tell you —"

"Please tell me you haven't done anything rash." He'd donated his savings to a legal fund for refugees. Without telling Maman, he'd given the food in our pantry to the poor, down to the last speck of flour. She and I had rushed to the market to get dinner on the table before Papa arrived home, so he wouldn't find out and scold Rémy.

"You used to understand." He strode to his room and slammed the door.

I flinched at his accusation. I wanted to yell that he never used to be so impetuous, but knew that fighting would lead nowhere. When he calmed down, I would try again. For now, I wanted to forget Papa and Paul and even Rémy. *Hard Times*. I took the book from my shelf.

CHAPTER
FOUR

LILY

Froid, Montana, December 1983

Dad and I hovered at the side of Mom's hospital bed. She tried to smile, but her mouth just quivered. The colour had gone from her lips, and she blinked in slow motion. Around her, machines beeped. Why hadn't I gone straight home after school? Maybe if I had, Mom wouldn't be here now.

I closed my eyes and took her away from the bowl of half-eaten green Jell-O, away from the sterile hospital stink, to the lake. Inhaling the marshy scent, she and I tramped around, her face flushed from the warmth of the sun. She noticed something in the grass. Moving closer, we found a copse of Coors cans. She pulled a plastic sack from the pocket of her Windbreaker and picked them up. Wanting to just enjoy the moment, I said, "Come on, Mom. Forget the trash," but she ignored me. It was important for her to leave a place better than we found it.

Dr Stanchfield brought me back. He'd come to translate the specialist's diagnosis: the EKG showed that Mom had had several silent heart attacks, which

44

had caused extensive damage. I didn't know how we'd travelled from Mom insisting she just had trouble catching her breath to heart attacks. It seemed like a long stretch of road with no warning signs, no "Falling Rocks", no "Dangerous Crosswinds". How did we get here? And how long would Mom have to stay?

For supper, Dad heated Salisbury steak frozen dinners and set up TV trays. He said it was so we could watch the news, but I knew it was so that Graham Brewster, the grandfatherly anchor, would do the talking for us. Tonight, he interviewed a member of the Union of Concerned Scientists about what would happen in the event of a nuclear war.

"Is Mom getting better?" I asked Dad.

"I don't know. She seems less tired."

Over 225 tons of smoke would spew into the air, said the MIT physicist.

"When will she be home?"

"I wish we knew, hon, but Stanch didn't say. Real soon, I hope."

The smoke would black out the sun, triggering an ice age.

"I'm scared."

"Eat something," Dad said.

No matter how bad things are now, the scientist concluded, they can always get worse.

I moved the meat around with my fork. My belly had stiffened into a boulder, and it beat long and slow, like a confused heart.

After dinner, Dad disappeared into the den. I twirled the telephone cord around my finger and called Mary Louise. The line was busy. If her sister Angel wasn't on a date, she was on the phone. I glanced around to make sure Dad wasn't nearby before dialling 5896. Please let Robby be home.

"Hello," he answered. "Hello? Is anyone there?"

I wished I could talk to him, but didn't know how. I eased the receiver on to the cradle but didn't let go right away — his voice, deep and velvety, made me feel less lonesome.

At my bedroom window, I stared up at the full moon. It stared back. The wind snatched at the brittle branches. When I was little and scared of a storm, Mom had pretended that my bed was a boat and that the gusts were waves, the sea slicing to and fro over our lawn, taking us to a faraway land. Without her, the wind was just the wind, howling past on its way to somewhere better.

Ten days later, when Mom came home, she sank on to the bed. Dad prepared a cup of chamomile. I lay beside her under the lemon-yellow afghan. She smelled of Ivory soap. Icicles dangled from the roof. Snow tight-roped the telephone lines. The big sky was blue, our world white.

"We're lucky today." She gestured towards the window. "Plenty of hawks."

Sometimes they glided high over the pasture across the street. Sometimes they flew low, searching for mice. Mom said bird-watching was better than TV.

"When I was pregnant, your dad and I cuddled on the window seat and watched robins. I loved their bright breasts, a sure sign of spring, but he didn't like the way they slurped down worms. 'Think of it as spaghetti,' I told him."

"Ew!"

"You were almost a Robin. After you were born, I told the nurse that was your name, though I knew your dad preferred Lily, because lily of the valley was in bloom when we bought the house. Then I saw you with him, your fingers clasped around his pinky. They reminded me of the tiny flowers. He leaned down and kissed your belly. The way he looked at you . . . with such love — I changed my mind." She told the story often, but today for some reason, she added, "When Dad works, it's not for himself. He wants us to feel secure. He was poor growing up. Deep down, he's scared he could lose everything. Do you understand?"

"Kind of."

"People are awkward, they don't always know what to do or say. Don't hold it against them. You never know what's in their hearts."

People are awkward. Don't hold it against them. You never know what's in their hearts. What did she mean? Something about herself? Or Dad? I heard Mary Louise's mom say that my dad took himself for a Wall Street stockbroker and that he liked money more than people.

"Dad's gone an awful lot," I said.

"Oh, honey, what a pity that babies don't have memories of how they were cherished. Your dad held you all night long."

47

He was an eagle, she said, calm and brave. I'd learned about eagles — both the male and female take turns sitting on the eggs.

"Humans have families," she continued, "but what about geese?"

I shrugged.

"We say a gaggle of geese."

"How about sparrows?"

"A host of sparrows."

"Hawks?"

"A cast."

Like a bird TV show. I giggled.

"Do you know what they call a group of ravens? An unkindness of ravens."

It sounded too silly to be true. I scoured her face for the truth, but she seemed serious. "What about crows?"

"A murder of crows."

"A murder of crows," I repeated.

It felt like the good old days, back when everything was okay. I hugged her tight, so tight, wishing everything could be like this always. Us, together on the big brass bed, warm inside.

In the morning, Dad and I lingered at the kitchen counter with Mom. He said it wouldn't hurt me to miss a day of school.

"I don't need babysitters!" Mom said.

"Stanch said you should still be in the hospital," Dad replied.

We ate our bacon and eggs in silence. The minute we finished, she pushed us out the door.

48

At school, all I could think of was her — at least in the hospital, she hadn't been alone. In the middle of math, Tiffany Ivers kicked my chair. "Hey, spaz," she said. "Mr Goodan asked you a question." I lifted my head, but he'd moved on. When the last bell rang, I rushed home. From outside, I could see my parents on the window seat. I went around to the back door, entering quietly through the kitchen.

"Stanch suggested getting a nurse's aide," I heard him say.

"For heaven's sake! I'm fine."

"Would it hurt to have some help around the house? I think Lily would breathe easier."

He was right, I would.

"Who would you ask?" Mom asked.

"Sue Bob?"

My ears perked up even more when I heard Mary Louise's mother's name.

"I don't want friends to see me like this," Mom said.

"Just an idea," Dad backtracked.

Maybe Mrs Gustafson could help. I knocked on her door. This time I didn't barge in.

"Mom's still sick," I told her.

"I'm sorry to hear that."

"And we need some help around the house, so she doesn't overdo it. Could you —"

"Lil?" I heard Dad say behind me. "What are you doing? We should get back to your mom."

"I suppose I could help out," Mrs Gustafson said.

"No need," Dad said. "We'll manage."

49

She looked from him to me, "Let me make dinner. I'll just gather a few ingredients," She went inside and came back with an armful of vegetables and a carton of cream.

At our kitchen counter, she peeled potatoes so finely that the skins were see-through.

"What are you making?"

"Leek and potato soup."

"What's a leek?"

"In eastern Montana, a most neglected vegetable."

She cut off the curly roots before splitting its slender white body. It smelled like a meek onion. She sliced the leek and scraped the pieces into the pan where they basked in bubbling butter while the potatoes boiled. Then she puréed the leeks and potatoes in the blender before adding a dollop of cream and pouring the white soup into bowls.

"Suppers ready," I called.

Dad walked beside Mom, his hands hovering near her waist like a hospital orderly. Before, I'd rolled my eyes when my parents kissed, but now I wished they could go back to the touchy-feely way they used to be.

After we said grace, I hunched over my bowl and shoved a spoonful into my mouth. The soup felt silky good. I wanted to eat fast, but it was hot.

"Soup teaches patience," Mrs Gustafson said. Her back was straight as she brought the spoon to her mouth. I stretched my spine taller.

"Delicious," Mom said.

"It was my son's favourite." The light in Mrs Gustafson's eyes momentarily dimmed. "It takes just a few ingredients to make a healthy meal, yet industrial food companies have Americans convinced there's no time to cook. You eat bland soup from a can, even though leeks browned with butter taste like heaven.

"Going without has made me more appreciative. During the war, my mother missed sugar more than anything, but I missed butter."

"So food was hard to come by?" Dad said.

"Good food was. I'm not sure which 'war delicacy' was worse — baguettes baked with woodchips because there was a shortage of flour, or a tasteless soup made of only water and swede, what you would call rutabagas in America. Endless queues for meat, dairy, fruits and most vegetables, but vendors couldn't give rutabagas away. And when I came to Montana, do you know what my mother-in-law put in every one of her stews? Rutabagas!"

We laughed. She made us laugh as she talked about this and that, giving us a break from the unnatural quiet that had descended on our family. When she rose to leave, Mom said, "Thank you, Odile."

Our neighbour looked surprised. I wondered if it was because she wasn't used to hearing her given name. Finally, she said, "My pleasure."

When Mary Louise and I got home from school, we could hear laughter coming from my parents' bedroom, Odile had kicked off her high heels and moved the rocking chair closer to the bed. Mom's hair had been freshly washed and curled, and she wore the same brick-red lipstick as Odile. She was beautiful.

"What's so funny?" Mary Louise asked Mom.

"Odile was telling me her in-laws had trouble pronouncing her name."

"They called me Ordeal!"

"Marriage: for better or worse, and however loony the in-laws are," Mom said, and they both laughed.

As Mary Louise and I went to my room to study, we heard Mom ask, "If you don't mind my asking, where did you and your husband meet?"

"At a hospital in Paris. In those days, an enlisted man had to ask his superior's permission to marry. When Buck's said no, he challenged the major to a game of cribbage — if he won, we could marry, if he lost, he had to clean bedpans for a month."

"He was determined!"

Their words became whispers, so Mary Louise and I moved closer to the door.

"He didn't tell me," Odile continued, "and when I arrived, there was a scandal. I wanted to return to France, but had no money for a return ticket. I thought people would forgive ... Not that I needed their forgiveness!"

"What scandal?" Mary Louise whispered. "Was she one of those cancan dancers? Is that why people don't talk to her?"

"*She* doesn't talk to them," I huffed.

Mom hibernated the winter away. After school, I lay down beside her and told her about my day. She nodded but didn't open her eyes. Dad stayed close, ready with chamomile in her favourite china cup. Dr

Stanchfield prescribed more pills, but Mom didn't feel better.

"Why can't she get up?" Dad asked him. We three lingered at the front door. "Even the smallest effort tires her."

"There's been too much damage to the heart," Stanch said. "She doesn't have much time left."

"Months?" Dad asked.

"Weeks," Stanch replied.

Dad put his arms around me as the truth closed in.

My parents insisted that school was too important to miss, but Dad took a leave of absence from work and watched over Mom, never leaving her side.

"You're suffocating me!" I heard her tell him. They'd never fought, but now he couldn't seem to do anything right. When she got riled, she had trouble catching her breath. Scared to make things worse, he went back to work, slipping out at sunrise and returning after dark. Not wanting to disturb her, he slept on the couch. At night, when the house was quiet, I heard Mom moan. Every scrape of her breath, every cough, every sigh scared me. Huddled in bed, I was afraid to go see if she was okay.

After I told Odile about Mom's raspy breathing, I felt better. Odile knew what to do. She even moved a cot next to Mom's bed so she could spend the night. When Mom protested, Odile assured her that it was no trouble. "I slept with dozens of soldiers."

"Odile!" Mom exclaimed, her gaze twitching towards me.

"Next to them in the hospital ward, during the war."

At 9p.m., the back door creaked. Dad coming home. Odile crept from the cot to the kitchen. Tiptoeing behind her, I plastered myself to the panelling in the hall.

"Your wife needs you, so does your daughter," Odile said.

"Brenda says seeing me so miserable makes her feel like she's already dead."

"That's why she won't let friends visit?"

"She can't stand the tears, even if they're for her. She doesn't want pity. I wanted to be there for her, but now I figure it's best to give her the distance she wants."

"You don't want to have any regrets." Mrs Gustafson's tone had turned from tart to tender. Like a mom's.

"If only it were up to me."

Down the hall, Mom coughed. Was she awake? Did she need me? I rushed to her room. Suddenly scared, I stopped at the foot of the bed. Behind me, Dad said, "Brenda, honey?"

Odile nudged me towards Mom, but I resisted, my shoulder blades pushing against her palms. Mom reached out. I was scared to take her hand, I was scared not to. She hugged me, but I stayed stiff in her arms.

"There's so little time," she said, her words whispery, "too little time. Be brave . . ."

I tried to say I would, but fear stole my voice. After a long moment, she pushed my body from hers and looked at me. Trapped in Mom's mournful stare, I remembered things she'd said: babies sleep through the

54

love. A gaggle of geese, a murder of crows. People are awkward, they don't know what to do or say. Don't hold it against them; we never know what's in their hearts, I wanted you to be Robin but you're Lily. Oh, Lily.

CHAPTER
FIVE

ODILE

Paris, March 1939

"Mademoiselle Reeder rang," Maman told me as Rémy and I walked in the door. "She wants to see you."

Turning to Rémy, I saw my whirl of hope and relief reflected in his eyes.

"Are you certain taking a job is a good idea?" Maman asked me.

"Certain." I hugged her.

Rémy gave me his green satchel. "For luck. And for the books you'll be bringing home."

Rushing to the Library before Miss Reeder could change her mind, I sprinted through the courtyard, up the spiral stairs, and slid to a stop at the threshold of her office, where she was reviewing documents, silver pen in hand. Eyes tired, lipstick long gone, she looked peaked. It *was* after 7p.m. She gestured for me to be seated.

"I'm finalising the budget." As a private institution, she explained the Library did not receive government funds — it relied on trustees and donors for everything from buying books to paying for heat.

"But you won't need to worry about that." She closed the folder. "Professor Cohen speaks highly of you, and I'm impressed with you. Let's talk about the job. The fact is, we've hired candidates who haven't been able to continue for one reason or another, so we ask employees to sign a two-year contract."

"Why didn't they stay?"

"Some were foreign, France simply too far from home. Others found dealing with the public difficult. As you wrote in your letter, the Library's a haven; staff work hard to make sure it remains so."

"I believe I can handle it."

"The salary's modest. Is that a problem?"

"Not at all."

"One last thing. Staff takes turns working weekends."

No more Mass or suitors? "I want to work Sundays!"

"The position is yours," she said solemnly.

I jumped up. "Truly?"

"Truly."

"Thank you, I won't let you down!"

She winked mischievously. "No bashing in subscribers' heads!"

I laughed. "I won't make promises I can't keep."

"You start tomorrow," she said, and returned to the budget.

I dashed out, hoping to catch Rémy before he left for his political rally, and slammed into him on the pavement.

"You came!"

"What's the verdict?" he asked. "You were in there for ever."

"Twenty minutes."

"Same difference," he grumbled.

"I got the job!"

"Told you!"

"I thought you'd be at your rally," I said.

"Some things are more important."

"You're the president. They need you."

He covered my foot with his. "And I need you. Without *toi*, there's no *moi*."

At home, I entered the sitting room, where Maman was knitting me a scarf.

"Well?" She set aside her needles.

"I'm a librarian!" I drew her up and waltzed her around the room.

ONE-two-three.

BOOKS-independence-happiness.

"Congratulations, *ma fille*," she said. "I'll bring Papa around, I promise."

Intending to prepare for work, I went to my room to review my Dewey Decimal notes. Yesterday, in the Luxembourg Garden, I saw several 598 (birds). Some day, I'll learn 469 (Portuguese) . . . Was there a number for love? If I had my very own number, what would it be?

I thought about Aunt Caro — it was she who first introduced me to the Dewey Decimal System. How I'd loved sitting on her lap during Story Hour as a child! Years later, when I was nine, she introduced me to the card catalogue, an unusual piece of wooden furniture made of tiny drawers, each with a letter on it.

"Inside, you'll find the secrets of the universe." Aunt Caro opened the N drawer to reveal dozens and dozens of stock cards. "Each has information that will open entire worlds. Why don't you take a peek? I bet you'll find a treat."

I peered inside. Flipping through the cards, I came across a sweet. "Nougat!"

She taught me how to find the next clue, a call number that would lead us to the section, to the shelf, to the exact book. A treasure hunt.

Aunt Caro had the tiniest waist and the biggest brain. Like Maman's, her eyes were periwinkle, but while my mother's had faded like one of Papa's navy dress shirts, Aunt Caro's were bright with life. As a reader, she was an omnivore, devouring science, maths, history, plays and poetry. Her bookshelves ran over, so her dressing table was a mixture of pink blush and Dorothy Parker, mascara and Montaigne. Her armoire held Horace and high heels, stockings and Steinbeck. Her love of books and her love for me imbued my being like the amber scent of Shalimar she dabbed behind our ears.

Memories of Aunt Caro reminded me why I *needed* the job.

On my first day, I felt more nervous than I had at the interview. What if I disappointed Miss Reeder? What if someone asked a question I couldn't answer? If only Aunt Caro were still with us. I'd have told her not to come on my first day, but she would have anyway. Laden with Shelley and Blake, she would have winked at me, and my nervousness would have melted away as I remembered what she'd said: the answers were here, one simply had to seek.

"Introductions," the Directress said briskly and presented Boris Netchaeff, the urbane Franco-Russian head librarian, impeccable as always in his blue suit and tie. At the circulation desk, subscribers lined up to pass before him the way they did their parish priest — for communion, for a private word. The glint in his green eyes never dimmed, not even when he listened to subscribers' long-winded stories. He knew where to buy the finest clothing ("My man at the Bazaar de l'Hôtel de Ville won't steer you wrong") as well as what to look for when purchasing a horse. Stern Mrs Turnbull said he was an aristocrat who'd owned a stable of purebreds. Mr Pryce-Jones said Boris had been in the Russian army. There were as many rumours as books in the Library.

Boris was famous for his bibliotherapy. He knew which books would mend a broken heart, what to read on a summer day, and which novel to choose for an adventurous escape. The first time I'd returned to the Library without Aunt Caro, ten years ago now, the tall stacks seemed to close in on me. The titles embossed on the spines of stories didn't speak to me like they usually did. I found myself with tears in my eyes, staring at a blur of books.

Looking concerned, Boris drew near. "Your aunt didn't bring you?" he said, "We haven't seen her in a while."

"She won't be coming back."

He selected a book from the shelf. "It's about family, and loss. And how we can have happy moments even when we're down."

I am not afraid of storms, for I am learning how to sail my ship.

Little Women was still one of my favourites.

"Boris started here as a page — a sort of Library apprentice — and knows absolutely everything about the ALP," Miss Reeder said.

He shook my hand. "You're a subscriber."

I nodded, pleased to be recognised. Before I could respond, Miss Reeder whisked me to the reading room, where we approached a woman writing near the window. Grey hair framed her face, black glasses balanced on the tip of her nose. Before her, books on Elizabethan England covered the table. Miss Reeder introduced the trustee, Countess Clara de Chambrun. I knew her name. I'd recently finished *Playing with Souls*, one of her novels. A countess *and* a real-life writer!

"Researching another book on the bard?" the Directress asked. "Why don't you use my office?"

"No need for special treatment! I'm a subscriber like anyone else."

The Countess's accent was most definitely not French, nor was it British. Did America have countesses? The mystery would have to be solved another day. The Directress steered me towards the periodical room, which was to be my post. On the way, she introduced her secretary Mademoiselle Frikart (French-Swiss), the bookkeeper Miss Wedd (British), and the shelver Peter Oustinoff (American).

I surveyed the long shelves that held 15 dailies and 300 periodicals from America, England, France, Germany and countries as far away as Japan. When Miss Reeder told me that I'd also be responsible for the bulletin board, newsletter and "ALP News" column in the *Herald*, I panicked, thinking there was no possible way I could manage it all.

"You know," she said, "I started in this section, and look where I am now."

We enjoyed a moment of complicity as we watched subscribers read, heads bowed, books held reverently in their hands.

Mr Pryce-Jones approached. He reminded me of a spry crane sporting a paisley bow tie. With him was a subscriber who resembled a walrus with bushy white whiskers. "Hello, gentlemen, please welcome the newest addition to our staff," Miss Reeder said, before returning to her office.

"Thank you for the advice about laying out an argument," I told Mr Pryce-Jones.

"Glad you got the job," he said, his bow tie bobbling. Gesturing to his friend, he added, "This conniving journalist is Geoffrey de Nerciat. He thinks the Library's copy of the *Herald* belongs to him."

"Spreading lies again, old boy?" asked Monsieur de Nerciat. "That's all you diplomats are good for."

"I'm Odile Souchet, librarian and referee," I joked.

"Where's your whistle?" Mr Pryce-Jones asked. "With us, you'll need one."

"Our shouting matches are legendary," Monsieur de Nerciat bragged.

"The only person who can bellow louder than us is the Countess."

"Which we learned when she managed to insert herself between us and insisted we take our differences outside." The Frenchman gazed at Clara de Chambrun.

"Quite scared me! Thought she was going to take me by the ear."

Monsieur de Nerciat grinned. "That fine lady can take me anywhere she likes."

"Doubt her husband would agree to that."

"And him a general! Better watch my step."

The duo continued to spar; I put out the dailies and familiarised myself with the magazines. Soon I was lost in the tables of content, my mind full of history, fashion and current events.

"Mademoiselle? Odile?"

Deep in the fog of work, I barely heard.

"Excuse me. Mademoiselle?"

I felt a hand on my upper arm. Glancing up, I saw Paul.

He looked dashing in the uniform of *les hirondelles*, the swallows, policemen who patrolled on bicycle. His navy blue cape emphasised his broad chest. He must have come directly from work.

Once, when I was reading on a gusty day in the park, the wind took hold of the pages and I lost my spot. Paul made my heart flutter like those pages rushing past.

Then a horrific thought occurred to me: what if Papa had sent him?

"What are you doing here?" I demanded.

"I'm not here because of you."

"Didn't think you were," I lied.

"Many tourists ask the police for directions. I need a book to improve my English."

"Did my father tell you I got the job?"

"I heard him grumbling about uppity women."

"Following up on a clue," I said tartly. "He'll soon make you lead detective. Just what you want."

"You've no idea what I want." He drew a nosegay from his messenger bag. "These are to wish you well on your first day."

I should have thanked him by kissing him on each cheek, but I felt shy and buried my nose in the blooms. My favourite flowers, daffodils held the promise of spring.

"Shall I help you find some books?"

"It'll be good practice to find them on my own." He held up a Library card. "I plan on spending time here."

Paul strode towards the reference room, leaving me adrift in the aisle. His card had been newly issued. Perhaps he'd come for me.

Over the course of the morning, most subscribers waited patiently as I helped them find periodicals; only one complained. "Why can't anyone here keep track of the *Herald?*" he grumbled. Later, I found the newspaper crumpled under Monsieur de Nerciat's briefcase.

A scuffle brought me out of the periodical room to the circulation desk, where a red-faced woman waved a book in Boris's face and shouted that the Library must stop lending "immoral" novels. When he refused to censor the collection, she stormed out.

"Don't look so shocked," he told me. "It happens at least once a week. Someone always thinks our job is to protect morals."

"Out of curiosity, which book was she talking about?"

"*Studs Lonigan.*"

"I'll make a note to read it."

He laughed, and, watching him, I couldn't help but think how odd — and wonderful — it was that we were now colleagues.

"I have something for you," he said.

"You do?" I hoped he'd selected a novel for me. Instead, he tendered a list of seventy books that I was to gather and wrap for out-of-town subscribers. I consulted my watch. Already 2p.m. I'd been so busy, I'd forgotten lunch. Too late now. From *Summer*, 813, to *Alcools*, 841 the treasure hunt took me throughout the three floors of stacks. By 6p.m., my feet ached and so did my head. I'd never felt a fatigue like this, not even during exam week. I'd met twenty people and couldn't remember a single name. I'd spoken English all day, answering dozens of enquiries: *is it true that Frenchmen eat frog legs, and if so, what do they do with the rest of the frog? May I access the archives? Where's the restroom? What did you say, girl? Speak up!* By the end of my shift, the language deserted me. It was like opening a novel, only to find the pages blank.

Clutching my droopy daffodils, I stepped into the cold night air. Frost covered the pebbles of the path and made them slick. The blisters on my feet throbbed. The walk home seemed as if it would take fifteen years instead of fifteen minutes. Limping along, I noticed that across the way, under the dim light of the *lampadaire*, a black car chugged. My father got out and opened the passenger door.

"Oh, Papa, *merci*." Relieved to slip back into French, I slid on to the seat, sitting for the first time since breakfast.

"Are you hungry?" He presented me with an Honoré pastry box. Opening it, I savoured the buttery aroma of the *financier* before taking a bite. The cake came apart in my mouth; I closed my eyes and chewed slowly.

"*Ça va?*" he asked. "The first day, and you're already exhausted. You don't have one of your headaches, do you?"

"I'm fine, Papa."

"At your age," he said, his tone tender, "Maman and I had just survived the war and were mourning the loss of friends and family. You're only twenty — we want you to enjoy your youth, find a beau, go to dances, not slave away in some book factory."

"Papa, please, not tonight . . ." My whole life, my parents' talk of war had ricocheted around me — tanks and trenches, mustard gas and mutilated soldiers.

"All right, we'll talk about something else. Now I know you work Sundays, so I've invited a fellow for dinner on Wednesday. This one says he reads!"

CHAPTER
SIX

ODILE

Paris, March 1939

Each morning, before the Library opened, I paid a visit to a different department. Monday, I had an appointment in accounting, where Miss Wedd, the bookkeeper, was known for her keen mind and scrumptious scones. When she leaned over her ledger, I saw three pencils tucked in her brown bun. After she explained the expenditure lines — everything from coal and firewood to books and glue for bindings — I asked if I could interview her. I had an idea for the monthly newsletter Miss Reeder had assigned to me. In addition to the usual scholarly reviews and the list of books that had been borrowed the most, I wanted to include something more personal about subscribers and staff.

"What kind of reader are you?" I asked, notepad in hand.

"I liked maths at school. Numbers always made more sense than people. That's why my favourite books are by the ancient Greeks: Pythagoras and Heraclitus. We're still using their work, their ideas.

"I'm not like Boris and Miss Reeder. I'm not good with the public" She slid a fourth pencil into her hair. "But I hope that in some small way my contribution here matters. For over a decade, I've filled entire books with tales of generous donors and knowledgeable staff who work long hours, only I write vertical columns instead of horizontal lines."

Interviewing her was like watching a rose bloom: she opened up, the petals of her cheeks pink with passion. "Thank you," I said, glad I chose her. "Readers will love your answers, and I'm eager to discover Heraclitus."

I was also enjoying getting to know my colleagues. Tuesday, I spent time with Peter-the-shelver, the only one tall enough to reach the top ledges. By arranging the books on the cart by their call numbers, he shelved ten books in the time I replaced two. He had the fine physique of a boxer, but when matronly Madame Frot's foghorn of a voice blared through the stacks, "Peter dear, oh, Peter," he dived into the cloakroom to avoid the amorous subscriber.

Wednesday, I went to the children's room, where low bookshelves bordered the walls, and tiny tables and chairs were grouped in front of the crackling fire. Though I'd never met the children's librarian, Muriel Joubert, I felt as if I knew her, because the neat script of her signature appeared on each of the cards of the books I borrowed. In the last week alone, she beat me to *Belinda*, *The Interesting Narrative of the Life of Olaudah Equiano* and *My Ántonia*. Given all she'd read, I'd pictured a white-haired lady. Instead, I found a girl my age observing me with keen violet eyes. Even with the black braid crowning her head, she didn't measure five feet.

"Mademoiselle Joubert?" I asked.

She told me to call her Bitsi, that everyone did, ever since a subscriber from Texas had taken one look at her and proclaimed, "Why, you're just an itsy-bitsy thing!" She said she'd wanted to make my acquaintance ever since she'd noticed my name scrawled on the cards of her favourite novels.

"We're bookmates," she said, in the decisive tone one would assert, "The sky is blue," or "Paris is the best city in the world." I was sceptical about soulmates, but could believe in bookmates, two beings bound by a passion for reading.

She proffered *The Brothers Karamazov*. "I wept when I finished." Her voice swelled with emotion. "First because I was happy to have read it. Second because the story was so moving. Third because I'll never again experience the discovery of it."

"Dostoevsky's my favourite dead author," I said.

"Mine, too. Who's your favourite live one?"

"Zora Neale Hurston. The first time I checked out *Their Eyes Were Watching God*, I gorged on the chapters, wolfing down the words, I needed to find out what happened next: would Janie marry the wrong man? Would Tea Cake live up to my hopes for Janie? Then, with a handful of pages left, I started to dread the fact that this world that I loved was coming to an end. I wasn't ready to say goodbye. So I read slowly, just savouring the scenes."

She nodded. "I do the same, to make each page last as long as possible."

"I finished the novel in four days, but kept it the full two weeks. On the due date, I placed it on the circulation desk, but my hand remained on the cover, not ready to let go. Boris found me three other books by Miss Hurston."

"I gorged on those, too, like chocolate cake, like love. I cared so deeply about the characters that they became real. I felt I knew Janie, that one day she might enter the Library and invite me for coffee."

"I feel that way about my favourite characters, too," Bitsi said.

A mother approached. "My son chose these" — she held up two storybooks — "but they appear to be . . . well-thumbed."

"They're well-loved," Bitsi replied. "If you prefer, we have brand-new books on our 'latest arrivals' shelf."

When Bitsi mouthed, "Back to work," and led them to the display, I peeked into the reference room, hoping to see Paul, but he wasn't there.

Disappointed, I continued to my desk, where a subscriber tapped her foot, wanting her *Harper's Bazaar*. "Where have you been?" Madame Simon scolded.

When I handed her the latest issue, still in its brown wrapping paper, she softened, confiding that at home she was always the last. Dentures wiggling as she spoke, she explained that everything she owned — the matted mink from a dead aunt, the false teeth that had belonged to her mother-in-law — had served someone else. But here, she was the first to take pleasure in fashion, though there was nothing she could afford. "Or fit into," she lamented, her beefy hand skimming her stout figure. She settled in next to Professor Cohen.

Observing Boris, Madame Simon said, "They say that during the Russian Revolution, his family fortune was lost. He had to start again here in France. Penniless as a pauper."

"Whatever his situation, he's a prince of a man," the Professor said.

"His wife's the princess, or was. Now she's a cashier. How the mighty have fallen!"

"Spoken by someone who's never had to earn her own keep."

Clara de Chambrun strode past, laden with papers. "And speaking of nobility," madame sniggered, "there's the Countess from Ohio."

"You've a bee in your beret today, and quite a sting. Clara's an excellent trustee, knows how to raise funds. We wouldn't be sitting here if it weren't for her. Since you're enamoured by fashion, I'll say this: snark isn't a good look on anyone."

71

CHAPTER
SEVEN

MARGARET

Paris, March 1939

Patting her morning pearls nervously, Margaret hesitated at the threshold of the American Library. It was as quiet as a cathedral, and she wasn't sure she should enter. Margaret certainly wasn't American, nor was she interested in books. But after four months in Paris, she was desperate for English in any form. The French language was a nasal bog that she had to wade through in the shops, the hairdresser's and the bakery. No one in those places spoke English. Reduced to sign language, she pointed and held up a finger to signal she wanted one croissant. She nodded to show she grasped the meaning, she shrugged to show she didn't.

At home, her husband Lawrence did most of the talking. Nanny minded Christina, and Jameson ran the flat with the same efficiency here as in London. No one needed her. Margaret barely spoke at all.

She'd assumed she would love Paris. The haute couture, the lingerie, the perfume. But shopping alone wasn't amusing. When she tried on dresses, no friends admired her figure. More than anything, Margaret wanted her mother's opinion — was this gown her colour, should she have a heart-to-heart with Lawrence or let him be? What surprised Margaret most about Paris wasn't Jeanne Lanvin's gorgeous dresses or the posh hats that women wore, it was how much she missed her mum.

Margaret didn't understand the unfamiliar money. And the shop girls cheated her! When she bought stockings, they told her, in their convoluted language, that 75 francs was the price for each one, not the pair. Yet when a Parisian behind her in the queue purchased the same stockings, she paid half. Margaret couldn't fight back, she couldn't insist. She could only stamp her foot, which made the shop girls giggle. Jokes at her expense were quite costly.

She stopped going out, stopped trying. She paced the flat, or curled up and cried under her evening gowns in "*le dressing*," though it was perfectly ridiculous to be miserable in the most fabulous city in the world. How she'd bragged to her friends! *I'll be in the romance capital of the world! Oh là là! Frenchmen will flirt with me! Oh là là! Champagne! Chocolat! You must visit!* How embarrassed she was by the truth! She would die before she told her friends. Not that they rang or wrote. When Margaret left London, she'd fallen off the face of their earth.

This morning, the consul's wife, a kindly woman, if a bit of a frump, had come to call. When Jameson announced her arrival, Margaret dashed to the mirror. She couldn't remember the last time she'd washed her hair. Her eyes were bloodshot. She was ashamed of how pathetic she'd become, and would have had the butler refuse Mrs Davies, but she was desperate for friends, and this was her first caller. She changed from her stained peignoir into a smart ivy dress. The consul's wife took one look at Margaret and insisted she visit the American Library, this very afternoon. And now here she was.

There was an easy camaraderie here that she'd never seen before. Women didn't ask, "What does your husband do?" Rather, they wanted to know, "What are you reading?" Margaret sighed. Yet more flurries of conversation that didn't include her.

"Welcome to the Library."

The librarian's dress was drab, but she was pretty enough with her hair swept up by a black bow. Her eyes sparkled like the gems Marjorie Simpson's second husband gave her for their third anniversary. Lawrence no longer gave Margaret jewellery like that.

"May I help you find something?"

Margaret gnawed on her stiff upper lip, wishing for once she could say what she wanted. Instead, she asked, "Would you have any books for my daughter? She's four."

The librarian tilted her head. "How about *Bella the Goat?*"

"You can't know how relieved I am to be in a place where English is spoken. Paris is so foreign." Margaret paused. That came out wrong. Everything she said came out wrong. "Of course, I realise that in France I'm the foreign one . . ."

74

"You'll fit in here," the librarian soothed. "We have many subscribers from England and Canada."

"Lovely. Would you happen to have anything for me?"

"A novel by Dorothy Whipple? *The Priory* is one of my favourites."

Actually, Margaret had meant magazines. She hadn't opened a book since dreary George Eliot at finishing school.

"Or *Miss Pettigrew Lives for a Day*, a Cinderella story for grown-ups."

Margaret could do with a fairy tale.

"If you're having trouble understanding French, we have some wonderful books on grammar. Lets see . . ."

Margaret was touched by this attention. At embassy events, when people chatted with Margaret, they kept one eye on her, the other on the room. The second they saw someone more important, they broke away mid-conversation.

"If you prefer," the librarian added, "we have *Vogue*."

She seemed disappointed, so Margaret said, "I'll take the books."

The librarian positively shimmered with enthusiasm. "Let's go get them. I'm Odile, by the way."

"I'm Margaret."

But instead of moving towards the stacks, Odile climbed the stairs. Margaret followed, and as they passed through the "Employees Only" door, she asked, "Where are we going?"

"You'll see."

In the tiny staffroom, Odile set the table with two mismatched teacups and a plate of plain scones. When the librarian turned to set the kettle on the hotplate, Margaret ran her finger over the rough surface of a scone, so like the ones her mum made. Yes, Paris was full of culinary delights, and she'd feasted on decadent pastries. Yet Margaret craved something familiar.

Odile sat and gestured to the seat beside her. "*Raconte*. It means 'tell me'."

For the first time since arriving in Paris, Margaret felt happy, she felt at home.

CHAPTER
EIGHT

ODILE

Paris, April 1939

L'heure bleue, that magical time between day and night, had fallen. As subscribers borrowed books and left for the day, stillness weaved its web over the tables and chairs. I loved the Library like this, when all was tranquil and it felt like mine.

In the thick leather ledger, I helped Boris tally how many subscribers had come in today (287), how many books had gone out (936), and details of Library life (another pregnant woman fainted — she read page 43 of *Prospective Mother*).

"It's late," he said. "You don't have to stay."

"I want to."

Boris gestured to the empty reading room, his elegant hand covered in paper cuts. "Heaven, isn't it?" And so began our nightly ballet, its choreography perfected over the last month. He made sure the windows were locked and closed the curtains; I dimmed the lights to warn the steadfast scholars in the reference room that the Library would soon close. Neither of us said anything as we realigned the chairs.

There were problems to discuss, tasks to assign, but all that would wait until tomorrow. After a day spent answering questions, this silence was our reward. I wondered if Madame Simon was right, that he was an aristocrat. I wondered if he would ever trust me enough to tell me anything about his life . . .

It was my turn to shoo out subscribers, so I made the rounds. Meandering along the rows of non-fiction, I saw titles I never noticed during the day. (This evening, I found *How to Boil Water in a Paper Bag*.) In the reference room, I peered into the stacks and made the best discovery — Paul. He was reading an English grammar book.

As he kissed me on each cheek, I tried to breathe him in. His skin smelled of tobacco, smoky like Lapsang Souchong, my favourite tea. I supposed I should step away, but the books were indulgent chaperones.

"Is it closing time?" he said. "Sorry to keep you."

"It's quite all right." Keep me. Keep me all to yourself.

"I've come in several times . . ."

"You have?"

"But you were busy with other subscribers."

We stood centimetres apart, yet it felt too far. As I moved closer, his lips brushed against mine. I let my fingers graze his cheek. Yesterday, if someone had told me that we would be kissing in the stacks, I'd have accused the person of inhaling glue fumes. Yet, this tender collision felt perfect and even right.

I'd read about passion — Anna and Vronsky, Jane and Mr Rochester — and felt the shivering sensations, or I'd thought I had. No passage on a page could convey the pleasure of this kiss.

Hearing the clip of high heels along the parquet, Paul and I both took a quick step back. Though we'd barely touched, every part of me — my skin, my blood, my bones — still felt him.

"There you are." Miss Reeder glanced from me to Paul.

"Thank you, er, Mademoiselle Souchet," he said. "Now I know where to find information on, er, the past participle." He held up the grammar book and rushed from the room.

The Directress's mouth twitched in amusement, "Miss Wedd is expecting you."

"Miss Wedd?"

"It's pay day."

Of course! Pay day. How could I have forgotten?

"What will you do with your first month's salary?"

"Do?" My mind was muddled.

"Of course, you'll want to save most of it — having a nest egg is important, but it's equally important to mark the occasion, perhaps to give a gift to those who've encouraged you along the way."

"That's very considerate." I wished I'd come up with the idea on my own. "Who did you thank?"

"My mother and best friend — I treated them to novels," she said. "Now please don't keep Miss Wedd waiting."

I joined the cheerful bookkeeper at her desk. Only two pencils in her bun tonight. "You were right about that Greek philosopher Heraclitus. I loved what he said about how 'No man ever steps in the same river twice'."

"The one thing we can count on is change," she agreed.

She counted out my salary. Each franc represented victory when I answered a question, embarrassment when I floundered, days speaking a foreign language, nights reading in order to offer book recommendations. I knew I'd love my job, but was surprised at how challenging it could be.

I tucked the notes into my pocket. This was the real reason I'd wanted the job: money equalled stability. I refused to end up destitute and alone like Aunt Caroline.

The following afternoon, I went to the bank and deposited my salary, keeping a few francs as spending money. Next, I went to the train station to purchase two tickets to Fontainebleau, something for Rémy to thank him for his steadfast support. More than music and books, he loved tramping around the forest, I thought to give him the present at dinner, but he took only a few bites before slipping away.

"He doesn't eat anything any more," Maman grumbled. "Doesn't he like my cooking?"

Papa grasped her plump hand in his. "It was a fine meal."

"These days, you prefer to dine out," she said sharply.

"Now, Hortense," he cajoled.

"Why don't you go and check on Rémy?" Maman told me.

He was at his desk, papers spread before him. I gave him the tickets, thinking he'd insist we go straight away. But he just kissed my cheek absent-mindedly. More and more, he was . . . gone. Even when he was with us, he wasn't. I missed him. He didn't say anything now, though he didn't go back to writing his tract.

"Did you go to class today?"

"What's the point of studying laws when no one respects them? Germany taking over Austria, Japanese soldiers marauding in China, The world's gone crazy, and no one gives a damn."

In a way, he was right. Skirmishes between subscribers felt more real to me than distant conflicts. Remembering the latest argument, I pinched a piece of paper in the middle and held it to my neck. "Here's Mr Pryce-Jones, with his paisley bow tie." I moved the paper to my mouth. "And this is Monsieur de Nerciat, with his woolly walrus moustache."

Bow tie: "Rearmament is the way to go! We need to prepare for war."

Moustache: "We need peace, not more guns."

Bow tie: "Ostrich! Stop burying your head in the sand."

Moustache: "Better an ostrich than a jackass. In the Great War —"

Bow tie: "Don't know why you bang on about the war! The only thing that's stayed the same is that awful haircut of yours."

Rémy laughed.

"If you think that's funny, you should catch a live show at the Library."

"I've got a tight deadline for this article."

"Come," I cajoled. "You'll see people do care."

Thursday was Story Hour, my favourite event of the week. I loved watching little ones immersed in stories, the way I had been with Aunt Caro. On my way there, I peeked into the reference room, hoping to see Paul, He wasn't there. *The Death of the Heart*, 823. I told myself that he couldn't visit the Library every day. Remembering our kiss, I touched my fingers to my lips. But maybe one day soon?

In the children's room, I moved to the hearth where a few mothers had gathered. Most chatted together, but one stood off to the side.

"Hello," she said, fiddling with her pearl necklace. "Lovely to see you again."

It was the lonely English woman. Margot? No, Margaret.

"*The Priory* was wonderful," she continued. "I liked it so much that I borrowed three other books by Mrs Whipple. I wasn't much of a reader before, but now I'm determined that my daughter and I will read together every day."

"Which one is she?" I asked.

Margaret pointed to the blonde, who was sitting next to Boris's little girl, Hélène. The girls spoke animatedly while waiting for Bitsi to begin, any moment now. I squinted at the clock above the doorway and was surprised to see Rémy enter. He skirted around the children to my side.

"I'm glad you came," I told him.

"How could I resist after your one-woman play? I wanted to spend some time with you in your favourite place. We've both been so busy . . ."

"You're here now, that's what counts."

Perched on a stool, Bitsi flipped through the pages of a book. She cleared her throat, and the room went silent. Twenty tots inched closer to her. As she read *Miss Maisy*, Bitsi's tone deepened, and her gaze hypnotised the audience. Enthralled, a boy touched her skirt, which billowed about her ballet slippers.

Glancing at Rémy, I saw that Bitsi had another fan — his eyes never left her face. When she finished, he clapped, and others joined in.

"So that's your 'bookmate'," he said. "Is she really as well-read as you?"

"Probably even more."

"She's talented," he said.

"She made the characters come alive."

"No, she became the characters." He strode to Bitsi's side.

I followed.

"*Vous êtes magnifique*," he said.

"*Merci*," she whispered, gaze now glued to the floor.

Wanting to introduce him to Mr Pryce-Jones and Monsieur de Nerciat, I tugged on his sleeve. He didn't notice.

"You must be parched," he told her. "Would you like to go for a *citron pressé*?"

It was the first time I'd seen him intent on a woman. At least six classmates had befriended me in order to meet him. Whenever I introduced him to a girl, he was polite, he listened, but never initiated a conversation.

I hoped Bitsi would accept his invitation. It wouldn't hurt if she left work early, this once.

Bitsi placed her hand in the crook of his arm. He closed his eyes for a fraction longer than a blink, a silent *merci*, before he escorted her out. Feeling forgotten, I tried to tell myself it was natural that Rémy was taken with her. They didn't mean to leave me behind.

Boris tapped me on the back. "The good news," he said, "is that we're donating books."

"What's the bad?"

"There are over three hundred, and your job is sorting them."

He handed me a list, and as I read the titles, I returned from the land of feeling sorry for myself. So Rémy's visit hadn't ended up as I'd expected. There would be another time.

"When I learned that the Library distributed thousands of books to universities, I found it admirable. Of course, that was before I was the one who packed them!" I joked.

Boris laughed. "Rather you than me."

The back room was bursting with empty crates and jumbles of books. "Safe journey," I said to a hardcover as I placed it in the crate for the American College of Tehran, Persia; another went to The Seamen's Institute in Italy; a third, fourth and fifth would travel together

84

to Turkey. I kept on for what seemed like hours, but when I consulted the clock, only ten minutes had gone by. It would be an endless, lonely afternoon.

There was a rap at the door. "I asked the man at the front desk where you'd disappeared to, and he sent me up here," Margaret said.

"I'd love some company. Would you mind lending a hand?" I said, then noticed her pink silk dress. It would be covered in dust if she stayed, and, anyway, women in couture didn't work.

"Why not? I've nothing better to do."

I offered to fetch her daughter, but she said Christina had seemed happy to make friends with Hélène and her father. I showed Margaret how to find the destination for each volume. She weaved between the crates gracefully, packing the books with care. "*Bon voyage,*" she whispered to each one.

I stared at her.

"You must think I'm crazy for talking to books," she said.

"Not at all."

"*Bon voyage* is the only French I remember from school. My mother was right, I should have worked harder."

"It's not too late! I'll teach you a few phrases. *Bon vent* means 'fair wind'. We say it to wish someone Godspeed or good luck. We say *bon courage* to give someone courage."

"*Bon courage!*" she told a chemistry manual.

"*Bon vent!*" I said to a maths primer.

We giggled as we wished the books well.

"What brought you to Paris?"

"My husband is an attaché at the British Embassy."

"A nice circle to be in."

"It's rather a vicious circle," She winced. "Oh, please don't tell anyone I said that. You can see why I'm not the diplomat."

Suddenly shy, Margaret went back to sorting books.

"You must attend glamorous events," I said, hoping she'd tell me about the parties.

"Yesterday, there was tea at the residence of the Dutch Ambassador, but I'm having more fun now."

"How can that be? You must encounter people from all over the world."

"They're interested in my husband, not me." Tears fell down her rouged cheeks. "I miss my mum, miss meeting my friends for tea."

I didn't know how to respond. Miss Reeder said foreigners often felt homesick in Paris and that staff could ease feelings of loneliness.

"I didn't mean for this to happen." Margaret dabbed her tears. "My mum calls me 'the teapot with a leaky spout'."

"She'll soon call you *la Parisienne*." I put the lid on the last crate. "You were a big help."

"Truly?"

"You should volunteer here."

"I haven't any training. What if I make a mistake?"

"It's a library, not a surgery! No one will die if you put a book in the wrong place."

"I'm not sure —"

"You'll make new friends, and I'll teach you French."

I accompanied Margaret to the courtyard, where her daughter was playing with Hélène. A shadowy dusk fell over the city and crept over the wall, on to the lawn, past the ivy in the urn, towards the Library. Darkness could come only so close — the lamps in the reading room shone brightly. Through the window, Margaret and I saw Madame Simon glance about furtively before taking a poodle from her bag. Placing him on her lap, she and Professor Cohen rubbed his belly. Engrossed in their own happiness, they didn't notice Boris and his wife Anna in the corner, dark heads tilted together. The two never touched, but a tender love radiated from them. Bony finger at her mouth, stern Mrs Turnbull shushed some students. Poor Peter-the-shelver dived into the stacks to avoid the matron who tracked him like prey. Observing him, our bookkeeper covered her mouth to muffle her laughter.

There was a longing in Margaret's gaze as she watched the unfolding scenes. Something told me she needed the Library. Something told me the Library needed her. Over dusty books, our conversation had flowed like the Seine. I hoped more than anything that Margaret would join our cast.

CHAPTER
NINE

ODILE

Paris, July 1939

It was exam week, and the tables were full, all but one spot taken. Monsieur Grosjean, in his tangerine earmuffs, planted himself in the middle of the reading room. Observing him, Boris and I braced ourselves, "What's our irregular regular going to do?" he asked me.

" 'Call me Ishmael,' " monsieur began to read aloud. " 'Some years ago — never mind how long precisely — having little or no money in my purse, and nothing particular to interest me on shore, I thought I would sail about a little and see the watery part of the world . . .' " When Boris pointed to the empty chair and invited him to read quietly *to himself*, monsieur replied, "I'll be damned before I sit by those perfumed Jews."

Miss Reeder approached, lips pinched in a frown. It was the first time I'd seen her angry. Monsieur took a step back. "I'll get to you in a moment," she said tersely. The Directress gathered the young women — students from the Sorbonne — and apologised, promising they'd be able to study in peace. She admonished Monsieur Grosjean, telling him, "There's no place in this Library for that kind of talk."

"I'm saying what others are thinking," he muttered.

"Think again," she said.

"Don't tell me what to do!" Monsieur waved his hand, nearly hitting her.

Boris gripped Monsieur Grosjean's arm and escorted him to the door. In his sleeveless jumper and tie, Boris was surprisingly proficient in the role of bouncer.

"I wanted to read out the passage about the 'damp, drizzly November in my soul'!"

"What soul?" Boris said.

"Unhand me —"

"You're not a victim," Boris said as he forced monsieur outside. "You're an unpleasant man who's offended a great many people. Say another syllable, and I'll make sure you never return."

Miss Reeder soothed the subscribers upset by the outburst; I decided to check on Boris. I found him at the far end of the courtyard, near the crimson roses that the caretaker spoke to as though they were his children. Boris leaned against the wall, a Gitane clenched between his fingers.

"*Ça va?*"

He didn't answer; I leaned against the wall, too, and we watched the smoke unfurl and rise.

"After the Revolution, I was forced to say goodbye to my country," he said. "It was painful to leave, but my brother and I believed that in coming here we'd be in a better, smarter place. Isn't France the country of the

Enlightenment? In Russia, many people were killed in pogroms. Our neighbour was killed, just for being a Jew. So when I hear talk like that . . ."

"I'm sorry."

"I guess hatred is everywhere." He took a drag on his cigarette; when he blew out the smoke, it seemed like a sigh. "Even in our Library."

Papa had been right — working with the public could be demoralising. Feeling particularly weary, I took the bus home and plunged into the pages of my faithful friend, 813, *Their Eyes Were Watching God*, turning towards the window to capture the faint light. *She knew things that nobody had ever told her. For instance, the words of the trees and the wind. She often spoke to falling seeds and said, "Ah hope you fall on soft ground," because she had heard seeds saying that to each other as they passed. She knew the world was a stallion rolling in the blue pasture of ether. She knew that God tore down the old world every evening and built a new one by sun-up. It was wonderful to see it take form with the sun and emerge from the grey dust of its making. The familiar things and people had failed her so she hung over the gate and looked up the road towards way off.* When the bus screeched to a stop at a red light, I fell out of my book.

Where were we? I searched for a familiar landmark and found my father's *commissariat*, an immense, brooding building. I was far from home but maybe I could get a ride with Papa if he was still at work, I scanned the street for his car; instead, I found him, fedora low on his brow, some woman on his arm. Perhaps he was consoling the victim of a crime, a shopkeeper who'd been robbed. I noticed the name of the building behind them, the Normandy Hotel. No, she was a receptionist or a maid. Papa grinned at something she said, and kissed her, not on each cheek, but full on the mouth.

How could he do that to Maman? The harlot wasn't even pretty with her thinning hair and door-knobby cheeks. Mercifully, the light turned green, and the bus lumbered over the cobbles, taking me away.

Feeling ill, I alighted at the next stop. On the walk home, I tried to make sense of what I'd seen. How long had this been going on? What had Maman done to deserve this? What hadn't she done? I flipped through the pages of my memory. One evening at dinner, Maman had said that Papa preferred to "dine out". Was an affair what she meant?

In the hall, I dropped my book bag and bellowed Rémy's name. He was reading *Of Mice and Men*. "Steinbeck can wait," I said. We went to our secret place, away from our parents, away from the world, under my bed where the light didn't quite reach. Rémy, then I, scooted along the parquet. It felt good to slip back into childhood, to the last place anyone would search for us.

Having trouble catching my breath, I sputtered, "Papa. With a woman. Not Maman."

"Why are you surprised?"

His nonchalance hurt as much as seeing Papa with the harlot. "You knew? Why didn't you say?"

"We don't have to tell each other everything."

Since when?

"Important men have mistresses," he continued. "It's a status symbol, like a gold watch."

Did Rémy really believe that? Did Paul? Papa's affair felt like a betrayal, not just of Maman, but of our family. How could Rémy not see that? I glanced over, but I couldn't make out his expression. I didn't know what he was thinking. I didn't know what to think. My fingers clung to the mattress coils.

"Bitsi said part of growing up is realising parents have their own lives, their own desires," he finished.

Bitsi said.

I remembered the other time Rémy and I had not seen eye to eye. The summer we turned nine, because of a lung ailment, he stayed in bed, and Maman coated his gaunt chest with mustard plasters to ease the congestion. I stayed with him — reading aloud or watching him doze — every day except Sunday, when Maman and I went to Mass with Uncle Lionel and Aunt Caro. I liked Uncle Lionel because he always said he wished he had a daughter like me. That made Aunt Caro weepy, and Maman insisted that they'd soon be blessed with a child. But, Maman — who said she was always right — would find that this time she was only half right.

When my uncle stopped attending Mass, Aunt Caro explained it so glibly — he had the flu, or he needed to take clients to Calais — that no one realised anything was wrong. That last time, as we left the church, Maman even said, "I'm glad it's just us girls."

I skipped ahead, dreaming of dessert.

"I'm relieved you feel that way," Aunt Caro said, "I have some news."

It was the thorn in her tone that made me stop, I didn't look back. I didn't want Maman to accuse me of eavesdropping.

"Lionel has been distant," Aunt Caro continued.

"Distant?"

"I had a feeling there was someone else. When I asked, he admitted he had a mistress."

"It's the way of our world," Maman said. "I'm surprised he told you the truth."

She sounded so bitter that I turned around. Neither noticed me.

"He had to." Aunt Caro's eyes welled with tears. "He got her pregnant. I've begun divorce proceedings."

"Divorce." Maman blanched. "What will we tell people?"

My mother's mind always went straight to *What will people think?* She glanced nervously at Monsignor Clement on the church steps.

"That's all you have to say?" Aunt Caro said.

"You won't be able to attend Mass."

"It's a pity, but I can read scripture on my own. Let's go."

Maman didn't move. "You need to go to your own home, tend to things there."

"I was hoping to stay with you."

"You need to go to your own apartment."

"I can't. Lionel's moving her into our place."

"That isn't my *affair*."

93

How shocking to see Maman, who hated confrontation, arguing in front of the church, before God and everyone. How could she be so cruel to her own flesh and bones?

"Please," Aunt Caro said. "I can't bear to be on my own."

Maman's gaze skittered to mine. I expected her to embrace her sister like she did me when I fell and scraped my knee, but Maman merely said, "I don't want the children to be influenced."

A divorcee was beneath a fallen woman. My mother believed what the Church told her to believe, but surely she'd make an exception for her own sister.

"I don't have anywhere to go," Aunt Caro said. "I don't have any money."

"Please, Maman," I said. But her expression only hardened.

"Divorce is a sin."

"We can ask forgiveness for a sin at confession," I replied.

When Maman couldn't win with logic, she used force. She grabbed my arm and dragged me down the street, towards home, I looked back at Aunt Caroline, who watched us go, hand trembling at her breast.

When we arrived, I went straight to Rémy's room, but as I twisted the knob, Maman propped herself against the door, "Don't upset your brother."

Over the next days, I asked about Aunt Caro, certain Maman would relent. She said, "Mention her one more time, and I'll send you away." I believed her.

For two weeks, I held my silence, or my silence held me. Unable to keep a secret from Rémy any longer, I perched beside him on the bed. His complexion was ashen, and I knew that he was exhausted from the incessant coughs that racked his body. "That mustard plaster makes you smell like a Sunday roast," I teased.

"Very funny."

"Sorry." I moved to tousle his hair. If he let me, he forgave my joke. If he didn't, he was still angry.

He let me.

"Feeling better?"

"Not really."

"Oh." I didn't dare tell — Maman had warned me not to upset him. My parents and I lived in fear of a relapse. We whispered when we believed Rémy might be sleeping, we tiptoed past his room.

What is it? I felt him ask.

Nothing, I replied.

Tell, he insisted.

Sometimes we communicated like that.

He listened as my pain poured out: I'd believed our mother's love flowed unconditionally, yet she'd turned it off like a tap. And what would become of our aunt?

"Maman told me that Aunt Caro wanted to move back to Mâcon," he said slowly.

My head reared back. Wanted to?

"Then why didn't Aunt Caro say goodbye?" I argued, "Why hasn't she written?"

For once, my chatty brother didn't have an answer.

"You'd rather believe what's convenient than what's true," I accused.

"You must have misunderstood. Maman could never be so cruel."

His refusal to believe me was as devastating as our mother forsaking her own sister.

"You weren't there," I said. "Playing sick, as usual."

His face flushed. He sat up and opened his mouth. I braced myself, expecting him to let me have it. Instead, he hacked and hacked, a deep cough that brought black blood. Helpless, I handed him my handkerchief and stroked his back, all thoughts of winning the argument gone.

Two months later, Rémy was back to attending Mass. Like Maman, he knelt lovingly before the crucifix, convinced his faith had brought him through, I let him believe what he needed to. I had learned that love was not patient, love was not kind. Love was conditional. The people closest to you could turn their backs on you, saying goodbye for something that seemed like nothing. You could only depend on yourself.

My passion for reading grew — books wouldn't betray. While Rémy spent his pocket money on sweets, I saved mine. He was the class clown, I was the dux. When his friends asked me out, I said no. Love was out of the question. I would learn a trade, get a job, and save money, so that when the inevitable happened, I could save myself.

Bleary-eyed after a restless night, I tried to help subscribers as best I could. It was hard not to dwell. Papa had a mistress, Rémy spent every second with Bitsi, and Paul hadn't returned to see me. I stopped at the circulation desk in the hope that Boris would have a book for me.

"You've been blue today." He handed me 891.73. "Go to the Afterlife. No one will bother you there."

Holding Chekhov to my chest, I slid up the stairs, past the scholars on the second floor who hadn't noticed it was summer, to the serene third floor, where we kept the books that were rarely borrowed, the Afterlife.

As I floated through the stacks, the silence filled me with peace. Hidden among the books, I read: *He had two lives: one, open, seen and known by all who cared to know; and another life running its course in secret. And through some strange, perhaps accidental, conjunction of circumstances, everything that was essential to him was hidden from other people.* We could never know our loved ones, and they would never know us. It was heartbreaking, it was true. Yet there was solace: in reading other people's stories, I knew that I wasn't alone.

"There you are!" Margaret said. Her face — usually perfectly powdered — shone with the effort of handling heavy tomes, and with contentment. The hesitant waif I'd first met had been replaced by a confident, capable woman.

"What was the task today?"

"Relocating the encyclopaedia sets." Rubbing her upper arms, she said, "One must be strong to work here."

"You're kind to give so much time."

"It's easy when you believe, and I believe in the Library."

I wondered about giving my heart to Paul. "What if you don't receive anything in return?"

"I'm not sure one should expect something when giving." She regarded me quizzically. "What are you doing up here on your own?"

"Taking inventory."

"You're rather pensive."

"I'm fine."

"Yes, I can see that," she said lightly. "It's stuffy up here. You need some fresh air."

Once outside, *The Lady with the Little Dog and Other Stories* tucked under my arm, I led Margaret up side streets.

"Where are we going?" she asked.

I frowned. Was Paul's precinct on rue Washington?

I'd seen love go wrong. Now I wanted to see love go right. I needed to know if he felt the same way I did: hopeful, cautious. I had a job and was growing more independent. Perhaps I could take a chance.

"Is everything all right?"

"I . . ." I didn't know how to say all that I felt, and anyway, she was so cosmopolitan, my problems wouldn't interest her.

"Would you like to attend the embassy party on Bastille Day?"

I turned to her. "Truly?"

"Of course! I want to cheer you up. Come to my flat, we'll get ready together. You can borrow one of my frocks, Er, not that you don't have frocks of your own . . ."

I barely heard. There was the precinct. Hurrah! I stopped short, Margaret regarded the bars of the windows warily. When a handful of handsome policemen exited, a dawning expression crossed her face. "Is there perchance a certain subscriber you're hoping to run into? I do hope he's a constable, not a robber!"

"He is."

"Go say hello."

"Papa wouldn't want me to. He says precincts are full of criminals."

"Is your father here?"

"No."

"Then I don't see why you can't go in!" She opened the wooden door and pushed me inside. The dim light barely cut through the fog of cigarette smoke. On the bench beside me, a man in a soiled undershirt leered. I clutched *The Lady* to my chest. He inched closer; I moved away. Perhaps Paul had taken the position Papa offered and no longer worked here. Perhaps he'd never worked here. I was an idiot. I shouldn't have come. On my way out, I felt a hand on my elbow. I jerked away, ready to thwack the tramp with Chekhov; instead, I found concerned blue eyes.

"When I dreamed of seeing you again, it wasn't here," Paul said.

I lowered the book. "You wanted to see me again?"

"Of course. But after I embarrassed you in front of your boss . . ."

"You didn't. Anyway, we've missed you . . . at the Library."

"I've missed . . . the Library, too," he said.

I waited for him to say something else, but when he didn't. I said, "I should go. A friend's outside . . ."

"My shift just ended, may I treat you both to dinner?"

In the bistro, the waiter, so dapper in his black blazer and bow tie, led us to a quiet table near the back wall, away from the cops who eyed us over their beers. Though none of them looked familiar, I wondered if any had been to Sunday lunch.

The mouth-watering scent of caramelised apples wafted out from the kitchen.

"What is that glorious smell?" Margaret asked.

"*Tarte tatin*," I answered. "My third-favourite dessert, after profiteroles and Maman's chocolate mousse."

"My fourth favourite," Paul said.

"I haven't tasted it," Margaret said, "but I'm convinced it's my new favourite."

Suddenly shy, I brushed the breadcrumbs off the checked tablecloth. She mouthed, "Talk to him." The silence grew louder as I tried to think of something to say. Perhaps I could ask about his job. I thought of Papa, who came home from work in a foul mood, complaining about the miscreants he dealt with, Rémy and I were never sure if he meant criminals or colleagues.

"Why on earth did you want to be a policeman?" I blurted out.

"She means it's such a dangerous job," Margaret said. "She was telling me how much she admires our men in blue."

"It's what I always wanted to do," he said. "To help people, to keep them safe."

"How rewarding!" she said.

"Why on earth would you want to be a librarian?" he asked, an *étincelle*, a sparkle, in his eye.

"Sometimes I like books more than people."

"Books don't lie or steal," he said. "We can depend on them."

I was surprised, and heartened, to hear an echo of my own feelings.

"What kind of reader are you?" I asked.

"Is this for you, or the Library newsletter?"

I felt my face flush with pride. "You read my newsletter?"

"I loved Miss Wedd's answer, and looked up old Heraclitus."

" 'We never step into the same river twice,' " he and I said together.

"I'm asking for me," I said shyly.

"I like non-fiction, mainly. Especially geography. I've enjoyed studying English grammar again, something with rules. Something I can point to and say, yes, exactly like that. I suppose it's because I need things to be true."

I was ready to argue that novels could be truer than life, but he continued, "Probably because I spend time with criminals who ignore rules. Felons don't care who they hurt. They tell good stories, and you want to

101

believe they had a reason for doing what they did. It's hard when you learn that someone you'd trusted lied to your face."

"It is painful," I said, thinking of Papa and his harlot.

The waiter cleared his throat. I'd forgotten we were in a busy restaurant, forgotten dear Margaret at my side. After *le serveur* took our order, Paul told her in halting English, "I'm not sure I could live so far from home. I admire you."

"That's kind of you," she said. "I was terribly homesick, but then I met Odile."

"Margaret has been an amazing help at the Library."

Blushing, she said, "Do you have holiday plans?"

"Each summer, I help my aunt on the farm," he said.

"Near Paris?" Margaret asked.

"In Brittany."

"You're going away?" I said glumly. The waiter brought our *steak frites*, but I was no longer hungry and picked at my chips.

After dinner, Margaret thanked Paul and climbed into a taxi. Under the soft glow of the streetlights, he walked me home. I didn't know if I should hurry like I usually did or match his pace. I didn't know if I should shove my hand in my pocket or let it dangle at my side so he could hold it, if he wanted to. Ascending the stairs, I wondered if he would lean down until his lips were on mine, until I could breathe him in like air. On the landing, he didn't come closer. I hid my disappointment by bowing my head to search for the key, lost in the bottom of my clutch.

As I tried to fit it into the lock, Paul touched my wrist. I froze.

"I was going to ask you out," he said.

"You were?"

"Then your father offered me a job, again."

I dropped the key.

Paul liked me because of Papa. What a fool I'd made of myself, hunting him down at the police station. I felt queasy. I needed to move to the other side of the doorway and close the door between us. Bending down, my fingers swiped at the key, but Paul was faster, grasping it in one hand, my elbow in the other.

"I'm qualified," he said, righting me, "and frankly, need the pay rise to afford somewhere decent to live."

I stared at the small blue button of his shirt. "Congratulations. When do you start?"

"I turned him down."

"You did?"

"I never want you to doubt my feelings."

My heart began to bloom. He covered my mouth with his. At first, my lips pursed like a starlets in the movies, then my mouth opened, and his tongue caressed mine. When Paul raised his head, I gazed at him in wonder, feeling that in the space of a languorous kiss I'd plummeted into *Wuthering Heights*.

On Bastille Day, when I arrived at Margaret's flat, a butler led me to the sitting room, where portraits of snooty men looked down on me. Intimidated, I moved from them to the grand piano parked in the corner. It was as big as Papa's car. My fidgety fingers hit a few notes. No one I knew had a butler or a grand piano — elements of novels, not real life. At the window, I could see the golden-domed chapel where Napoleon was buried. Indeed, the neighbours here were high-ranking. At home, we rarely opened the windows because of the coal dust that wafted over from the train station. The low ceilings made our dim apartment feel cosy on good days, claustrophobic on bad. The view from my bedroom was into the building opposite ours — ten feet away — where a line of limp girdles dried above Madame Feldman's bath. Sunlight and splendid views were a luxury. Margaret wasn't exactly the waif I'd pictured.

"Did we keep you waiting? Christina didn't want to get out of the bath," Margaret said, her daughter in her arms. The little girl hid her face in the collar of Margaret's blouse, and all I could see were damp ringlets.

"We met at Story Hour," I reminded her. "It's my favourite time of the week."

She perked up. "Mine, too."

A nanny came for Christina, and I trailed Margaret through her powder-blue bedroom to the dressing room, which was the size of Miss Reeder's office. One wall was lined with couture day dresses, another with evening gowns, each worth more than a year's salary. It was hard to believe that one woman had so much, and impossible not to gawk. The colours! Candy-apple red, toffee, peppermint, liquorice! I couldn't stop touching the gowns.

"Would you like to try one on?"

104

"Would I!"

I couldn't decide, so Margaret handed me a black gown. I held it to my torso and floated around the dressing room. "Come on," I said. "What are you waiting for?"

She pulled a green gown from the hanger and joined me in a bout around the room. I began warbling the words to "La Vie en Rose", and Margaret sang along, until we were out of breath from dancing and singing and giggling, and we fell into a heap under the silken gowns.

"Am I interrupting?" The man spoke English with a strong French accent. His thin black moustache rivalled that of the provocateur Salvador Dalí.

Margaret and I stood, and she introduced us.

"*Enchanté*," he said to me.

Because of his posh clientele, society papers called Monsieur the "Heir Dresser". He did not confer with *clientes* about what they wanted. He simply knew what had to be done. I offered Margaret dull days repairing books, she offered me a date with Paris's most sought-after stylist.

Margaret had me try on the black gown so her maid could hem it, then she sat me down at her Art Deco dressing table.

"Paul's a nice chap," she said as Monsieur Z began to comb my hair.

"Do you think he and I have enough in common? He's a policeman, and I'm, well, me."

"Lawrence and his Cambridge cronies can recite sonnets. It doesn't mean they know anything about love, Paul clearly cares for you, and that's more important than his job title or the books he reads."

I should have told her I appreciated her reassurance, but Monsieur Z massaged my scalp, and I gave in to the pleasure. I didn't realise how anxious I'd felt — about my burgeoning feelings for Paul, the painful distance between Rémy and me, my father neglecting us for his mistress — until the tension melted away. When Maman cut my hair, her comb tore through the tangles. Monsieur's slid through my tresses like a knife through butter.

This was the first time I'd had my hair professionally styled, and I was mesmerised by monsieur wrapping locks of my hair around the heated tong to create a sea of rippling waves.

When he finished with a flourish of his hands and a resolute "*Voilà!*" Margaret proclaimed, "Just like Bette Davis. You'd make one hell of a femme fatale."

As Monsieur Z tied Margaret's hair in an elaborate topknot, she asked, "Do you think Miss Reeder has a beau?"

"The ambassador escorted her to the Library gala."

"They say Bill Bullitt is a keen negotiator but that he has a roving eye. I know a Norwegian consul who's perfect for her. I'll advise him to become a subscriber."

"He'll have to join the queue."

When Monsieur Z finished styling Margaret's hair, she didn't look at the mirror, she looked to me.

"What do you think?"

"Gorgeous," I said wholeheartedly. "Inside and out."

106

She blushed, and I wondered how long it had been since she'd been complimented.

"Lawrence will fall in love with you all over again," I said.

"Hardly . . . he's very busy."

"Too busy to tell you you're beautiful?"

"Not everyone sees me the way you do." She rose without a glimpse in the mirror.

She donned the strapless green dress and handed me the hemmed gown. The silk slid along my skin, so unlike the scratchy wool I wore in winter, the stiff linen in summer. She fastened my zipper, and for an instant, as I admired my reflection, I couldn't breathe. My own dresses drooped over my torso like a tablecloth. This gown worked, cinching in my waist, pushing up a bust I didn't even know I had. Though I told myself the bodice was tight, I knew the cold sensation coiling around my ribs was envy. Margaret had so much, and I had so little.

"Today's the first time I've enjoyed getting ready for a party in Paris," she said. "I hope you'll come again."

Gowns and house-calls from hairdressers — I could get used to luxury. Her invitation to return dissolved the whorl of jealousy.

When we floated down the hall to join Lawrence in the den, the silk of my dress whispered a sensual *yes, yes, yes* as it caressed my calves. I wished Paul could see me.

Lawrence lounged in an armchair, half hidden by the *Herald*. Beside me, Margaret cleared her throat. He set down the paper. Dusky lashes shrouded his turquoise eyes. *Mon Dieu*, he was dashing in his dinner jacket! "You're ravishing!" He rose and kissed my hand. I expected him to kiss Margaret, but he kept his focus on me, my hand still in his. "If I weren't already married . . ." He waggled his brows, and I giggled, entirely charmed.

"Do you happen to be acquainted with Mr Pryce-Jones?" I asked, wanting to show that I, too, knew someone in exalted diplomatic circles.

"The mans a legend! He wrote the protocol for Franco-British relations, and he hasn't lost a debate since 1926. How do you know him?"

"He's one of our habitués," Margaret said proudly.

Lawrence kept his gaze on me. "It's kind of you to let her play at being a librarian."

Beside me, Margaret stiffened. It made me think of a line from *Their Eyes Were Watching God. She starched and ironed her face, forming it into just what people wanted to see.*

"She doesn't 'play at' anything," I responded, snatching my hand from his and tucking it around her waist. "Margaret's extremely competent."

There was a peculiar current in the air. He'd gone from charming to condescending; she'd become wooden. I remembered Maman's advice to cousin Clotilde: *Make the courtship last as long as you can. Once you marry everything changes.* Was this what Maman had meant?

"You look handsome." Margaret spoke the line as if it were from a tired drama she no longer wished to play.

"So do you," he said distractedly as he consulted his pocket watch. "Shall we? The chauffeur is waiting."

At the residence of the British Ambassador, under the brilliant light of the chandeliers, women in jewels dazzled. Like Lawrence, each gentleman wore a black *smoking*. It was the kind of party I'd dreamed about. I was dying to hear about the places the other guests had seen, the books they'd read.

Deserting us, Lawrence rushed towards a busty brunette. "If you weren't happily married, I'd whisk you away."

"Darling, don't let that stop you!" She stroked his chest as if Margaret weren't there.

It's a vicious circle. Margaret's remark about diplomatic circles finally meant something. I scowled at Lawrence, furious at him for humiliating Margaret in this way, furious at myself for having been taken in by his generic flattery.

"Don't let him spoil your evening." She gestured to a stout matron. "That's the consul's wife. She's in charge of lost souls.

"Mrs Davies," Margaret called out. "Lovely to see you. Thank you for your advice to visit the Library."

"You're looking better," she replied warmly.

"Have you met my new and dearest friend?"

"One friend can make all the difference," Mrs Davies said. "Yes, we've crossed paths at Professor Cohen's lectures."

I hadn't known that Mrs Davies was an unofficial yet vital delegate of the diplomatic corps, and watched as she greeted each new arrival personally. "How pretty you are," she said to a pallid lady who blossomed with the compliment. "How are you adjusting?" she asked a lone *Italienne* who glanced around nervously. "France can be a woman's dream, but the reality takes some getting used to."

"We can't let Hitler steamroll his way across Europe!" Mr Pryce-Jones said, his opinion echoing through the ballroom like it did at the Library when he and Monsieur de Nerciat argued, "We must band together and fight."

"Doesn't he realise it's a party?" I said.

"War is all he ever talks about these days," Margaret replied.

"Did you see *Othello* last week?" asked Mrs Davies.

Several guests spoke simultaneously, relieved to discuss something other than war. "How queer to see Shakespeare in French!" "*Très bizarre!*" "Poor Desdemona."

"France's army is the strongest it has ever been, that's what Général Weygand says."

"Général Weiss says that the French air force is the best in Europe. We've nothing to worry about!"

"We must create alliances," Lawrence insisted. "Italy used to be an ally, but Mussolini's signed a treaty with Hitler."

"Does anyone know the name of a reputable dressmaker?"

"You simply must go to Chez Geneviève, Emma Jane Kirby did, her gown is sumptuous!"

"Can you believe that Emma, flirting with a man thrice her age," Margaret whispered, staring at the blonde beauty. "He must be terribly rich!"

"The old goat is lapping it up," I replied.

"Young Lawrence is right!" Mr Pryce-Jones said. "We need to observe what's happening around us."

110

"Nonsense. We must appease Hitler," the ambassador replied.

"Silly old fool!" Margaret whispered.

"Incompetent fool!" Lawrence roared.

"Champagne!" the consul's wife cried out. "More champagne."

Fantastique! The last time I'd had a glass was at New Year's. Popping corks — the sign of celebration, my favourite sound in the whole world — heralded servants who swirled around the room, proffering flutes. Everything was held out to me on a silver tray. Bubbles glistened in my glass, icy rivulets slid down my throat. I was so dazzled, I forgot Lawrence's boorish behaviour, forgot the fighting diplomats. I took in the dewy Turner landscapes on the walls, tasted the caviar that men in white gloves offered. Margaret had all this, all the time; thanks to her, I had one night, and I meant to enjoy it. A burst of fireworks exploded in the sky. Wanting to watch, I drew her outside, where we joined other revellers on the lawn. The wafting scent of roses surrounded us. High stone walls hid the city from us. The stately residence — its windows lit — glowed. Above, flecks of light soared then fizzled, and a hazy happiness imbued me, all worries of war, of Rémy, of Papa, of Paul forgotten.

CHAPTER
TEN

ODILE

Paris, August 1939

Paul came to the Library so often that Miss Reeder began referring to him as "our most faithful subscriber". On the afternoons he was on patrol, he parked his bicycle in the courtyard and helped me with tasks such as ripping through the heavy paper that protected magazines like *Life* and *Time* as they made the ocean crossing. Alas, under the nosy watch of Madame Simon, sneaking a kiss was impossible.

Home was no better. Sitting thirty-two centimetres apart, Paul and I left our tea untouched. "Do you think the rain will stop?" I asked, aware that Maman was listening in around the corner.

"The clouds are clearing."

He was leaving for Brittany tomorrow, yet here we were, discussing rainfall like strangers at a bus stop.

"Let's go for a walk," Paul said. "I want to take you to my favourite place in Paris."

"I'm not sure," my mother said from the hallway.

"Please, Maman." Longing turned my tone ragged. "He'll be gone most of August."

112

"This once then. But don't stay out too long."

His hand warmed the small of my back as he whisked me along the avenue, through the symphony of honking horns, past a shopkeeper smoking a cigarette just outside the door, to the Gare du Nord. Under its immense glass roof, porters in blue overalls hauled luggage. Travellers shouted and shoved as they made their way to the trains.

Paul pointed to the platform where a bespectacled young man kissed a woman who'd alighted from a carriage. "I come here to be in the presence of love. You probably think I'm crazy, spying on people . . ."

I shook my head. It was why I read — to glimpse other lives.

A musician with a trumpet case rushed by. A group of Scouts gawked at a locomotive. A mother let go of her toddlers' hands, and they ran to a man in a trench coat. He picked them up and spun them about.

"How darling," I said.

Paul was riveted by the homecoming.

"What is it?" I asked.

"Nothing."

"Nothing?"

He watched as the family left the station. "My parents and I used to live a block from here."

"You did?"

"Until my father left . . . I was seven. My mother said he'd taken a long trip on the train. Convinced he'd return, I came here." He turned to me. "I'm still coming here."

I drew him closer, and he buried his face in my hair. I felt his shaky heartbeat against mine. Perhaps it wasn't dangerous to trust.

"I've never told anyone," he said.

On the way home, neither of us said a word. We inched up the stairs to the landing.

"Can you stay for dinner?" I asked.

He kissed my temple, my cheek, my lips. "And pretend I'm not miserable about leaving in the morning? I can't."

As I watched him disappear down the steps, the door opened behind me.

"I thought I heard someone," Rémy said. "Were you talking to yourself?"

"To Paul." I wanted to tell Rémy that one moment I felt joyful and as light as a firefly, yet sometimes, like now, separated from Paul, I was miserable. "I can't stop thinking of him." I'd tried to keep Paul in the margins of my mind, but he'd moved to the middle of the page, to the centre of my story.

"You're in love," Rémy said. "I'm glad for you."

"I hope you're as happy."

"That's what I came to tell you. I'm in love with Bitsi."

They were perfect for each other, and I felt proud that I'd played a small part in bringing them together. "I tried to set you up with Monsieur de Nerciat and Mr Pryce-Jones, but perhaps Bitsi was the better choice."

"Perhaps?"

"Have you told her?"

"I wanted to tell you first."

We shared so much. He was the first reader of my newsletter, and I was the only person he allowed to edit his articles for the law review. Over tea in the kitchen, we talked until the small hours. We knew each other's secrets. Rémy was my refuge.

Yet everything was changing. I was with Paul; he with Bitsi. I had a job; soon, he'd graduate. This might be the last year we'd live under the same roof. We'd been together since before we were born, but eventually we would live separate lives. I wondered how long we had left together.

I quizzed Margaret on yesterday's French lesson as we finished work for the day. "Verbs are divided into three families. To love, to speak and to eat are in which?"

"*Aimer, parler* and *manger* belong to the -er family," she said. "Families — what a lovely way to view words."

"Don't forget your French when you're in London."

"I'll only be gone two weeks."

We continued to the courtyard, where Rémy's bicycle waited against the wall.

"*Merci* for suggesting that I volunteer," she said. "I finally feel part of something."

"*Merci à toi!* Without you, I'd still be stuffing crates. Or standing in front of the precinct."

"Nonsense!" Her cheeks flushed, and she looked pleased.

"I don't know what I'd do without you." There was more I could have told her, but in my family we didn't discuss our feelings. *Without you, I never would have worked up the courage to seek out Paul. Tutoring you*

115

has reminded me of the beauty of French, a beauty I'd taken for granted. The dullest tasks — shipping books, repairing rips in magazines, moving old newspapers into the archive room — go by quickly with you by my side.

When she said, "My dear friend, I don't know what I'd do without you, either," I wish I'd kissed her on each cheek. Instead, my mind on dinner, I hoisted myself on to the seat of Rémy's bike.

"You know how to ride?" she asked.

"You don't?" I pulled my foot from the pedal. "I can teach you!"

"I won't be able to, and when I fall, I'll make a fool of myself."

"What do you care if a few Parisians see you scrape your knee? Isn't that the best thing about being abroad? You can do what you want and no one back home will ever know."

I held the bike steady. Margaret flipped her leg over the bar. The bike wobbled as it coasted, and she clutched the handlebar with one hand and my arm with the other.

"I can't do this."

"You already are. Hold on to the handlebars."

"I'm not sure this is a good idea —"

"You're learning French and living in a foreign country — riding a bike is nothing compared to that," I said, giving her a gentle push, "Bon vent!"

As Margaret gained speed, her skirt flew above her knees. "If I fall, I'll get right back on."

"That's the attitude!"

She pedalled slowly. "I'm scared."

"Trust me!" I scampered alongside her. "I won't let anything happen to you."

"I trust you," she shouted. Exhilaration outweighed the uncertainty in her voice.

My arms were out, ready to catch her if she fell.

Paris was hot and humid in August, so many subscribers went sunbathing in Nice and Biarritz, or home to visit relatives in New York and Cincinnati. At my desk, Miss Reeder and I enjoyed a rare moment of calm. She looked cheery in her polka-dot dress. Her hair was coiffed in a chignon, and her silver pen was poised in her hand, ready to compose a speech or write a thank-you.

Most people in my life — from my father and my teachers to officials to waiters — said "no". I'd like to take ballet classes. "No, you don't have the right body." I'd like to take a painting class. "No, you don't have the necessary experience." I'd like a glass of red wine. "No, white goes better with the dish you've ordered." Miss Reeder was different. When I'd asked if I could make some changes in the periodical room, it had been shocking to hear Miss Reeder say, "Yes."

There was so much I was dying to ask her. What do your parents think about you living here? Where did you find the courage to live in a foreign country? Will I ever be that brave? Though I could hear Maman say, *Don't pry. Mind your own onions!*, questions simmered inside me, until one spilled out: "What brought you to France?"

117

"A love affair." Her hazel eyes shone.

I leaned closer. "Really?"

"I fell in love with Madame de Staël."

"The writer?"

"In her day, people said that there were three great powers in Europe: Britain, Germany and Madame de Staël. She insulted Napoleon by saying that 'Speech happens not to be his language'. He responded by banning her book and banishing her."

"She wasn't afraid of anyone."

"Would you believe that I sneaked into the mansion where she used to live? I only intended to enter the courtyard, but when a servant said, '*Bonjour*,' as if I belonged there, I strode in and slid up her stairs, running my hand along her banister, gawking at the walls that had once held her family portraits. That probably sounds fanciful."

"It sounds like love. Did you really come for a writer?"

"I was already in Spain to organise the Library of Congress stand at the Iberian fair. There was a job opening here, and I seized it. What about you? Do you long to travel? Did you always want to be a librarian?"

"I always wanted to work here. In my letter, I told you that I wanted to work at the Library because of my memories of coming here with my aunt. You remind me of her, actually — not just your chic chignon, but the way you both treat others so kindly and the way you share your love of books."

The Countess approached, files under her arms. Her hair reminded me of the sea on a cloudy day: white wisps curled like waves above strong currents of grey. The reading glasses perched on her nose made her look as if she were going to lecture us.

"We must talk," she said to Miss Reeder.

"We can continue our conversation later if you like," Miss Reeder told me before accompanying the trustee to her office.

While I straightened the newspapers, Boris read to me from *Le Figaro*. "Monsieur Neville Chamberlain motioned for the adjournment of Parliament, from the 4th of August to the 3rd of October, unless extraordinary events necessitate its convocation."

"I want to go on holiday," I said, wishing I could be with Paul.

"Get elected to Parliament," Boris joked.

At least I could look forward to Sunday lunch for once. Rémy had invited Bitsi, tantamount to announcing an engagement. I just worried that Papa would ruin everything by humiliating him.

I collected last week's papers and took them upstairs to the archives, past Miss Reeder's office. The door was ajar, so I peeked in.

The Directress's expression was grim. "I received a letter from the university library in Strasbourg. Monsieur Wickersham wrote that he and Madame Kuhlmann packed and evacuated 250 crates of books."

"War is coming." There was a catch in the Countess's voice.

Strasbourg was dangerously close to Germany. Librarians had moved books to safety when politicians hadn't said anything about evacuating people?

"The crates were shipped to the Puy-de-Dôme region," Miss Reeder said. "We need to plan ahead, too."

Was the south-west safer than Strasbourg? Safer than Paris?

"I'll take our finer things to my country house — Alan Seeger's letters and poetry, the collection of first editions, that sort of thing. They'll be out of harm's way."

"We'll stock up on canned goods, bottled water and coal. Sand to put out fires."

The Countess sighed. "And gas masks, if this war is anything like the last. Ten million dead, and as many wounded and mutilated. I can't believe it's happening again."

Dead . . . wounded . . . mutilated . . . I'd avoided talk of war, changing the subject when Rémy brought it up, nipping into the children's room when Mr Pryce-Jones banged on about it. But now it seemed the Library's collection might be in danger. We might be in danger. I had to face the fact that war was on the way.

CHAPTER
ELEVEN

ODILE

Paris, August 1939

At 11.55 on the day of Rémy and Bitsi's anticipated engagement luncheon — *les fiançailles* — my parents and I perched on the divan. I wore a pink silk blouse that Margaret had lent me. Maman's rouged cheeks resembled luscious plums, and she'd put on her cameo brooch, which she brought out on the most special of occasions. Papa's suit was too tight, and he tugged at his tie. The doorbell rang, and Rémy, pulling on his blazer, rushed to let Bitsi in. As always, her hair was a braided crown, but she wore a lime-green dress instead of her everyday brown one. She and Rémy gazed at each other. I felt breathless, something akin to pain, and wished Paul was with me.

When Bitsi finally noticed us standing there, she didn't meet my eye. Was it shyness, or was she cross for some reason? I sometimes left my teacup in the sink, and she'd reminded me more than once that no one wanted to clean up after me.

Maman beamed at Bitsi. "Odile and Rémy have said such fine things about you."

Papa drew himself up. "I hear you're one of those career girls, too."

"I help my family, sir." Bitsi met his gaze straight on.

"A fine thing," he said.

Maman exhaled shakily. Perhaps Papa would behave.

"You work with children," he said. "That must mean you'd like some."

Bitsi blushed, and Rémy put his arm around her protectively.

"Ignore the *commissaire*," he said.

I glared at Papa. Never able to put water in his wine, he always had to say what was on his mind.

"Do you knit?" Maman asked Bitsi, jerking the discussion back to decent ground.

"After reading, it's my favourite pastime. I also like to fish."

Papa gestured to the sitting room, where he'd set out the decanters for the aperitif, but Maman pointed to the dining room. She couldn't stop Papa from badgering Bitsi like he would any new recruit, but she could curtail the interrogation.

Papa presided at the head of the table. I was beside Maman, the happy couple across from us, with Bitsi next to Papa. When the maid brought out the roast and potatoes, Papa served Bitsi, Maman and me, then Rémy and himself. As we ate, Bitsi continued to avoid my eye. I could sense Maman mentally rifling through her jewellery box, searching for Grandmother's opal ring for Rémy to present to Bitsi. There would be a wedding feast, a honeymoon. I wondered if the newlyweds would live here, at least at first.

122

Rémy looked to Bitsi, who clasped his hand. With her at his side, he was more confident.

"I have an announcement," he said.

This was it. They were engaged. Bitsi had had trouble meeting my eye because she'd been keeping a secret. Well, it was no secret! I lifted my wine glass to congratulate the couple.

"Yes?" Papa grinned at Bitsi.

"I've joined the army," Rémy said.

Maman put her hand to her mouth. Papa went slack-jawed. My arm remained frozen in mid-air. The cold defiance, the finality in Rémy's tone hurt me. It felt as though he'd emptied a canister of bullets on to the table, into our water glasses and what was left of the gravy. I didn't realise I was shaking until I noticed the wine quivering in its glass. Only Bitsi remained serene. Rémy had discussed his plans with her. She clearly approved. Perhaps she'd encouraged him.

"What?" Maman said. "But why?"

"I *can't just sit at home*," Rémy had said. "*Someone has to do something*."

"I want to make a difference."

"Do something here." She gestured to Papa. "Join the police."

I could read Rémy's thought: *the last thing I want is to be like him*.

Papa pushed himself from the table. His chair scraped across the floor and fell over.

I expected him to attack with the arsenal he had at his disposal. Derision — how could you possibly be a soldier? You can barely stand up straight. Contempt —

if you refuse to help me chop down a Christmas tree, I doubt you can fell a man. Guilt — what will this do to poor Maman? Machismo — do you think the army will take a weakling like you? They only take real men like me. Fury — I'm the head of this household. How dare you enlist without informing me!

Without a word, he left the room. A second later, the front door slammed. Maman and I exchanged bewildered glances, Bitsi whispered something to Rémy. He regarded me.

Well? I heard him say.

He waited for me to give my blessing, but all I could get out was, "Don't . . ."

There was hurt in his eyes. He'd trusted me to support him.

I didn't want there to be distance between us. Not now. "Don't you know how much I'll miss you?" I said with forced cheerfulness. "We'll have to make the most of our time together before you go."

"I leave in three days," he said.

"What?" I asked.

"Papa has contacts everywhere, and I didn't want to give him time to find someone who'd kick me out of the army before I even made it to the base."

Maman rose and righted Papa's chair.

CHAPTER
TWELVE

LILY

Froid, Montana, March 1984

My mother's funeral was on the first day of spring. At
the front of the church, red roses smothered her casket.
It was hard to believe that Mom was in there instead of
at home, perched on our window seat. Dad and I
hunched in the front pew, Odile and Mary Louise next
to us. My lower lip wouldn't stop trembling, so I
covered my mouth with my hand. Odile clasped the
other. I didn't want her to let go.

Dad looked everywhere but at the casket — to the
faded painting of Jesus, to the stained-glass windows
that wouldn't let us see out. He resembled someone
who'd boarded the wrong train and ended up
somewhere completely unexpected. Behind us, I saw
Dr Stanchfield, his satchel beside him like a faithful
wife. Robby, between his parents. Mary Louise's dad
with wintergreen snuff tucked into his cheek. Sue Bob
swearing under her breath. Even Angel came. So did
every teacher I had ever had.

With wobbly voices, women read scripture. Then,
one after another, Mom's friends spoke. Sue Bob said

she had the best sense of humour. Kay said Mom was the softest shoulder to cry on. Snot leaked from my nose, spit wallowed in my mouth, grief churned in my gut. Trying to keep it in, I choked and started coughing. Mary Louise hit me on the back. Hard. The pain felt good.

The braying organ signalled the end of the service; its mournful moans ushered us out. The congregation crossed the street to the hall. Usually, men complained about taxes; ladies complained about each other; and freed from the fetters of Mass, kids shouted and roughhoused. This time, we walked in silence. Angel slipped a mixtape into my pocket. Dad's boss put his arm around his stout wife, as if worried she could be taken, too. Robby drifted over. He wore black Wranglers instead of blue jeans. He held out a handkerchief. I took it. Fists jammed into his pockets, he returned to his parents, who nodded their approval. I guessed they were teaching him how to be a man.

A long table was laden with food. One of the ladies sat Dad and me down, another made up plates for us. Slices of roast, mashed potatoes and gravy. He hadn't organised any of this. The ladies, old hands at death, did what was needed, serenely, efficiently. They cooked, they served, they cleaned up. Behind the buffet or in the kitchen, they did all they could to make the worst day of our lives go smoothly.

Around us, people talked, trying to act like life would go on.

"A nice service."

"So young . . ."

126

"What'll he do about Lily?"

Afterward, Father Maloney, Dad and I followed the hearse to the cemetery. At the gravesite, as Father said the blessing, I was glad that it was just me and Dad for this quiet moment with Mom. A few feet away, a robin pecked at the grass. When Dad noticed, he put his hand on my shoulder, and my tears fell.

We woke to darkness. Mom had always been the one to thrust open the curtains, so I'd wake to a kiss on the forehead and sunlight streaming in. Since the funeral, Dad downed his coffee and I ate cereal in a gloomy fog. It simply did not occur to us to let in the light.

Once, our home had felt full and loud. Dinner club. Mom and her girlfriends giggling on Saturday afternoons. She'd always been there when I got home from school. Now I returned to a silent house. When I walked down the hall to bed, no one called out, "Sweet dreams!" At school, in front of the row of lockers, kids stepped back when they saw me, scared that what happened to me could happen to them. Teachers never asked about homework. On Sunday, as Dad and I straggled down the aisle to our pew, God didn't say a word.

Every day, I came home with so much to tell Mom. I missed her questions about my day, I missed her. I ran my finger along the rim of her cup, nestled in the kitchen cabinet. Afraid to break her best thing, I never used it. I wished I could go back to that last moment. I would say, You were the best mom in the world. I need you. We need you. I loved the way we watched robins

127

and hoped for hummingbirds. I wished we had one more morning. One more hug. One more chance to say I love you.

I spent weekends lounging on beanbag chairs at Mary Louise's house. As usual, we complained about the only things we knew: school and family. "Dad can barely open cans of Campbell's Soup," I said, rolling my eyes.

"Neither can you doofuses," Angel said as she slipped on her satin jacket.

"If you're such a genius, why are you flunking math?" Mary Louise asked.

"At least I have a life, unlike you." She stomped out.

Their bickering was better than the silence at home. Only Mary Louise's mom treated me the same as always. It was a strange comfort to be told, "Don't be so damn lippy."

The whole town pitched in to feed Dad and me. He bought a deep freeze to store the casseroles. At dinner, we barely spoke — the news anchor, our constant companion, did the talking. Our conversations were stilted, and pauses lasted as long as commercial breaks.

When school let out for the summer, Angel introduced Mary Louise and me to Bo and Hope on *Days of Our Lives*. Their soap-opera love story let me forget my loss for an hour as I absorbed its lessons: love is longing, love is agony, love is sex. I imagined Robby and me, our bodies and souls entwined.

My soap opera binge lasted a month. When the thermometer hit a hundred degrees, Dad took off early from work, and came to get me at Mary Louise's. He

128

looked past us to the television, where the lovers were locked in their signature tongue-on-tongue embrace.

Dad's brows shot up then settled into a scowl. "I came to take you out for ice cream," he said. He had meant for the invitation to include Mary Louise, but now he was mad, blaming her for a choice I'd made. She saw that and stayed put. I stalked out to the station wagon and pouted the whole way to the Tastee Freez. A strawberry milkshake did nothing to cool my temper.

"Why can't I watch what I want?"

"Your mother wouldn't like it," he said, the best way to silence me.

When we got home, Dad marched over to Odile's. Leaning on the haunch of our car, I listened to him complain about the perils of daytime television and Mary Louise's permissive parents. Towering over Odile on the porch, he opened his wallet and held out some bills. He thought everyone was as interested in money as he was. She shoved his hand away.

"I need someone to look after her," he said, adding the caveat, "No soaps."

"I don't need a babysitter!" I shouted.

The following morning, I found myself right where I'd always wanted to be, at Odile's, but the reason I was there filled me with resentment. She understood and stayed busy in her garden. Over lunch, I tried to remain sullen, but the ham and cheese sandwiches she served broke down my reserve. We ate the *croque-monsieurs* with our forks and knives since there was a layer of bubbling Swiss cheese on top. Everything about Odile was elegant, even the way she ate her sandwich. In

129

Froid, she stuck out like a sore thumb, but maybe in Paris she was just an ordinary finger. I longed to see her world. Would she ever go back? Would she take me with her?

As we washed the dishes, she asked me to teach her to make my favourite dessert — chocolate chip cookies. Surprisingly, she didn't know basic things, like the fact that you're supposed to lick the beaters clean. That's the whole point of baking.

Mom had let me eat as many cookies as I wanted, but Odile let me have two. When I tried to take more, she replied, "Two feed your stomach, the rest your soul. We'll find another way to soothe your heart." She handed me a book. "Literature, not sweets."

I groaned and plunked myself down on her brocade couch. She sat in what she called her "Louis the 15 th" chair. Its carved wooden legs made it seem expensive. Maybe she'd been rich, and when she was my age her governess made her walk around the castle with the musty family Bible on her head. I'd lived next to Odile for ever, well, my for ever, and knew nearly nothing of her life. I eyed the drawers of the buffet and wondered what was inside. Maybe I could sneak a peek . . .

"Read," she ordered.

The Little Prince began with a boy who made simple drawings. When he showed them to adults, they didn't understand. I knew how he felt; no one understood how much I missed Mom. "Jesus needs her in heaven, hon," the ladies said, as if I didn't need her down here. I continued reading. "It is such a mysterious place, the land of tears" — the words from a dead aviator comforted me more than trite phrases from folks I knew. "It is only with the heart that one can see rightly; what is essential is invisible to the eye." The book carried me to another world, to a place that let me forget.

Odile said *Le Petit Prince* had been written in French and that I was reading a translation. I wanted to read the original, to understand the story the way it had understood me. I wanted to be eloquent like the prince, elegant like Odile. I told her I wanted to learn French. "I'd love to teach you!" she said. In a notebook, she wrote: *le mariage, la rose, la bible, la table*. When I asked why there was a "*le*" or "*la*", she said French nouns were either masculine or feminine.

"Huh?"

"Let me put it another way. They're either . . . boys or girls."

"In France, tables are girls?"

She laughed, a pretty, tinkly sound. "Something like that."

La table? I imagined tables wearing dresses. A denim mini-skirt or floral gown that grazed the ground. It seemed silly, but then I remembered Mom combing her hair at her vanity, knees brushing its gingham skirt. The idea of a table being a woman made sense.

It had been four months since Mom died, and for the first time, I didn't feel heartbroken when I thought of her.

In the evenings, I was alone: Dad shut himself away in the den. At my desk, I revised each day's French lesson,

131

repeating the words until they no longer felt foreign. Odile got me my own French-English dictionary — an orange is *une orange*, a lemon is *un citron*. *Je voyage en France. Je préfère Robby. Odile est belle. Paris est magnifique.* Basic sentences, simple pleasures, one word at a time, every sentence in the present tense, no sadness of the past, no worries about *le futur*. I loved *le français*, a bridge to *la France*, a world that only Odile and I knew, a place with mouth-watering desserts and secret gardens, a place I could hide away. I could not master heartache — too dense, too overwhelming — but I could conjugate verbs. I begin — *je commence*; you finish — *tu finis*. In this secret language of loss, I spoke of my mother: *j'aime Maman*.

On the first day of school, Mary Louise and I yawned amid the mustard-yellow kitchen units. Our homeroom was Home-Ec, mandatory for eighth graders. I prayed Robby would be in our class, and sighed with relief when he walked in.

Consulting her clipboard, Mrs Adams paired up students. "Lily and Robby."

I elbowed Mary Louise, unable to believe my luck. Inching towards him, I couldn't think of a single thing to say. Not "How was harvest?" Not even "Hi." He kind of smiled at me. It was enough.

When Mrs Adams held out a recipe card, neither Robby nor I moved to take it, so she placed the card on the counter next to the canisters of flour, sugar and salt. Side by side, he and I read the instructions, and I felt the heat from his body. I measured the ingredients,

132

he stirred them together with a beat-up spatula. We spooned the batter into the moulds, then, like proud parents, we peered into the oven to watch the cupcakes rise.

When they were golden brown, I pulled them out. Though they were hot, Robby bit into one. He chewed twice and said, "Gross!"

"Quit goofing around." I popped a piece into my mouth. It tasted like a mouldy sponge drenched in salt. I spat it into the garbage. "I must have mixed up the salt and sugar."

"It's not a big deal."

"Are you kidding?" I said, practically in tears, mostly from the way the salt burned, but also because I didn't want us to flunk.

"You're worried about your 4.0."

Robby scarfed a cupcake, barely chewing before forcing it down. His eyes watered but he grabbed another. I shoved one into my mouth, too, gagging on the yellow lump.

Mrs Adams complimented Tiffany and Mary Louise on their masterpiece before moving on to us. She held up our empty pan. "How am I supposed to grade you?"

Grimacing from the sharp taste of salt, Robby and I shrugged.

"Well, don't just stand there!" she said. "Start cleaning up."

At the sink, we plunged our hands into the warm, soapy water to wash the pan and utensils. A tiny bubble rose in the air, and we watched it float away. I'd never been so happy.

In social studies, Miss Davis bristled about the Soviet boycott of the Olympics in LA. "Probably afraid their athletes would defect! How are we supposed to win the Cold War if they won't compete?"

Barely listening to our teacher's bitter soliloquy, Mary Louise and I passed notes, "I'm starving," she wrote. "Cheese fries for lunch?"

At my locker, I slathered on some of her lipstick before we crossed the street to the Husky House, I pushed open the smudged glass door, and there in the middle of the diner sat Robby with Tiffany Ivers balanced on his lap, her turquoise cowboy boots dangling an inch from the floor, I felt my eyes widen as I stopped dead.

Mary Louise crashed into me. "Hey!" Then she saw what I saw: Robby squirming; Tiffany Ivers's triumphant smirk.

"Why him?" I asked. "She can have anyone she wants."

"You don't choose who you love," Mary Louise said.

"Why are you always defending her?"

"Why do you let her get to you?"

The salt gave me heartburn. Or maybe it was seeing Tiffany Ivers on Robby's lap. "I'm going home."

"Don't let her win."

I ran to Odile's and let myself in. "Why aren't you in school?" she asked. "Did something happen?"

I was a sweaty mess. "I saw something . . . and now I'm sick."

While she got me a glass of water, I flipped through her French-English dictionary. I took a gulp, then asked, "What are the worst French words to describe someone?"

"*Odieux, cruel*. Odious, cruel."

I'd wanted slut and bitch, but guessed those would do.

"Why focus on the negative, *ma grande?* Does this have anything to do with that boy you moon over after church?"

Jesus, did the whole congregation know?

"Well?" she said.

When I told her, she said, "Sometimes we misread signs. I assumed much about Paul, my first . . . boyfriend, but I was wrong. Perhaps Robby squirmed because she made him uncomfortable."

"Doesn't matter." I crossed my arms. "I'm done with him."

"Don't close your heart."

I thought about the loved ones she'd lost and felt foolish complaining. "You made it through a war, I can't even make it through junior high."

"We have more in common than you think. Let me tell you which words describe you. *Belle, intelligente, pétillante.*"

I felt better. "What's the last one?"

"Sparkling."

"You think I sparkle?"

She smiled wryly. "You came into my life like the evening star."

If Robby wanted to be with Tiffany, fine. In class, I watched the teacher the whole time. I wouldn't look at him. I couldn't. Mary Louise passed me a note, whispering, "It's from Robby." Probably an invitation to his wedding. I tossed it in *la poubelle. Je déteste l'amour. Je déteste* Tiffany Ivers. *Je déteste* everyone.

I dreaded seeing Robby and Tiffany on a date — his arm around her at the choir concert or sharing a doughnut after church, but that day never came. Around Halloween, I realised Odile had been right about misreading signals. I tried to catch his eye, but he no longer looked in my direction.

But someone else was dating. The ladies of Froid pushed every single single woman in Dad's path. In the church hall, they set him up with a giggly blonde teller who'd recently started at the bank.

"He's nothing but skin and bones," said old Mrs Murdoch.

"Lost his appetite," Mrs Ivers said. "But his savings account is plump."

During the fall band concert, they stuck him next to a florist with greasy hair. "He's a good provider," Mrs Ivers whispered during *Danse Macabre*. At the firemen's spaghetti fundraiser, they paired him with my English teacher. Listening to her yammer on about *Macbeth*, Dad didn't seem happy, but he didn't rush through dinner, either. Mary Louise and I were the first to leave.

"Revolting," I told her, kicking at the dead leaves on the sidewalk.

"Gag me," she agreed.

"Your dad goes on more dates than you," Tiffany Ivers said as she slithered by.

136

In Mary Louise's room, we sang "You May Be Right" at the top of our lungs, using Angel's Aquanet as a microphone. Something in the angry twitch of Billy Joel's voice spoke to me. At midnight, Sue Bob pounded on the door and told us to shut up.

In the morning, Mary Louise and I trotted down the alley — the quickest way to my place. Two houses from home, we froze like antelope when we saw Dad at the back door with the blonde bank teller, who blushed as she stroked the arm of his shirt. He wound his fingers through hers.

"Gross!" Mary Louise hissed. "They're having hand sex."

"She spent the night."

"Do you think he'll marry her?"

It had only been eight months since Mom died.

Grief is a sea made of your own tears. Salty swells cover the dark depths you must swim at your own pace. It takes time to build stamina. Some days, my arms sliced through the water, and I felt things would be okay, the shore wasn't so far off. Then one memory, one moment would nearly drown me, and I'd be back to the beginning, fighting to stay above the waves, exhausted, sinking in my own sorrow.

A week later, after church, Dad, Mary Louise and I were picking out pastries in the hall when the blonde approached and regarded him expectantly. He kept glancing from me to her. "Girls," he finally said, "I'd like you to meet Eleanor. She's . . . This is Lily and Mary Louise, her partner in crime."

"Nice to meet you. Heard so much about you," she squeaked like a demented parakeet.

"Lily?" I heard Dad say. "Are you okay?"

I shook my head. He could move on. I would stay with Mom. I remembered her hand, dusted with flour, passing me the beaters covered with chunks of cookie dough; her laugh as I twirled my tongue around the metal, trying to get what I could. I remembered the clown costume she made me for Halloween, her foot on the pedal of the sewing machine, head bent in concentration. I remembered things I could not possibly remember. Mom watching over me as I slept. Mom with a tender expression, patting her enormous belly, me nestled inside, I remembered that I wouldn't wear the sweater she'd crocheted because it wasn't store-bought like Tiffany Ivers's. I remembered the way Mom smiled to hide the hurt. If I could find it, I'd wear the sweater every day.

For my fourteenth birthday, Dad took me to Jeans 'n Things, which was owned by Mrs Taylor, who sat three pews in front of us and had a brown bouffant. Angel and her friends had designed their own T-shirts with their names printed on the back, and that's what Dad decided to get me. I was impressed he came up with the idea himself.

The T-shirts came in five colours; orange was the only one in my size. Next, the decal. Pictures of bunnies, birds or rock bands. Before, Dad would have checked his watch twenty times, worried about time away from work, but now he examined each one with me.

"Your mom would have chosen the eagle," he said, so softly I barely heard.

That's what I picked. Mrs Taylor brought out the velveteen letters — big, medium and small, and red, black and blue. He and I felt them all.

"Your mom took care of the presents. I didn't realise everything she did . . ."

"Thanks, Dad," I said, hugging him tight, the way I wished I'd hugged Mom that last day.

I wore the T-shirt home.

Odile brought over a cake — *chocolat!* — and Mary Louise and a few other girls from school watched me blow out the candles. The smoke was still rising when Eleanor Carlson barged in without knocking.

Scowling, Mary Louise said, "What's *she* doing here?"

"What a nice surprise." Dad kissed Eleanor Carlson's cheek.

"Happy Birthday!" she chirped.

"Lovely to see you." Odile nudged me.

"Lovely," I muttered.

Mary Louise crossed her arms and wouldn't say a word.

Dad and Eleanor Carlson were careful not to touch, careful to stand well apart. But he smiled at her more than he smiled at me, and it was my party. Wanting the day to be done, I horked down the cake and tore open my gifts.

Afterward, as Mary Louise and I stuffed the paper plates into the trash, Dad brewed a fresh pot of coffee. His girlfriend opened the exact cabinet for the cups. Out of all of them, she chose my mother's favourite with the dainty blue flowers. Of course she did. Dad didn't seem surprised.

Mary Louise took everything in, my pain written on her freckled face. She knew that I'd never used the cup. In a low, fierce tone, she spoke my anger, my hurt, my heart. "That bitch thinks she can just come in here and take anything she likes?"

Eleanor set the cup and saucer on the counter, then reached for the coffee pot. Mary Louise swiped the porcelain on to the floor, the sound of it shattering at once sad and satisfying. White and blue snowflakes scattered across the linoleum. No one moved. We watched the last piece skitter to a stop under the fridge.

"You did that on purpose," Dad shouted at Mary Louise. "Why would you do such a rotten thing?"

On and on he continued, but she was used to getting bawled out. Eyes half closed to protect from his spittle, she took it stoically.

Dad's girlfriend watched, maybe wondering why he was getting all worked up.

"For heaven's sake, it's only a cup!" Eleanor said. Taking the broom and dustpan from behind the door, she swept up my mother's remains.

CHAPTER
THIRTEEN

ODILE

Paris, August 1939

Rémy prepared to join the army the same way he got ready for school, by slapping some cold water on his face and throwing a few books into a messenger bag. I perched glumly on his bed. Resentment swam between us: I felt that he was abandoning me, and bolting headlong into danger; he was disappointed by my lack of enthusiasm for his plan. I didn't think he should go; he couldn't wait to leave.

"Take a jumper," I said. "You don't want to catch a cold."

"They'll supply me with everything I need."

Earlier, I'd gone to the bank and withdrawn my seeds of security. "Here," I said, pressing the francs into his hands,

"I don't need your money."

"But you'll have it."

"I'll be late." He set the notes on the bed.

I followed him to the hall, where our parents waited. Maman fussed, straightening Rémy's collar and asking, "Do you have a clean handkerchief?"

Papa gave Rémy a brass compass. "From my own army days," he said, his voice hoarse.

"Thanks, Papa." He flung the compass into the air and caught it before slipping it into his pocket. "I'll show those Krauts."

"Promise you'll write," I said.

He kissed my cheeks. "Promise."

Bag slung over his back, he bounced down the stairs as though he were nipping out to buy a baguette.

As a precaution against air raids, the City of Light stayed pitch-black at night — no streetlights, no neon lights of the cabarets, no lamps lit in the reading room. Parisians had been advised to carry gas masks. Many people, like my cousins, crammed belongings into their cars and left. Miss Reeder helped distraught compatriots book passages back to America. Teachers curtailed their summer holidays to help evacuate pupils to the country. The calm of the children's room was chilling.

Home was quiet, too. This was the first time Rémy and I had been separated for more than four days. Like the sunrise, like the bread on our table, he'd always been there, slurping his *café au lait*, gurgling after he brushed his teeth, humming while he and I read together. Rémy provided the musical score of my days. Now, life was silent.

He'd been serene in his choice to join the army, and that should have been some comfort. Instead, I drew my solace from Maman and Papa. Before, Rémy and I had been on one side, our parents on another like we were at the dinner table. Now, we three became united in our worry, in our anxious glances at the empty chair. Rémy hadn't written.

"When's Paul returning from Brittany?" Maman asked. She did her best to smooth over awkward silences.

I tucked my hand into my pocket and touched his latest letter. He wrote every day, telling me how much he missed me, how many hectares left to harvest.

I sighed. "Not soon enough."

In the cloakroom, brown leather gas masks — with "The American Library in Paris" printed on the top — slumped against the wall. As I flung mine on to the floor, Bitsi breezed in and chirped a friendly *bonjour*. I didn't reply.

"What are you reading these days?" she asked. "I just finished *Emma*."

"With Rémy away, I'm too distracted to read!"

"It's not a competition to see who misses him more," she said on her way out the door.

I didn't know what to say, or rather I had too much to say. How dare you encourage Rémy to enlist? What if he's in danger?

Margaret entered and hung her straw hat on a peg. "What's wrong?" she asked.

"Bitsi is what's wrong."

Margaret said she'd fix a tea tray and meet me at my desk, "Now what's all this about?" she asked as she poured the Darjeeling.

"Rémy's always been fragile — the first to catch a cold, the last one picked in gym class. Yet Bitsi encouraged him to put himself in harm's way. And he didn't even tell me that he was enlisting."

"Is there a reason he didn't confide in you?"

Margaret's eyes were so earnest that I found myself telling her a truth that I just now understood. "He did try to tell me," My teacup trembled in my hand, "I wish I'd listened. He's always been there for me, yet the one time he needed me . . ."

"Don't be so hard on yourself."

"I could have talked him out of enlisting."

"Perhaps this is something he felt he had to do."

"Perhaps . . ."

Margaret gestured to the scene before us. Peter-the-shelver was orienting Helen, the newest member of staff, a reference librarian from Rhode Island with a frizzy bob and dreamy eyes. Gliding along the stacks, the two of them reminisced about New England, 917.4, the most magical place on earth; I'd read enough love stories to know the beginning of one when I saw it.

Boris approached with a long roll of paper and said we needed to cover the windowpanes to protect against the glass shattering in case of a bombing.

"How's your brother?" he asked as he laid the roll over the table.

I cut a large swathe. "He still hasn't written."

"How long has it been?"

"Two weeks."

"When I joined the army," Boris said, spreading glue on to the paper with an old paintbrush, "we cadets trained so hard that at night we fell into our bunks dead tired. There was no time for correspondence. The

144

sergeant wanted it that way, wanted us to leave our former lives behind."

"You're probably right . . ."

"But it's hard to be the one left behind."

Boris understood. We said little, but much, as we enveloped the Library in darkness. With so many windows, it took two days.

Then, on 1 September, the army called up men aged eighteen to thirty-five. Boris, the neighbourhood boys I'd grown up with, the pasty doctoral students who practically lived in the reference room, the baker who burned the baguettes — all were mobilised. Papa asked to keep his police officers in Paris; Paul received a dispensation to keep working on his aunt's farm — for now.

Everywhere, I saw evidence that war was imminent: in the army, which had swelled its ranks; in the *Herald* with its ominous headlines; and on the Library bulletin board, alongside the bestseller list, a newly posted paper embossed with the US Embassy seal declared: "In view of the situation prevailing in Europe, it is advisable that American citizens return to the United States."

Would Miss Reeder follow the embassy's directive? What if the British Ambassador issued a similar statement and I lost Margaret?

I ran past the card catalogue, where Aunt Caro had introduced me to Dewey and a whole constellation, past the stacks where Paul and I had first kissed, past the back room where Margaret and I had become friends, to Miss Reeder's office.

The Directress swivelled slightly in her chair, pen in hand, her attention on the documents spread over her desk. The scent of her espresso filled the air. There were no boxes, no sign of packing. She was here. As long as she was here, everything would be all right. My panic receded, and I took a slow, deep breath.

"You're not going home?" I asked.

"Home?"

"You're not leaving?"

Her brows came together, and she regarded me quizzically, as if the thought had never occurred to her. Miss Reeder replied, "I am home."

1 September 1939

Dearest Paul,

I miss you so; I want to feel your arms around my waist, your whisper of reassurance at my temple. My chest has ached since Rémy enlisted. I hate how I left things with him. When you return, things will be better.

Since most local men have been mobilised, your aunt surely needs you now more than ever, but I need you, too, and count the days until you come back.

All my love,
Your prickly librarian

I couldn't escape the fact that Rémy had a new confidante, but I could escape *her* by remaining in the periodical room as much as possible. Today as always, I

146

was buoyed by seeing my habitués. Swathed in a purple shawl, Professor Cohen sighed over a beautiful passage of *Voyage in the Dark*. Beside her, Madame Simon's dentures clicked as she swooned over the fashion in *Harper's Bazaar*. Across from them, Monsieur de Nerciat and Mr Pryce-Jones bantered.

"The best whisky's made in Scotland," the Englishman said. "I'm half Scotch myself."

"Yes, I know," the Frenchman murmured. "And the other half is soda."

"Glendronach is the best!"

Never willing to admit that Great Britain produced anything of value, the Frenchman argued, "George Dickel out of Tennessee is the finest."

"A taste test is the way to find out who's right," I told them.

"Odile, you're ingenious!"

Bitsi sidled up to me, "My brother was called up," she said. "He left yesterday."

"Mine left weeks ago," I said. "But then you knew all about it, didn't you?"

"Rémy would have been called up anyway."

"Is that supposed to make me feel better?" I snarled.

Subscribers gaped in surprise. "We're all worried," Professor Cohen soothed.

Turning away from Bitsi, I opened the *Herald* and read the editorial: "For all the present anxiety, a great war may never come. Certainly no one, with the possibility of Herr Hitler, can say that it will." I didn't realise I'd said the words aloud until I saw Madame Simon grimace.

"What war?" she tittered. "Europe is tired, no one wants to fight."

"You're delusional," Professor Cohen said. "Children fight over toys, men over territory."

"Let's not think about that right now," said Monsieur de Nerciat, eyeing me worriedly. He nabbed the *Herald* and opened it at the society pages, where two full columns announced the news of Paris's American colony. "Mr Eli Grombecker, of New York, flew to Europe on the Clipper. Mr and Mrs E. Bromund, of Chicago, among those who visited Berlin recently, are at Le Bristol. Mrs Minnie K. Oppenheimer and Miss Ruth Oppenheimer, of Miami, are at the Continental."

"War won't stop socialites from shopping," Mr Pryce-Jones said.

"And the news from the British colony," Monsieur de Nerciat continued. "The Maharaja of Tripuria and the Yuvaranee of Baria are at the George V. The Countess of Abingdon joined the Earl at Le Prince de Galles."

My habitués and I laughed. The socialites took themselves so seriously, but allowed us to briefly forget the tense political situation.

After work, I went home, hoping for a letter from Rémy, but the tray on the hall table remained empty. I heard voices in the sitting room and peeked in — Paul! Seeing me, he jumped up. Aware of my parents, I allowed my hand to settle briefly on his upper arm as he gave me a peck on the cheek.

148

On the divan, twenty centimetres apart, I whispered, "I missed you."

"I missed you more. You had your habitués for company. Aside from my aunt, I had cows, chickens and goats."

"One could argue that Mr Pryce-Jones is a stubborn old goat."

"Yes, but he's never bitten you!"

My father regarded us with smug benevolence. "I knew Paul was the one for you."

"Yes, Papa, the fourteenth suitor you brought home was the charm."

"Soon you'll have more time together," he replied. "With this talk of war, your colleagues will leave Paris, and the Library will close."

"Miss Reeder says we'll stay open," I said, "No one's going anywhere."

"You'll be able to rest." With a teasing wink, he added, "Maybe you'll even be on time for dinner."

When Papa spoke of his job, he spoke of duty. He couldn't understand that I loved the Library. The extra hours spent with Helen-in-reference to learn how to find answers for subscribers wasn't a chore, it was a treasure hunt. "It's important to remember how hard it is to ask for help," she reminded me. "Never be impatient; all questions have value." She and I dug through specialised bibliographies and encyclopaedias to find everything from the population of Cuba to the estimated value of a Chinese vase. Every day brought questions that wanted answers. After writing dozens of academic papers, Professor Cohen decided to try her

149

hand at a novel and was researching sixteenth-century Italy. "What did Venetians wear? What did they drink? What did they put in their pockets?" she asked.

"Are you sure they had pockets?" Helen asked.

"Not at all!" the Professor replied, and we three set sail for Venice, navigating through the stacks.

I was needed at the Library. I was happy there.

"I can't rest," I told my father, "Miss Reeder says books promote understanding, which is important now more than ever."

When he opened his mouth to argue, Maman ushered him from the room, closing the door behind them.

I moved closer to Paul. "He's impossible!"

"He worries about you."

"I suppose . . ."

Paul kissed my hands, my cheeks, my lips. I wanted more. His skin on mine, our bodies entwined. Kissing was the prologue of a marvellous book, one I wanted to read until the end.

The doorknob rattled; we leaped apart. Maman rushed to the planters, where she watered her ferns.

When I was little, I'd loved to read in bed. Every evening, after Maman said, "Lights out," I begged to finish the chapter, but it was no use. Maman, now as then, decided when it was time to stop.

As I set out the afternoon editions of the newspapers, I saw Miss Reeder — white as a sheet — stumble into the reading room. Immediately, we all knew something was wrong. Mr Pryce-Jones and Monsieur de Nerciat stopped arguing. Professor Cohen looked up from her book. Standing in front of the shrouded windows, the Directress said, "The embassy called." Her voice trembled. "England and France have declared war on Germany."

When Papa spoke of his years in the trenches, I could only imagine the fighting as faded photos taken from a distance. Now, the pictures of tanks and wounded soldiers were in technicolour. Was Rémy in combat? Was he injured?

"Did they say where the fighting is?" Bitsi asked before I could.

"I wish I knew more," Miss Reeder said. "Ambassador Bullitt will keep us informed."

After reassuring subscribers, she gathered staff in her office. "You should leave — back home, or to the countryside, where you'll be safe," she told us, her tone so authoritative that in my mind, I threw my yellow dress and blue scarf into a suitcase.

"What will you do?" stern Mrs Turnbull demanded.

"I'll remain," Miss Reeder responded without hesitation.

"I'll man the circulation desk," Bitsi said.

"I want to stay," our bookkeeper Miss Wedd said.

"Me, too." I mentally put my clothes back in the armoire. My place was here. I wanted to do everything I could to make sure that our Library would remain open.

"I can't return to Rhode Island so soon," Helen-in-reference said.

Peter-the-shelver gazed at her. "I don't want to leave."

Miss Reeder regarded us gratefully. "Nonetheless, we must do what we can to keep subscribers safe."

Peter-the-shelver lugged pails of sand to the top floor in case air raids caused fires. Miss Wedd pasted directions to the closest shelter — the Métro station — on the wall. During the safety drill, Miss Reeder cleared the reading room, tucking her arms around scared students. I herded my habitués from the periodical room. Snatching *Good Morning, Midnight* from the shelf as if she were saving her best friend from a burning building, Professor Cohen proclaimed, "I'll not leave Jean Rhys." Helen-in-reference carried bottles of drinking water; the caretaker cut the electricity. At the door, Bitsi waved the lantern. And a cortège of dazed booklovers trudged two blocks to the safety of the station. In the dim Métro tunnel, we wondered what would happen, and when.

CHAPTER
FOURTEEN

ODILE

Paris, September 1939

Boris strolled into the reading room as if he'd gone for a long lunch, not six days with the army. Subscribers swarmed, vying to welcome him back. Monsieur de Nerciat and Mr Pryce-Jones were the first to pump Boris's hand in vigorous handshakes. Professor Cohen was next. "We're glad you're home safe. Your wife and daughter must be relieved." I tried to reach him, but a scrum of bookworms surrounded him. I withdrew to the trolley and grabbed a book to reshelf. The call number on the spine was 223. Was that religion or philosophy? The things I knew for sure grew muddled. Since Rémy had left, I often found myself in the middle of a room, unable to figure out where I belonged.

Boris found me deep in 200. "How are you?" he asked.

"Scared for Rémy."

He tucked my book on to the shelf. "I know the feeling. My brother Oleg enlisted in the Foreign Legion."

"I hope he'll be safe. At least you were able to return."

"Thanks to Miss Reeder, who wrote to the army. Apparently, I'm indispensable."

153

"Indispensable. That has a nice ring to it."

She'd also managed to keep the caretaker. Thankfully, Papa received permission to keep his police officers in Paris. He wanted to shield his men, even if he wasn't able to protect his own son. I was worried sick about Rémy, but grateful, so grateful that I wouldn't lose Paul.

Boris tucked another book into place. "I'd have done my duty in the French army. After all, I've already fought one war."

"You have?"

"I was in cadet training when the Russian Revolution broke out. Some of us were barely fifteen years old, but we sneaked away to join the army."

"Fifteen . . ."

He explained that he and his comrades thought that shooting a strawberry to smithereens at ten paces made them men, and that when he and his best friend planned to steal away, their biggest concern was which uniform would make them appear more dashing. "We wondered if we should go on foot or take a horse. Go hungry, or raid the pantry and risk waking the surly cook. It was easy to enlist," he concluded. "Like most children, we could envision no more than a week ahead."

That was the way Rémy had left home, eager for an adventure, anxious to prove to Papa that he was a man.

"My captain wasn't much older than me. He ordered us to shoot to kill, but it's hard to kill your fellow countrymen." Boris swallowed. "Hard to kill anyone."

154

The stacks were tall, as hallowed as a confessional. He stared at the row of books lined up like soldiers. "Across the river from us, there was a lookout, one of theirs," he continued. "A fellow Russian, the enemy, I pulled the trigger and grazed his earlobe."

"His earlobe?"

Boris shrugged, "I was a decent shot, I didn't want to kill the chap. Merely warn him away."

"You did the right thing."

He took another book and ran his hand over the cover sombrely. "Later, my regiment came face to face with his, and that soldier killed my best friend."

"I'm sorry."

"I was shot twice." His finger followed a scar along his cheek. The mark was so faint that I'd thought it a laugh line, "But typhus almost did me in. The infirmary was worse than the front. I grew up in a boisterous family and went from military school to the army, I'd never had a second of solitude, never had to face my own thoughts. Being alone in the hospital was the lowest point in my life. One thing got me through — thoughts of my sisters together."

He gestured to the children's room where Bitsi paced.

"She and I are *not* sisters," I said.

He regarded me with such sorrow. "Back to the circulation desk," he said in a resigned tone, and left me alone with my regret and resentment.

155

CHAPTER
FIFTEEN

ODILE

Paris, September 1939

Three days after war was declared, Miss Reeder created the Soldiers' Service. Wanting to comfort French and British troops, to offer escape, and to let them know that their friends at the Library cared, we prepared collections of books for canteens and field hospitals. Paul and I delivered the crates to La Poste. Paris was strangely calm, like a grand hotel with very few guests, yet the Library bustled with subscribers who took it for granted that we would remain open. They continued to scour the paper for news and to borrow books.

"People read," the Directress said. "War or no war."

She launched an appeal for donations, penning letters to loyal patrons like the Countess Clara de Chambrun. Calling me into her office, Miss Reeder explained that she'd invited journalists to the Library and wanted me to tell them about the programme. They were waiting in the reading room.

"Me?" I said. "Newspapermen are . . . unruly." When I'd delivered my first "ALP News" column to the *Herald*, one of them noticed a typo — "pubic" relations

156

instead of public relations. Each time I dropped off a new column, one of them asked about my "special" relations.

"They can be rash," Miss Reeder admitted. "They're rushing all over France to describe war efforts. But if one is rude, whack him over the head."

Remembering the interview where I'd threatened to do exactly that, I felt my face flush. "Oh, no, I . . ."

"I know. You're not that girl any longer. You've grown up and are doing a marvellous job. Everyone loves your column in the *Herald*, and your newsletter is delightful, especially your 'What kind of reader are you?' interviews. It's wonderful to get to know someone by the books they love."

On my way to the reading room, I allowed myself to bask in Miss Reeder's praise. At the hearth, I rubbed one foot over the other, working up the courage to talk to the blasé newspapermen in rumpled trench coats. But before I could address them, they addressed me.

"Are the French so interested in American books?" a journalist with thinning grey hair demanded. His mien was tired — no, jaded. "And do soldiers have time to read?"

"One general sent trucks from the Maginot Line to collect reading material," I said briskly. "The soldiers do have time, and our aim is to support those who are ill, wounded, or lonely. We must serve in the field of morale."

"Morale? Then why books? Why not wine?" a redhead quipped. "That's what I'd want."

"Who says it's either or?" I asked.

They laughed.

"But seriously, why books. Because no other thing possesses that mystical faculty to make people see with other people's eyes. The Library is a bridge of books between cultures."

One by one, they shrugged out of their coats and settled into their chairs as I explained how people could get their donations to us. Some journalists jotted down information, others seemed to reminisce about books they'd read. The jaded one contemplated the stacks, perhaps remembering a novel that had brought solace after a difficult day.

"We all have a book that's changed us for ever," I said. "One that let us know that we're not alone. What's yours?"

"*All Quiet on the Western Front*", he said.

833. "Help spread the word. Help get the books that you've loved to our soldiers."

As information got out, donations poured in. Staff assembled libraries of fifty magazines and one hundred books for each regiment. At 9p.m. one evening, Margaret, Miss Reeder and I finished up for the day. The Directress wrote out address labels, Margaret typed up the catalogues of each collection, and I placed books in the crates.

Bitsi burst into the room, waving a letter. "It was there when I got home."

Rémy wrote to her first?

"Oh, how wonderful to hear from him," Margaret said.

158

"And wasn't it kind of Bitsi to come back to share the news?" Miss Reeder gave me a pointed look.

She was right. It wasn't a competition to see who got a letter first. And yet . . .

"He's stationed near Lille," Bitsi said. "He's far from the danger."

"For now," I said sharply.

"He wanted to enlist."

"You encouraged him."

"To follow his beliefs."

"What if they get him killed?" I heaved hefty unabridged Victor Hugo into a crate, where he landed with an indignant thump.

"Please." Her alabaster hands, so delicate, grasped mine, smudged with blue ink. "I need to be with someone else who loves him."

"I should tell my parents." I untangled my fingers from hers. "They'll be relieved."

"Odile, dear . . ." Miss Reeder's head tilted in sympathy.

Kindness would only make me cry, so I gasped a quick, "See you tomorrow," and hurtled down the stairs. When I told my parents about the letter, there must have been a bitter twinge in my tone because Maman said it wasn't Bitsi's fault that he'd enlisted. With all the political tracts he'd written, his choice should have been no surprise. Papa said I'd better be nice to Bitsi, for Rémy's sake.

Two days later, a letter arrived. *My regiment is stationed on a farm. A barn cat tags along with us like a dog, even during field exercises. We haven't seen fighting of any kind, except over which of us is going to do the washing up.*

Breathing was easier.

Requests poured in from all over France, as well as Algeria, Syria and British headquarters in London. Staff and volunteers from the Red Cross, YMCA and Quakers crammed into our back room to help get books to soldiers. Carefully noting book preferences (non-fiction or fiction, mysteries or memoirs) and languages (English, French, or both), we made sure each serviceman who'd requested one received a care package twice a month.

Miss Reeder snapped photos of volunteers packaging books, Bitsi wrote notes of encouragement to soldiers, and Margaret and I opened requests. I read out one from a professor of English, now a French corporal, who wanted textbooks in order to teach his regiment.

"Which shall we send?" Bitsi asked me.

I pretended not to hear.

Eyeing Bitsi and me nervously, Margaret read aloud: "I am in the east of France and there are ones of us who read English, may we have some books and magazines, also some girls (not too old) who would agree to correspond with us?"

Completely charmed by the requests we received, I read out another: "We are some comrades and me, in the French countryside, between Saar and Moselle. And as you might think, our pleasures are limited. If possible, will you send us any old copies of the *National*

160

Geographic? This magazine shall make our pleasure, because we appreciate this beautiful review."

"It must be hard for the soldiers to be far from home," Margaret said. "What a relief to be able to do something for them."

"Thank you for your dedication," Miss Reeder said, her voice as comforting as a cup of cocoa. "We're fortunate to have you."

"What would I do without all of you?" Margaret teared up, "Oh, dear, the leaky teapot is back."

"We've all been emotional lately," Miss Reeder responded, eyes on me.

Few shots were fired in France, though the situation remained tense along the Maginot Line, where generals were certain the enemy would attack. We'd dispatched hundreds of books to the soldiers there. Several wrote back, kindly sending tokens of appreciation: a watercolour of a kitchen on the Maginot Line, sketches of an enemy plane they'd shot down, a packet of cigarettes. Margaret and I read a letter from a British captain:

> It was so kind of you letting me have that wonderful packet of books. I do so appreciate what you are doing for us and consider it most important to give the men all the recreation possible.
> We want to express to you all our gratitude for the beautiful work you're doing among us soldiers. For what you did in the

161

last war and for what you are doing now, we're most thankful.

Our Soldiers' Service operation had grown so large — thousands of donated books, dozens of volunteers — that businessmen in the neighbouring building lent us an entire floor. Piles of novels and magazines reached to the ceiling, a literary Tower of Pisa. Miss Wedd baked us scones and recorded statistics about the books we sent. That autumn, we shipped 20,000 tomes to French, British and Czechoslovakian troops as well as to the Foreign Legion. Like Miss Reeder, I felt especially proud of our service to individual soldiers, I felt less proud of the fact that I'd barely spoken to Bitsi.

Maman grumbled that I was never home any more, and Paul joked that he had to volunteer if he wanted to spend time with me, but I found that, like Rémy, I 'needed to do something'. As bereft as I felt without him, I knew it had to be worse for the soldiers who were far from home. I tucked cards of encouragement into their books.

Feeling uncertain about the future, I often checked the last page of a novel, hoping for a happy ending. In *Villette, 823: Here pause: pause at once. There is enough said. Trouble no quiet, kind heart; leave sunny imaginations hope. Let it be theirs to conceive the delight of joy born again fresh out of great terror, the rapture of rescue from peril, the wondrous reprieve from dread, the fruition of return.* I wished I could tear ahead in the story of my own life to reassure myself.

162

The war would end. Rémy would come home. Paul and I would marry.

Exhausted again tonight, I fell into bed with a book. *Mr Rochester crossed the floor and seized my arm, and grasped my waist. He seemed to devour me with his flaming glance . . .*

"Never," said he, as he ground his teeth, "never was anything at once so frail and so indomitable. A mere reed she feels in my hand! [And he shook me with the force of his hold.] I could bend her . . . the savage beautiful creature!

"Of yourself, you could come with soft flight and nestle against my heart, if you would: seized against your will, you will elude the grasp like an essence — you will vanish ere I inhale your fragrance. Oh! Come, Odile, come!'

"Odile!" Maman banged on the door. "It's past midnight."

Picking up a pen and paper, I wrote:

Dear Rémy,
I could read all night, but Maman will
pester me until I turn out the light. Today
was another hectic day. The Library is as
busy as ever — subscribers who left at the
end of August are back, and we're doing
our best to get books to you all. Paul comes
to take crates to the station. Margaret says
he's there for me, but I'm not sure. I don't
know how he feels. We've never said "I love
you." We're never alone. Perhaps I keep

him at arm's length. It hurts to hope. I
worry his feelings for me will disappear.

I remembered how Papa and Uncle Lionel had both
found someone else.

I mean, don't sparks die?

"Lights out, Odile!"

1 December 1939

Dear Odile,
Thanks for the book! Jane Eyre is as feisty
as you. How clever to write your impres-
sions in the margins! Turning each page
feels like we're reading the novel together.
Why on earth do you sympathise with Mr
Rochester? He's a cad! I'm starting to doubt
your taste in men.
Margaret's right — Paul volunteers to be
close to you. It shouldn't hurt to hope. It
should give you thrills, like a plateful of
stars set before you, shimmering with pos-
sibility.
I didn't ask for leave at Christmas. Many
soldiers in my squad have children, and I
want them to be able to spend the holidays
with family. I'll try to get back to Paris in
the spring.
You didn't mention Bitsi. There's
something gloomy about her letters. I get

the impression she doesn't spend time with friends, doesn't ever have a laugh. She goes to work and back home. With her brother mobilised, she's doubly miserable. It kills me to think she's unhappy. I don't want her to be alone. Please take care of her for me.

Love,
Rémy

CHAPTER
SIXTEEN

ODILE

Paris, January 1940

For the first time, my family greeted the New Year without my twin. We three ate our duck confit in silence. These days, my inner metronome ticked back and forth: I was in tears, I was serene, I was befuddled, I was fine. At the Library, we continued to send packages to our soldiers. Staying busy — wrapping books, aiding subscribers — contained my fears.

Paul helped haul crates to the station, where they would be shipped on trains. Today, when he saw me, his whole face lit up. My breath caught in my chest. Aware that gossipy Madame Simon was watching (and she was always watching), Paul and I said hello like we did the first time we met, with quick pecks on the cheek.

From the threshold of the children's room, Bitsi watched us manoeuvre a cart towards the door. I pretended not to see her. I'd received Rémy's last letter two weeks ago, and still hadn't done as he'd asked.

At the Library entrance, Miss Reeder took in the scene. "You didn't greet Bitsi," she said.

"I said hello to her this morning."

"You used to be friends."

"The train will depart soon," Paul interceded. "We'd better get the books to the station."

"We'll talk when you get back," Miss Reeder told me pointedly.

I wasn't worried. The minute she entered her office, she'd be swept into a whirlpool of demands from subscribers and trustees, and she'd forget about me.

Paul pushed the cart along the pavement. "Did you notice that Boris uses his gas mask as a lunch box? Maybe it's a sign that despite the war life has gone back to normal."

"The true sign is that he's back to writing *The Passion of Boris*."

"What's that?"

"The history of the Library. Funny stories and statistics. He could dedicate an entire chapter to various ways people ask for *The Grapes of Wrath*: Grapes of Rats by Steinbaum, Grapes of Gravity, Grapevine Wrath, Vines of Grapes, Gabe's Wrath, not to mention The Rapes of Wrath."

Paul chuckled. "I don't know how he keeps a straight face."

In front of the station, I tripped on the kerb. Paul put his hands on my hips to steady me, and I forgot about the books. All I saw was him. All I wanted was him. I longed to say *I love you*, but was scared. Scared he didn't feel the same.

He stroked my back. "*Ça va?*"

"*Oui.*"

"*Je t'aime*," he whispered.

"I love you, too."

I expected a roar of thunder or a solar eclipse, some magic to mark the moment. Instead, an old man knocked into us and shouted, "Watch where you're going!"

Paul and I laughed — the absurdity of the situation, the relief of finally saying what we felt. "Well," I said.

"Well," he said.

We continued into the station.

After dropping off the books, we meandered back to the Library. Like the scent of baking bread, love was in the air. I noticed the heart-shaped ironwork of the balconies. A ballad playing on a distant radio. Cafés with tables for two. Paul — my love — kissed me at the entrance of the courtyard. Dreamily, I strolled up the pebbled path.

At the circulation desk, Miss Reeder sat alone. The set of her mouth was sad.

"Is everything all right?" I asked. "Where's Boris?"

"I told him I needed to speak with you."

"Me?"

"Petty quarrels are bad for staff morale, and subscribers deserve better."

I was in trouble because of Bitsi? "She started it!"

"The American Hospital needs volunteers," she said. "I want you to go there."

I want you to go.

"But we have so much work here," I argued.

"True."

"I haven't said a word to Bitsi!"

"That's the problem. You haven't said a word." Her eyes didn't move from mine as she searched for wisdom that wasn't yet there. "You need to grow up. A week of hospital work will put things into perspective."

"When do you want me to go?"

"Now, please. You'll receive your pay as usual. At the hospital, report to Nurse Letson. She's expecting you."

I felt small, a fleck of dust Miss Reeder had wiped off a shelf. Too stunned to speak, I nodded to her and passed under the drooping French and American flags into the courtyard, along the border of wilting pansies, to the street. At Métro Monceau, I trudged down the jagged stairs, where I ran into Margaret. When I told her I'd been banished, her head tilted in sympathy.

"You respect Miss Reeder so much," she said. "Is it possible she has a point?"

"Why does everyone think she has all the answers?"

"If you could talk to Bitsi . . ." Margaret continued. "Isn't it what Rémy would want?"

What about what I wanted? Why couldn't Miss Reeder see she was being unfair? I didn't deserve to be banned like Jean Moreau, who blew his nose in books he didn't approve of. I hadn't done anything wrong.

"I should go."

In the chic suburb of Neuilly, under the bare chestnut trees on Boulevard Victor Hugo, I opened the hospital's iron gate and hurried up the path. A nurse in a white cap and apron gave volunteers a first-aid lesson before giving us a tour. "If we were like the French," she said, "we'd have plaques all over the place. 'Josephine Baker sang in this exact spot.' 'Here's where

Hemingway started writing *The Sun Also Rises* after we removed his appendix.'"

She introduced Dr Jackson, who explained, "Things are calm in the combat zone, but we must be ready."

Paper had been pasted on the windows, but he decided it wasn't enough to hide the light. In charge of the fourth floor, I smothered the panes with blue paint, getting more on my dress than on the glass. Though I missed my habitués and being surrounded by books, I threw myself into the task, trying to forget the hole in my heart, the one I'd dug myself.

The ward, made up of 150 beds, housed a dozen soldiers who'd been injured by shelling along the Maginot Line. They were in pain. They had no privacy. No family or friends were able to visit. Their spirits were flagging. I made sure the soldiers had books and magazines on their bedside tables. Reading offered escape, something else to think about, a privacy of the mind.

A curly-haired Breton quickly became my favourite because he was cheeky like Rémy. While I cleared away the lunch trays, he asked, "Will you read to me, mademoiselle?"

"Do you have a favourite author?"

"Zane Grey. I like cowboy stories."

Grabbing the dog-eared copy of *Nevada* from the library in the corner, I sat beside him and began to read. Finishing the first chapter, I asked, "What do you think?"

He grinned. "I think I could have read it myself — my leg's busted, not my brain. But your voice is so pretty, you're so pretty . . ."

"Scamp!" I reached over to muss his hair, like I would my brother's. Hand mid-air, I stiffened. What if something happened to Rémy and he ended up in a hospital, injured or worse? He'd asked one thing. I needed to make things right with Bitsi.

I wished I could have blamed my rudeness to her on the war, but the truth was that I *was* immature. If I wanted to have a better relationship with my brother and Bitsi, I needed to change, I wanted to. But would I be able to?

"Are you all right, mademoiselle?"

"Better than you," I teased. "My leg's in one piece."

After my shift, I rushed to the Library, where I breathed in the heavenly smell of books. I found Bitsi shelving children's stories.

"Let's take tea."

Her violet eyes brimmed with hope, "What about work?"

"Miss Reeder won't mind."

"I miss him," Bitsi whispered.

I slipped my foot over hers, like I would have Rémy's.

CHAPTER
SEVENTEEN

ODILE

Paris, May 1940

In the courtyard, the roses were in bloom, and the sweet scent wafted into the Library. Despite the balmy days, everyone was touchy — worrying about loved ones far from home, about war communiqués that reported on deadly battles in Norway, about the likelihood that France might be next. Mr Pryce-Jones told Monsieur de Nerciat to "sod off". Boris complimented Professor Cohen on her new briefcase, but Madame Simon muttered, "When I see what *you people* have while *good Frenchmen* like my son work for a pittance . . ." At least Bitsi and I were getting along.

Deep in thought, I didn't hear the whisper of her ballet slippers until she was beside me. "Miss Reeder wants a word. Staff meeting."

Bitsi and the caretaker were the last to arrive; she moved to my side.

At her desk, Miss Reeder cleared her throat. "I have news. German troops penetrated Belgium, Luxembourg and the Netherlands. They've bombed the north and east of France."

172

The north. Rémy was in the north. *Please let him be all right.* I sought Bitsi's hand and held it in mine.

Miss Reeder said we must be prepared for bombardment and even warfare. There was simply no way to know. Parisian staff should leave the city, foreign staff the country.

"Return home?" Helen-in-reference asked.

"I'm afraid so," Miss Reeder replied.

"Are you leaving?" Boris asked.

"Please don't go," Bitsi mumbled to herself.

"No," the Directress said. "The Library will remain open."

Thank goodness. Bitsi squeezed my hand. We were scared, but at least we still had the Library.

"That will be all." This phrase, used to signal the end of meetings, scattered us like billiard balls — to share the news, to have a cry in the cloakroom. Dazed, I stumbled to the periodical room, where Paul paced near the magazine rack.

"I just heard," he said. "You must be worried sick about Rémy."

He opened his arms, and I slid into his embrace.

A week later, Miss Reeder approached, her brow creased with concern, "The American Hospital is overwhelmed," she told me, "Why don't you lend a hand for a few days? It's a long shot, but you might encounter someone who knows your brother or his regiment."

"What about the Library?"

"Books will outlast us all. Go and find out what you can."

Nurses rushed from one operating theatre to another, starched caps askew, aprons drenched in blood. Soldiers in soiled bandages slumped on chairs in the corridors. Volunteers washed the men's faces and feet. I filled a basin with warm water and knelt before a serviceman, and another, then another. Each time I cleaned the blood from the face of a dark-haired soldier, I hoped Rémy's intelligent eyes would be revealed. Countless faces later, I rose to stretch, to see if I could be of assistance in the ward, where the wounded lay on narrow beds. I didn't know whether to be relieved because Rémy wasn't here among the injured or scared that he was out there fighting.

At dawn, I fell on to a cot in the staffroom only to wake two hours later to serve breakfast. In their pyjamas, French and English soldiers were stripped of uniforms, rank and nationality. Social order was based on the severity of injuries. This was how I gauged the wounds: if a man flirted, he was feeling better; if he stayed silent, he was hurting.

On a trolley, straight out of surgery, one moaned. I moved closer, smoothing his creased brow with my handkerchief, which Maman had dipped in lavender water.

"You," he said.

"Me," I replied.

"You washed my face. Your touch was tender . . ." He dozed off, then startled awake, "I love you."

"With everything they pumped into you," I replied, "you'd love a goat."

In the ward the next evening, I helped him write a letter home to America. He'd crossed into Canada and signed up with the Royal Air Force. "I was never one to sit on the bench," he said. He gestured to my hands, raw from washing the wounded, "You aren't, either."

"I'm used to patching up books, not people."

"Books?"

"I'm a librarian."

"Do you shush people?"

I gave his arm a playful poke. "Only impertinent soldiers."

"Wish we were in a library now."

"What kind of reader are you?" It was the first time in weeks that I'd asked the question.

"The Bible. Where I'm from, they're big on the Bible."

"Do you want me to bring you one?"

"God, no! I mean, no thank you, I've already read it."

"How about I bring you something to read tomorrow?"

"I'd like that."

He yawned, and an instant later, he fell asleep. It was nearly 9 p.m., and I needed to get home before Maman picked apart her ferns in worry. As I walked towards the door, a private named Thomas reached out, his fingers grazing my bloodied dress. He was nineteen. A barber, before. Yesterday, when I'd brought him a copy of *Life* with Lana Turner on the cover, he refused to open the magazine, "No need to look further," he insisted.

"Don't leave, Mademoiselle Bookworm." He clutched at my hem.

I brushed his hair — brown like Rémy's — from his forehead.

"Don't leave," he whispered again.

Maman would have to wait. I tucked the blanket underneath his chin.

"Talk to me," he said.

"About what?"

"Anything."

"I wish you could meet my habitués at the Library. There's an Englishman — imagine a crane wearing a paisley bow tie. And his French friend — a walrus with a bushy moustache. Each day, they light a stinky cheroot and debate. Today's topic: Proust's madeleine, should it have been a croissant? Yesterday's: who's the greatest athlete with a J in his name? Johnny Weissmuller or Jesse Owens?"

I was rewarded with a small smile. "They're both wrong — it's the rower Jack Beresford. I want to hear more."

"There's Madame Simon, with hand-me-down dentures that don't fit her big mouth. Oh là là, she loves to gossip . . ."

"Like the women at my church. More."

"The latest chinwag is about my favourite subscriber, a professor with a mysterious past. 'She married a man half her age,' Madame Simon began, but our cataloguer, stern Mrs Turnbull with her crooked blue-grey fringe, interrupted, 'No, he was twice her age.' Well, they were both right — the Professor's first husband was twice her age, and the second half her age. Then they speculated about the third."

"The third?" he said. "What a life."

I glanced at the clock. Nearly eleven.

"Don't go," he said.

His voice had become hoarse, so I lifted his head and gave him a sip of water. "You'll never be alone," I promised. "Shall I tell you more? You'd recognise the Professor from a distance because she always wears purple. She talks about books like they're her best friends . . ."

"I want to meet her."

I stayed through the night, telling tales, calming his fevered dreams, holding his hand until he died.

CHAPTER
EIGHTEEN

ODILE

Paris, 3 June 1940

I was blocks from the Library, fetching books for my soldiers at the hospital, when the city went still. No pigeons warbling, no Parisians chatting. Just a loud whirr. I looked up and saw planes, dozens and dozens of them. My heart boomed in the hollow of my clavicle. In the distance, I heard the crash of shattering glass as bombs exploded. An alarm screeched its way through the streets. People ran around me, they ran into me. I tasted smoke and knew I should run for cover. Frozen on the pavement, I felt numb as I gaped at the raiders in the clear blue sky. All I could think of was Rémy. Where was he? Were these the smells and sounds that he faced?

When the bombardment was over — was it an hour? Or two? Or was it only twenty minutes? — I clung to the sides of buildings all the way to the Library. At the front desk, staff gathered around me. I looked at Bitsi who said, "Oh, dear!"; at the Directress, who now had a delicate line between her brows; at Margaret, who gripped her pearls; and at Boris, who said, "She's going to faint!"

Miss Reeder sat me down. Boris poured a teacup of whiskey to calm my nerves.

"You're safe," he told me, "for now."

"German troops will never make it past the Maginot Line," Margaret said.

"We've done our share of wishful thinking," Miss Reeder said, "now plans must be made."

"Are you saying we should leave?" Bitsi said. "I don't know where my mother and I could go."

The siren still screeched in my ears, and I couldn't take in what they were saying. I only knew I had to return to the hospital: my soldiers needed me. I rose from the chair.

"You should sit tight," Bitsi said.

No. I needed to get back to the wounded.

The Hospital had sustained no damage, but inside everyone was shaken. Reading material in trembling hands, I made my way through the ward, weaving between the beds, between the worried faces. At dinnertime, no one had much of an appetite. The nurses and I proffered bowls of soup and persuaded the soldiers to eat.

At home, Maman fussed. "You get home later each evening. Paul's here, and the roast's been ready for an hour."

"Has Rémy written?"

"Not yet," Papa said.

"A hell of a day," Paul said as we picked at our plates. Needing the reassurance of his touch, I moved my leg so it rested between his.

"Good news in Dunkirk. 'An obstinate battle continues . . .'" Papa read from the war communiqué. "'Magnificent resistance of the Allied troops.'"

"I pray the war will end, and that he'll soon be home," Maman said, one hand on her aching temple, the other on the back of Rémy's chair.

When I arrived at the Library the next morning, Miss Reeder was alone at a reading room table, poring over the paper. Impeccable in her blue jersey dress, mascara dusting her lashes, lipstick just so, she didn't let her fears stop her from coming to work.

Perhaps feeling my gaze, she glanced up. In her expression, I saw so much: concern, curiosity, courage, affection. "Was anyone in your family hurt during the bombing?" she asked.

"No."

"Good." She held up telegrams. "I'm afraid that mine is begging me to go home."

I didn't blame them. Sometimes, even I wanted to leave. "How can you stay?"

Gently, she cupped my cheek, "Because I believe in the power of books — we do important work, by making sure knowledge is available, and by creating community. And because I have faith."

"In God?"

"In young women like you and Bitsi and Margaret — I know you'll set the world right."

Habitués gathered around to read the news. *Le Figaro* congratulated Parisians on their sangfroid. It stated that 1,084 bombs were launched, killing 45

180

civilians, injuring 155. A photo showed a bombed building, rooms open to the world like a doll's house.

"Every battle's either a 'magnificent struggle' or a 'valiant fight'," Monsieur de Nerciat said.

"Each day, more news articles are blacked out," Professor Cohen said. "What are the censors hiding?"

Mr Pryce-Jones asked if he could speak with me in private. His milky blue eyes clouded with concern. "If I had a brother, I'd want to know."

In the cloakroom, among broken umbrellas and wibbly chairs, the retired diplomat confided that the communiqués weren't telling the real story.

"But . . . the newspapers say we re winning."

No, he said. According to his source at the embassy, tens of thousands of French and British soldiers had been captured. At Dunkirk, the Germans surrounded the Allied troops, who had their backs against the Channel. Braving attacks from the enemy, English ships sailed over to pick up their soldiers. Soon there would be almost no British military presence left on the Continent.

I sank on to a chair, unable to reconcile the gulf between what we'd read and what he was telling me. The British were withdrawing mere weeks after the real combat had begun. What would happen to the French troops? What would happen to Rémy?

"I'm sorry, *ma grande*."

"You were right to tell me. Why couldn't they save our soldiers?"

"According to my sources, they helped as many as they could. Remember, we're talking about fishing

181

boats and dinghies as well as naval vessels trying to evacuate 300,000 men."

The Maginot Line would keep us safe, France had the best army — nothing but lies. *Oh, Rémy, where are you?* If something happened to him, I assumed I'd *know*, but I didn't feel anything.

A few days later, on my way home, I turned on to the leafy boulevard, expecting to weave around mademoiselles delighting in the window displays of Kislav gloves (silk or cotton, leather or lace) and Nina Ricci ensembles (trimmed with squirrel tails, *bien sûr*). Instead, the pavements and cobble-stones were crowded with thousands of people, so many that I couldn't see across to the other side of the street. All wore dazed, haggard expressions. I couldn't imagine what these people had gone through, the horrors of war they'd run from.

Some families rode wagons pulled by oxen, mattresses piled behind them. Others trudged along on foot, lugging bundles or pushing prams crammed with plates. There were country folk in work boots, city dwellers in brogues and pumps. A granny in a sweat-stained dress cradled a cast-iron skillet, while her husband held a hessian sack. Even children carried something — a Bible, a bag with clothing spilling out, a birdcage. Many walked in small groups, but others were alone. A soldier with a soiled bandage wrapped around his arm nearly bumped into me. Plodding along, a girl my age held an infant out in front of her, as if she didn't quite know how to carry him. Perhaps her husband had been called up, and she'd been left alone

182

with the baby. She shook him gently, as if she wanted him to wake up. His cheeks were a sickly green, his limbs frozen in time. Unable to face the truth, I turned away.

Beside me, a farmer beseeched his bull to move. A mother murmured to a toddler. But mostly people were silent, as if they had no words for what they'd seen. In their haunted faces, I saw that life would never be the same. I stood on the street, staying with them out of respect, as one would a funeral procession, before stumbling home.

At dinner, Papa said he and his staff had taken trays of coffee to the sudden refugees. Most were from the north-east of France. Many had never left their villages. "They were fleeing German soldiers. The men I spoke to — simple farmers and tradesmen — received no help or instruction. Their mayor was the first to leave."

"What's the world coming to?" Maman said. "Those poor people. Where will they end up?"

Kneading her hand, he said, "The south, which is where you and Odile shall go. I must do my duty here, but I want you to go where it's safe."

What he said made sense. I expected Maman to acquiesce, but she reeled back as if he'd slapped her with a demand for a divorce.

"Non!"

"Now, Hortense —"

She snatched her hand from his. "This is where Rémy will return. I won't leave."

Point final.

★ ★ ★

We Parisians were a blasé breed. We walked quickly but never rushed. We didn't bat an eyelid at seeing lovers in the park. We were elegant even when taking out the rubbish, eloquent when insulting someone. But at the beginning of June, with the news that German tanks were just days from the city, we Parisians forgot ourselves. There was so much to say — finish packing, lock the door, hurry up — that we stuttered. Some ran to the station to ensure that loved ones were put on trams to safety. Others joined the forlorn procession of wagons and wheelbarrows, cars and bicycles as cobblers, butchers and glove-makers boarded up their windows and left. Each apartment shuttered, each closed door was proof that something terrible was going to happen.

The British Embassy advised their staff to quit Paris, so Lawrence and Margaret planned to drive to Brittany with their daughter. "Until things blow over again," Margaret said, insisting they'd only be gone a few weeks. Recalling the frightened faces of the French who'd become refugees in their own country overnight, I wasn't so sure.

Though the city was a ghost town, my habitués still haunted the periodical section. Huddled around the table, we scoured the newspapers. Would Paris be bombed again? Could the Germans get this far? Even the generals didn't know. Maybe that was the most frightening — we didn't know what would happen.

"Will you go to England?" Professor Cohen asked Mr Pryce-Jones.

184

His head reared back. "Certainly not! Without Paris, I don't know where I'd be."

Monsieur de Nerciat asked about Rémy, but I merely shook my head, afraid I'd cry if I opened my mouth.

"Politicians have fled." Mr Pryce-Jones kindly changed the subject.

"So have the diplomats."

The Englishman harrumphed, and monsieur added, "Present company excluded."

"Paris without politicians is like a brothel without *filles de joie*."

"Are you comparing Paris to a house of ill-repute?" I asked.

"Worse!" Monsieur de Nerciat said. "He's comparing politicians to prostitutes."

"If the shoe fits . . ." I said, and the men laughed.

"Bill Bullitt's still here," said Mr Pryce-Jones, pointing to the photo in *Le Figaro*. "Said no American Ambassador had ever fled — not during the French Revolution, not when the Boches came in 1914 — and damned if he'd be the first."

"A poster said Paris would be an open city," I said. "What does that mean?"

"Paris won't defend herself, and the enemy won't attack. It's a way to ensure the safety of the inhabitants."

"So no more bombs?" I asked cautiously. War communiqués weren't always to be believed, but I had utter faith in Mr Pryce-Jones.

"Bombs, no," he replied. "Germans, yes."

Margaret ran into the Library. Pale as her pearls, she scanned the room and rushed over to me. "I had to ask one last time," she said. "Are you certain you don't want to come?"

"If Rémy returns . . ."

"I understand." She clasped my hands. "What if we never see each other again?"

It was a question with no answer. I could only tell her, "You're my dearest friend."

"I don't know what I'll do without you. I love the Library, but I love you more."

A car horn blared.

"It's Lawrence. Christina must be fussing," she said shakily. "I'd better go. *Bon courage.*"

I love the Library, but I love you more. It was exactly how I felt. We were just like Janie and Pheoby in my favourite book. We could tell each other anything.

Watching my best friend leave turned me into a leaky teapot. Not wanting my habitués to see me lose control, I blinked rapidly as I hurried to the card catalogue. Flicking through the cards, I let my tears soak into them, all angst carefully concealed in the O drawer.

"Margaret's doing the smart thing." Professor Cohen draped her shawl over my shoulders.

"Are you leaving, too?"

She smiled wryly. "*Ma grande,* no one's ever accused me of doing the smart thing."

A library is a sanctuary of facts, but now rumours made their way into the periodical room, where Professor Cohen and Madame Simon chatted at the table. "I

186

heard that from now on in schools, they'll only teach German," madame told me as I tidied a pile of magazines. "We won't be allowed on the pavements, just Germans. Are you listening to me, girl?" She poked my chest. "They'll rape anything with legs. Especially pretty ones like you." Fear churned in my stomach as I tried to ignore her. "Cover yourself in mustard so they won't want to have their way with you."

"Enough!" Professor Cohen said.

The Directress had arranged for vehicles to take colleagues to Angoulême, where they would assist staff at the American clinic, I wanted to see them off, but Papa ordered me to stay at home.

"I need to say goodbye!"

"Absolutely not."

"If I don't go, Miss Reeder will be alone." I remembered how a sobbing subscriber had collapsed into her arms. The Directress was staying, and it wasn't even her country at war.

"I'm not worried about her. I'm worried about you."

"Miss Reeder says —"

"Miss Reeder says! What about what I say?"

"What about the Library?" I asked.

"What about the Library?" he said, exasperated. "Do you not understand the danger?"

"Papa . . ."

"Not another word."

The following morning we awoke to blasts from loudspeakers. "Protests and hostile acts against German troops are punishable by death!"

CHAPTER
NINETEEN

MISS REEDER

Paris, June 1940

Was this really Paris? Miss Reeder did not think so. The avenues were deserted, market stalls empty. Even the sparrows had fled. She walked briskly towards the bus stop, past the flower shop, where she spied spidery carcases of hydrangeas, then past a boarded-up bakery. She longed for the ordinary, magical smell of croissants. Usually, she took the number 29 to the Library, but public transport had ceased. Continuing on foot, briefcase and gas mask in tow, she cringed at the sight of a trio of German soldiers on patrol. Worried about where else she might find such men, Miss Reeder moved faster, one thing on her mind: the Library.

She crossed the Seine. There was not another soul on the vast Place de la Concorde, not a single car motoring down the Champs-Élysées, France's grandest traffic hazard. In the liveliest city in the world, she could hear a hairpin drop. The stillness was strange. She'd never felt so alone. Nonetheless, seeing the embassy reassured her, and she was tempted to go in to inform Ambassador Bullitt that the Library remained

188

open — after all, he was the honorary president. But she knew that before the French government had taken to the road, the Prime Minister had asked the American Ambassador to deal with the arriving German generals and to maintain order. The heaving swastika atop the opulent Crillon Hotel, directly across the street from the embassy, indicated that the ambassador had work to do.

The Directress entered the Library courtyard as the caretaker opened the shutters. She was just in time to see the sleepy eyes of her world awaken.

"I'll be in my office. No visitors until nine, please," she told the caretaker as usual before preparing a pot of espresso. At her desk, she reread the telegrams, hoping they'd changed overnight, like everything else. "Fund solicitation has been withheld," the third vice-president of the board had written from New York. "Uncertainty might arise in the minds of our friends as to whether the Library could continue." Another wrote: "We assume that the Library has closed. I doubt it can have any existence in the immediate future."

"I haven't left my post!" she wanted to shout, "We're here." She needed to convince them that the ALP must remain open. "Libraries are lungs," she scrawled, her pen barely able to keep up with her ideas, "books the fresh air breathed in to keep the heart beating, to keep the brain imagining, to keep hope alive. Subscribers depend on us for news, for community. Soldiers need books, need to know their friends at the Library care. Our work is too important to stop now." She reread the lines: too true, too sentimental. She composed herself, and she composed more letters, this one to Mr Milam of the American Library Association, that one to the board in New York: "We are giving the students what they need, the public the books they want, and the soldiers what we can. It is, after all, something, to continue to hold on, to hope for a wider contribution to humanity."

She poured herself an espresso.

"Any left?" asked Bill Bullitt, sticking his bald head into her office.

"Ambassador."

"Directress," he said. "You know why I'm here."

"To advise me to return to the States," she said flatly.

"President Roosevelt ordered me to leave Paris, and I'm still here. I won't advise you to do something I refused to do myself."

"Where is our common sense?" she said with a little smile.

"We must have left it in the States."

She watched as he served himself a cup of espresso.

He sat down. "Take refuge at Le Bristol, where the other Americans are staying."

"I can't afford it."

He took a sip. "Let me worry about that."

"I'll be fine at home."

"Does your building have a basement shelter to protect against poisonous gas?"

She gestured to the gas mask slumped in front of the bookcase.

"Transport will be disrupted for a time," he said. "Le Bristol is just four blocks away."

It would be convenient to be closer.

The stalemate brought silence.

"Can you tell me anything?" she finally said.

The confident tone he'd struck slipped away. "We've had a hell of a time dealing with the Germans. Promise you'll be careful. And that you'll move to the hotel."

"I'll go tonight." She handed him the correspondence to be sent by diplomatic pouch.

"I won't keep you." He saw himself out.

A small part of her wished she'd listened when her parents had begged her to board a ship. She carried a photo of them in her handbag. Each time she bought a baguette or fished around for her handkerchief, Mom and Dad's eyes implored her to come home. She wished she could make them understand that Paris was home. She'd made her life's work, her life here.

Remaining had been the right choice. If her parents had taught her one thing, it was to stand her ground, whether dealing with a malicious schoolmate or the domineering cataloguer at the Library of Congress. You're nothing without principles. Nowhere without ideals. No one without courage. Even as they begged her to come home, they were proud she stayed. *Dear Mom and Dad*, she wrote. *There are many things I should like to say to you, many thoughts I should like to send, but alas, I shall have to depend upon your heart and understanding to know all that I carry inside . . .*

Le Bristol. Her parents would be reassured that she was staying with compatriots. The hotel had a long list of esteemed guests: movie stars, heiresses, lords, ladies and now a librarian. After work, she walked home to 1 rue de la Chaise to collect her things. As she unlocked the door, Madame Palewski rushed to her. The concierge's olive skin was chalky.

"What's happened?" Miss Reeder asked.

"My husband was at the Polish Library. They came." Madame began to weep. "They stomped in. Demanded the keys. Went through the entire building. The archives, the rare manuscripts. The director, he tried to stop them. Soldiers threatened to take him away."

"Is your husband all right?"

"Yes. But they stole everything . . ."

The Nazis had been in Paris for three days, and it was starting. Miss Reeder had hoped that churches and libraries — quiet places of devotion — would not be disturbed.

She realised that soon she would face the enemy.

CHAPTER
TWENTY

ODILE

Paris, 3 July 1940

Dear Rémy,
Where are you? We long to see you, to have news from you. All is well with us. After keeping me home for ten long days, Papa finally allowed me to return to work. I was worried sick about the Directress, alone at the Library, but she insists she got "quite a kick" out of being the sole guardian. It felt terribly lonely without the others, who only just returned. When I laid eyes on Bitsi, I screamed with joy; Monsieur de Nerciat took great pleasure in shushing a librarian. But the good news was followed with bad: Boris explained that the Nazis had arrived in Angoulême, too. Stern Mrs Turnbull is travelling back to Winnipeg directly from there. Canadian and thus a British subject, she's considered an enemy alien.

Here, Nazis are buying up everything from soap to sewing needles. We call them "tourists" because they take photos of monuments as if they're on holiday. When they ask for directions — Where is the Arc de Triomphe? Where is the Moulin Rouge? — we tell them we don't know. With the 9p.m. curfew, the city is silent in the evening. We've been forced to move our clocks an hour ahead to their time zone. Every time I check my watch, it's a reminder that we live on their time, on their terms.

No one can believe that France has lost and so quickly. At the pulpit, the priest shook his Bible at us and bellowed that defeat is God's punishment for our lack of moral values.

Papa said that a few people were arrested for writing graffiti or throwing rocks at German soldiers, but other than that the situation's calm. Paul looks angry enough to kill someone. He says his job now consists of directing traffic for the Nazis. They ordered him to wear white gloves, which make him feel like "a goddamn butler". Soon he'll help with harvest on his aunt's farm. The change will do him good.

It must be hell for you not to be able to hold Bitsi in your arms. She misses you terribly. I swear that while you're gone, I'll take the best, sweetest care of her.

We haven't had news from Margaret and hope she's safe. The few subscribers who remain are borrowing more novels than ever before, perhaps as a way to escape this unsettling metamorphosis — Boris calls it "France Kafka".
Love,
Odile

"British Fleet Scuttles Two French Battleships — Over 1,000 French Sailors Killed", read the headline. According to the *Herald*, across the Mediterranean in Oran, the British feared that the French navy would allow the Nazis to confiscate their ships. The British admiral gave the French an ultimatum — surrender your vessels or we'll sink them — and six hours to relinquish the ships. When *l'admiral* refused, the British attacked. I read the article twice, but still didn't understand. Allies were fighting each other?

"Traitor!" Monsieur de Nerciat shouted at Mr Pryce-Jones. I didn't need to read the newspaper to know that France had cut diplomatic ties with Britain. For days, I watched monsieur stomp through the Library, muttering about finding a seat that hadn't been tainted by betrayal.

I felt Boris beside me. "Phone call," he said, his green eyes mournful. "Your father."

I ran to the circulation desk and grabbed the receiver. "Papa? Is it Rémy?"

"Come home, dearest," he said.

I fetched Bitsi, who was reading to a handful of children. One look at me, and she dropped her book. Rushing out of the Library, I grabbed her hand and tugged her along. We raced down the street, raced towards . . . I stopped.

"What is it?" she asked.

I shook my head. Suddenly, I wanted to take as long as possible, afraid that Rémy was . . . I couldn't say it, I couldn't even think it. Right now, he was alive. Perhaps when we got home, he wouldn't be.

Our life together played out before me. Our fifth birthday, when Maman had baked the chocolate cake with burned edges. The day Papa took us to ride ponies in the Bois. The time Rémy and I filled the sugar bowl with salt, which caused Maman and her friends to choke on their tea. When she complained to Papa, expecting him to scold, he doubled over with a big belly laugh I wasn't sure I'd heard since. Maman, no fool, only used sugar cubes after that. Endless Sunday lunches where a wink from Rémy was the only thing that kept me sane. The most important meal of my life, when I met Paul. Every memory included Rémy.

Until he'd joined the army, he was the first person I spoke to in the morning, the last at night. My best friend, my other half. Not that I'd ever told him. What if we'd spoken our last words to each other? I remembered the day he'd left home. What had I said? Take your jumper, you'll catch cold? Hurry up, you'll miss the train?

"Stop it," Bitsi said.

"What?"

"Whatever you're doing."

At home, Papa sat Bitsi and me down next to Maman, who was as pale as an aspirin. He braced himself against the hearth.

"We've received news of Rémy," he said.

CHAPTER
TWENTY-ONE

LILY

Froid, Montana, April 1985

Dad and I got to the church at three thirty. Dipping my fingers into the rancid holy water, I noticed the swarm of pink roses that adorned the pews. There were almost as many flowers for the wedding as there were for Mom's funeral, a little over a year ago now. I had a headache. I wished I could crawl into bed and pull memories of Mom over me like a comforter.

Eleanor's mother rushed over. "Ready for the big day?" she asked Dad. She hugged me. My nose landed in her carnation corsage and I sneezed. She said, "Call me Grandma Pearl," and led me into the back room where she introduced me to three giggly bridesmaids, who, like "Grandma Pearl", had come from Lewistown. My dress was the same Pepto-Bismol pink as theirs. Eleanor preened at the full-length mirror, a lace veil obscuring her face and chignon.

"You're as pretty as Lady Di," I said. It was the honest-to-God truth — they both had those doe eyes.

I wanted to like her. I wanted her to like me. Yet when she pulled me to her sequinned bosom and held me tight, my arms flailed, not ready to hug her.

"Hon," she said, "I promise to look after you like my own."

It was nice as far as promises went, and I knew how to respond. After my lesson on *les adjectifs*, Odile had said, *I'll teach you words in English. Words you'll be expected to say.* "I hope you and Dad will be happy," I told Eleanor. Though I'd practised, the sentence sounded stilted.

In French, there are two forms of "you", the informal and formal. *Tu* for friends and loved ones, *vous* for acquaintances and people we want to keep at a distance. I would use *tu* with Dad, but *vous* with Eleanor.

The organ boomed out Pachelbel, and we scurried to the back of the church. Mrs Olson — the only organist in town — waited for no bride; weddings followed her schedule. Slipping down the aisle, I spotted Robby in the fourth row from the back. He watched me. Just me, I wiped my sweaty palms on my dress and slid between Odile and Mary Louise in the first pew. In neat pairs, the bridesmaids and groomsmen followed. The overbearing notes of "Here Comes the Bride" filled the church. Dad stood in the exact spot where Mom's coffin had been. Her ivory casket had been carried up the same aisle that Eleanor and her father were walking down now.

"Dearly beloved . . ." Iron-Collar Maloney began, and tears filled my eyes. Scared that Dad would be upset if he saw, I hunched down and stared at the kneeler. Odile placed her foot on mine. The pressure gave me something to focus on.

"Married and Brenda barely dead," Sue Bob said.

"And James taking up with someone so young," Mrs Ivers said, though she'd been the one to set them up.

"He's doing this for Lily," old Mrs Murdoch said. "That girl needs a mother."

Whisper, whisper, whisper. I tried not to listen.

"You may now kiss the bride," is usually the best part, because it's romantic and close to the end, but watching Dad kiss another lady felt weird. Mary Louise elbowed me, like she couldn't believe it, either.

In the hall, pastel streamers floated between the fluorescent lights. "All this pink makes me want to barf," Mary Louise said. Slouching on the metal folding chairs, we watched the bride and groom glide along, greeting guests. It was only a matter of time before they had a kid so they could replace me like they'd replaced Mom.

The cake, nearly as tall as Eleanor, echoed the frothy form of her Cool-Whip dress. She and Dad cut the cake, his hand over hers on the silver knife. They tucked crumbs into each other's mouths. Cameras flashed. Dad gestured for me to come get a slice. Of course, Tiffany Ivers got there first.

"At least the cake's good," she said.

"Shut up." I grabbed two plates, one for Mary Louise, one for me.

"Just trying to be nice." She turned to Dad. "Congratulations, Mr and Mrs Jacobsen."

He'd seen the exchange and probably wondered why his daughter couldn't be as sweet as Tiffany Ivers. The

200

plates in my hands trembled. Before Dad could scold, I rushed off, weaving between wedding guests.

Robby appeared before me. "Sucks, huh?"

I heard so much in those words. I'm sorry your mom died. Today must be hard for you.

"Yeah."

He carried my plates back to Mary Louise, lingering at the table for a minute before heading back to his parents. She ate my cake and hers. When the DJ put on a slow song, I stared at the blinking exit sign above the door, not willing to watch Mr and Mrs Jacobsen smoosh up against each other.

Dad tapped me on the arm, "Father-daughter dance, Lil." He led me to the dance floor where Mr Carlson gently spun Eleanor around. We were supposed to dance, but just stood there. "In church," Dad said, "I saw you with your head down."

I tensed.

"I'm a little sad, too," he admitted.

He took my hand. We swayed slowly, together, and for the rest of the reception, his confession stayed in my ears.

Dad and Eleanor drove off in our station wagon, decorated with a "Just Married" sign. Relieved the ordeal was over, I trudged home with Mary Louise. In my room, I changed into my eagle T-shirt. She kicked the pink dress under the bed.

Chez Odile, I awoke to the aroma of buttery croissants. Feeling out of sorts, I didn't eat much. I couldn't help but wonder what life would be like when Dad and

Eleanor got back from their *lune de miel*, moon of honey. Things would change, and I worried there wouldn't be room for me.

"You seem pensive." Odile handed me *The Outsiders*. "It's about family, the one you're born with, and the one you create with kindred souls. It's about how we make a place for ourselves in this world."

"Your books are lucky," I said, eyeing her shelves. "They have an exact place they should be. They know who they're next to. I wish I had a Dewey Decimal number."

"I used to wonder what my number would be if I had one. We could create our own."

This spurred a conversation. Should we be in literature or non-fiction? Should Odile's number be French or American, and was there a French-American number? Could we share the same number so we'd always be together? We added 810 (American), 840 (French) and 302.34 (friendship), and created our shelf of 1955.34-worthy books. Some favourites were *Le Petit Prince*, *Little Women*, *The Secret Garden*, *Candide*, *The Long Winter*, *A Tree Grows in Brooklyn*, *Their Eyes Were Watching God*. When we finished, I felt like no matter what happened, I'd always have a place with Odile.

The next morning, Mary Louise and I lounged on Odile's couch and drank *café au lait* that was mostly *lait* while she hoed her garden. When we finished, I peeked into the drawers of her buffet.

202

"Do you still think she was a spy?" Mary Louise asked.

I shrugged. From the bills, I learned her clothes came from a boutique in Chicago. Not exactly a discovery — I knew they weren't from Jeans 'n Things, In a faded Christmas card, someone named Lucienne urged Odile to contact her parents before it was "too late".

"She's right outside," Mary Louise hissed. "You're gonna get caught."

"Something happened in Paris. There's a reason she stayed here."

When the sliding door opened, I slammed the drawer shut.

When the honeymoon was over, Dad came to get me at Odile's, just as she and I finished my quiz on *les verbes*. She invited him in but he declined. We lingered on the porch, the spring sun warming us. I worried about what he was going to say. Numbers came easy to Dad. They always added up. Words were trickier. He never understood their weight.

"Thanks for taking care of Lily," he said.

"My pleasure." Odile beamed at me.

"Now that Ellie's here, you can step back," he said.

"Step back?" she repeated.

"Lily should spend more time at home."

No way was I giving Odile up. She was on my side, no matter what. I could tell her anything. Dad bossed me around, but Odile never did. She trusted me to make the right choices. I'd wash her car, mow her lawn, water her ferns — anything to keep taking lessons with her.

Before I could tell her so, she said in French, "Same time tomorrow."

"*Oui, merci*," I said, my thanks gushing out gratefully.

Eleanor quit her job and Dad's life went back to normal. After a long day at the bank, he came home to a wife, a daughter and a hot dinner. On Saturday mornings, Eleanor made me vacuum and run a rag with lemon Pledge over every surface. "A young woman needs to learn these things. You'll thank me later." When I complained, Dad said I needed to "listen" to Eleanor. By that he meant "obey".

Even when school let out for the summer, she got up early and sculpted her curls with mousse. Before Dad left for work, she straightened his tie ten times. Mom had never ironed my shirts, but Eleanor did. "No one'll ever be able to say that I didn't take care of you." At dinner, when I spilled creamed corn on the tablecloth, she darted to the sink and returned with a rag to wipe up the blob.

I wanted a vacation from her, and couldn't wait to start high school. I hoped that Robby would finally fall in love with me, that Tiffany would move away (or better yet, come down with a case of *choléra*). At night, in my room, I revised the day's French *leçon*, then said what I was too *timide* to say in English: *je t'aime*, Robby, *je t'adore*.

204

On the first day of class, I slipped on my eagle T-shirt. Though it was two sizes too small and the decal had mostly peeled off, wearing it made me think of Mom.

In the kitchen, Dad jangled the car keys. "Ready to go?"

"We bought you a new outfit," Eleanor huffed. "Will you please go put it on?"

I crossed my arms. "No."

We looked to Dad, the unwilling referee.

"I can hear them! 'And that waif, Lily,'" Eleanor mimicked, "'wearing high-water pants and a ratty T-shirt. What would her dear mother say?'"

"Folks talk, doesn't mean we have to listen." Dad pointed to his watch. "If we don't leave now, we'll be late."

"Fine," she said.

It was no real victory.

In homeroom, I sat in the front row, Mary Louise behind me. Robby slid into the seat across the aisle from me. When I said, "*Bonjour*," he glanced around, like he thought I was talking to someone else.

"Maybe stick to English," Mary Louise advised.

"Hush," Miss Boyd snapped, "or I'll assign extra homework for everyone!"

Bref, le lycée was the same disappointment played out in front of other teachers in a bigger building, and at home Eleanor greeted me with a new list of chores. "I'm not the one who promised to love, humour and obey," I muttered, barely swishing the mop over the linoleum.

Sometimes I dreamed of Mom. Of the way we watched geese soar. The way we sang "Jingle Bells" at the top of our lungs. The way we baked cookies. When my alarm went off, Mom went away. Grief hit so hard, I curled up in a ball.

"Get up, lazybones!" Eleanor banged on my door. "You'll be late for school."

"I don't feel good," I whimpered.

"You sound fine to me."

Still, at Thanksgiving, Eleanor thought to include Odile, who made the dry turkey easier to swallow. When she confided that she'd spent the holidays alone since her husband died, Dad patted Eleanor's hand, and we could see that he was proud of her. As I moved chunks of chalky pumpkin pie around my plate, Eleanor asked Odile to take a photo for a Christmas card. My fork stilled. Dad and Eleanor rose, ready to have their pictures taken, but my heart burned at the thought of Mom being scratched off the family map.

Christmas vacation. Homework finished. Tiffany Ivers back east visiting family. Not a cloud in my sky. Mary Louise and I sculpted a snowwoman (with marbles for her eyes, mouth and earrings) as a surprise for Grandma Pearl. Each time she called Eleanor, she always asked to talk to me, too. And each month since the wedding, she'd sent me something — a funny card, a subscription to *Seventeen*, mauve moonboots. I wasn't too sure about Eleanor, but I liked Grandma Pearl.

"What do you think?" I asked Odile, who'd stepped out to get the mail.

"She needs some colour."

Mary Louise untied the fuchsia scarf she'd "borrowed" from her sister and wound it around the snowwoman's icy neck. Unfortunately, Angel drove by and saw we'd used something of hers. She grabbed a shovel and beat our creation into a heap of dented snowflakes. After she was done, we couldn't even find the marbles.

When Eleanor's parents drove up, I hugged Grandma Pearl before she got out of the car. Taking the luggage, Dad and Mr Carlson evaporated into the living room, while we women got to work on our ginger cookies. At the kitchen counter, Odile hummed "Silent Night" as she flattened the dough with the rolling pin; I sank the Santa moulds into the sticky molasses mass. Grandma Pearl stirred the hot cider. Eleanor bounced around like she had to pee.

"Girl, what is wrong with you?" her mother asked.

"I can't keep it inside any more!" Eleanor squealed. "I'm expecting!"

"My baby's having a baby!" Grandma Pearl said.

Say what?

"When's the due date?" Grandma Pearl asked.

"April 28th."

Did Dad know? Why didn't he tell me?

"A baby!" Odile clapped her hands together. "How wonderful!"

"Your christening gown is in my hope chest," Grandma Pearl said. "I'll send it."

"I've got some yarn that would be perfect for a baby blanket," Odile added.

We didn't have an extra bedroom. Where would they put it? Sparrows steal nests from martins, forcing their young ones out. Starlings steal from sparrows. Sneaky, but Mom had said it's nature's way.

Out went the metal desk and banged-up filing cabinet. Out went bank statements and phone bills. Out went programmes from band concerts and photos of birds — any reminders of life with Mom. Maybe to Eleanor they looked like old papers, but to me they were memories. Luckily, I saw them in the trash and hid them in my room.

Dad's den was now a nursery. Eleanor held up pastel paint swatches that resembled the Easter eggs we'd just coloured. In the end, we painted the room a sunny yellow. Mom would have said that the wooden bassinet resembled a nest, but I didn't tell Eleanor. I no longer mentioned Mom to her because when I did, her nose wrinkled as if my words stank.

On May Day, Eleanor — so enormous — saw me off to school, hand twitching above her big belly. That evening, she lay in the hospital bed, looking tired but happy, like she'd run a long race and won. Men offered Dad cigars and slapped him on the back. He grinned like Dopey the dwarf. Mrs Ivers gave the baby a savings bond. Crotchety Mrs Murdoch had crocheted bootees. The whole town crammed themselves into the sparse visiting hours. When Mary Louise came by, we rolled our eyes and mimicked what we heard.

"A boy! Praise the Lord!"

"The name will be carried on!"

Later, when I held the baby, I thought of my mother, and melancholy washed over me. Then Joe snuggled into the crook of my arm, and I bent down to breathe him in. He smelled like sugar cookies. Maybe things would be okay.

Back home, Eleanor barely slept. If she could have stayed awake all night long to watch over Joe, she would have. Mom had been right. Babies didn't know how lucky they were — they slept through most of the love. After three months of no rest, Eleanor yawned constantly, no longer a perky parakeet, but a plump pigeon that waddled from the crib to the rocking chair. Her skin became blotchy and her hair clumped together in tufts.

"You're a mother, but also a woman," Odile told her, "Take care of yourself. You need rest and exercise." She and I took turns holding Joe so Eleanor could dance to her Jane Fonda aerobics tape. We peeked into the living room to watch Eleanor in her pink unitard, legs kicking as high as they could. Odile whispered, "Like the cancan in Paris."

While Eleanor and I waited for Dad to get home from work, she asked, "How much did your mother weigh?"

"I have no idea."

The following day, she cornered me at the counter. "What kind of diapers did she use? Did she breastfeed?"

Next she'd ask what the milk had tasted like. We didn't have a scale until Eleanor moved in. She used to weigh herself once a week. Now, puffy and trying to "lose the baby weight", she stepped on the scale ten times a day.

"Did she breastfeed?" Eleanor asked again. "Did she use cloth diapers?"

"She used silk ones. Yeah, and she breastfed me five times a night. Grandma Jo came, but Mom wouldn't accept help. Said she didn't need it."

I expected that to be the end of it, but Eleanor started in again: "How much did she weigh?"

"Ask Dad."

"How much?"

Her stupid questions drove me nuts. It took me a while to understand that she was comparing herself to Mom. Well, Eleanor could cook in my mother's pans, eat off her plates. She could live in her house, she could mother me all she wanted. But Eleanor would never be my mother. I gave an impossible answer: "One hundred pounds."

"One hundred pounds?" Eleanor's mouth quivered.

After school, I liked coming home to see Eleanor and Odile having tea at the table, because Eleanor never pestered me when we had company. Today, with Joe slobbering in the bassinet beside them, they talked about faraway things: some day Eleanor would go back to college, some day Odile would visit Lucienne, her war bride friend in Chicago. When Odile held out a plate of grapes, Eleanor patted her stomach and said, "I'm trying to slim down."

I smirked. Like a grape would make her fat.

"You won't lose weight for several months," Odile said.

Eleanor frowned. "Why would you say that?"

"You're pregnant."

Another baby? I quit smirking.

"But I just had Joe five months ago," Eleanor protested.

"I've seen enough women to know the symptoms."

"James told me it would be safe."

"How old are you, and you believe what a man tells you?"

Eleanor laughed, kind of. A joke? And there was . . . something in Odile's voice. Something tart. Something that made me wonder what a man had told her.

Eleanor got as big as a *château* with a belly so huge it made her head seem small. Her maternity clothes fit funny; her bosom and bottom rebelled against the tight cotton. She stopped dyeing her hair, and dark roots took hold. Only trashy women let that happen.

"It wasn't like this with Joe." She sounded dazed.

Pasty and swollen, like her whole body was pregnant, not just her stomach, she felt dizzy the second she stood. When she stayed in bed all day like Mom, I remained at Eleanor's side. I remembered a line from *Bridge to Terabithia: Life was as delicate as a dandelion. One little puff from any direction, and it was blown to bits.* As a kid, I thought only old people died. Now I knew differently. Why hadn't I been nicer to Eleanor? I felt awful about the sick satisfaction I'd taken in hurting her. She wasn't so bad. She'd even convinced Dad to give me an allowance, telling him, "A banker's daughter should learn how to budget." *Please don't die*, I prayed.

Odile came over. I liked that she didn't knock, she just walked right in, like family.

"You're like a Madonna," she told Eleanor.

"Really?"

Honestly? More like Jabba the Hut. I knew the truth wouldn't help, so I nodded.

"But let's call Dr Stanchfield to be on the safe side," Odile said.

He took Eleanor's blood pressure twice and said she had to go in for testing, the same thing he'd said about Mom.

"Is she going to be okay?" I asked.

"Your stepmom has high blood pressure, which isn't healthy for her or the baby."

While Joe and Eleanor dozed, Odile tried to take my mind from my worries by teaching me *bébé* vocabulary — bassinette, *couffin*; diapers, *couches* — but with Eleanor stuck in bed, I didn't give a *caca* about all that.

"How do you say 'high blood pressure'?" I asked.

"*La tension.*"

Tension. That word said it all.

"Shall we go for a stroll?" Odile said.

She was a big believer in fresh air. The cruel north wind whipped around us as we walked down Main Street, past the church, past the pygmy pines, ending up in the graveyard. Like the other ladies, Odile was a cemetery person. Not me. Seeing *Brenda Jacobsen, Beloved Wife and Mother* etched in granite made me

212

ache. Mom had been gone more than two years. Chrysanthemums lay at the foot of her headstone, like the ones on Odile's son's and husband's graves. I knew I should bow my head and pray, but I peered over at Odile. Her head was bowed, her expression bleak. It dawned on me that she missed her family, Buck and Marc, but also her parents and twin. I longed to know what had happened to them.

CHAPTER
TWENTY-TWO

ODILE

Paris, August 1940

"Perhaps I shouldn't have called you home," Papa said, "but I assumed you'd want to know as soon as possible . . ."

"Monsieur?" Bitsi prompted.

"Rémy's alive," Papa said.

I exhaled sharply.

"Where is he?" Bitsi asked. "Is he on his way home?"

"He's been taken prisoner," Papa replied.

"Prisoner?" Bitsi repeated.

"He's in what they call a Stalag," Papa said, "a prisoner-of-war camp."

Maman wept, and I put my arm around her.

"He's alive," I told her.

"We know where he is," Papa said. "Try to let that be a comfort."

He was right. Poor Bitsi hadn't had a letter from her brother in months.

"I wish we had news of Julien," Papa told her, his voice tender.

214

She bit her lip, and I could see that she was trying not to burst into tears.

Papa drew a card from his blazer. I prised the paper from his hand and read the faint type: *Je suis prisonnier*. I'm a prisoner. Below, there were two lines:

1. I'm in perfect health.
2. I'm injured.

The second had been circled. Rémy was alone and hurting.

Blanching when she read the card, Bitsi said she should let her mother know. Papa and I saw her to the door. She kissed his cheek, which brought a shadow of a smile to his face.

We returned to Maman, Papa knelt beside her and gently wiped her tears. He and I tucked our arms around her waist and helped her to bed. In their room, Papa paced, and Maman continued to weep.

"Shall I call Dr Thomas?" I asked.

"All the medicine in the world won't help," Papa said. "I'll stay with her. You should rest."

For once, I didn't argue. I felt guilty about leaving Maman in her grief, yet relieved to contend with my own. Stalag, A new word in the vocabulary of loss. Until today, we'd been able to tell ourselves that Rémy was making his way back to us. What would we tell ourselves now?

At my desk, with his fountain pen, I wrote: "*Dear Rémy, We hate that you're a prisoner, hate that you're hurt and far from home. We're so worried.*" Pouring out my feelings brought relief, but the letter would offer

Rémy no comfort. I opened the pen and let the ink drip over the page. I began again. "*Dear Rémy*."

Dear Rémy was as far as I got.

In the morning, I dressed and went to my parents' room. Maman was tucked under the duvet. Eyes closed, she whimpered as if she were unable to wake from a nightmare. In front of the armoire, Papa buttoned his shirt.

"I'll stay with her," I said.

"Maman wouldn't want you to see her like this." He escorted me to the front door. "I know of someone who can look after her."

Outside, there were few people on the pavement, and no cars on the cobbles. The Library was strangely calm, too. I missed Margaret. I missed Paul. I even missed the sound of stern Mrs Turnbull shushing students.

"I heard about Rémy. I'm so sorry." Professor Cohen proffered a novel by Laura Ingalls Wilder called *The Long Winter*. "I've marked a particularly memorable passage. During a snowstorm, a pioneer family huddles together in their shack, unable to get warm. Pa begins to play the fiddle and tells his three daughters to dance. They giggle and prance, and this keeps them from freezing to death. Later, Pa must tend the livestock, or the animals will die. When he steps outside, he can't see six centimetres in front of him. He holds on to the clothes-line to make it to the barn. Inside, Ma holds her breath, waiting." When I took the novel, Professor Cohen covered my hands with her own. "We can't see what's coming. All we can do is hold the line."

★ ★ ★

216

Before dinner, I peeked into my parents' room, where Maman was sleeping. A nurse was seated near the bed. Thinning brown hair framed a ruddy face. She looked familiar. A subscriber? A volunteer at the hospital?

"I'm Odile."

"Eugénie," she said.

"How is she?"

"Your mother hasn't stirred. I'm afraid she's in shock."

Days went by. After work, Bitsi and I tramped around the Tuileries.

"How's your mother?" I asked.

"She waits at the door like my brother will come home any minute."

Parisians got used to the occupiers. Some did business with them, selling film for their cameras or beer to quench their thirst. Others refused to acknowledge them, pretending they weren't there. Some women accepted compliments and invitations to dinner. Others pursed their lips in distaste. In the Métro, I scowled at a skinny German soldier until he lowered his gaze.

It was reassuring to know that Eugénie was at home, one eye on Maman, the other on her knitting. Still, I wondered how I knew her. Someone who'd helped with the Soldiers' Service? The mother of a school friend?

Then one evening, as Papa and I saw her off, he helped her don her jacket and proposed seeing her home, an offer he'd never made to the charwoman. Eugénie gave a rabbity huff and scurried down the stairs. Suddenly, I knew — this "nurse" was the harlot with him at the hotel.

"How could you bring her here?" I hissed.

For a second, he appeared taken aback. Then with a calculating glint in his eye, he added up what I might know, subtracted his own guilt, and hypothesised how he could divide the attention between his mistress and my mother. After considering the elements of this chaotic equation, he chose his argument as well as Rémy did at one of his law school debates.

"What choice is there? Ask your Aunt Janine to come back from the Free Zone? Bring in some stranger?"

"Maybe we could try to find Aunt Caro. She would want to know. Would want to help."

"Your mother would have a fit if we talked to Caroline behind her back."

"But Papa —"

"Perhaps you'd like to tend Maman?"

I was afraid of drowning in the bottomless depth of her grief. "Can't we hire a nurse?"

"The ones who didn't have the good sense to flee are working ten-hour shifts in hospitals. Eugénie's doing a fine job."

I snorted. "I'm sure you've enjoyed her bedside manner."

"Don't discuss matters you know nothing about! Besides, Eugénie's practically a nurse."

"Working in a library doesn't make me practically a book. Maman needs a *real* nurse."

I stomped down to my bedroom. Bringing his mistress into his house. If only Paul were here, he'd talk sense into Papa. I wrapped my arms around my ribs, wishing it were Paul holding me. When my father disappointed me, when I had a trying time with a snippy subscriber, when I missed Rémy so much I ached, Paul was the balm I rubbed into my bruised soul.

At 8p.m. my father knocked on my door. "Dinnertime."

"I've lost my appetite!"

All night. I lay awake and pictured myself cornering the harlot. Face red with shame, she would apologise for daring to breathe the same air as my mother. She would promise never to darken our doorstep again. She would never again speak to Papa.

Before I left for work, I looked in on Maman. Tender as a lover, Eugénie stroked Maman's hair; tender as a mother, she wiped her nose. I hadn't once changed Maman's nightgown, hadn't emptied the bedpan. This stranger had stepped in and done all that I couldn't. Slowly, my outrage dissipated.

I kissed Maman's cheek. She didn't stir.

"No improvement?" Still, I found it hard to meet Eugénie's gaze.

"Eight handkerchiefs yesterday. Better than the day before, when she used a dozen."

"Oh, Maman . . ."

"I know how she feels."

"Your son, too?"

"In the Great War. He was a toddler when they bombarded our village. I hope your mother never learns how I feel." Eugénie stroked Maman's arm. "Hard, so hard this life, Hortense. But your children need you. We could write to your son. Your daughter's here, wouldn't you like to see her?"

Maman lifted her head and stared at me with helpless eyes.

25 August 1940

Dear Rémy,
We miss you and hope you'll be able to
come home. If you've written, I'm afraid the
letters haven't yet arrived. Maman and Papa
are well. Paul's away, helping with harvest. I
miss him so and can't imagine how much
you must miss Bitsi.

More and more people are coming to the
Library, for community, for respite. Though
many subscribers fled (with our books!),
we're at capacity. Miss Reeder refuses to
turn anyone away.

I haven't heard from Margaret, but Bitsi
finally received a card from her brother, so
that's reassuring. She's well, though she
pines for you.

Will this letter find you? There's so much
I want to tell you.
    Love,
    Odile

25 August 1940

Dearest Paul,
Please thank your aunt for her kind invita-
tion. I'd love to meet her and long to see
you, but must stay in Paris in case we hear
from Rémy.

220

Yesterday, Bitsi received a card from her brother. He, too, is a prisoner of war. I wanted to weep when I heard. As much as I love the Library, sometimes work is unbearable. Coming face-to-face with Bitsi is like looking in the mirror: I see my own worry in her puckered brow, my misery in her chalky complexion. It's twice as hard for her, since both her sweetheart and her brother have been imprisoned. I put a teacup full of posies on her desk. I wish I could do more. I wish I had better news, fewer maudlin thoughts. When will you return?

All my love,
Your prickly librarian

25 August 1940

Dear Margaret,
I write to you often, but haven't yet received a letter from you. I hope that you are well. It's been difficult here. Rémy's in a Stalag. Maman had a breakdown, and Papa brought in his mistress to care for her. Bet she didn't realise emptying bedpans would be the kind of favour she'd be granting! Ah, well, every position has its drawbacks. Maman's recovered enough, but not too much. She likes to be waited on. Or she knows who the "nurse" is and wants to

make her suffer. Knowing Maman, a bit of both.

Nazis have swarmed Paris, and even the National Library. At the ALP, we receive requests from prisoners of war, but Nazi authorities won't allow us to send books to Allied soldiers imprisoned in Germany. It's heartbreaking.

Look at me, as dour as Madame Simon. I'll include some pleasant news. Peter-the-shelver and Helen-in-reference have been spending so much time together — picnicking in the courtyard on their lunch hour, holding hands when they think no one sees — that they have become Helen-and-Peter. They are in love, and it's lovely to see.

Come home! The Library's not the same without you.

Love,
Odile

Come September, Miss Reeder tore off the brown paper that shrouded the windows. When I looked out, I no longer saw the pebbled path or the urn filled with ivy. All I saw were lost letters and faraway friends. I saw Margaret, crunching along the path!

"Rémy?" was the first word out of her mouth, which made me love her even more, "Have you had more news of him?"

"Not since that one card."

"My dear friend." She hugged me. "I worried about you and Rémy, about the Library . . ."

"*Raconte!*" we said at the same time. Tell! I want to know everything.

She recounted the flight from Paris. "The roads were flooded with cars. German pilots fired on civilians, so any time a plane flew overhead, cars screeched to a stop and people dived into the ditch. We ran out of petrol rations and had to walk the last ten miles to Quimper. Christina howled the entire time. How to explain war to a child?"

Lawrence had wanted to send them back to London, but Margaret refused. "For the first time, I feel important, as if my work — well, my volunteer work — matters."

"You *are* important," I insisted. "We need you here."

"*Sincèrement,* I'm thrilled to be back to repairing books!"

"Is Lawrence happy to have returned?"

Margaret picked at her pearls. "He's in the Free Zone."

France had been slashed in two, with the north under German control and the south governed by the hero of the Great War, Marshal Philippe Pétain.

"A pity Lawrence is so far away," I said. "Is he working there?"

"He's with a . . . friend."

"How long will he be gone?"

Margaret searched for words the way I did after a long day spent swerving between French and English, "Oh, who cares about him!" she finally said. "Let me tell you about the trip back. To ensure we had enough petrol, I filled old teapots."

"Not leaky ones, I hope!"

A week later, when Paul arrived at my door — his hair sun-bleached the colour of hay, his cheeks ruddy, I simply stared. In bed at night, I'd imagined our reunion many times. Throwing myself at his chest, covering him with kisses. His hands on my bottom, making my body thrum. Yet when he took me in his arms, I remained stiff. Tense for so many months, I couldn't unwind. "*Je t'aime*," he said. Feeling his lips on my temple, my body softened, and I wept. Cradling me, he brought me on to the landing, knowing I didn't want to worry my parents. I'd put up a good front for them, for Bitsi, for subscribers, but with Paul I didn't have to pretend.

"We'll get through this together," he said.

My sobs subsided and I nuzzled closer. I could stay in Paul's embrace for ever. Well, until Maman joined us. Noting the baskets of potatoes, butter and cured ham that he'd brought, she told him, "The way to Odile's heart is through her stomach."

"A good provider," Papa said.

At the table, in the sitting room, my parents hovered. A few of Maman's worry lines faded, and Papa laughed for the first time in a month.

"I've missed you," Paul whispered to me. "I wish we could have five minutes alone."

"Let's meet at your place tomorrow."

"Four colleagues have rooms on my floor. If they saw you, your reputation would be ruined."

KRIEGSGEFANGENENPOST   15 August 1940

Dear Maman and Papa,

All is well. My health is improving. In the barrack, a doctor from Bordeaux has a bunk near mine. He snores, but his presence is reassuring. Thank you for your cards. Could you send a few things? A warm shirt, underwear, handkerchiefs and a towel. Some thread. Shaving soap and a razor. If it's not too much trouble, food that keeps well, perhaps some pâté.

Please don't worry. We're treated fairly and have no complaints under the circumstances.

Your loving son,
Rémy

KR1EGSGEFANGENENPOST   15 August 1940

Dear Odile,

How are you? And Bitsi and Maman and Papa and Paul? My shoulder is healing. Near Dunkirk, I was hit by enemy fire. Hurt like hell! Of course, when you used to kick me under the table, I complained that hurt like hell, too. Several men in my unit were captured. We felt resentful about our fate until we learned how many had been killed.

We — French soldiers and some British, too — were marched through what felt like most of Germany with very little food or rest. You know me, I've never been athletic. After weeks of walking, many of us were relieved to arrive here and sleep on a bed — even if it's just wooden planks — instead of the cold, soggy ground.

Thank you for your letters. I'm sorry I wasn't able to write before now.

Love,
Rémy

30 September 1940

Dear Rémy,

Thank goodness you told us what you need — Maman wanted to send rosaries, so you and the others could "pray properly". Today, for the first time in ages, she attended Mass. She hadn't been well, so Papa found a nurse for her.

At first, I wasn't sure about having a stranger care for Maman, but then I saw how well they get on. Eugénie wears a cardigan with a white blouse, an ordinary woman with rounded shoulders and melancholy eyes. Every so often, a wistful smile touches her lips. Kind of like Maman.

In the evening before Papa arrives, we three take tea.

He arrives later and later. His car was requisitioned, so he takes the bus. Unfortunately, there are very few because there is almost no fuel available.

With you gone, Papa picks on me twice as much. And he's become overprotective — he doesn't like me going out, not even to see a matinee. The Nazis have their own cinemas and brothels, so surely Bitsi, Margaret and I are safe. The lights dim, and we express our true feelings: when the newsreels show Hitler, everyone hisses.

With the Soldaten telling us what is verboten, German seeps into our skulls. And their soldiers are learning French. A cross-eyed Kommandant attempted to converse with our bookkeeper — remember her, the intrepid scone baker with a love of dead Greek mathematicians? "Bonjour, mademoiselle. Vous êtes belle," the officer said, to which Miss Wedd replied, "Heave, ho!" When he didn't understand, she added, "Auf Wiedersehen!"

Love,
Odile

It wasn't easy to keep letters light, especially when the Nazis were all over Paris. At a staff meeting, Boris informed us that they'd seized over 100,000 books from the Russian Library near Notre Dame.

"Over 100,000 books," Margaret repeated weakly.

Once, when I was little, Aunt Caro and I had gone there. After Mass at Quasimodo's cathedral on the island in the River Seine, we crossed over to the Left Bank and meandered down the rue de la Bûcherie to a *hôtel particulier*. The doors of the mansion were open, so we peered inside. "Welcome, welcome," we were told. The librarian, who wore reading glasses on a silver chain around her neck, handed me a picture book. Aunt Caro and I marvelled at the words, not just in a foreign language, but in a foreign alphabet.

The walls were covered by bookshelves from floor to ceiling — so high that one needed a ladder to reach the highest shelves. Aunt Caro let me climb it all the way to the top. That day, like any day with my aunt, was heaven.

Now, I imagined those shelves bare. Imagined the librarian with tears in her eyes. Imagined a subscriber coming to return a book, only to learn that it was the only one left.

"Why are they looting libraries?" Bitsi asked.

Boris explained that the Nazis wanted to eradicate the cultures of certain countries, in a methodical confiscation of their works of science, literature and philosophy. He added that the Nazis had also pillaged the personal collections of prominent Jewish families.

"Jewish subscribers," I said, "including Professor Cohen."

Yesterday in the reading room, at the table in the corner, I'd spied piles of books. Behind them, I could make out white hair and a peacock feather. It was almost as if the Professor had created a barricade of Library books — works by Chaucer, Milton and Austen, to name a few.

The Professor didn't seem to notice when I drew near.

"Revisiting the classics?" I asked.

"The Nazis seized my books. They stormed in and shoved my entire collection — my first editions, even my article about Beowulf whose last page was still in the typewriter — into crates."

"No . . ." I wrapped my arm around her shoulder. "I'm so sorry . . ."

"I am, too." She gestured helplessly to the piles. "I wanted to sit with my favourites again."

At the staff meeting, Margaret said, "Forty years of research gone."

"We know her favourites," Bitsi said. "I can scour the booksellers to replace some."

"What about our other subscribers?" Miss Reeder asked.

"And the Russian Library?" Boris added.

"What about *our* Library?" I said.

"She's right," Miss Reeder said. "The Nazis will be here soon enough."

In October, school began, proof that life went on, no matter what. Mothers ironed shirts and made sure their children had notebooks and pencils. Certain foods were

229

becoming scarce, and housewives waited in long queues at butcher shops. Fashion magazines churned out tips on how women should wear their hats (tipped to the back). Margaret and I boxed books to send to internment camps in the French countryside, where Communists, Gypsies and enemy aliens — civilians whose country happened to be at war with Germany — were imprisoned.

The *Propagandastaffel* worked overtime, trying to stir up resentment. Posters plastered on buildings, Métro stations and theatre lobbies showed a French sailor flailing in a red sea of blood. Clutching the tattered Tricolore, he implored, "Don't forget Oran!" where the British navy had scuttled our ships. How could we forget? They'd killed over a thousand French sailors. Monsieur de Nerciat still wouldn't speak to Mr Pryce-Jones.

Refusing to be swayed by Nazi propaganda, Parisians had defaced the posters, covering "Oran" and scribbling other words, so the line read, "Don't forget your bathing suit."

At lunchtime today, Paul and I went to Parc Monceau. Rigid with anger, he strode along the sandy pathway, and I had a hard time keeping up.

"I've been ordered to repair the posters," Paul said. "It's worse than directing traffic in those damn white gloves. When people see me mopping up graffiti, they snigger."

"That's not true." I tucked my arm through his, but his stance didn't soften.

"It's humiliating. Cops used to have weapons. Now we have sponges. I used to keep people safe. Now I erase scribbles."

"At least you're here."

"I'd rather be with Rémy."

"Don't say that," I said.

"At least he fought. At least he's still a man."

"You're doing your part."

"By keeping their propaganda pristine?" He kicked a twig out of our way. "It's humiliating."

KRIEGSGEFANGENENPOST 20 October 1940

Dear Odile,

Thanks for the pâté. Everyone enjoyed it. Though most who receive food from home share, there are a few hoarders. How disappointing that even in such conditions we can't pull together.

Paul sent news clippings and a sketch he did of Story Hour. Bitsi's holding an open book over her head, like it's a roof. I can practically hear her tell the children that books are a sanctuary. I was glad to have some news from Paris. Don't be afraid to tell me what's going on. I want to know what's happening there. It takes my mind from what's happening here. We're all getting frantic, wondering how long we'll be prisoners. One of the fellows has taught me to play bridge. It seems that all we have here is time.

Love,
Rémy

12 November 1940

Dear Rémy,
I'm glad you liked the sketch. Paul's
talented, isn't he? Maman invites him and
Bitsi over often. At dinner last week, Papa
showed her your baby pictures. With her,
he's not gruff. I wish you could see how
she's won him over. I wish you could come
home, full stop. Yesterday, nearly 2,000
lycée and university students protested
against the occupiers. Old men like Marshal
Pétain may run the country, but the young
people will lead the way.
     Love,
     Odile

I didn't tell Rémy that the pâté we'd sent was our family's meat ration for the week. I didn't tell him that the demonstration didn't last long because the authorities broke it up. I didn't tell him that the Nazis had seized the Czechoslovakian Library, I didn't tell him that the *Kommandantur* wrote to inform us that in a week's time the Bibliotheksschutz would "inspect" our Library.

Miss Reeder, Boris, Bitsi and I gaped at the diktat.

232

"What's a *Bibliotheksschutz*?" Bitsi asked.

"Literally translated, it means 'Library Protector'," the Directress said.

"That's a good thing, right?" I said.

Miss Reeder shook her head sadly, "It's quite an ironic term. I imagine they're going to seize our books."

"It's the Book-Gestapo," Boris explained.

On the day of the "inspection", Boris smoked a pack of Gitanes before noon. Miss Reeder threw herself into paperwork, wanting to be sure there could be no technical reason to close the Library. I gathered books to be re-shelved. *The Great Gatsby, Greenbanks, Their Eyes Were Watching God*, these novels were dear friends. Glancing at Margaret, I knew we were thinking the same thing: *how can we go on without the Library?*

"Lets take tea to Miss Reeder," she said. "We must do something or we'll go mad!"

I felt jittery, so Margaret carried the tray. As she placed it on a table near Miss Reeder's desk, I asked, "How are you?"

"Sick to my stomach, and shattered to the core," the Directress replied. "Waiting for his majesty, the Bibliotheksschutz. Praying that somehow we'll stay open."

Margaret poured the chamomile tea. The hot porcelain warmed my clammy hands. I was about to take a sip when I heard heavy heels hit the hardwood floor and echo through the stacks.

In her chair, the Directress squared her shoulders. Three men in Nazi uniforms entered. No one said anything. Not hello, not *bonjour*, not *guten Tag*, not you're under arrest, not *Heil Hitler*. Two of them — no older than me — were brawny soldiers. The third was a slim officer wearing gold-rimmed glasses. He carried a leather briefcase.

The trio sized up items in the office: the papers on the desk; the empty shelves, where rare manuscripts and first editions had been held until they'd been sent into exile in anticipation of this moment; the Directress, her alabaster skin, her glossy chignon, her pursed lips.

If Miss Reeder was scared, no one in the room knew it. I'd never seen her sit so rigidly, never seen her face devoid of warmth. She always rose to welcome visitors, ignoring the gender protocol which allowed her to remain seated and merely extend her arm to shake hands. But these uninvited guests did not deserve her usual attentions.

The "Library Protector" must have expected a director, not a directress. Staring at her, the Bibliotheksschutz spoke in German, his tone dark, his orders quick. The younger men left, quietly closing the door behind them like parlour maids. When the Directress remained taciturn, he said in flawless French, "What a fine library. I am most impressed, Mademoiselle Reeder. Nothing in Europe can compare with it!"

Upon hearing her name, she focused her gaze on his face. "Dr Fuchs? You're here in Paris? I had no idea." She clapped her hands together as if happy to see an old friend. "I confess, I saw the uniform, not the man."

"I was assigned this post just last week, and am now in charge of intellectual activity in Holland, Belgium

234

and French-occupied territory," he boasted, almost boyishly hoping for her praise. His shiny cheeks and fine sandy hair gave him the appearance of a Sunday school teacher.

"You must be missing your library." Her head tilted in sympathy.

"Indeed. The Staatsbibliothek can undoubtedly do without me. Whether I am able to do without it is another question."

I'd assumed the Nazi would be an illiterate brute. Instead, he worked at the most prestigious library in Berlin. Margaret and I waited for a directive from the Directress, but she and the Bibliotheksschutz were completely absorbed by each other.

"You are now the Directress?" he continued. "My warmest congratulations."

"We're lucky to have a dedicated staff and volunteers." She frowned. "Well, we had . . . things have changed. Colleagues have had to leave."

"It must be difficult on your own." He jotted down his phone numbers on a scrap of paper and put it on her desk. "At home, at the office, and in Berlin — in case you need to contact me."

"It's been ages," she prevaricated.

"Since the International Institute of Intellectual Cooperation colloquium," he murmured. "Simpler times."

"If they'd told me the name of the Bibliotheksschutz, I could have saved myself a week of worry. I've been perfecting my tirade since we learned of the 'inspection'."

"What were you going to say?" he asked, still standing at attention.

"Stay for tea." She gestured to a chair.

Margaret fetched another cup. I knew I should have gone, but was too fascinated by this turn of events.

"I was going to tell the Bibliotheksschutz that a library without members is a cemetery of books," Miss Reeder said. "Books are like people, without contact they cease to exist."

"Beautifully said," he replied.

"I was ready to humbly beg to keep the Library open. How could I have guessed that it would be you?"

"You must know I would never allow the Library to be closed. However . . ."

"Yes?" she prompted.

"You'll be bound by the rules imposed on the Bibliothèque Nationale, Certain books may no longer circulate." He pulled a list from his briefcase.

"Are we required to destroy them?" Miss Reeder asked.

He looked at her, appalled. "My dear young lady, I said that they must not circulate. What a question between professional librarians! People like us don't destroy books."

Margaret returned with a cup of Earl Grey. The citrusy smell of bergamot infused the room with hope. *People like us.* A fellow librarian, a kindred spirit. Yes, this war had divided us, but a love of literature would reunite us. We could meet over tea and talk like civilised people. Miss Reeder let out a shaky sigh, perhaps feeling the worst was over. She and the Bibliotheksschutz reminisced about conferences they'd attended and people they knew: *oh, my, the ALA event in Chicago was so interesting; ah, yes, she's retired now; he transferred to another branch and just isn't the same.*

With a start, Dr Fuchs consulted his watch and said he was late for his next appointment. "It was a pleasure to see you," he told the Directress as he rose. At the door, beaming about a meeting that had gone well, he turned to us. I expected a comment about the collection or a bland farewell. "Of course," he said, "*certain people* may no longer enter."

CHAPTER
TWENTY-THREE

ODILE

Paris, November 1940

Digging her fingers into her temple, Miss Reeder murmured, "I must think. There must be a way . . . Perhaps we can deliver books somehow . . ."

Staff filed in, one by one. Bitsi bit her lip. Boris frowned. Miss Wedd had twelve pencils in her bun. I pulled *The Dreamers* from Miss Reeder's shelf. I needed something to hold on to. I didn't have to turn the pages to know what was written: *This book is a map, each chapter a journey. Sometimes the way is dark, sometimes it leads us to the light. I'm afraid of where we're going.*

"Well?" Bitsi said. "What did the 'Library Protector' say?"

"We must take forty works from our shelves," Margaret replied.

On the list: Ernest Hemingway, who'd written for our newsletter, and William Shirer, who researched articles in our reading room.

"When you consider their banned-book list includes hundreds of works," Boris said, "it's a small price to pay."

I wasn't so sure. Without these books, Paris would lose a part of its soul.

"We can lend them to subscribers we know well," Peter-the-shelver said.

Subscribers we know well . . . I thought of Professor Cohen, of the students from the Sorbonne, of the little ones who came to Story Hour. Holding the book to my chest, I wondered how we could tell the Professor that she was no longer welcome. I wondered how we would face our other Jewish subscribers, I wondered if we would deny children books. Of course, the diktat went deeper than books. The Bibliotheksschutz demanded that we cut subscribers from the fabric of our community.

The Countess Clara de Chambrun arrived and settled into the chair that Dr Fuchs had vacated. She was the only remaining Library trustee still in France — the others had sailed back to the safety of the States. She'd lived in America, Africa and Europe. A Shakespeare scholar, she held a doctorate from the Sorbonne. I could see vast experience in her shrewd eyes, and hoped that with her help we'd find a way forward.

Reading glasses perched on the tip of her nose, she said, "Now, what did you need to tell me?"

We turned to the Directress. Usually, she spoke briskly, aware time spent in meetings was time away from tasks, "I . . . That is . . ."

"Go on," the Countess urged.

"No Jews are allowed in the Library by Nazi police regulations." Miss Reeder's voice was small. She shook her head, as if she couldn't believe the words had come out of her mouth.

"You can't be serious!" Bitsi said. Chin jutting out, she resembled Rémy, raring to fight for those in need.

"The books of the Alliance Israélite Universelle were seized," Boris said, "in a complete and total amputation. The Nazis not only seized the collection of the Ukrainian Library, they arrested the librarian. God only knows where he is. If we don't follow orders, they'll close this Library and arrest us. At best."

We looked to Miss Reeder.

"'Certain people may no longer enter,'" she repeated. "Several are our most loyal subscribers. There *must* be a way we can keep contact with them."

"Think of the story of Mahomet and the mountain." the Countess replied. "I possess a pair of feet, so do Boris, Peter and Odile, I am ready and willing to carry books to subscribers, and feel sure that every member of staff will be happy to do the same."

"We'll make sure all readers have books," Margaret said.

"There's danger involved," Miss Reeder said gravely. She regarded each of us to make sure we understood. "The rules we've lived by have changed overnight. Delivering books could be perceived as defying authorities, and we may be arrested."

"I arrived in Paris on the eve of war in order to put books into the hands of readers," Helen said, "and I'm not about to stop now."

"I'll carry the entire contents of the Library to subscribers," said Peter.

"We won't let readers become isolated," Miss Wedd insisted. "I'll take them books. And scones, too, if I can scrape up enough flour."

"Delivering books will be our way of resisting," Bitsi said.

"We need to do this," I said.

"It's the right thing to do," Boris said.

"Then let's get to work," Miss Reeder said.

She and the Countess wrote to Jewish subscribers, Bitsi called those who had a telephone. Seated at Miss Reeder's desk, the receiver nearly as large as her head, I heard her voice catch. "Until things go back to normal . . . I'm sorry . . . Which books may we bring you?"

Boris prepared requests, tying the books together with twine. He proffered me a bundle for Professor Cohen, and I set off into a very different world.

I tried to avoid Nazi checkpoints, but a new one had sprung up two blocks away. On a narrow street, *Soldaten* — always armed, always in packs of five — prodded Parisians through metal barricades in order to verify our papers and search our belongings. As I stood in line, I realised I'd scribbled the Professor's address on a scrap of paper and tucked it in my satchel. Why hadn't I just memorised where she lived? What if I led the Nazis to her apartment?

A soldier demanded that I open my satchel. I just stood there. My breathing became so shallow that I thought I would pass out. He grabbed my bag and rummaged through the books and papers inside.

"Nothing interesting here," the soldier declared in German, "just a handkerchief, her house keys and some books."

At any rate, that's what I thought he said. The only words I understood were *nichts, interessant,* and *Buck* He eyed my papers, ogling the photo on my *carte d'identité*, before thrusting the documents at my bosom and growling, "Be on your way!"

When I rounded the corner, I scoured my satchel for the scrap with the address. Vowing to be more careful, I ripped it up. I didn't want to endanger readers. After my breathing returned to normal, I started off again.

I'd always wondered where the Professor lived, and imagined her in an airy study that bordered a rose garden. Not that she'd invite me in. This was not a social visit and, given the circumstances, I had no idea what to say. It's not right? The Library sends its regrets? This is strange business?

Nothing?

It was a twenty-minute walk to Professor Cohen's. Inside the blond Haussmannian building, the staircase curved like an escargot's shell. I made my way to the second floor, where I heard the rat-a-tap-tap of the typewriter. Afraid to disturb her, I considered leaving the bundle outside the door, but knew Boris wouldn't like it if books were abandoned. Finally, I knocked. The Professor ushered me in with a swish of her shawl. Following her into the sitting room, my gaze moved from the peacock feather in her hair to the skeletal wall of shelves that had once held a thousand volumes. The

242

Nazis had plunged a bayonet into the body of the Professor's research.

"They even stole my diaries — my happy times with loved ones, my moments of despair."

They'd confiscated her private thoughts. Hurricanes, 551.552; censored books, 363.31; dangerous animals, 591.65.

She pointed to a pile of books on the chair. "Friends have stopped by. They know my taste, and little by little I'll rebuild my collection, maybe with a novel I've written myself. I spoke to an editor about my work-in-progress, and he seems most keen."

Hope, 152.4. I glanced at her typewriter. "What's your book about?"

"It's about us. Well, about us Parisians. Like most, I love people-watching, but sometimes I think we're too aware of each other. It creates a corrosive jealousy."

Before I could respond, she left the room and returned with a tray of tea and biscuits. I peeked at my watch — four o'clock. Other subscribers were expecting deliveries, and I didn't want Boris to be cross. Yet I couldn't leave after she'd gone to such trouble.

While the Orange Pekoe brewed, I nibbled on a Russian cigarette. My tongue seemed to swell as I savoured a rare substance — butter. Where on earth had she found it?

"My nephew's best friend owns a creamery," she said.

I grimaced. "Whoever thought we'd feel obliged to justify having kitchen staples?"

"And it's going to get worse."

I had trouble imagining how things could get worse. "Miss Reeder promised to stop by tomorrow," I said, hoping news of the visit would cheer her up.

"How are things at the Library?"

I heard the questions she didn't ask. *Will my friends notice I'm gone? Will they miss me?*

The Professor's expression, unguarded, was filled with an immense sorrow. How odd to see this internal landscape — the inside of an apartment, the inside of a life. To enter a subscriber's home and see things meant to remain private. I didn't know what to say. Neither did she. In the end, it was the author who found the words. "Thank you for bringing the books. I must get back to my novel."

News from the outside world rarely reached the Occupied Zone, Though Miss Reeder's mother had written weekly since 1929, the Directress hadn't received a letter in six months. No foreign books or periodicals arrived; I imagined them stacked up in a New York warehouse.

Even with rations, food became hard to find. At the market, Maman queued for an hour to buy three puny leeks. Miss Reeder's polka-dot dress, once form-fitting, now hung on her slight frame. Helen-in-reference still had frizzy hair and dreamy eyes, but she'd lost twelve pounds. Like them, I'd become too thin. I told Dr Thomas that I hadn't had my period in months; he said I wasn't the only one.

Famished, I moved at half speed, delivering reading material throughout Paris, from posh apartments bordering Parc Monceau to modest rooms in Montmartre. Today at the checkpoint, one of the soldiers — the officer in charge — took a closer look at the contents of my satchel. "*Call of the Wild? The Last of the Mohicans?* What's a French girl doing with novels in English? Show me your papers!"

The Kapitän ran his finger over the photo of my *carte* d'identisé, perhaps convinced it was counterfeit. He asked the other soldiers a question in German. They moved closer, until I was surrounded. I'd never felt smaller. Examining the books, the *Soldaten* spoke quickly; I could only make out a few words: *Gross. Roman. Gut.* What were they saying? Did they think I was carrying messages? Would they arrest me? What excuses could I offer? That I was a librarian at the ALP? No, they might visit. That I had an English friend? No, they might detain Margaret.

"A 'French girl' can be interested in other cultures, you know," I told them. "My brother and I appreciate Goethe."

The Kapitän nodded approvingly. "We Germans have good writers."

He handed back my belongings; I hurried away before he changed his mind.

It was difficult to avoid these spot checks because the Nazis set up barricades on random streets. When I finished my deliveries. I returned to the Library and warned Margaret about the danger of being arrested as an enemy alien.

"I know. On my way home yesterday, I spied a checkpoint and darted into a milliner's. Three hours and four hats later, the Nazis left." She wound her pearls around her finger. "It feels as if there's a noose around my neck."

When our bookkeeper missed work, we feared the worst. We searched Miss Wedd's apartment building, hospitals and police stations, before Boris learned what had happened: the Nazis had arrested her and sent her to an internment camp in eastern France. Imprisoned because she was British.

Miss Reeder decided that foreign staff members should leave France, "One of the hardest things I've ever had to do is ask Helen-and-Peter to leave," she told subscribers and staff at the farewell party. "I know it's the right decision. My head — and heart — will function much easier when I know they're safe."

Helen's complexion was ashen, but there was a light in her eyes. Peter had proposed. Knowing that their Library love story would endure made us feel less blue as we raised a glass to bid them adieu.

"Thank goodness Miss Reeder is staying," I told Bitsi.

"For now," she replied.

February, March, April. Winter wouldn't let go. Grey clouds groped the sky, a dreary rain drizzled day and night. On his daily round, Paul brought me a bouquet of lilacs. "You've been so glum," he said. "Have you heard from Rémy recently?"

I pulled an envelope from my pocket and unfolded his latest letter as if it were priceless linen.

246

Dear Odile,

Happy Easter! I'm thinking of you.
Thanks for *Villette*. I'm beginning to think
of the Brontës as dear friends.

We've been forced to work on farms.
Their men are fighting on the Eastern
Front, so mostly it's women and old folks
here. We prisoners are trotted into town,
where the landowners sniff around us, wanting a brawny worker.

Fellows sabotage what they can — the
farmers are the enemy, after all. I wish you
could meet Marcel. When an old frau led
him to her barn and shoved a pail into his
chest, expecting him to milk the cow, he
yanked on its tail as one would pump water
from a well. Startled, the heifer kicked him.
Now he's laid up with me in the barrack.
He insists the look of disgust on the frau's
face was worth a couple of broken ribs.

Love,
Rémy

He put on a good front for me, the way I did for him.
"What's wrong?" Paul asked.
"Where to begin? There's a German soldier billeted
at Bitsi's apartment. He sleeps in her brother's room. I

don't know how she bears it. Yesterday after work, she wept in the children's room, and I didn't know if I should comfort her or pretend I didn't see. She has her pride, after all. Monsieur de Nerciat and Mr Pryce-Jones still aren't speaking — I hate that the war has ruined their friendship. We worry for Miss Reeder, who gets gaunter by the day —"

"At least you have a boss you can admire."

He looked troubled. I wanted to take him in my arms, wanted to forget the war for five minutes, but Madame Simon's dogged stare unnerved me. Would Paul and I ever be alone?

From the escargot staircase, I could hear Professor Cohen's keystrokes. This time, as always, her landing was imbued with the inky scent of typewriter ribbon. Despite feeling melancholy, I grinned when she answered the door — in a dinner jacket.

"What on earth?" I asked.

"I'm trying to get into the mind of my character, so I put on my husband's dinner jacket."

"It is working?"

"I'm not sure, but it's great fun."

Behind her, the bookshelves were nearly half filled. Bitsi, Margaret, Miss Reeder, Boris and I had brought books from our own collections, as had the Professor's friends. The pile of paper next to the typewriter had also grown.

"What's new?" she asked.

I sighed. "I've been promoted to reference librarian."

"Isn't that a good thing?"

"The previous one returned to the States. This wasn't how I wanted to work my way up. I'd rather stay in the periodical room for ever and keep my colleagues."

"People make plans, and God laughs," she said. "A cup of tea? And a more suitable attire?"

We chatted on the divan, teacups balanced on our laps, she in her dinner suit, me with a black bow tie around my neck. I touched the silk. It did make me feel better.

Visiting Professor Cohen each week was one of the great joys of my job, of my life. She even let me read her work-in-progress, some of which took place at the Library. The chapters were so witty, so insightful, so her. The Professor had become my favourite writer, all categories combined.

Paris
12 May 1941

Monsieur l'Inspecteur,
Why aren't you looking for undeclared Jews
in hiding? Here is the address of Professor
Cohen at 35 rue Blanche. She used to teach
so-called literature at the Sorbonne. Now
she invites students to her home for lectures
so she can cavort with colleagues and
students, mostly male — at her age!
*   When she ventures out, you see her*
coming a kilometre away in that swishy
purple cape, a peacock feather askew in her
hair. Ask the Jewess for her baptism

249

certificate and passport, you'll see her
religion noted there. While good Frenchmen
and women work, Madame le Professeur sits
around and reads books.

My indications are exact, now it's up to
you.

Signed,

One who knows

CHAPTER
TWENTY-FOUR

ODILE

Paris, May 1941

In the barren courtyard of our building, Maman winced as she tipped her beloved ferns from the window boxes. Beside her, Eugénie and I sowed carrot seeds in the soil. Helping Maman made me feel useful, and the sunshine felt heavenly.

"We could have planted vegetables last year." She ran her fingers over the helpless ferns splayed over the cobbles. "But I liked having something beautiful."

"Who knew the Occupation would continue?" Eugénie asked.

"What if it never ends?"

"We said that about the Great War. All good things come to an end, bad things, too."

Maman read us a letter from country cousins, who promised to send provisions. When she finished, she said, "All my life, I've been embarrassed by my rural roots. When Papa's bosses and their wives came for dinner, I always felt . . . not quite as fine as the Parisian ladies. Fatty mutton next to smoked salmon."

"Oh, Hortense —" Eugénie took Maman's dirt-caked hand.

"But now my roots may well save us."

"In the form of carrots," I joked.

"Why did you have to say mutton?" Eugénie lamented. "Now I'm starving."

Chuckling, she and I carried the planters up the stairs and set them on the window ledges. Maman followed, her fist full of baby fronds that curled like question marks.

"I suppose we should see about dinner," Eugénie said. "Why don't you invite Paul over?"

"He'll have to come for the company, not the meal," Maman said as she set her ferns in a glass with a little water. "Swede again."

"Baked this time," Eugénie said pertly.

After we ate, Maman pretended to tidy the desk, and Paul and I sat on the divan. Since we couldn't speak freely, I showed him a page of *The Age of Innocence*, our torsos nearly touching as we read. *When we've been apart, and I'm looking forward to seeing you, every thought is burnt up in a great flame. But then you come; and you're so much more than I remembered, and what I want of you is so much more than an hour or two every now and then, with wastes of thirsty waiting between.*

Eugénie swept in and tugged Maman's hand. "Oh, let them have some fun."

"When they're married, they can have all the 'fun' they want," she replied.

252

"Where's your father?" Paul said, bringing our communication back to the public domain.

"Still working. He comes home at night with files, but won't tell us a thing. When I see the dark circles under his eyes . . ."

"You worry about everyone else, but I worry about you." Paul said. He explained that he'd saved an entire year for a special surprise.

"What is it?"

"Tomorrow, we're going to a cabaret."

"A cabaret!" Maman gasped.

"They'll be surrounded by dozens of people," Eugénie soothed.

I threw my arms around Paul's neck. Music! Champagne! No chaperone! We'd dance all night, since partygoers got around the curfew by staying at the cabaret all night, leaving only at sunrise.

"It won't resolve our worries," he said, "but we'll be carefree for a few hours."

The following evening, Maman tucked a dewy frond in my hair while Paul fidgeted in his corduroy suit. At the cabaret, he and I sipped bubbly as buxom *danseuses* in brassieres and bloomers shimmied on stage, offering an occasional glimpse of cleavage. I was more interested in the chicken breast on my plate. The knife and fork quivered in my grasp. It had been so long since I'd had any kind of meat. Picking it up, I bit into the moist flesh and slid my tongue along the bone. Not willing to waste a drop of sauce on my napkin, I licked my fingers. After dinner, surrounded by couples on the dance floor, Paul and I clung to each other.

At first light, revellers — sated and sleepy — filed out of the cabaret. Paul and I meandered through the empty streets, passing the *mairie*, where banns were posted. *Mademoiselle Anne Jouslin of Paris will wed Monsieur Vincent de Saint-Ferjeux of Chollet.*

"Odd to think of people getting married," I said, thinking of Rémy, so far away, of Bitsi, who spent her evenings alone.

"Life goes on." Paul gazed at me.

I suspected that if it were up to him, we'd already be married. I tugged him along through the winding streets of Montmartre. As the sun rose, we settled on the steps of the Sacré Coeur church. Cradled in his arms, I watched the orange and pink clouds blossom like flowers.

"From the beginning, I knew you were different from the others," I said contentedly.

"How?"

"You defended Rémy, and me when I wanted to work."

He drew me closer. "I'm glad that you're independent. It's a relief."

"A relief?"

"I've taken care of my mother ever since my father took off."

"But you were so young!"

"When I was a kid, I never knew what state she'd be in when I got home — drunk, weepy, half-naked with some man. Later, I had to drop out of school to get a job. Most of what I make, I send to her. Honestly, I see why my father left."

"Oh, Paul."

He pulled away. "We should go."

"Let's talk."

"I don't want your parents to worry."

He remained aloof on the way home. I wanted to close the distance that had grown between us. On the darkened landing, I embraced him. I could feel his pounding heart, and revelled in the feel of his lips on mine, the taste of his champagne in my mouth. My hands roamed his body, as he kissed my cheek, my neck, my décolletage. In thrall to this tender, wild magic we performed together, I wanted him around me, inside me. It was time to write a new chapter in our relationship.

I loosened his tie. "Let's."

"Are you sure?" he asked, but his belt was already unbuckled.

I loved feeling him stir beneath my fingers, loved hearing his quiet groan, knowing I had the same effect on him that he had on me. I let my foot trace a trail along his calf, his knee. He grabbed my thigh and hauled my body to his. My tongue met his, stroke for stroke. He wrapped my legs around his waist. Blood pounded through my veins.

"Odile, is that you?" Maman's voice was muffled behind the door.

Slowly, Paul lowered me back to earth. Thrumming with desire, I teetered in my heels. He held me steady with one hand and tugged the hem of my dress down with the other. My body ached. I hadn't wanted to stop. Passion had made me reckless, and I liked it.

255

The front door swung open. "Did you forget your key?" Maman asked.

"Find a way for us to be alone," I whispered to Paul. I rubbed my swollen lips. The risk we'd taken . . .

At the Library, I hung up my jacket, tipsily humming a ballad the band had played. My belly was full, my body still sang. When Bitsi — cloaked in her coat of melancholy — entered, I sobered immediately.

Bitsi could see my distress. "What's wrong?"

"Nothing." I couldn't bear to meet her gaze.

"Something."

"With Rémy gone, it's not fair that I go on with my life."

"Who said life is fair?" she said gently.

"How can I let myself be happy when he's miserable, when you're miserable?"

"I hope you and Paul aren't postponing getting married."

I looked at her. "He's hinted at it . . ."

"Your happiness isn't at Rémy's expense. You and Paul belong together."

"You really think so?"

"I do."

When Bitsi turned to go to the children's room, it seemed to me that her braided crown of hair had become a halo.

Before I could follow, Boris gave me a bundle of books to be delivered. On my way to Professor Cohen's, I passed a flower girl on the street corner. I thought of how, when the Professor and I chatted, she sometimes cast a melancholy glance at her empty crystal vase. Hoping to cheer her, I bought a bouquet.

When I proffered the purple gladiolas, the Professor beamed. She chose a jug from the sideboard and arranged the flowers.

I pointed to the vase. "Why didn't you use that one?"

"I've never put anything in it."

"Why not?"

"The first time my third husband invited me to his parents', it was for an interminable Sunday lunch. I needed a break and stepped from the room."

"I can understand that."

"When I returned, his mother was criticising me: 'She's cold. Too intellectual. So old she's barren.' Before he could reply, I told them I was leaving. The next day, he came by my office with that vase. When he said it reminded him of me, I replied, 'Cold, hard and empty?'"

"What did he reply?"

"That it was a work of beauty. Full of life, yet able to hold so much. Perfect all by itself."

I could see why she'd married him.

"How are things at the Library?" she asked.

I heard the questions she did not ask. *Do they know that Jews can no longer teach, and that I lost my job? Do they care?*

"Monsieur de Nerciat and Mr Pryce-Jones will drop in this afternoon," I said.

She perked up. "Together? They made up?"

Indeed. Last week, sick of the standoff, the Frenchman had asked Miss Reeder to mediate.

"The Directress is formidable," Mr Pryce-Jones had told me. "We were no match for her."

"When she puts her foot down," Monsieur de Nerciat added, "the entire Library shakes."

Once again, the reading room resonated with their debates:

"The US will enter the war!"

"Americans are isolationists. They'll stay out of it."

How I'd missed their bickering!

"I'm glad you made up," I told Monsieur de Nerciat, who stopped by my desk to say *bonjour*.

"Well, I had to put myself 'in his *shoes*'."

I smiled at the idiom, since we French would say "in his *skin*".

"Was it hard to take the first step?" I asked.

"It would have been harder to lose a friend."

In the reference room, a queue of subscribers formed, and I answered queries ranging from "How do I make hominy?" to "Will you tell the woman over there to quit talking so loudly?" When Paul approached, next in the queue, he had a question, too. "Can you get away for lunch?"

My gaze shifted to the children's room. Paul and I could be together. Bitsi had said so, and her blessing meant more than any priest's.

Near Parc Monceau, a posh neighbourhood known for its embassies, Paul guided me into a majestic limestone building.

"Where are you taking me?" I asked as we ascended the marble staircase.

He grinned. "You'll see."

On the second floor, he unlocked the door to an apartment even grander than Margaret's. Cinched velvet curtains set off tall windows. In the sunlight, the prisms of the chandelier sparkled.

"Who lives here?" I whispered in awe.

"Probably a wealthy businessman who fled to the Free Zone."

"How'd you get the keys?"

"A friend's in the same situation as us. He meets his girl here."

An apartment of romantic assignations!

Paul nuzzled my neck. "I love you," he said. "I'd do anything for you, anything at all."

I wanted this more than anything, but I was scared. Scared that this would change everything, scared there would be pain, scared making love would tie us together for ever, scared that it wouldn't.

"It's my first time, too," he said.

Looking into my eyes, he waited for my answer.

I caressed his cheek. "I want to."

His fingers trembled as he unbuttoned my dress. How divine to bare my body. How divine to see his without worrying about Maman bursting in. He caressed my tired silk stockings. "*Que tu es belle*," he said and drew me on to the divan.

I brought my legs up, and he slid in slowly. At first it hurt, but gazing at Paul, I was glad it was him. When he moved inside me, my hips rose to meet his. For once, my mind stopped analysing every little thing.

259

Afterwards, nestled against his body, I wondered why books skip over this part. It had felt perfect, and more than that — right. Being with Paul felt dreamy and important and right.

When he stirred, I lifted my head and looked about. I wondered where the hallway would take us. Naked, I bounded over the sunbeams warming the parquet. Paul followed. The first door led to a den with a gilded desk. Rémy would have loved the collection of ornate fountain pens that we found inside the top drawer.

"Why didn't they take their treasures?" I asked.

"When war broke out, people left in a panic."

I didn't want to remember those terrible days. I pulled Paul from the room, leaving all questions behind. The door on the left led to a pink boudoir, where we climbed on to the four-poster bed. We bounced tentatively, one foot to the next, before we began to jump. Up and down, we giggled like children. Paul stopped first, suddenly serious. I loved the way he regarded me, with such admiration in his eyes.

Breathless, I flopped on to the bed and dived under the duvet, knowing he'd follow me into the downy heaven. His legs entwined with mine, and he whispered, "We're home," into the tangled cloud of my hair.

When we left the warmth of the bed, we skated along the slippery parquet to the sitting room, where we donned the clothes we'd left in an impatient heap, Paul showed me his pocket watch. "We should get back before that scold with the oversized dentures complains about how long you've been gone."

"Promise we can come back," I said as we closed the door behind us.

He tucked a stray hair behind my ear. "Every day, if you like."

We lingered in front of the Library. "I'd better go in," I said shakily. My body felt as if it had been asleep and was now wide awake. I noticed every blink, every breath, every heartbeat. I wondered if anyone would see a change in me.

CHAPTER
TWENTY-FIVE

ODILE

Paris, June 1941

The circulation desk sat unattended. How odd. It wasn't like Boris to abandon his post. I continued to the reading room, where my habitués sat motionless. No one spoke, no one read. I asked Madame Simon if she'd seen Boris. She shook her head, not even bothering to chastise me for returning from lunch five minutes late.

Something was dreadfully wrong. I rushed through the Library, The reference section was deserted, so was the children's room. Miss Reeder's office was locked. The Afterlife was empty. Finally, I found Bitsi in the cloakroom, huddled in the corner, knees drawn to her chest.

I knelt before her. "Is it Rémy?"

"No." She stared at the parquet.

"Your brother?"

She met my gaze, her violet eyes drenched in sorrow. "Miss Reeder announced she's leaving."

It couldn't be true.

"She and Boris went to get her travel passes," Bitsi added.

"Why is she going now, after all this time?" I asked.

"The trustees in New York sent a cable ordering her to leave France immediately. They think it's only a matter of time before America enters the war, and they're afraid she'll be arrested as an enemy alien."

I sank on to the floor next to Bitsi. I couldn't imagine life without the Directress in the next room, where I could peek my head in and ask her advice. If it hadn't been for her, Bitsi and I wouldn't be friends. Miss Reeder offered me a chance to grow. She hadn't lectured. She'd trusted me to learn my own lessons. What would I do without her?

Two days later, I helped Miss Reeder pack her belongings. Though I knew that her safety mattered more than anything, and that this was for the best, I moved slowly, wanting to keep her with us for as long as possible. In the drawer, a red address book teemed with *cartes de visite* from the likes of the Swedish Ambassador and the Duchess of Windsor. I slid it into her briefcase.

"What will you do in the States?" I asked.

"Hug my family and hear about the moments I've missed. Beyond that, I haven't given it much thought. Perhaps rejoin the Library of Congress, or apply to the Red Cross."

"I wish . . ."

"I wish, too. It's painful to leave. I'm so proud of the Library and the fact that we've remained open. But when you have no news of the outside world — not even from your own family . . ." Tears glinted, and she returned to packing her private collection — favourite books she'd brought from home, signed first editions from admirers, and several French volumes.

There goes Rilke, there goes Colette, and when the books were boxed, there goes Miss Reeder. Watching her empty the shelves was painful, so I turned to the desk. In the bottom drawer was a cache of correspondence. I knew I shouldn't snoop, not with Miss Reeder right there, but couldn't resist when I saw her bold, curving script. It was a letter to "Mom and Dad".

> One cannot plan more than a day in advance, so what the future holds, I do not know. I do, however, have the feeling that our Library will always continue. We're doing a good piece of work, considering the handicaps. It's not easy when you have to stand in line for food before going to work; when everything is extremely hard to get, including clothing, shoes, medical supplies, etc.; no heat and no hot water; and everything very expensive. Seeing the lines makes your heart sad. No soap — no tea — no nothing. The iron clamp is working — granted in a very polite way — but hard — oh, very hard . . .
>
> But physical hardships seem small when compared to those of the heart. We at the Library had our share like all others, but somehow it touches more closely when it

takes place in your own building among
your own staff. Someday I hope to tell you
the story.
      Love,
      Dorothy

The missive reminded me of the ones I'd written to Rémy. Filled with the stark truth of the Occupation, I'd tucked those letters inside the musty classics on my bottom shelf. I wanted to shield him, the way Miss Reeder had her parents. There was so much we did not tell.

"It's been wonderful to work with you," she said.

"Truly?"

"Just promise that you'll think before you speak. You may have the Dewey Decimal System memorised, but if you can't hold your tongue, that knowledge is wasted. Your words have power. Especially now, in such dangerous times."

"I promise."

When she finished packing, only the paper with Dr Fuchs's phone numbers remained. "He said we could call day or night. I hope you'll never need to."

At the going-away party, the Countess had her servants proffer glasses of wine, but my habitués didn't have the heart to partake.

"Who will step into the Directress's shoes?" Mr Pryce-Jones asked.

"Our Odile," Monsieur de Nerciat said.

"She's too young," Madame Simon said, dentures clinking. "The board of trustees will never allow it."

"Perhaps they'll offer the job to Boris," Mr Pryce-Jones said.

"A Russian at the helm of the American Library?" Madame Simon said. "Face facts. The Library will close."

"Let's have a toast," the Countess said, to stop the mood from becoming morose.

We raised our glasses.

Though Miss Reeder was gaunt, her smile was radiant. "To all of you, it's been an honour. The finest tribute would not begin to tell of my devotion, deep affection and high regard."

"May you only remember the brightest days," Boris said as he presented our gift, a snow globe with an Eiffel Tower inside. When she shook it, bits of gold foil twirled about.

Standing off to the side, Margaret, Bitsi and I watched subscribers bid the Directress farewell. Margaret pulled at her pearls. She hadn't been able to contact her family in London and didn't know how they fared in the Blitz, Bitsi clutched Emily Dickinson to her chest. With that German soldier billeted in her apartment, she couldn't even escape the war at home.

Tomorrow, Miss Reeder would make her way out of the Occupied Zone, cross through the Free Zone to Spain, then Portugal, where an ocean liner would sail her back to America. I thought of Rémy, of Bitsi's brother Julien, and the other prisoners of war. Of cheery Miss Wedd, whose crime was being born British. Our Canadian cataloguer, stern Mrs Turnbull, Helen-and-Peter and now Miss Reeder, a world away. 823. *And Then There Were None.*

CHAPTER
TWENTY-SIX

LILY

Froid, Montana, August 1986

Each time I perused Odile's shelves, a different book spoke to me. Some days, a title in bright letters beckoned; other times, a thick tome cried out to be read. This afternoon, Emily Dickinson called my name. Mom had liked one of her poems. The line I remembered was: *Hope is the thing with feathers that perches in your soul.* Inside the slim volume, the "American Library in Paris Inc., 1920" bookplate showed the sun rising over an open book, a horizon as wide as the world. The book lay on a rifle, almost burying it — knowledge slaying violence. As I flipped through the pages, a black and white photo stashed between the pages floated to the floor.

Odile, back from getting the mail, picked it up. "That's Maman, Papa, Rémy and me."

Her father's moustache dominated his face and made him seem stern. Her mother practically stood behind him, and I wondered if she was shy, Odile and her mother wore dresses, the men wore suits.

"Was your dad a businessman?"

"No, a police commissioner."

I grinned. "Does he know you stole a library book?"

She didn't smile back. "He knows I'm a thief."

I was dying to know what she meant, but just as I was going to ask, the phone rang. I knew it was Eleanor before I heard the shrill neediness. "Is Lily there? I sure could use some help . . ."

"So much for today's French lesson," I said. Slipping the photo back into the book, I noticed there were a few other pictures, and I wished I could stay.

"Is the baby still colicky?"

"*Mais oui.*"

For two months now, no one had been able to get any sleep. Worse, the baby wouldn't suckle. The nurse said the tenser Eleanor was, the longer it would be for Benjy "to take". With Dad always at work, I took care of Eleanor, patting her back, the way I did when I burped Joe.

Barely a year apart, both boys wore cloth diapers under rubber pants. Eleanor had shown me how to change a diaper then plunge the poopy one into the toilet before throwing it into the wash. I didn't know why she insisted on using cloth when everyone else used disposable. Maybe she thought more work was more love.

I found Eleanor in the kitchen, which was ninety degrees. Sweat poured down her face, and Benjy was bawling in her arms.

"Why won't he stop? Is it my fault?" Eleanor wailed. She cried almost as much as the baby.

"Have you eaten today?" I sniffed to see if I needed to change his diaper. He smelled fine. She didn't. "Or showered?"

Eleanor gawked at me like I was speaking Farsi. I scrambled three eggs with one hand and cradled Benjy in the other. While she scarfed down the omelette, I wiped his nose with his bib.

When Dad got home, he did the only thing he could. He flipped on the fan and aimed it towards Eleanor. After listening to her fret, he called Grandma Pearl, who drove out the next day, "It stinks to high heaven in here," she said, setting a cardboard box full of baby bottles and rubber nipples on the counter.

"Bottle feeding?" Eleanor protested. "What will people think?"

She told Eleanor to go and rest. I hid my smile behind my book. When Grandma Pearl told you to rest, she needed a rest from you. Tightening the belt of her scruffy pink bathrobe, Eleanor shuffled into the living room. Grandma Pearl prepared the formula and screwed on a nipple. She marched in and thrusted the bottle at Eleanor. "Now feed that child."

"But Brenda breastfed."

"Quit comparing yourself to a ghost!"

"Mother!" Eleanor gestured towards me.

Disparaître means to no longer be visible, to cease to exist. I wrapped French around me like a shawl and went to see Odile, who was rooting around in her garden. She rose and wiped her hands on her smock. "*Bonjour, ma belle. Comment ça va?*"

She was the only adult who asked how I was. The others asked about my brothers.

"How do you say ghost?"

"*Le fantôme.*"

"What about 'sad'?" I'd learned the word a while back but needed it again now.

"*Triste.*" She hugged me. "School starts tomorrow?"

"Yeah. Mary Louise and I signed up for the same classes."

"It's a gift to spend time with your best friend. I can't tell you how much I miss mine." She put the leeks she'd plucked from the ground into her basket. Her expression seemed *triste*.

"Do you have time for a French lesson?" we said simultaneously.

Airport, *un aéroport*. Plane, *un avion*. Plane window, *un hublot*. Flight attendant, *une hôtesse de l'air*. Hostess of the air. Side by side at our desk, Odile's kitchen table, I wrote the vocabulary. Usually, we studied everyday words like sidewalk, building, chair.

"Why are you teaching me travel vocabulary?"

"Because, *ma grande*, I want you to fly."

At dinnertime, as Eleanor set the meatloaf on the table, Grandma Pearl followed, picking at her like a hen pecking at feed. "The whole world won't stop if you take a nap. Don't you have more than one shirt? When was the last time you washed your hair? Where's your pride?"

Eleanor slammed down the creamed corn. "Muuuther!"

270

In moments like this, I remembered that Eleanor was only ten years older than me.

"And where're those friends of yours?" Grandma Pearl continued. "Why don't they help?"

"Lily said Brenda did everything on her own."

"How would she remember?"

Eleanor turned on her mother. "Lily wouldn't lie!"

I felt my face redden. "Actua —"

"I'm not saying she did," Grandma Pearl said quickly. "But I'm telling you, a woman with three children needs a hand."

"I can do it myself." Eleanor sounded as sullen as Mary Louise's sister, Angel.

As usual, Dad came home from work two minutes before dinnertime. We ate in silence, except for Benjy's cries, Eleanor didn't even say grace.

While she and Grandma Pearl bathed the boys, I washed the dishes, picked up toys, folded the laundry, and counted the hours until school started.

For a week, Grandma Pearl did the cooking and lectured Eleanor on how store-bought baby food never killed anyone. Before climbing into the Buick, she told Eleanor, "You lean on Lily a lot. Isn't there someone else who could help? What about that nice Odile?"

Eleanor crossed her arms. "I can do everything by myself. Besides, Lily is family."

She considered me family? Suddenly, helping out didn't seem like such a sacrifice. Yet I could hear Mary Louise's voice as if she were standing beside me. "Eleanor keeps you slaving away. Is that how you'd treat a real daughter?"

In geography, we learned about China, where the government tells couples they can only have one child. Seeing how worn out Eleanor was, it didn't seem like a bad policy. "Girls don't count in China. Parents want boys who can work in the fields," Miss White rattled on, somehow never noticing that our farm community was the same.

"Ever notice the only thing they teach about Communist countries is that they suck?" Mary Louise whispered.

"Yeah, like Froid's so great."

In China, I would have been enough. If I'd been a boy, Dad would have let me take driver's ed. I'd already be driving. I'd already be gone. As the teacher droned on, I lay my head down for a minute, the desk cold against my cheek. My house was China. I imagined taking a bath, imagined my father and Eleanor seizing my shoulders and holding my body underwater, imagined the life seeping out of me.

"Lil?" Mary Louise patted my back.

I woke up. Everyone else was heading out the door.

"Didn't you hear the bell?"

Yawning, I covered my mouth and felt a thread of saliva stitched to my chin.

"Slobbering over Robby," Tiffany Ivers said on her way out.

I prayed, *Please God, don't let him have seen.*

"Ignore her," Mary Louise said. "Want to come over?"

"Eleanor needs me to baby-sit."

"What about Friday? Spend the night like you used to."

I wanted to. I really did. "Can't."

I trudged home, where diapers would need to be changed and Weeble Wobbles were scattered over the linoleum like landmines. *Bien sûr*, Benjy screamed. At the kitchen table, in the scabby shirt she'd worn all week, Eleanor rocked him while Joe whimpered at her feet. I cuddled with him before attacking the dirty dishes that languished on the counter.

"You don't have to," she protested weakly. *Lily is family*. I sterilised the things that needed sterilising. I rocked Benjy until he dozed off. Even in his sleep, he sniffled. Passing him to Eleanor, I ran to Odile's for a quick lesson.

Lord, I loved the calm there. No babies bawling. Not a thing out of place. Newspapers folded in the basket beside her chair. Our books arranged according to the Odile-Lily Decimal System. The small framed photos of her husband and son.

"Tell me about Mr Gustafson."

"Buck?" She squinted, as if she hadn't thought about him in a long time and wasn't sure who I meant, "A man's man. Handsome in a rugged way, with stubble on those ruddy cheeks of his. He liked to hunt, which is how he got his nickname. He killed his first deer, a six-point buck, when he was ten. Its mangy carcase was our first fight. Buck wanted the head of that poor animal over the mantle; I wanted it nowhere near me."

"Who won?"

"Well, *ma grande*, that was the first lesson I learned as a young wife." She got up from the table and moved to the sink. "Sometimes, when you win, you lose. I got rid of the stuffed head — the bin man picked it up

273

when Buck was at work. But he was angry for a good long while."

"Oh."

"Oh, indeed." Her back to me, she tucked the plates on the dish rack into the cupboard.

"What did you and Buck like to do together?"

"We raised our son."

"And after he was grown?"

She turned to me. "Buck and I didn't have much in common. He loved attending football games, I preferred to read. But we both liked brisk walks. He was romantic. He never stopped holding doors open for me, never stopped holding my hand. At midnight, we sometimes went to the park and played on the swings, like children."

It was the most she'd ever said about her life, and I stayed silent, hoping she'd continue.

"After he died, I donated most of his things to charity — his tools, the truck. But I kept his rifle. I needed something important to him to remain."

The phone rang. Eleanor again. I headed home. After cooking dinner and cleaning up, I fell into bed still wearing my jeans, too tired to study. Anyway, calculus paled next to Odile's lesson: love is accepting someone, all parts of them, even the ones you don't like or understand.

When Eleanor got home from the fall parent-teacher conference, she slammed the back door. "Lily?" she hollered. "Where are you?"

In the living room, watching the boys, where else? On my lap, Joe tugged at my hair; laying on the blanket I knit for him, Benjy noticed his toes for the first time.

274

Eleanor strode in. "Miss White said you fall asleep in class. She made it sound like *I* was somehow at fault, I'm not a bad mother! Why don't you get dinner going while I feed Benjy?"

She hiked up her shirt over her sagging belly, past a spidery web of stretch marks. I fled to the kitchen before she undid her bra and released her chapped nipple. Seeing it once had been enough. I wished that Eleanor trusted me less. I wished she'd go back to the aerobics tapes and chatting with Odile, but she spent most of her time making home-made baby food and sobbing at the sink. "You're a mother but also a woman," Odile had told her. It seemed to me like Eleanor had given up on the woman she used to be.

Little by little, I had stopped doing homework and hanging out with Mary Louise. Even French was *fini*. Eleanor needed me. Sometimes, she just sat and contemplated the wall. "Don't you want to hold Benjy?" I'd say. Or, "Look, Eleanor, Joe's teeth are coming in." She would barely nod.

When I got my report card, I realised how the situation had devolved. Math: C-. English: B-. Science: C-. History: C-. "What happened?" Mr Moriarty wrote in red ink. I trudged home, afraid that, like Eleanor, I'd given up on the girl I'd been.

"Lily?" Odile said from her porch.

I continued on.

"Lily, what's wrong?" She steered me into her house and pried the report card from me.

"Oh la la," she said.

"I have to go, Eleanor needs my help."

The aroma of chocolate filled the air. Odile held out a tray of cookies. Hunkered on her couch, crumbs spilling on to my clothes, I gorged, not even tasting them.

She watched sadly. "What's going on at home?"

"*Rien.* Nothing." I didn't want to complain.

"You must stand up for yourself."

"Can't *you* talk to them?" I asked.

"In the long run that won't help. You must learn the art of negotiation."

I snorted. "Like they'd listen to me."

"Talk to them."

"Eleanor has a full plate."

"Tell your father how you feel."

"He won't care."

"Make him care."

"How?"

"What does he want?" Odile asked.

I considered the question. "To be left in peace."

"What does he want for you?"

Mom had wanted me to go to college. She almost went, but got married instead. If Dad wanted anything for me, I didn't know about it. And there was no way I could ask, at least not at home, where Eleanor and the boys ate all his attention, "Maybe . . . maybe I could go to his office. But he might be mad."

"He might not. You must try."

The following morning, I dressed with the same care that I did for church. What would I say to Dad? It was eight blocks to the bank, and I practically ran, hoping no one would report me for skipping school. When Mr

Ivers saw me pacing outside Dad's office, he guffawed and said it must be urgent if I had to make an appointment to see my own father.

When Dad came out, he was confused. "Why aren't you in class?" Then scared: "Did something happen to the boys?"

Of course. The boys.

"Lily's here for a father-daughter chat," his boss chuckled, but Dad didn't laugh. Embarrassed, he shoved me into a chair in his office.

"This better be important," He folded his hands on his immense desk.

"I . . . I . . ."

"Well? What is it?"

His anger made it easier. "I miss learning French and seeing Mary Louise and doing homework and reading. I'm sick of dirty diapers."

"Ellie needs your help."

"Am I the only one who sees that all she does is cry? She needs more than I can give."

"She'll be fine."

"She might need a psychologist."

"Psychologists are for crazy people."

"For depressed people."

"You need to help out more."

"What about you? They're your kids."

"I work here."

"And you need to work at home." I slapped my report card on to the desk. "Even when Mom died, I made the honour roll. You might be fine with me being a nanny, but it's not what Mom would have wanted."

His head jerked back as if my truth had walloped him.

"I'm happy to help out. I am. But I want French lessons. I want to go to college."

He gestured to the door like I was someone who would never qualify for a loan. "I'll drive you to school."

We didn't talk. I stared out the window, wishing it were the window of a plane, that Odile was right and that some day I'd fly away.

Dad always came home at ten to six, just before dinner. For the first time, he was late, Eleanor asked if I wanted to eat, but since she held off, I said I would, too. We kept the roast in the oven. At the dining room table, Joe bounced in my lap, and Eleanor held Benjy, who'd stopped crying, like magic. Usually, we bathed the boys at seven o'clock, but tonight we were still waiting for Dad. In that brief moment of peace, Eleanor asked me the question she always asked him: "How was your day, dear?"

"I went to the bank."

"The bank?" she said, all confused, like she'd forgotten Froid had one.

"I needed to . . ." What did I need? Eleanor regarded me intently, listening as never before. "I needed to get through to Dad. About college."

She let out an odd kind of laugh and said, "At least one of us is brave enough to say what we want."

I sniffed. "Do you smell smoke?"

She shoved Benjy into my arms and ran to the kitchen. I followed, Benjy balanced on my hip and Joe glued to my leg. Smoke billowed from the oven.

"I give up," Eleanor wailed, taking out the scorched pan.

278

Dad walked in, briefcase in hand. It was 8p.m., which was like midnight anywhere else in the world.

"Not even a phone call to say you'd be late?" she yelled and chucked the charred roast at him. He held his briefcase in front of his face and ducked. The charred hunk hit the wall and fell to the floor, sliding to a stop at his feet.

I was proud of Eleanor.

"You leave me to do everything," she told Dad.

I carried my brothers to their room.

"You're never home," she said. "Are you there with Brenda or here with me?"

Brenda. No one said her name any more. "Oh, Mom," I whispered. "I miss you."

"Why you sad?" Joe asked. I caressed his hair, downy like the feathers of a baby chick.

My father murmured soft words but Eleanor wasn't having any of them. "What do you mean, I bite off more than I can chew?" she yelled. "When I bought disposable diapers you said *she* used cloth. I never measure up to Saint Brenda!"

"There weren't other options back then," he yelled back. "I wasn't saying you should use cloth. I was remembering things were different. There's no need to do everything on your own. Folks have reached out. Stop swatting their hands away."

Silence.

"The person I want help from is you."

When I told Odile that Dad decided to take Saturdays off to help take care of the boys, and that Eleanor bought a truckload of Pampers, she said, "See how standing up for yourself feels? There's not always a solution, but if you don't try, you'll never know."

"I'm not sure it was the trip to Dad's office." I told her about Eleanor and the flying roast.

Odile clapped her hands together. "It sounds like you inspired Eleanor to speak up, too. Brava!"

Now that Odile and I had uninterrupted time, I got out the book with the photos again. On her couch, we looked at the picture of her family. "How I miss them," she said as she moved to the next photo, which showed a dark-haired beauty in a polka-dot dress. Odile beamed as if she'd unexpectedly run into a friend. "That's Miss Reeder. She was my boss at the Library and the person I admired the most."

The next picture showed a lady in a turban talking to an officer with wire-rimmed glasses who wore a swastika armband.

"No use thinking about the past," Odile said, her tone as stony as her face. She shoved the photos back into the book.

Why did she have a picture of a Nazi?

"You knew a Nazi?"

"Dr Fuchs came to the Library."

When I'd imagined Nazis, they were killing people in concentration camps, not checking out books. It seemed unseemly that she knew his name.

"Paris was occupied," Odile explained. "We couldn't avoid them, and not all people wanted to. He was what the Nazis called a 'Library Protector'."

"So he saved books?"

"It's not so simple."

280

I thought about what I'd learned at school. "My history teacher said Europeans should have known about the camps. She said it was obvious . . ."

"I learned about them after the war. At the time, my family merely tried to survive. I worried about Anglophone friends and colleagues, who were arrested as enemy aliens. Though Jewish people were barred from libraries, it never occurred to me that they, too, would be arrested and that many would be killed."

Odile was quiet for a long time.

"Are you mad that I asked?"

"*Mais non.* Forgive me, I was lost in my memories. During the war, we librarians delivered books to Jewish friends. The Gestapo even shot one of my colleagues."

Shooting a librarian? Wasn't that like killing a doctor? "They killed Miss Reeder?"

"She'd left by then. The Nazis arrested several librarians, including the director of the National Library. We feared Miss Reeder might be next. I was broken-hearted when she left. But saying goodbye is a fact of life. Loss is inevitable."

I was sorry I'd dug out the photos, they'd only made her sad. But then she cupped my cheek gently and said, "Sometimes, though, good things come from change."

Paris
1 December 1941

Monsieur l'Inspecteur,
I am writing to inform you that the
American Library houses more <u>enemy aliens</u>
than an internment camp. To start with,

there's the arriviste American, Clara de Chambrun. She spends more time at the Library than she does at home like a good wife should. She devotes her days soliciting funds from fancy socialite friends in order to sustain the Library. I doubt she declares this revenue.

She does not like Germans (or "Huns" as she calls them) and flouts their regulations. Just because she's a countess doesn't mean that she needn't follow the rules. I believe she smuggles books to Jewish readers. Who knows what else she is up to? She's very evasive.

Pay a visit and see for yourself. You'll see she thinks she's above the law.

Signed,

One who knows

CHAPTER
TWENTY-SEVEN

ODILE

Paris, December 1941

Clara de Chambrun, our new Directress, had helped found the ALP in 1920. Along with Edith Wharton and Anne Morgan, she'd been one of the original trustees. The Countess not only wrote several works on Shakespeare, she also translated his plays into French. She and Hemingway shared the same publisher. More recently, these past months, she sought donors to cover expenses from coal to payroll, and she wrote letters to prevent Nazi authorities from forcing Boris and the caretaker to work in Germany as a part of the *Relève* plan. I worried that as a prominent foreigner she could be arrested.

At the circulation desk, I shared my fear with Boris and Margaret as he stamped Madame Simon's *Harper's Bazaar*. He said that Clara had married Count Aldebert de Chambrun, a French general, in 1901. She had dual citizenship, and would not be considered an enemy alien.

Just then, Monsieur de Nerciat burst in, Mr Pryce-Jones on his heels.

"Kamikazes hit Pearl Harbor!" Monsieur shouted.

We gathered around him.

"What on earth is a kamikaze?" Margaret asked. "And where's Pearl Harbor?"

"Japan attacked an American military base," Mr Pryce-Jones translated.

"Does this mean the United States will join the war?" I felt a glimmer of hope that soon the Germans would be defeated.

"We believe so," Monsieur de Nerciat said.

"The Americans will annihilate the Nazis!" I said.

"They can hardly do worse than the French army," Margaret said.

My head reared back. How dare Margaret criticise soldiers like Rémy, when *she'd* been one of the first to flee Paris. "British forces were certainly quick to retreat to that puny island."

We glared at each other, and I waited for her to take back her words.

"We shouldn't talk politics, should we?" she finally said.

She offered an olive branch, not an apology. I tried not to be angry. She didn't mean to be tactless. Afraid to say something I'd regret, I hurried to the typewriter in the back room, hoping that working on the newsletter would distract me. Before the Occupation, I'd cranked out 500 copies on our mimeograph, but with the shortage of paper, I now posted one lone copy on the bulletin board.

Mr Pryce-Jones scooted over to a chair beside mine. "We can hear you pounding away from the reading room."

I pointed to the ribbon. "It's so old, the lettering is fainter and fainter."

"I thought you might be working out your anger. What Margaret said about the French army wasn't kind."

"I know she didn't mean it, but it hurts." I covered the r, e, m, y keys with my fingers. "I miss my brother so much, and I know he fought hard."

"Margaret knows it, too. She sometimes speaks without thinking."

"We all do." I needed an interviewee for this month's newsletter. "What kind of reader are you? What are your prized books?"

"The truth?"

I leaned closer. Would he confess to reading scandalous novels?

"Just last week, I discarded my entire collection."

"What?" Giving away books was like giving up air.

"I'd had my share of Sophocles and Aristotle, of Melville and Hawthorne, books assigned at university or offered to me by colleagues. I've spent enough time in the past. I want today, now. F. Scott Fitzgerald, Nancy Mitford, Langston Hughes."

"What did you do with your books?"

"When I heard Professor Cohen's collection had been pillaged, I boxed up my books and took them to her. Stealing books is like desecrating graves."

Though Mr Pryce-Jones made it seem as if he were content to give away a collection built over a lifetime, I sensed the truth. He parted with his books because the Professor had been forced to part with hers. I reminded myself that there were people with bigger problems, bigger hurts.

But I was still miffed with Margaret.

KRIEGSGEFANGENENPOST   12 December
1941

Dear Odile,

Do you know how I can tell that you are holding back in your letters? You haven't complained about Papa in ages, and you rarely mention Paul. Perhaps you feel you can't write about him because I can't hold Bitsi close. You're wrong. I want to hear Papa bluster and Maman chinwag. I want to know you in love. Tell me what you truly feel, not what you feel I can bear to hear — I need your honesty as much as your love. Having only a little of you, sensing you censor each sentence is killing me. We're not together, but we needn't be distant. Bitsi hesitates when she writes. I do, too. I want to shield you. I don't want you to know. I want you to know.

Things are hard here. We're hungry, we're tired. Our heads are bowed, our clothing threadbare. We long for home. We worry our fiancées will forget us. We weep when we think no one can hear. What bothers us most is the word "prisoner", associated with criminals. All we did was fight for our beliefs and our country. Barbed wire is always in our peripheral vision.

Love,
Rémy

20 December 1941

Dear Rémy,
I'll try not to hold back. Paul and I escaped Maman's spying. He found us an abandoned apartment for afternoon trysts. We've decorated our boudoir with my books and his sketches of Brittany. There's no heat, and we've both come down with colds, but it's worth it! I never expected to find a pursuit more thrilling than reading.

Now that Germany has declared war on the US, and Americans in France are enemy aliens, I fear the Nazis will close the Library for good. Though staff try to put on a good face, we're tired and frightened. We move like toys winding down. Sometimes I get angry for no reason. Sometimes I find it hard to think. Sometimes I don't know what to think.

At any rate, we have the Christmas party to look forward to. The Countess said we may bring family if they are of "superior quality", so I've invited Maman and "Aunt" Eugénie. Papa can't come, he has meetings.

That's why I don't complain about him —
he's never home.
    Love,
    Odile

The scent of Boris's hot spiced wine wafted through the Library, Chestnuts crackled in the fireplace. Bitsi helped children cut up old catalogues to make ornaments for the fir tree. Margaret and I fetched the festive red ribbons from the cupboard and decorated the reading room.

"It's cold in my flat," she said. "I could use a few of these fusty books as firewood."

Instinctively, I grabbed a novel and held it to my chest. I'd die of hypothermia before destroying a single one. Many of these books had been sent from America to soldiers of the Great War. Read in trenches and makeshift hospitals, their stories brought comfort and escape.

"I was joking," Margaret said. "You do know that?"

"Of course . . ." Still, it was a horrible thing to say. I moved to a secluded corner, cradling *The Picture of Dorian Gray*, 823. I inhaled the novel's slightly musty odour, imagining it was a *mélange* of gunpowder and mud from the trenches. Whenever I opened a worn book, I liked to believe I released a soldier's spirit. "Here you go, old friend," I whispered. "You're safe now, you're home."

"Talking to yourself?" Bitsi teased, Maman and Eugénie in tow.

288

"So this is where you work," Maman said. "It's not as grim as I expected."

Eugénie giggled. "Did you think she worked in a coal mine?"

Maman tapped her playfully on the arm.

Each attendee brought a delicacy that was scarce and dreadfully expensive, obtained either from the black market or country cousins. A creamy camembert. A basket of oranges. Eugénie passed the plate of foie gras she and Maman had prepared with the goose liver that Paul had brought from Brittany.

A hush fell over the room as the Countess, in her ermine wrap, entered the party on the arm of her husband, a white-haired gentleman in a dinner suit. Even without medals on his breast, it was clear from his deportment — chest thrust out, coolly surveying the guests as if they were his troops — that he had been a general.

Near the refreshment table, Madame Simon cornered Clara de Chambrun, giving a long-winded explanation of how she'd fashioned her tatty turban from a bathrobe. The Countess shot her husband a "save me now" look, and like an obedient lap dog, he scampered over to whisk her away.

"He commanded soldiers on two continents," Mr Pryce-Jones said.

"But there's no mistake about who's in charge now," Monsieur de Nerciat observed.

"The Général has met his Waterloo."

"Met his Waterloo? He married her."

Paul led me to my favourite section of the stacks, to 823, where we joined Cathy and Heathcliff, Jane and Rochester. I gazed at his lips, rosy from the wine. Slowly, he knelt before me. "You're the woman of my life," he said. "The first face I want to see when I awake, the one I want to kiss at night. Everything you say is so interesting — I love hearing about the autumn leaves that crunch under your feet, the cranky subscriber you set straight, the novel you read in bed. I can tell you my deepest thoughts, my favourite books. The thing I want most is a continuation of our conversations. Will you marry me?"

Paul's proposal was like a perfect novel, its ending inevitable and yet somehow a surprise.

From the reading room, I could hear my mother ask, "Where did Paul and Odile go?", could hear Eugénie respond, "Oh, for once, let them be."

"I wish we were at the apartment," I whispered, "in our rosy boudoir."

"I love being alone with you, too, only . . ."

"Only what?"

His Adam's apple bobbed nervously. "We shouldn't be sneaking around, it's not right. I'm not sure how much longer I can —"

"Papa won't find out."

"Why do you make everything about your father?"

"I don't!"

"Let's not fight," he said.

Caressing his face, I took in the changes that war had wrought: dusky shadows gathered under his eyes; lines formed bitter parentheses around his mouth. So much

had changed, I wanted some things to stay the same —
my work at the Library, our afternoon trysts.

"You're the person getting me through the war," he
said, "through my work duties. I want us to be
together."

"Yes, my love. When Rémy's released."

I slid to my knees. Paul started to say something,
maybe *I love you*, maybe *I don't want to wait*, but I
kissed him and his words were lost beneath my tongue.
He drew me to his chest. My hands slipped under his
jacket, his jumper, his shirt, to the heat of his skin. In
the background, friends sang "Silent Night", but Paul
and I remained entwined, eyes closed to everything but
our passion.

My family continued to count the days of Rémy's
captivity as the year turned, 12 January: *Dear Rémy,
You're the only one I can tell: Paul proposed! We'll
have the wedding when you come home*; 20 February:
Dear Odile, Don't wait for me. Be happy now; 19
March: *Dear Rémy, Margaret and I have no more
stockings, so we pat our legs with beige powder. Bitsi
thinks we're crazy*; 5 April: *Dear Odile, Bitsi's right!
Thanks for the package. How did you know that I
wanted to read Maupassant?*

Everyone had to register for something: housewives
for rations; foreign and Jewish people with the police.
Though Mr Pryce-Jones signed in weekly at the
commissariat, Margaret hadn't gone once. Scrawled on
the sides of building's, I saw Vs — for Victory over the
Nazis, but I also saw "Down with Jews". Marshal

291

Pétain, the First World War hero who'd been appointed Chief of State, transformed the French motto "Liberty, Equality, Fraternity" to "Work, Family, Fatherland". It felt as if Parisians' state of mind was "Tense, Angry, Resentful".

Paul and I strolled under the leafy shade of the Champs-Élysées, past cafés filled with Nazis and their gaudy girlfriends. *Soldaten* had Deutschmarks to buy beer and trinkets like bracelets and blusher. The men were away from the Eastern Front and wanted to forget the war in the company of lovely, lonely *Parisiennes*.

I didn't blame the girls. At eighteen, who didn't long to dance? At thirty, mothers needed help with the bills. Their husbands had been killed in battle or were stuck in Stalags. The women went on with their lives as best they could. Still, next to them, I felt like a frump, I pinched my cheeks, hoping to bring out a little colour, and reminded myself, *It's chic to be shabby.*

"I can only dream of offering you a piece of jewellery." Paul scowled at the couples. "Not being able to give you the sweet somethings you deserve — it's damn humiliating!"

"How I feel about you has nothing to do with trinkets."

"Those sluts get everything while we go without. They're whores, sucking off —"

"There's no need to be crude!"

"They should be ashamed, plastering themselves over the damn Krauts, sucking up to the enemy. I'd like to teach them a lesson they'll never forget."

He stepped towards the *Soldaten* and their girls. His jaw was clenched. His fist clenched. He didn't look like himself. For the first time, he frightened me.

"Don't pick a fight. It's not worth it." I grabbed his arm and held on tight.

Soldaten were becoming impossible to avoid. They loafed at our favourite cafés, they set up more and more checkpoints on our streets. It was difficult to know where they'd turn up. On my way to Montmartre to deliver scientific works to Dr Sanger, I passed through a metal barricade that had not been there just the day before. One of the soldiers grabbed my satchel and dumped the contents on to the ground. I winced as the heavy tomes hit the pavement and fell open. He picked one up and leafed through the pages. Perhaps he was looking for top-secret codes or a knife hidden in the binding; perhaps he was just bored. Glancing at the title, he smirked. "Mademoiselle is reading treatises on physics?"

It had been a long time since my physics class at the *lycée*. If he asked a question, I was in trouble. I could say the works were for a neighbour, or I could ask a question of my own.

"Are you saying women should stick to books on embroidery?"

He handed over my satchel and told me to pick up my books.

When I returned to the Library, I tried to warn Margaret, but she refused to acknowledge the danger she was in, even as we filled crates intended for internment camps where foreigners like our Miss Wedd and the Left Bank bookseller Miss Beach were imprisoned.

"Have you registered with the police yet?" I asked for the tenth time.

"I feel French, that should be enough," Margaret said, gently laying *Christmas Pudding* over *Pigeon Pie*.

"Perhaps you should join Lawrence in the Free Zone."

"His mistress wouldn't appreciate it."

Mistress? No, it couldn't be, I revisited our conversations, searching for clues I'd missed. She'd said he was with a "friend", and I'd taken the word at face value, Margaret had never spoken of receiving letters from her husband, never mentioned missing him. I felt a fool, blathering about Paul while she suffered in silence. I could read books, but couldn't read people.

I knew that a mistress could bring about a divorce and worried that Margaret might move to London, or, worse, disappear like Aunt Caro. I must have appeared distraught, because Margaret placed her hand over mine. "Diplomatic ties between France and Britain were cut," she said. "He stayed for her. Lawrence and I live separate lives. It's not what I wanted — especially for Christina, who never sees her father — but I've accepted it."

"He's an idiot. He must be if doesn't see how lovely and brave you are."

Margaret smiled tremulously. "No one's ever seen me the way you do."

294

My hand tightened around hers. "Do you think he'll want a divorce?"

"Couples like us don't divorce, we 'muddle through'."

"So you'll stay?"

"I'll never leave the Library."

"Promise?"

"The easiest one I've ever made."

"I'm thrilled you're staying, but don't want you to get into trouble. What if you get arrested like Miss Wedd? Please think about signing at the *commissariat*. It's the law."

"Not all laws are meant to be obeyed." She untangled her fingers from mine and set the lid firmly on to the crate of books. Case closed.

CHAPTER
TWENTY-EIGHT

MARGARET

Paris, May 1942

In the silver evening light, Margaret ascended the steps of the Métro station, wondering which book she would read to her daughter at bedtime. *Bella the Goat* or *Homer the Cat*? Too late, she spied a new checkpoint. She retreated slowly.

A soldier demanded, "*Vos papiers.*" He spoke French with a harsh German accent.

She held out her papers.

He assessed them, then glared at her. "*Anglaise?*"

English? The enemy.

He took hold of her arm. His knuckles brushed against her breast, and she shrank back, manoeuvring her bosom away from his touch.

Margaret was the only foreigner they found. Prodding her along, they moved down the pavement She'd never been so scared. She knew the men could shove her into an abandoned courtyard and have their way with her, and her life would change for ever.

Six blocks later, they entered a requisitioned police station. Inside, there were desks on one side of the room, and on the other a holding cell where three grey-haired ladies slumped on a bench. Their smeared mascara and creased dresses told Margaret that they'd been imprisoned for several days.

"My daughter . . ." she said when the soldier shoved her into the cell. "May I please telephone?"

"This isn't a country club," he replied. "You aren't our guest."

The ladies made room on the bench, and Margaret perched primly on the edge. Normally, she would introduce herself as Mrs Saint James, but it seemed silly to stand on formality in a cell.

"I'm Margaret, My crime is being English."

"Ours, too."

"They caught us on the walk home from our book club."

"We were quite a catch!"

"Those strapping soldiers must feel proud of stopping ladies from reading Proust."

Eventually, the officers left for the day, leaving only a young soldier, who read at his desk.

"*Entre nous*, I think that guard is taken with our new friend."

Margaret had noticed his gaze travel from his book to them. But in this dank police station, what else was there to look at?

"How long have you been here?" Margaret asked.

"A week. When there are enough of us, they'll send us to an internment camp. No water, no food, just lice and bored soldiers."

As the evening went on, and they prepared to spend the night again, the ladies became distressed. "What if they never let us go?"

Margaret drew *The Priory* from her bag. "I'm going to read a story." The women settled in, "'It was almost dark. Cars, weaving like shuttles on the high road between two towns fifteen miles apart, had their lights on. Every few moments, the gates of Saunby Priory were illuminated.' It's a grand old house. I promise, you'll feel comfortable there."

At the end of the chapter, one of the ladies yawned. The three of them crouched down and made their beds for the night, bodies on the cement floor, heads on their handbags. Margaret joined them.

"Take the bench, dearie."

"You don't have as much padding as us. Stay up there."

She was moved by this simple kindness. "I'd rather be with you."

Head resting on *The Priory*, Margaret fiddled with her morning pearls. The necklace had been her mother's and wasn't worth anything, not like the jewels Lawrence had expected her to flaunt at parties. But when Margaret wore the pearls, she knew she was encircled by her mother's love, like a child when she'd felt the whisper of Mum's lips upon her brow.

Study hard so you won't have to do factory work like me, her mother said, but Gran told Margaret that she could have any man she wanted, that her regal appearance made up for the fact she was from an inferior class. Gran compared catching a man to reeling

298

in a fish: go where there are plenty about, use your best lure and be still. Margaret and her friends lingered outside a fine restaurant, gliding demurely past the entrance. When she saw Lawrence, so dashing in his navy suit, she dropped her bag. He picked it up. Hook, line and sinker.

At their wedding, she wore a silk dress by Jeanne Lanvin. Her mouth hurt from smiling. She hadn't given any thought beyond the ceremony, and didn't know anything about the wedding night. The shock of it was so intimate, so awkward, that she didn't mind that they couldn't go on a honeymoon. Lawrence was a young diplomat, and he and Margaret were invited to an important dinner, which would hopefully lead to peace talks.

At the Putney, cocktails were served. Hand on the small of Margaret's back, Lawrence showed her off — "*Voici ma femme!*" — moving from the Italian Ambassador to the German contingent. She was surprised that everyone spoke French; they were in England, after all. "It's the language of diplomacy," he explained. "You said you studied French."

And that's exactly how she'd phrased it when he'd asked. She'd been careful not to lie. The truth was that she'd failed four years of French. But during their courtship, he did most of the talking, and managed to fill in all her blanks. She hadn't thought it would matter.

Gulping down her cocktail, Margaret watched the other wives use witty phrases to coax begrudging smiles and even outright laughter from stiff diplomats.

At the dinner table, she was unable to communicate with the gruff Russian on her right, the timid Czech on her left. She hoped for a small show of support from Lawrence, but he regarded her as his mother had, with disdain. Mercifully, the women withdrew to a salon while the men puffed on their cigars. Margaret expected to discuss fashion, but the ladies spoke of the prevailing political situation. She couldn't keep track — a *duce* in Italy, a chancellor in Germany, a president *and* a prime minister in France. It was confusing.

When the debacle was finally over, it wasn't over. In front of the hotel, while she and Lawrence waited for the Jaguar to be brought round, a Frenchwoman in a sequined dress kissed him on the cheek (very close to his mouth), and said in perfect English, "You'll have to buy little Margaret a newspaper subscription so she'll have something to contribute."

In the car, Margaret said, "It didn't go so badly. I'll get a tutor to brush up on my French."

He didn't reply. In the lamplight, she saw he wore the same expression as her mum, just home from the market, after she realised the plump raspberries she'd bought had mould inside. It was a look of disgust, but of disgust for oneself, for allowing oneself to be swindled.

"Tell me what to do and I'll do it," Margaret pleaded.

He didn't look at her. He never touched her again.

The following week, she invited friends to tea. They were thrilled for her — a posh house, a rich husband, a diamond ring. "You got everything you wanted!"

In the cell, one of the women moved closer, and her warmth lulled Margaret to sleep. As she drifted off, she realised it was true, she'd got everything she wanted. She wished she'd known to want more.

In the middle of the night, Margaret was roused from her sleep. Someone was poking her shoulder. The guard crouched over her. She reared back, away from him, but there was very little room to manoeuvre.

"I'm letting you go," he whispered.

The door to the cell was open. She moved to wake the ladies.

"Not them, just you."

"Why me?"

"You're beautiful. You shouldn't be here."

He was like Lawrence. He saw what he wanted to. She lay back down.

"I'd let you all go if I could," he said, "but I can't explain an empty cell."

She glared at him, angry he'd dangled the possibility of freedom in front of her, only to fling it away. "The war hasn't taught you to lie?"

"I'll get in trouble."

"Your commander will shout and you'll feel ill at ease. What's the worst that will happen to us? Sent to a prison far from loved ones, with no food, no heat, no books."

"I'll let the four of you go —"

"*Merci. Danke.*"

"I'll let you all go, if you read me the novel."

"What?"

"We'll meet once a day. On the steps of the Panthéon, or wherever you want."

"That's absurd."

"One chapter per day."

She wished she could see his expression, but he was facing away from the dim light. "Why?"

"I want to know what happens next."

Paris
9 May 1942

Monsieur l'Inspecteur,

I am writing to inform you that at the American Library, the Directress Clara de Chambrun née Longworth writes lies and excuses to keep both the head librarian and caretaker in Paris, rather than allowing them to be dispatched to work in the Fatherland.

Boris Netchaeff visits the homes of Jewish readers. Each evening, he carries away several batches of books. It wouldn't surprise me if he were smuggling obscene books to people. He has no morals, and refuses to keep the Library's collection pure. He says he took French nationality, but I have my doubts.

Do your job — rid Paris of these foreign degenerates.

Signed,
One who knows

CHAPTER
TWENTY-NINE

ODILE

Paris, June 1942

Breakfast was a few spoonfuls of oatmeal and an egg that Maman split three ways, careful to place the crumbled bits of yolk back on the white. Her cheeks, once plump plums, were now sunken prunes. Papa had lost so much weight that she'd taken in his trousers. His broom-shaped moustache could no longer hide the sad sweep of his mouth.

"You should be married instead of a spinster librarian," he told me. "What's wrong with you?"

I stared at Rémy's chair. I missed his support.

"Paul is a wonderful young man," Papa continued.

"Then why don't *you* marry him?"

"Enough!" Maman said.

For once, my father shut up. I could almost hear Rémy say, *That's all it took? One word? If only we'd known!*

At work, I barely made it past the threshold before Boris loaded me down with books. I didn't mind. We all faced checkpoints, and I knew that he and the Countess delivered just as many. On the way to Professor Cohen's, I tried to enjoy the lush June morning, but Papa's criticism echoed: *What's wrong with you? What's wrong with you?*

I slumped on the Professor's settee. My gaze moved from the grandfather clock that burped the hour to the always empty vase to the clouds of concern in the Professor's eyes.

"Is everything all right?"

It wasn't professional to vent, but she did ask. "Papa thinks I should get married."

She leaned forward on her chair, "Are you and Paul engaged?"

"Yes!" It felt good to share my secret with her. "But only Rémy knows. And now you."

The clouds lifted. "This calls for champagne. Alas, cherry wine will have to do." At the sideboard, she took out a bottle and emptied the last drops into two glasses.

"To you and your young man."

We sipped the sweet wine.

"Why haven't you told your parents?"

"The minute I do, Papa will pick the wedding date and name the grandchildren. Maman has sewn so much that my trousseau takes up an entire room — you could drown in doilies. Mostly, though, I want to wait for Rémy. It's my decision, not my father's."

"I empathise, my dear. I do. But my mother used to tell me, 'Accept people for who they are, not for who you want them to be.'"

"What does that mean?"

"Your father's old, he won't change. And dogs don't have kittens, so you're as stubborn as him. The only thing you can change is the way you see him."

304

"I'm not sure that's possible."

"Talk to him," she said. "Tell him how you feel about Paul, and that you want Rémy at your side."

"Papa just wants to marry me off."

"He misses your brother, too. Surely he'll understand."

I pouted. "You don't know my father."

"When you're older . . ."

I bade her farewell, bristling as I stomped down the steps. *When you're older! What's wrong with you?* Barrelling down rue Blanche, I noticed a brunette in an elegant blue jacket, a yellow star on her lapel. I froze, hurt pride suddenly the furthest thing from my mind.

Jewish people could no longer teach, enter parks, or even cross the Champs-Élysées. They couldn't use phone booths. They had to sit in the last carriage of the Métro. Continuing in my direction, the brunette raised her chin, but her mouth quivered. I'd heard about the yellow stars, but this was the first one I'd seen. I didn't know how to react. Should I smile kindly to let the woman know that not everyone agreed with this bizarre identification? Should I stare straight ahead as usual, to let her know that nothing had changed? By not looking at the woman, I would prove that I viewed her just like any other. As we crossed paths, I averted my eyes.

Jewish people were not just banned, they now wore targets. And I'd complained to Professor Cohen about my insignificant problems.

All morning, Margaret and I repaired worn books. We could no longer order new ones, so each was precious. Tired and hungry, I pasted the glue over the binding, back and forth, back and forth, slowly, then slower still, like a record player winding down. She'd stopped working a while ago. The right corner of her mouth turned up in a smile. I called her name but she didn't answer.

"Margaret?" I nudged her knee.

"Sorry, I was lost in thought."

"Occupational hazard," I said.

She laughed. The light in her eyes spoke of love. Had she and her husband made up?

"Is Lawrence home?"

She gaped at me, aghast. "Heavens, no! What made you think that?"

"You seem happy." She was always beautiful, but her expression had changed these past weeks, become brighter. It was as if the morning fog had given way to the afternoon sun, the change so gradual that I hadn't seen it until now.

Haltingly, almost as if she were surprised, she said, "I suppose I am."

"Any special reason?"

"I'm rereading *The Priory*, aloud this time."

"Aloud?"

"To someone who couldn't otherwise."

Before I could find out more, our attention was taken by the sound of soldiers' boots. The Bibliotheksschutz and two lackeys had come to call. Subscribers stiffened. Parisians were used to *Soldaten* in the street, but not in our library. It had been several months since Dr Fuchs's last visit, and much had changed: Miss Reeder had left, and Germany was now at war with America. Was that why he was here?

Straightening his gold-rimmed glasses, Dr Fuchs asked to see the Directress, so I escorted the men to Clara de Chambrun's office. Bitsi trailed us cautiously.

Used to officers in full Nazi regalia, the Countess remained blasé when he was announced. The same could not be said of the Bibliotheksschutz. His eyes bulged at the sight of a stranger at Miss Reeder's desk. He glanced around the office, then scowled at me as if I'd sequestered the Directress inside the massive safe.

"What is the meaning of this?" he demanded.

"Please meet the Countess Clara de Chambrun, who directs the Library," I said.

"Where is Miss Reeder?" He sounded worried.

"She's gone home," the Countess replied.

"I guaranteed that she would be under my protection here. Why did she leave?"

"Doubtless she considered an order to return more imperative than your guarantee."

Joining Bitsi in the corridor, I asked, "Why is he mad?"

"The Directress went away without saying goodbye. He's not mad, he's hurt."

Ah. I couldn't help but like him for loving Miss Reeder.

He interrogated the Countess about her qualifications, the value of the collection, and the Library's insurance policy. Satisfied, he laid out the rules, from no pay rises for staff to no selling off books. "I gave my word that this Library should be maintained," he said.

"Should the military authority interfere in any way, you'll find my numbers here and in Berlin in Miss Reeder's drawer. Call in case of trouble."

KRIEGSGEFANGENENPOST   30 November
                                                1942

Dear Odile,

Sorry I haven't written — no paper to be had. Many of us have ailments. My wound still gives me trouble. The guards aren't trying to kill us, but they're not trying to keep us alive, either. One said they don't have medicine for themselves.

My bunkmate Marcel is at it again. After the cow-milking fiasco, he drove the old frau's tractor into a ditch. He's as banged up as the tractor — when it tipped over, his arm was crushed underneath. The *Kommandant* offered to replace him, but she didn't want any more French help.

Another fellow works for a young widow who has the body of Mae West and the face of an (Aryan) angel. They've grown close, and when he talks about staying here after the war, we feel sorry for him.

She slipped him a radio in thanks for bringing in the harvest. Some of the Germans are as virulent as Hitler, but others are anti-Nazi and listen to the BBC. It's been hard to be cut off from you, from the entire world. We're thrilled to have daily news, though we don't always have daily bread.

I live for your letters and the hope of seeing you. I'm fortunate to have a caring family. Many never hear from home. If you're able to send Marcel Danez a packet of sweets, I know he'd be pleased.

Love,
Rémy

In the children's room, Bitsi bit her lip when she read the letter. Rémy meant well, but how could we send food to a stranger when there wasn't enough for family?

"*Bonjour, les filles,*" Margaret said as she entered. "Odile, why aren't you at the reference desk? Subscribers are queuing."

"We've had some news." I translated the letter.

Her brow furrowed. "Each month, you'll be able to send a proper package, I promise."

The following day, she brought in a small crate of dry sausage, cigarettes and chocolate.

"How?" I asked in wonder.

"Don't you worry about that."

Remembering the gilded portraits on her wall, I imagined Margaret selling off ancestors one by one, in order to feed Rémy. She was the dearest of friends.

20 December 1942

Dear Rémy,

We hope the package we sent got through. Does the cardigan fit? Do you recognise the colours? The yarn is from sweaters Maman saved from when we were children. Sorry the sleeves weren't the same length. In my case, practice doesn't make perfect.

Last night, Paul and I went to the Countess's production of Hamlet at the Odeon Theatre. It felt wonderful to do something ordinary like we did before the war. Bitsi and I are going to pick holly in the woods so we can decorate the bundles of books we deliver. Lately, there've been fewer requests, which is odd.

Bitsi misses you terribly. We all do. We want you home.

Love,
Odile

KRIEGSGEFANGENENPOST 1 February 1943

Dear Odile,

Thanks for the delicious food! Even more wonderful was seeing Marcel's face when he received the package. Please don't deprive yourselves for us. I never should have asked.

Everything's fine here. Except that Marcel
almost got killed. In the common room, a
few prisoners were huddled around the
radio, listening to the BBC, the sound no
more than a sigh, when the guards charged
in. The rest of us high-tailed out of there,
but poor Marcel was so engrossed he didn't
notice. The guards shattered the radio and
lined up all 100 of us in the courtyard — no
coats on, of course — promising to go easy
if we confessed. None of us admitted
anything. The *Kommandant* forced Marcel
to his knees and held a pistol to his head.
"Tell me who was with you, or I'll kill you."
Do you know what that jackass replied?
"Then I'll die alone."
Love,
Rémy

Paris
31 March 1943

Herr Kommandant,
I have written to the French police with no
results. Now I turn to you.
The American Library has caricatures of
Hitler in their collection, and anyone can
see them. That's not all. As I mentioned to
the police, librarians smuggle books to
Jewish subscribers, including banned books
that no one should be reading.

Librarian Bitsi Joubert says vile things about German soldiers. She has one billeted in her apartment, and God only knows how she abuses him. Volunteer Margaret Saint James buys food from the black market. To look at her plump cheeks, you wouldn't know many people are practically starving. Subscriber Geoffrey de Nerciat donates money to Résistants and lodges them in his grand apartment.

In the back room of the Library, subscriber Robert Pryce-Jones listens to the BBC, though it's strictly forbidden. And that is not the only annoying noise one hears. The creaking of footsteps echoes from the attic — locked at all times — and I wonder what or who the librarians are hiding.

Pay a visit and see for yourself.
Signed,
One who knows

CHAPTER
THIRTY

ODILE

Paris, April 1943

When the post arrived, I set the fashion magazines on the shelves. *Mode du Jour* reminded readers that "Intelligence and taste aren't rationed", and that while shoes get worn out, hats never do, I missed *Time* and *Life*. I turned to commiserate with the man beside me, one I'd never seen before. Once I would have taken in his pinched lips and green tweed suit and assumed he was an uptight professor. Now, I'd say a mole. I swallowed. Paranoia. Nazi propaganda had got to me. Surely he was harmless, though he did tuck an old journal into his jacket.

I scowled. "Periodicals stay here."

He put it back on the shelf and stalked out.

"Brava!" Boris applauded. "You're as intimidating as Madame Mimoun at the National Library, a real dragon."

I curtsied. "I try."

When Bitsi arrived at work, she merely nodded in greeting. These days, she was so quiet that it frightened me. Wanting to keep an eye on her, I insisted that I needed help delivering books to Professor Cohen. We climbed the escargot stairs to the second floor, where the Professor lifted the hefty biographies from our arms.

"I've finished my novel." She gestured to the pile of paper on the table.

"Congratulations!" I said.

I was surprised to see that the jaunty spark in her eye was extinguished, and disappointment had taken up residence.

She sighed. "The editor won't publish it."

I was sure of the reason, and I knew she was, too. No French publisher could publish a work by a Jewish author.

"I'm sorry," I said.

"I am, too," she said. "In any case, I could never have finished it without you. Not only for the books you brought for my research, but your company and kindness. You became my window to Paris. Books and ideas are like blood; they need to circulate, and they keep us alive. You've reminded me that there's good in the world."

I should have been thrilled at such praise. Instead, a cold dread settled into my bones. "It sounds like you're saying goodbye."

"I'm saying we don't know what will happen." She presented me with the manuscript. "Please keep it safe."

Honoured by her trust, I kissed her on each cheek. "Are you sure you don't want to send it to a colleague?"

"This is the only copy. The novel will be safer with you."

"What's it called?" Bitsi asked.

"*La Bibliothèque Américaine.*" The American Library.

"Then it's definitely a drama!" Bitsi replied.

"Wait until you meet the characters. What a cast of originals!" The Professor winked. "You'll certainly recognise a few."

Light, 535; manuscripts, 091; libraries, 027.

By the time she saw us out, she seemed to be in better spirits. In the stairwell, Bitsi and I heard the spry tap-a-tat-tat of the typewriter. I hoped that the Professor was working on the sequel.

On the way back to work, Bitsi said, "It's a big responsibility."

I stuffed the pages in my satchel. "We'll put it in the safe."

Turning on to our street, we passed three giggly *filles de joie* in fishnet stockings. Yellow hair dishevelled, the plump trio sashayed past in a haze of pungent perfume.

"Sluts!" Bitsi swatted at the smell. "Some people don't know there's a war on," she continued loudly as we entered the Library. "Yesterday morning, I saw a gaggle of harlots staggering home. They reeked of alcohol. There's such a thing as showing good taste!"

In the back room, I set the manuscript on the table and sat Bitsi down. "The wrong people get the right things," she said, her voice raw. "I'm hungry. I can't think. Seasons go by, but I don't miss the days. Christmas, New Year, I'm glad they're gone. Now it's

Easter, and the only thing that will rise again are prices. I miss Rémy. If it weren't for him I might —"

"Let's write to him." Her despair frightened me. Rémy would help — thinking about him always made us feel better. I pulled a pencil from my bag. "You use small letters, I'll use capitals."

dear REMY, *greetings* FROM *the* LIBRARY *where* WE *are* MISSING *you.* ODILE *suggested* THIS *crazy* BRILLIANT *idea.*

"The letter resembles a ransom note," she said. "Who knows if he'll receive it?"

"At least we'll confound the censors."

Bitsi half smiled. It was enough.

"Do you think Professor Cohen would mind if we take a peek at her novel?" she asked.

Torn between respecting the Professor's privacy and comforting Bitsi, I turned over the title page and read aloud: "The Afterlife is filled with the heavenly scent of musty books. Its walls are lined with tall bookshelves full of forgotten tomes. In this cosy mezzanine between worlds, there are no windows nor clocks, though an occasional echo of children's laughter or whiff of a chocolate croissant wafts in from the ground floor."

"It's my favourite section of the Library," Bitsi said.

"Mine, too."

I was about to read the next line when we heard a woman shout, "I'm sick of waiting! Give me my books, or else!"

"Oh, dear. Another scuffle."

Rushing to the circulation desk, where half a dozen subscribers waited to borrow books, Bitsi and I found

316

that even Clara de Chambrun had emerged from her office. "What on earth is going on?" she demanded.

"Mrs Smythe is tired of waiting," Boris told the Countess. To the subscriber, he said, "Please be patient and go back to your place in the queue."

"I'll inform the police," she snarled.

"That we're inefficient?" He raised a brow. "You could turn in the entire country."

People in the queue chuckled at his observation.

"I'll denounce you for catering to Jews."

"That's it!" The Countess seized Mrs Smythe by the arm and led her to the door. "Never come back again."

The subscriber began to sob. "I cannot get along without the books I find here."

At the circulation desk, well before the Library opened to the public, while Boris and I tucked cards back into the pockets of returned books, I let my thoughts drift to Paul. At noon, we'd meet at the apartment, the one place where disappointment never walked through the door. We'd laze in the rosy boudoir, where his sketches of Brittany hung on the wall. I loved each one: a wheat field bordered by poppies, mounds of golden hay, the old swayback horse.

An insistent rapping brought me back. I saw Dr Fuchs peering through the window. Why had he come so early, and alone? We invited him in, but he wouldn't budge from the step.

"Be careful," he whispered. "The Gestapo is laying traps. Don't let banned works fall into their hands.

317

They'll use any pretext to arrest you." He glanced over his shoulder. "I can't be seen here."

"What kind of traps?" I asked, but he'd already rushed away.

"I've heard the Gestapo is taking control of Paris," Boris said as he lit a cigarette, "and that they're even more dangerous."

More dangerous than the Nazis who'd defeated the French army? More dangerous than the *Soldaten* who patrolled day and night?

We worked the rest of the morning in a troubled silence.

When I left the Library at lunchtime, I was surprised to find Paul in the courtyard. "Weren't we meeting at the apartment?" I asked. These days I muddled everything.

"My friend and his girl went yesterday. There was new furniture mixed with the old stuff, but he didn't think anything of it. They were, uh, kissing when they heard someone come in. They hid for a while, then sneaked out through the servants' stairs. He went back later, but the lock had been changed."

Our nest had vanished, the place we could hold each other; the place we could say anything, or nothing at all; the place we could forget the war.

"What about your sketches?" I asked glumly.

"I'll draw new ones." He put his arm around my waist. "Cheer up, I found us a new place."

On the street, we encountered Madame Simon. "Where do you think you're going?" she demanded.

318

Still distraught from losing the apartment, I tried to swallow.

"Mademoiselle Souchet has a right to take lunch," Paul answered.

"Just so you're back at one," madame told me.

"Mademoiselle doesn't answer to you," he said, his grasp tightening as he steered me down the pavement.

"You didn't need to be abrupt," I told him. "She's like crotchety Aunt March in *Little Women*. Gruff on the outside, but kind deep down."

"Not everyone has a deep down."

"And not everyone is a criminal," I said lightly.

"Some people are exactly what they present to the world." We stopped in front of a grand Haussmannian building. "This is the place."

In the foyer, our footfall was muted by a plush crimson carpet. Gazing at the golden chandelier, I had the tingly feeling of déjà vu. Perhaps I'd delivered books here.

Upstairs in the apartment, the brocade curtains were drawn. I didn't care about the view, I only cared about Paul. I wanted an hour when we could forget everything. As he kissed my breasts, my belly, my bottom, my whole body crackled.

Afterwards, still naked, we visited our new place as if it were a museum, admiring the Chinese vases on the mantle, the Old Masters on the wall. But the best was the kitchen: chocolate in the cupboard. The new place wasn't so bad — exploring was exciting.

But we were running late, so I tossed the dress shirt and trousers to Paul. He slipped them on but didn't fasten them; instead, he helped do up the back of my blouse. Behind me, almost reverently, he kissed my nape as he fastened the mother-of-pearl buttons. It was in these tender moments that I loved him the most.

Caught up in my feelings, I barely registered the click of the lock, the squeak of the hinges.

"Who the hell are you?" a barrel-chested man demanded.

Barefoot and dishevelled, Paul and I jumped apart.

"This is my place now."

I inched towards the door. Paul grasped my hand and pulled me to him. "We thought —"

"Get out! And stay the hell away."

Heads hung low, we slunk back to the Library, embarrassed to have been caught. Where would we meet now? Another question was forming, too. *Whose apartment was it?* "We didn't do anything wrong," Paul said. He gave me a peck on the cheek and continued on to the police station. *Whose apartment?* Flustered, I entered the periodical section before recalling I worked in the reference room. With no current newspapers, few people spent time here, so it was surprising to see someone digging through old magazines.

"May I assist you?"

"I notice some subscribers are foreigners." He looked familiar. Ah, yes, the man in tweed who'd tried to abscond with a journal.

"One of our many points of pride. Everyone feels at home here."

"I'd like to contact them."

320

"We destroyed our records. We didn't want them to fall into the wrong hands," I said tartly and strode to the circulation desk, where Boris and Bitsi chatted, heads tilted together.

"He asked where I'm from," Boris whispered. "I told him I'm Parisian."

"He comes here more and more," Bitsi said. "When he's behind me, I can feel his sour breath on my neck."

I slipped my foot over hers.

"What did he want?" Boris said.

"He asked about our foreign subscribers."

"Speaking of foreigners," Bitsi said, "where's Margaret?"

She should have arrived by now.

"Phone her," Boris said.

I called her throughout the afternoon but no one answered. What if she'd been arrested like Miss Wedd? No, there was a reason she hadn't come, a perfectly reasonable reason. I looked at my watch. Its face remained impassive, its hands refused to move. Holding my wrist to my ear, I listened for the watch's faint pulse. Panic rose in my chest, making it hard to breathe.

"Go," Boris urged. "We can take care of things here."

I made one more call, then rushed to Margaret's.

CHAPTER
THIRTY-ONE

ODILE

Paris, July 1943

The butler answered the door.

"Is Margaret in?" I asked, anxiously looking past him into the flat.

Imperturbable as ever, he led me to her room, where she lay in bed, surrounded by crumpled handkerchiefs. I embraced her.

"Thank God you're here. We feared you'd been arrested!"

"I'm ill," she rasped. "I tried to ring, but couldn't get through. The phone's been down all week."

I perched beside her. "I even asked Paul to come in case we had to file a missing-persons report."

"You needn't worry." There was a sureness in her tone.

"Of course I worry! The city's overrun with Nazis."

"I'm telling you, you needn't worry." She peered towards the hall to make sure no servants milled about, before whispering, "I met someone."

"We meet new someones every day."

"No, I *met* someone."

Was she trying to say she had a beau? "At the Library?"

"No. I didn't want to frighten you . . . but I was arrested."

"Arrested?" I shouted.

"Shh! This is exactly why I didn't tell you."

Grasping the blue silk of the bedspread, I wondered how she could keep such a thing from me. Of course, it didn't occur to me that I hadn't told her that Paul and I were engaged.

"After I was released, Felix gave me a document that allows freedom of movement."

She called him by his first name? Did that mean he was her beau? It was too much to take in. She kept company with the enemy. She'd kept a secret. My whole body tightened in anger.

"Did you say Paul is coming?" She moved to the dressing table and powdered her pink nose.

Now I was the one eyeing the hall. "You're not well enough for company," I said stiffly. "I should go."

"Don't do what Parisians do, when they conceal their true feelings behind a stiff veil of politeness."

"I don't know what you're talking about."

"If you want to go, go. But don't pretend it's because I have a cold." Our gazes met in the mirror. Mine was troubled, hers resolute. "If Felix hadn't freed me and three elderly ladies from that dank cell, we'd be mouldering in an internment camp. And what would my daughter have done then? Think about that."

Her words sank in. She could have disappeared like our Miss Wedd. I had to stop jumping to conclusions, stop judging. I was as bad as Madame Simon.

"I'm sorry," I said. "The most important thing is that you're safe. Are you certain you're up to having company?"

"I'm only dizzy when I stand. Ask Isa to ready a tea tray. I'll join you shortly."

In the sitting room, the gouty men in gilded frames were still here. Each time Margaret had proffered a package for Rémy, I'd felt guilty, imagining these paintings ripped from the wall, sold in order to purchase supplies. But if the portraits were here, how had she obtained the food?

She'd asked her Nazi.

Margaret and a Nazi. How odd to put the two together. They belonged in separate books, on separate shelves. But as the war went on, people became entangled. Things that were black and white — like print on the page — mingled to form a murky grey.

When Paul arrived, I pulled him close.

"What's wrong?" He kissed the top of my head.

"Nothing. I'm glad to see you, glad you're you."

"I can't believe these portraits. It's like the Louvre in here."

"All that glitters isn't integrity," I said.

"Huh?"

Margaret swept in. She did love to make an entrance. Paul and I stepped apart.

"Sorry to have taken you away from work, Paul. It was kind of you to come. Odile is lucky to have you."

His ears went red, and he grinned bashfully. "Always a pleasure to see you."

I elbowed him to remind him that we weren't here to make small talk. He needed to warn her about the danger — I wasn't convinced that a flimsy piece of paper from her beau could protect her.

"They say the Krauts have interned over two thousand foreign women," he said firmly in English.

"I know," she said.

"You're in danger here," he said. "You should leave."

"You two could have fled to the Free Zone in the south," Margaret argued. "You've stayed."

"I need to stay where Rémy can find me."

"I want to be with Odile," Paul said. "Think about your daughter."

"London isn't safe, either." Margaret coughed into her handkerchief.

"Be careful," he said. "If you see Germans coming, cross the street."

No one could avoid Nazis, not even at the Library, and I knew Margaret didn't particularly want to.

A week later, Margaret cornered me in the cloakroom and thrust a box with a silver ribbon at me. I opened it and smelled the chocolate — black-market gold. My stomach gurgled. I didn't want her ill-gotten goods, but couldn't stop myself from taking a piece. As the milky chocolate melted in my mouth, I wondered what she'd done to get such luxuries, I wondered what else she'd received. Silk? Steak? What were their Dewey numbers? The closest I got was 629 for silkworms and 636.2 for cattle. I couldn't find the right numbers. I couldn't believe all she had while the rest of us went without.

"During the Library's annual closure, Felix and I are going on holiday. Deauville is supposed to be delightful. Nanny will watch Christina, and if anyone asks, I'll say I stayed with you . . ." Still on her cloud of happiness, Margaret floated out to the reading room.

The chocolates were delicious. I'd send the rest to Rémy. I would. After one more piece.

That evening, while Boris and the Countess went over the budget in her office, I manned the circulation desk. When the phone rang, I expected to be asked to deliver books, "I demand to see Clara de Chambrun." The caller spoke in French with a slight German accent. "Let us say nine thirty tomorrow. Tell her to enter directly, and express my regrets at not being able to call at the Library." He didn't give me a chance to reply before hanging up. What did Dr Fuchs want with the Countess? Would we lose another friend?

Upstairs, I peeked into the Countess's office. When Boris noticed me, his brows rose in concern. Of course, he knew something was wrong, he was a librarian — part psychologist, bartender, bouncer and detective.

"I have a message," I said.

The Countess peered over her reading glasses. "Well, what is it?"

"I'm afraid Dr Fuchs insists on seeing you at his office tomorrow," I said.

"Oh, does he?"

"You and the General should leave town," Boris said.

"So they can arrest you in my place?" she replied. "What exactly did he say?"

I repeated his message.

"I'll accompany you," Boris said.

I didn't want him to go — he had a wife and little girl who depended on him. I tried to find a convincing argument. He had the keys, so he had to be here to open in the morning? No, he would simply hand them to me.

"From what I've seen," I said slowly, "Dr Fuchs has a soft spot for women. It's better if I accompany the Countess."

"I'm not taking you to pay a call on a Nazi!" she said. "What would your parents say?"

"Honestly, my father didn't want me to work with the capitalist foreigners here, either. Papa's a *commissaire*, so my family has already had dealings with Nazis." I said this only to win the argument. I never thought about how my father spent his days, or with whom.

"Are you certain about accompanying me?" she asked.

I was afraid to go to Nazi headquarters, but as I considered the leather-bound books on the Countess's shelves, the novels I delivered to subscribers, and Professor Cohen's manuscript hidden in the safe, I decided that words were worth fighting for, that they were worth the risk.

"Absolutely."

There was no time to dwell on what might or might not happen — we were too busy running the Library. I returned to the circulation desk, where Madame Simon demanded, "Where the devil have you been? I could have walked right out with these books!"

When the last subscriber had left for the day, I shoved Professor Cohen's books into my satchel and hurried up the boulevard. It was just past seven, but the murky silhouettes of buildings loomed. I'd grown up in the city and felt as safe on the avenues as I did in Maman's arms. But tonight, each time I glanced behind me, the man in the tweed suit was there. When I crossed the street, he did, too. I looked back; he stopped and leafed through a magazine at the kiosk. I walked briskly. He continued, as if on an evening stroll, a scowl on his sinister face. In the shadows, I saw his briefcase in one hand, and in the other . . . the glint of a gun, its barrel staring at me.

Taking a sharp right, I leaned against the grimy building. My legs twitched, urging me to break into a run. I peeked around the corner. As he drew closer, I saw that what I'd thought was a barrel of a gun was a rolled-up magazine, probably purchased at the kiosk.

I went out of my way to lose him, scurrying along posh rue du Faubourg Saint-Honoré, past Hermès, then the presidential palace, looking for a place to hide. I wasn't far from Le Bristol, where Miss Reeder had stayed at the beginning of the Occupation. I'd delivered books to infirm guests there. I broke into a run, and before the doorman could reach his post, I threw open the door and dived towards the front desk, where I begged the concierge to let me out the back way. He whisked me across the sumptuous oval salon, through a *trompe-l'oeil* door, into the cacophonous kitchen, and on to a side street.

As I caught my breath, I wondered if I should deliver the books or go straight home. I decided that I had a right to see whomever I liked.

"I wasn't sure you were coming," Professor Cohen said.

"I took the long way."

She ran a hand over the book cover as lovingly as Maman caressed my face. The Professor had borrowed *Good Morning, Midnight* at least ten times. When I asked why she liked it so much, she replied, "Jean Rhys is fearless. She tells the truth, and writes for the forlorn and the vulnerable."

I opened to a random page, the way I usually did to get to know a book. *Paris is looking very nice tonight . . . You are looking very nice tonight, my beautiful, my darling, and oh what a bitch you can be!* I cringed. That wasn't how I thought of my city, not at all.

Seeing my reaction, the Professor said, "Remember, Rhys is describing Paris as a foreigner with little money and no one to help her."

I loved Professor Cohen, and wanted to love what she loved. "Promise you'll let me read it when you've finished. Do you think I'll like it?"

She drew her shawl tighter around her, "I'm not sure. There's no happy ending."

At 9 a.m, the next morning, the Countess and her husband waited in their car in front of my building. The General's bowler covered most of his white hair. Like

329

many Parisians, he had bags under his eyes. When he pressed down on the accelerator, the Peugeot ambled over the cobbles like an old nag who didn't want to be ridden. From the back seat, I noted that he spent more time watching his wife than he did the road. We putted up the Champs-Élysées, past the Arc de Triomphe, and arrived at the Majestic Hotel, Dr Fuchs's office.

"Shall I come with you?" the General asked.

"We're perfectly capable of answering a few questions."

"Then I'll wait," he said, gripping the wheel.

The lobby was empty. A dowdy blonde — Parisians called these German women "grey mice" because of their drab uniforms — led us to Dr Fuchs's sparse office. Seated stiffly at his desk, the Bibliotheksschutz appeared as perturbed as we felt. When he didn't stand to greet us, as was proper, I knew something was very wrong. In French, he warned, "You must speak the truth."

The Countess drew herself up. "There's no question about the Library that we will not answer fully."

"We received an anonymous letter accusing the Library of circulating anti-Hitler tracts."

We'd been denounced?

"These caricatures were discovered in your collection." He thrust a file at the Countess.

She flipped through the pages. "The drawings date from before the war, and periodicals like these never go beyond the reading room." She placed the file on his desk. "I assure you that I would never betray the institution I promised to safeguard."

"If they've been circulated," I said tartly, "it's because one of your compatriots carried them off. I saw one try to steal a journal."

"Hush," the Countess whispered. "Think before you speak."

"I know that you also circulate banned books," he said.

"You told Miss Reeder that we didn't have to destroy them," I argued.

At the mention of the Directress, his stance softened. "That's true. But from now on, you must keep them under lock and key." He drew a long breath. "Mesdames, it appears we have found a solution." Switching to English, perhaps so the Grey Mouse eavesdropping in the corridor wouldn't understand, he added, "I am most happy for you. I will not conceal that I am also very happy for myself."

He rose, and we knew the meeting was over. Noting that even Dr Fuchs was cautious around the Grey Mouse, the Countess and I remained silent on the way out.

On the way back to the Library, I wondered about Dr Fuchs's odd declaration. Perhaps if we'd been found guilty of wrongdoing, so would he, as the administrator of libraries in the Occupied Zone.

When the Countess and I crossed the threshold, Boris drew a flask from the drawer and poured some bourbon into three teacups. The Countess eased on to a chair and took a sip. Quickly, I explained the allegations.

"Does Fuchs know about our special deliveries?" Boris asked.

"I don't believe so," she said. "But after such a close call, I've decided that instead of waiting until August for the annual closure, it would be best to close the Library to the public tomorrow."

Bastille Day. Another holiday with no reason to celebrate.

CHAPTER
THIRTY-TWO

BORIS

Paris, July 1943

Boris and Anna always played cards at the neighbours' on Tuesday evenings. War or no war, Occupation or no Occupation. They went to the Ivanovs' for a glass of wine and a light dinner that got lighter each week. Hélène played with Nadia in the bedroom. Behind closed doors, Bach on the gramophone, the shutters drawn, the couples unwound over slices of *solo*. At the table, able to confide, the way one may with old friends, Vladimir spoke of the pupil he and Marina hid in the attic of their school. His parents had vanished, and he'd hidden at home for three days before telling anyone. Though he was only thirteen, Francis ate like a workhorse, and it was hard to acquire extra rations.

Talk turned to their own children. Boris loved listening to Anna speak about Hélène. Her tone became tender. Her eyes, too. Though she was exhausted from queuing for bread, for butter, for everything, Anna hadn't let the war write anything on her face. No worry lines, no anger. At times, his shoulders slumped, defeated and, yes, bitter about this life — after all, they'd fled the Revolution only to be confronted with a war. But Anna sat straight as ever, until her strength became his.

After the plates were cleared away, Boris shuffled and dealt the cards, Anna beamed when she saw her hand, and he was glad.

A knock on the door. Startled, they looked at each other. Maybe it's something, maybe nothing. The person will go away. We'll wait.

Bam! Bam! Bam! on the door. Though their eyes met, the friends said nothing. Vladimir, Marina and Anna put down their cards. Boris kept his. Vladimir went to the door and squinted through *le judas*. His back stiffened, confirming what Boris knew. Gestapo.

Ah, they've caught us — playing cards and listening to Bach, while our children play make-believe in the bedroom. Vladimir opened the door slowly. Four Nazis pushed past. One pointed a gun at Vladimir. Two tore into the books on the shelves, another ripped the cushions from the divan. Damn snoops, they were never satisfied. Perhaps they'd found out about the boy. Vladimir and Marina were teachers, not revolutionaries, yet here they were, in trouble for helping a child. Why else would the Nazis be here? Not that Nazis needed a reason.

Boris was no longer surprised to see such men. Parisians had seen the Nazis at their best, boots polished, buying trinkets for their mothers back home. And at their worst. Too much to drink, stumbling down the streets. Red-faced after a blunt rejection by a *Parisienne*. Of course, Nazis had seen Parisians at their worst. Hungry and resentful, snapping at each other in the queue at the butcher's. No, they were intimate enemies. On top of each other, beside each other, beside themselves.

The Nazi with the pistol snarled something in German. Anna, Marina and Boris had remained seated at the table. This enraged him, why were they sitting there so calmly?

"Get up!" he shouted in French.

Anna rose with the grace of a czarina rising from a throne. She would not show she was scared. It would prove that they'd won.

"You, by the door," the Nazi told Vladimir. "Stand with the others. Hands up!"

They raised their hands, and Boris realised he still held his cards.

The gun was aimed at Boris. Would they arrest him? Russia and America were both at war with Germany, and he was a Franco-Russian working at an American institution. Yes, now he recognised the man brandishing the pistol, though the weasel had worn a tweed suit when he'd rifled through the collection, searching for evidence of betrayal. The snoop had been in the reading room so often that Odile said, "Someone needs to tell the bastard that the decent thing for him to do would be to pay for a Library subscription."

That Odile! He'd laughed. He laughed.

The Luger went off. Pain bounded through Boris's body. Blood soaked through his whitish shirt. He let go of his cards. They fluttered and fell to his feet. The pain was too much. He swayed. And in that last dance, he thought, *Tell the children I love them. Anna, oh, Anna. You know all that I feel.*

He didn't remember falling, didn't feel his head hit the floor. He sensed Anna beside him, saw the red run down his shirt over her ashen hands. He heard the Nazis shout. It was all too much. Boris longed to slip up the spiral staircase, to walk along secluded rows of books, to lose himself in the sweet quiet of the Afterlife.

CHAPTER
THIRTY-THREE

LILY

Froid, Montana, August 1987

Mary Louise's sister Angel reigned from the front page of the *Froid Promoter*. Homecoming queen. Bikini-clad car-wash diva raising money for orphans or cheerleading camp. Her gaze could turn a grown man's brain to manure. Mary Louise and I spent hours wondering how we could be like her. To get some conclusive answers, we snuck into Angel's room, ears pricked for trouble, like any sign of Sue Bob coming down the hall. A whiff of danger blended with the sickeningly sweet scent of Giorgio perfume.

Mary Louise pawed through the dresser drawers. On her finger dangled a black bra with cups so big they could hold softballs. We caressed Angel's angora sweaters, softer than skin, and held them up to our flat chests. What would it be like to feel Robby's hand creep under the sweater, wanting to get at me? Delicious. Under the bed, I found a shoe box filled with corsages of proms past and a pink plastic container. Inside, pills wound around like a snail shell. The birth control in my palm was like a gun — both had the power to stop the human body. I plucked a pill from the foil, but Mary Louise told me to put it back.

On the vanity, make-up was laid out on a tray like a surgeon's instruments. The blue liner made Angel's eyes seem like endless oceans. When we tried, it looked like someone had gone crazy with a Bic. Finally, we lost ourselves in the closet, full of silky Gunne Sax dresses. Feeling them was like holding hands with the heavens.

When I got home, Odile and Eleanor were on the couch, waiting.

"Sue Bob called," Eleanor said grimly as she rose.

I couldn't believe the intelligence report made it home before I did.

"You know it's wrong to snoop." Eleanor wasn't mad. She seemed . . . concerned. "How would you like it if I went through your things?"

"Go ahead!" I said bitterly. "I don't have any secrets."

"*Ma grande*", Odile said, standing as well, "everyone has secrets and private feelings. Your dad, Eleanor, me. Be grateful for what people tell you, when they're ready to talk. Try to accept their limits, and understand that their limits usually have nothing to do with you."

Seeing I didn't know what to make of Odile's advice, Eleanor simplified: "Don't snoop. You'll get yourself into trouble."

"Why am I the one getting lectured when Angel's the one with the birth control pills?"

Eleanor gasped, filling me with satisfaction.

Odile's fingers dug into my arms. "Listen carefully: there is nothing worse than divulging someone's secrets. Why would you tell us — or anyone — Angel's private concerns? Are you trying to get her into trouble? Ruin her reputation? Hurt her?"

"I guess I didn't think —"

Odile scowled at me. "Well, next time, think! And keep your mouth shut."

"No one likes a tattletale," Eleanor added. She and Odile settled back on the couch, back into their conversation.

"So you think I should go?" Odile asked. For once, she was the one who sounded unsure.

"Go where?" I asked.

"Chicago!" Eleanor squealed.

"Chicago," I sighed, wishing I could get away from people watching my every move, could go to a city full of skyscrapers and fancy restaurants, "You have to go!"

"I haven't taken the train since I came here over forty years ago. And that's how long it's been since I've seen my friend Lucienne."

"Why didn't you go before?" I asked.

"She invited us, but Buck never wanted to. After he died, I was in the habit of saying no."

"Think of the stores and theatres!" Eleanor said. "Why, if I had the chance . . . And wouldn't it be wonderful to see your friend?"

"She wants me to come for a whole month."

"Lily and I could drive you to the train station," Eleanor said.

"I'll think about it," Odile said, which in my experience meant no.

In bed that night, as I dozed while reading *Homecoming*, the sounds of an argument slid under the door into my room. "Sue Bob can't control her daughters and thinks she can tell me how to raise mine?" Dad said. "Angel's a lost cause, and Mary Louise is following in her footsteps."

"Nonsense," Eleanor said. "Mary Louise is just high-spirited."

Gratitude engulfed my sleepy heart. The door creaked open, and Eleanor's Isotoner slippers whispered along the carpet. She turned off my lamp.

"Thanks," I whispered.

"For what?"

For not getting mad about my snooping. For encouraging Odile. For seeing the best in Mary Louise. For understanding. I didn't say any of this, but only snuggled under the comforter feeling happier than I had in a long time.

Ten days later, Eleanor and I drove Odile to the station in Wolf Point. From the back seat, I watched the barren land pass by and wished I was the one leaving.

As we waited on the platform, Odile asked, "What if she's changed? What if we don't get along? I'll be stuck."

"You can come home early," Eleanor said. "Froid will still be here."

"It's not Froid I'll miss," Odile replied.

My foot slid over hers. "I'll miss you, too."

The Empire Builder chugged to a stop, and she boarded. On the empty platform, Eleanor and I waved as Odile slipped away.

* * *

Two weeks later, at dinner, as I cut Joe's chicken, I asked Dad about taking driver's ed again. "Mary Louise already has her licence."

"Why compare yourself to others? You're a beautiful, unique girl."

I dabbed at the ketchup that covered Joe's face. "I'm unique all right, the last one in my class to get a learner's permit." I wanted to tell him he couldn't keep me hermetically sealed in this house for ever. Mary Louise had taught me to drive on the dirt road that led to the dump. It wasn't that hard.

"After what happened to the Flynn girl, I'd be worried sick," he said. "I don't want you taking any chances."

Jess Flynn had been in a pick-up with boys who were drinking and driving. When the Ford flipped off the road, she was killed instantly. Our town had mourned her death for five years.

"Teens don't drink and drive to and from school," Eleanor argued. "Nothing wrong with a young woman having a little independence, and isn't it best that she gets some practice under her belt before she goes off to college?"

Dad accused her of being on my side so that I would like her. She started clearing the table, throwing the silverware on to the plates. Now I was stuck in the middle of their fight, one I'd accidentally started.

After dinner, Mary Louise came over. Cross-legged on the floor, backs against my bed, we listened to The Cure.

341

"Dad and Eleanor are at it again," I said. "Wish I could escape to Chicago."

"It'd take for ever to save up. You'll be able to when you're thirty."

"When I'm too old to enjoy it."

"Lily," Eleanor squawked from down the hall. "Turn down that music, it's scaring Benjy! Why don't you two go water Odile's plants? They're probably half dead by now."

Odile's living room seemed the same — a basket of yarn near the chair, the coffee table that displayed my crafts: a lavender sachet, a leather bookmark — but no Bach played, no one asked about our day. The house didn't smell like freshly baked cookies; the musty odour made the place feel empty. With the curtains drawn, with Odile gone, the room felt like a body without a soul.

The whole house was open to us. We could do anything we liked. And we'd never have this chance again. I opened a drawer, but there was nothing but old newspaper clippings.

"What are you looking for anyway?" Mary Louise asked as she drizzled water on the crispy ferns.

"Clues." I wanted to discover the things Odile would never tell. I grabbed books from the shelves, hoping to find another photo, a love letter, a diary. The forbidden was exciting. And how else do you find things out? *Don't snoop. You'll get yourself into trouble.* I felt a soupçon of guilt, but I continued to flick through the pages.

342

"You might not know Odile as well as you think. What if she was in love with a Nazi?"

I remembered the photo of the "Library Protector". He hadn't been bad looking, for a Nazi. I shook my head. "No way! She was in the Resistance, cracking codes hidden in books. I bet she was in love with one of the resisters, oh, and maybe he was killed on a secret mission."

"She didn't laugh for a whole year," Mary Louise added on to the story. "But then she saw Mr Gustafson, and he helped her smile again. How'd they meet, anyway?"

I took a guess. "He parachuted into France and was shot down by the enemy. He was taken to the hospital, where she volunteered once a week."

"But when she met him, she volunteered every day."

We studied Odile's wedding photo. Mouth tight, she looked at the camera. Buck stared down at her, his eyes dumb with love.

"Can't you see him lying in the hospital bed, gazing up at her in adoration?" I asked.

"And she liked him too, but she couldn't say, because back then women had to pretend to be shy."

"Definitely." I imagined Odile in a beret, defying the Gestapo the same way she stood up to Dad. I bet she hid Jews in her apartment. "If Odile had hidden Anne Frank, she'd be alive today."

"Totally," Mary Louise said. "Let's see what else she has!"

We left the books in a heap and headed to the bedroom, Mary Louise disappeared into the closet. "A jewellery box! Bet it's full of rubies from an old lover!"

I followed her inside. Both of us barely fit. My cheek brushed against the sleeves of Odile's blouses. On a peg, a black lace nightie — something so sensual that just seeing it made us blush — shimmered. Buck's gun was propped up in the corner. We shouldn't have been in Odile's bedroom, in her closet, in her things. I knew that. But I couldn't stop caressing her cashmere cardigans, folded like they were still in the store.

Mary Louise pointed to a white box on the second highest shelf. I grabbed it, and she opened the gold clasp.

"It's not locked," I marvelled.

"Bummer." She held up a bunch of paper.

"Maybe they're love letters!"

This was what I'd hoped for, a piece of Odile's past, penned by a beau. Buck or someone else, someone dashing and foreign. The paper was crisp as bacon and yellowed with age. I grabbed the first page. Its feminine, flowing handwriting resembled Odile's. Not from a lover, then. The French wasn't easy to understand. The letter was full of words like "cavort" that I'd seen once and long since abandoned in the back of my brain.

Paris
12 May 1941

Monsieur l'Inspecteur,
Why aren't you looking for undeclared Jews
in hiding? Here is the address of Professor
Cohen at 35 rue Blanche. She used to teach
so-called literature at the Sorbonne. Now

344

she invites students to her home for lectures
so she can cavort with colleagues and
students, mostly male — at her age!

When she ventures out, you see her
coming a kilometre away in that swishy
purple cape, a peacock feather askew in her
hair. Ask the Jewess for her baptism
certificate and passport, you'll see her
religion noted there. While good Frenchmen
and women work, Madame le Professeur sits
around and reads books.

My indications are exact, now it's up to
you.

Signed,
One who knows

Hatred from more than forty years ago rose from the page. Was this why Odile wouldn't talk about her past, because the words were so ugly?

I felt as if I were standing in a snow globe that someone had shaken, only the pieces inside weren't glued down, and everything swirled around — the brick house, the lamppost, the stray cat, the police car. We all went careening with the snow that was not snow, just jaundiced scraps of paper, decaying confetti that I'd made from the letter.

Mary Louise smacked me. "Why'd you rip it up?"

"What?" I said, still dazed.

She pointed to the scraps at our feet. "She'll find out for sure. We're in trouble."

Nothing made sense any more. "I don't care."

345

The photo of the "Library Protector" flashed into my mind. Odile kept it with pictures of loved ones. Maybe she'd dated the Nazi, and maybe she'd helped him in his work. After all, she'd never returned to France, and her family never visited. Maybe they'd disowned her.

"What did the letter say?"

I didn't want her to know how horrible people were, I didn't want to share my suspicions about what Odile had done. If she wasn't the one who wrote that letter, why did she have it?

"What'd it say?" she repeated.

"I don't understand."

"That's okay." She patted my back. "Maybe you don't speak French as well as you think you do."

We'd found the clue I'd wanted. And now . . . I felt cold. And sick to my stomach.

"If you don't understand that one, read another." She pointed to the letters in the box.

"There's nothing to understand. They're trash. Old trash." I tried to rip them up, but Mary Louise snatched the letters and folded them exactly the way we'd found them.

"I want to go home," I said.

"Maybe you're right. Maybe we should go."

"Yes, maybe you should," Odile said.

Odile.

We turned to face her. Her brows were raised, curled like question marks. What were we doing in her room? What were these bits of paper at our feet?

She was happy to see me. I could see it in the lift of her lips, in her gentle gaze.

Mary Louise and I were used to getting in trouble, though we'd never been caught red-handed. Part of me wanted to apologise to Odile for invading her privacy, but most of me wanted *her* to apologise for that nasty letter, for teaching me those horrible French words, for making me think she'd been in the Resistance when she was just a liar.

"Was it you who took my books from the shelves?" Her voice was gentle.

Dropping the letters, Mary Louise pushed past me and ran off. But if Odile had taught me one thing, it was to stand my ground. I looked her straight in the eye. Straight into her soft brown eyes. "Who are you?"

CHAPTER
THIRTY-FOUR

ODILE

Paris, 19 July 1943

Bitsi didn't bother with *bonjour*. She barged into my bedroom, where I was writing to Rémy at my desk. Bedraggled and out of breath, she announced, "Boris was playing cards!"

"Cards?"

"And then he was shot!"

"Shot?" My hand flew to my heart. "Is he . . . is he alive?"

"They hauled him off to Pitié Hospital for interrogation."

Under the control of the Gestapo, "Pity" Hospital was practically a death sentence. No, not Boris. I couldn't bear to lose another friend.

"At home, I pace and fret," Bitsi continued, "so I went to the Library to get some work done. The Countess had just come back from talking to Dr Fuchs. She said that Boris's wife rang her at midnight. In the morning, the Countess went straight to the Bibliotheksschutz. 'Boris Netchaeff has been with the Library for nearly twenty years,' she informed him. 'He would never do anything to compromise it. You promised to help if there was a problem.'

"He asked her to prepare a written report. Ha! The Countess knows about the Nazis and their reports! She presented a full account of the incident, typed and signed by a witness. He phoned someone, who informed him that Boris was scheduled to be deported."

"Deported!"

"But Dr Fuchs promised to intervene."

That was something. I knew he'd keep his word. The Bibliotheksschutz wasn't as bad as the rest of them. "How can we help Boris?"

"By helping Anna."

We bicycled to the Netchaeffs' in the nearby suburb of Saint-Cloud. Is Anna in? We were whisked into the apartment, filled with friends and relatives talking in hushed tones. Yes, Hélène had been in the next room and heard everything. Poor little cabbage, she's only six. What were the Nazis searching for? I hope they let Anna see Boris. Would you believe the Gestapo had the gall to come back, at three in the morning, no less? They wanted the cigarettes they'd seen on the table.

Late that evening, Anna returned, pale as the moon. The Gestapo had shoved her into a dank room in the basement and shown her photo after photo of men she didn't know — the same ones they'd shown Boris — before allowing her to see him. Still in his blood-caked shirt, he hadn't been examined by a doctor.

In August, Boris was transferred to the American Hospital, thanks to the intervention of Dr Fuchs. Boris had been shot through the lung, and because the wound wasn't treated for several days, a life-threatening infection had set in. After a month, doctors allowed him to have visitors other than his wife. In the Hospital's grand entrance hall, Anna told Bitsi and me, "He's feeling better. Yesterday, he teased me about bringing him a pack of Gitanes."

I smiled, not entirely sure he was joking.

"Hello, there!" Margaret said, rushing towards us. "Sorry I'm late."

I hadn't seen her for weeks. Tanned and insouciant, she brimmed with happiness.

"Poor Boris!" Margaret said. "Why didn't you tell me sooner?"

"I rang," I said tersely, "You never returned my calls."

"I was at the seaside with —" She glanced at Bitsi and Anna. "I was at the seaside. I should have stayed in better touch."

On the way to see Boris, one of the nurses greeted me warmly. It was touching to be remembered. She and I chatted in the hall while Anna made sure that he was awake.

Once in the room, I made a beeline for Boris. Fussing like Maman would, I tucked the blanket over his chest. His green eyes were soggy with painkillers, but the corner of his mouth lifted like it did when he was about to say something silly.

"Our country has truly become France Kafka."

"It's been a *Metamorphosis*." I tried to keep my tone light.

350

"Sorry to leave you on your own at the circulation desk," he said.

"I don't mind — I'm glad to help readers. Of course, our habitués didn't let the annual closure stop them from coming in every day! Now, promise you won't overdo it."

"Overdue?" he quipped.

Too emotional to speak, Bitsi kissed his cheek, then moved to the corner of the room.

"Boris, one has to admire your timing," Margaret said, "getting shot and recuperating during the annual closure."

"It wasn't the first time I've been shot," he said drowsily, "but I hope it's the last."

"What?" she cried.

His eyelids fluttered shut.

"He tires easily," Anna said as she accompanied us to the entrance, "but he insists he'll be back to work in no time."

"I believe him," Bitsi said. "When can we visit again? Do you need us to watch Hélène?"

As the two of them spoke, Margaret pulled me aside. "I can't introduce Felix to my daughter, she's too little to keep a secret. But I need one person to know him, to see how kind he is. I'd like you to meet him."

Did she truly expect me to take tea with her lover? "You shouldn't be seeing him," I snapped.

"He saved my life. He's saving Rémy's life."

She was right. But she was wrong.

"I'm asking for an hour of your time," she said.

Margaret often spoke without thinking, but to ask something so vile, she was not merely thoughtless, she was out of her mind.

"Even five minutes would be too much!"

"When you needed something from me, I didn't say no!" She huffed off.

"Are you two fighting?" Bitsi asked.

"It's nothing," I said, "You know how prickly I can be sometimes."

"Only sometimes?" She raised her brow.

KRIEGSGEFANGENENPOST   3 September 1943

Dearest Odile,
    This may well be my last letter to you. I've been ill, and the fellows tell me I've been delirious. My wound never healed, and without medicine, the infection keeps getting worse.
    Don't let this war, or anything, separate you and Paul. Marry him, sleep in his arms every night. There's no reason both of us should be miserable. If I were there, I'd be with Bitsi. I'd spend every minute with her.
    Whatever happens, please don't grieve. I believe in God. Try to have faith.
    Love,
    Your Rémy

352

I pictured him lying on cold wooden planks, far from anyone he'd ever loved. Oh, Rémy. Please come home. Please come home. My belly lurched, and I ran to the water closet where I crouched as my stomach heaved. Please don't die. Please don't die. When there was nothing left inside me, I moved to the corridor and leaned against the wall. My whole body hurt, my belly, my head, my heart. I ran my hands over my face, through my hair, down my neck, trying to ease the ache. There had to be something we could do. I tore open the medicine cabinet and grabbed ointments, mustard plasters, a bottle of aspirin (there were three pills left), anything that might help. Arms full, I went to find a box in the kitchen.

"What's all this?" Maman eyed the jumble on the table. "What happened to your hair? You look like a madwoman!"

I read her the letter.

"Oh, dearest . . ." She helped prepare the package, though we both knew we'd already exceeded the amount of what we were able to send that month. "The authorities may not accept it," she said, "but we will try."

How astonishing that she was the calm one. Until this letter, I'd been convinced that Rémy would come home. Maybe Maman, who'd been through the Great War, knew better, and that's why she'd taken the news of his imprisonment so hard.

A week later, upon returning home from work, I was surprised to find the apartment unlit, as if no one was there. I turned on the hall light and peeked into the sitting room. Alone, Maman sat dressed in black. "Word came," she said. Her cheeks and even her lips were a ghostly white. The emotion had drained from her face like blood.

A paper lay at her feet, and I knew that Rémy was dead.

Once, when he and I were ten, we tussled and I fell hard, so hard it knocked the breath out of me. On my back, unable to move, I couldn't raise my head, couldn't say, "It wasn't your fault." I'd thought I was paralysed, that something was severed. I felt like that now, unable to take off my jacket, to blink, to go to Maman. I stood there, so much frozen inside me.

"For so long, I hoped he'd be released," she said, "that he'd make his way back to us."

"Me, too, Maman." My voice caught. "Me, too."

It had hurt to hope, but now I knew it was more painful to give up hope. I sank beside her. She gripped my hand. Her rosary beads dug into my palm.

"But then, even before his last letter," she said, "I knew. Somehow, I knew."

"Were you on your own when word came?" I asked.

"Eugénie was here, thank goodness."

I turned on the lamp. "Where is she?"

"She wanted to put on mourning."

"We should send for Papa."

She turned off the lamp. "He doesn't deserve to know."

"Oh, Maman . . ."

"Rémy enlisted to prove to Papa that he was a man."

354

Even if it was true, blame wouldn't bring Rémy back. If she remained fixated on my father, Papa would be dead to her, as dead as Rémy. I had to move Maman away from her resentment.

"We need to tell Bitsi," I said.

"Tomorrow is time enough. Let her have one last night before we break her heart."

In silence, Maman and I were steeped in the shock of grief. For how long, I didn't know. *Of course he wasn't dead. He could never be dead until she herself had finished feeling and thinking. 813. Their Eyes Were Watching God*. I just had to keep thinking of him. Rémy penning an article at his desk. Rémy sipping coffee at our favourite café, calico cat on his lap. Rémy laughing with Bitsi. Rémy. Oh, Rémy, *The fellows tell me I've been delirious*. Rémy was gone. But how could that be, when there was so much I wanted to tell him?

CHAPTER
THIRTY-FIVE

PAUL

Paris, September 1943

At his desk in the *commissariat*, Paul had one thing on his mind: Odile. If he could focus on her, he could forget everything else. Odile when they'd first met — she was angry, and he didn't know why. Odile when he gave her a nosegay and her gaze softened. Her mouth, sweet and tart like cherries. The sway of her hips. Odile in her black dress, Odile without it. Her breasts. He loved to caress them, to taste them.

His boss pounded on the desk. "Don't you have work to do?"

Paul shifted in his chair. "Yes, sir. But why — "

"Yours isn't to ask questions. Yours is to shut up and follow orders. Here's the list."

Paul didn't understand it. When war had been declared, the police had arrested Communists, Kraut pacifists living in France, a bunch of English folks — even ladies — and then Jewish people. On the poster beside his desk, the regulation stated: "Jews of both sexes, French and foreign, are to be subjected to random checks. They may also be interned. Agents of the police force are charged with the execution of the present order."

Some colleagues had relished kicking people out of their apartments. Others feigned sickness to get out of the unpleasant work, but that wasn't Paul's way. He'd briefly considered fleeing to the Free Zone, but he refused to abandon his responsibilities like his father had. Paul wanted to take up the fight in North Africa with the Free French, but couldn't abandon Odile. He'd turned down the promotion her father had offered so she would know that *she* came first. He'd told her things he'd never confided to anyone. His choice: Odile or everything and everyone else. The decision was easy.

He set off towards the furthest address on the list. He didn't want to think about his job. Only Odile could push it from his mind. Odile on the bed. Odile, naked in the kitchen, whisking *chocolat chaud* in a stranger's copper pot. At first, the trysts had been exciting, but now Paul was tired of sneaking around. He wanted to marry Odile. What if Rémy never came back? No one dared bring up the possibility. What could Paul do? Get a special licence, and the second she said yes . . . He arrived at the address. He didn't want to think about what he was about to do, Odile saying, *je t'aime*. Odile fawning over his sketches. Odile reading Éluard aloud to him. Odile. Odile. Odile.

Paul tramped up two flights and rang the bell. A white-haired lady appeared at the door, and he said, "Madame Irène Cohen? I'm supposed to escort you to the police station."

357

"What have I done?"

"Probably nothing. I mean you're —" He would have said *old*, but it wasn't polite to remind a woman of her age. "It's a random check."

When she turned to take a book from the table, Paul noticed a peacock feather tucked in her bun, "You're right to bring a book along," he said. "Administration gets longer every day."

"I know you. You're Odile's fiancé." She thrust the slim volume at his chest. "Please give this to her, she'll know what to do."

Surprised, he fumbled, and the book fell. When its spine hit the floor, the pages fluttered, and Paul saw the American Library bookplate — *Atrum post helium, ex libris lux*. Odile had told him it meant "After the darkness of war, the light of books".

He picked up the book. "Madame, I'm a policeman, not an errand boy. You'll be home by dinner and able to return it to her yourself."

"You're naïve, young man."

Paul drew himself up, ready to tell her off. Naïve! He was a worldly fellow! Just because he wasn't a soldier didn't mean he hadn't seen anything. Why, he'd travelled all over France. He was the breadwinner for himself and his mother. Who was she to judge, crazy lady with a feather in her hair? Feather in her hair. He remembered her now; well, not her exactly. There were plenty of old folks at the Library, and he didn't know them all by name. He recalled Odile's awe as she spoke of her favourite subscriber, the Professor with a peacock feather in her hair.

Professor Cohen put on her coat. When Paul saw the yellow star on her lapel, he started to sweat, and beads of shame dripped down his body. He'd wanted to tell Odile about the round-up, that terrible morning in July when he and others on the force, including her father, had arrested thousands of Jews, entire families, even children. But it wasn't just his work, it was her father's.

Paul contemplated the Library book in his hands. Should he shield Odile, or confide in her? Should he do his duty and arrest Professor Cohen, or should he leave this apartment and never return?

CHAPTER
THIRTY-SIX

ODILE

Paris, September 1943

Since word had come, Maman hadn't let me go anywhere. For ten days, she trailed me throughout the apartment. I yearned for Rémy and for the solitude to mourn him, yet Maman stood watch. On the divan, I opened *The Silence of the Sea*, 843, and held it up like a shield. I just needed a moment of quiet, or better yet, to throw myself back into work. The Library needed me, and I was stuck at home.

"That book better not upset you," Maman said.

I put it down. "I missed Boris's first day back. I'm sure he isn't up to working."

"Neither are you! We've had a terrible shock."

The sole visitor Maman allowed was Eugénie. I watched them, both in black, as they coddled the carrots growing in the window boxes.

"Another day or two," Maman said.

"They'll be bigger then," Eugénie agreed.

On to the bathroom, where they prepared the laundry. The charwoman had fled Paris, and no one blamed her. But that did leave the washing. Maman and Eugénie donned old petticoats to do the dirty work. They poured boiling-hot water over the linens in the bath. Scrub, rinse, wring. The effort brought a sheen of satisfaction to their faces. The work gave Maman something to do, something better than crying.

I tried to help, but Eugénie brushed me aside.

"It'll ruin your hands. You'll have your whole life to do such tasks."

They wrung, I felt useless.

"This war," Maman said.

"This war," Eugénie agreed.

This war had made strange bedfellows.

"Let me." I wrestled with a wet towel, barely wringing any water out of it.

"She never would have made it on the farm," Eugénie giggled.

"My daughter's a city girl," Maman said proudly. "More brains than brawn. When I was her age, I could snap a chicken's neck without thinking about it."

Just when I thought I'd go mad, missing Paul, missing the Library, Bitsi thrust open the front door and pushed past Maman. Like us, she wore mourning, "We need you." She poked my chest in rebuke, as if she thought staying at home had been my idea. "The Countess is frail. Boris shouldn't be out of bed. We've all suffered."

Eugénie's gaze flitted towards Maman. "Odile needs her rest."

"So do I," Bitsi said. "So do you."

"I need Odile here." Maman trembled. "If anything happened to her . . ."

I embraced her, suddenly understanding why I'd been kept at home.

Leaning against the weathered doorjamb, I observed Boris, busy at the circulation desk. He was gaunt in his suit. Silver now threaded the hair at his temples. If it hadn't been for the Countess and Dr Fuchs . . . When he saw me, he rose slowly, unsteady on his feet. Worried about his injuries, I kissed his cheeks gingerly; he crushed me in his emaciated arms.

Soaking in the earthy smell of his Gitanes, I said, "Anna will kill you when she finds out you've been smoking."

"I still have one good lung," he protested.

I laughed. Not ready to stop touching him, I brushed a piece of fluff from his tie.

"I'm sorry about your brother," he said.

"I know. Me, too."

Soon we were surrounded. The Countess, Mr Pryce-Jones, Monsieur de Nerciat and Madame Simon expressed their condolences. So young. So sad. A pity. This war . . . Just when I thought I would start to cry, Mr Pryce-Jones said, "We've missed our favourite referee."

I smiled.

"Fighting's no fun without you," Monsieur de Nerciat added.

The tone was light, but the concern in their eyes told a story of its own.

I felt lucky to have such friends, to be back where I belonged. On my way to the reference room, I breathed in my favourite scent in the world — books, books, books.

Margaret stepped from the stacks, as hesitant now as she'd been on her first day. I cringed when I remembered that she'd wanted to introduce me to her Leutnant.

"I heard about Rémy," she said.

At the sound of his name, said so rarely now, I teared up.

"About before," she continued. "It was asking too much. I see that now."

"I'm sure Felix is lovely, and my family appreciated the food he got for . . ." I didn't want to say my brother's name in the same sentence as her lover's.

"I've prayed so hard for you and your family. I'm sorry I didn't go to see you at home — I wasn't sure I'd be welcome."

The war had stolen so much. Now I had to decide if I would allow it to claim our friendship. "It would have been a waste of time," I said. "Maman didn't allow anyone in."

"Not even Paul?"

"Not even Bitsi."

"You weren't kidding when you said she was strict."

"I'm sure there's a lot of work." I gestured to the files on my desk. "Would you like to help me field questions?"

"More than anything."

The cadence of the Library took over, and we spent the day solving puzzles. (Where can I find information on Camille Claudel? What is the history of Cleveland?)

I kept my hand in my pocket, on Rémy's last letter. I had the whole thing memorised, but as the last subscribers left for the day, one line came flooding back: *Don't let this war separate you and Paul*

I rang the precinct. "I'm free! Come to the Library."

As I paced the courtyard, the Countess approached. "I've tried to deliver books to Professor Cohen twice, but she hasn't been home. Could you try now?"

"I have plans with someone tonight. May I tomorrow?"

"I suppose," she said indulgently. "Does this someone have 'A lean cheek — a blue eye'?"

"Yes." I recognised the line and added, "But not an 'unquestionable spirit'."

She continued on, under the acacias, their whispering leaves illuminated by the dull light of the streetlamps. I remembered another line from *As You Like It: These trees shall be my books. And in their barks my thoughts I'll character.*

When Paul arrived, I slid into his embrace.

"I'm so sorry about your brother," he said.

I nestled closer.

"I tried to visit," he said. "Your mother's a dragon."

"The war's changed her."

"It's changed everyone."

I didn't want to think about war, of the loved ones we'd lost, of my beloved Rémy. On the way home, I asked, "How's work?"

"Bizarre."

The question used to be banal, but now it felt like a loaded gun. As we strolled, I asked after his aunt (I knew not to mention his mother), but he didn't answer. I asked if his colleague had returned from sick leave. No reply.

"Is everything all right?"

We stopped, I could see he wanted to say something. "Tell me."

"A few days ago . . . well . . . Your father says what we're doing —"

"My father?" I said. "What does he have to do with anything?"

Paul shrugged and stalked off.

I caught up with him. "What's wrong?"

He stared straight ahead. "Why should there be anything wrong?"

The following day, for the first time, Paul didn't stop in at the Library on his rounds, I hoped that nothing had happened to him. At work, he dealt with all kinds. He'd broken up more than one drunken brawl, and black-marketeers had been known to cudgel policemen who tried to seize their ill-gotten gains. Distracted by my worry, I forgot about the books I was supposed to deliver to Professor Cohen and went straight home.

For the second evening in a row, Paul didn't come. At closing time, I tucked the novels for Professor Cohen into my satchel. Climbing the escargot stairs, I expected to hear her typing away, but there was only an eerie hush. I knocked. "Professor?"

Nothing.

I put my ear to the door. Silence.

I knocked louder. "Professor? It's Odile."

Where could she be at this time of night? Was she visiting someone, or had something happened to her? Perhaps she'd gone to the country to see her niece. But she hadn't mentioned any travel plans. Perhaps she'd had a malaise, though despite the deprivations she'd remained hardy. I knocked again, then waited twenty more minutes before trudging home.

At work the next morning, I told Boris, "For the first time, the Professor didn't answer her door. I didn't know what to do. Should I have called someone? Should I return today?"

I expected him to tell me that I was fretting for nothing, but he said, "Let's go now."

On the way, he confided that three Jewish subscribers to whom he delivered books had disappeared. We didn't know what to make of it. Had they fled Paris and the menacing watch of the Nazis, or had something happened to them?

When we arrived, Boris knocked; I called out, "Professor! It's Odile," but no one responded.

When Paul stayed away for another week, I was devastated. Aunt Caroline had lost Uncle Lionel, Margaret had lost Lawrence. Perhaps Paul had lost interest in me. Since my family had received word about my brother, I hadn't been good company. I was teary-eyed and had trouble concentrating on what people were saying. Perhaps Paul was with someone else. Paris was crawling with eager women. I remembered the time we'd strolled past cafés full of

Soldaten and their girls, how he stared at the harlots in low-cut blouses.

At dusk, when I left the Library, Paul was waiting. Relieved, I moved to embrace him, but he held me at arm's length.

"What's going on?" I asked.

He didn't meet my gaze. "Don't be angry."

I knew it. He was going to break my heart.

"I'm sorry I haven't come by more, especially since you found out about Rémy. It's just work. It's been horrible."

What? All this wasn't about some hussy, it was about his job? I felt terrible for doubting him.

"I'm glad you're here." I reached up to caress his hair, but he ducked his head.

"I arrested someone we know. Professor Cohen."

That was absurd. "There must be some mistake." Cohen was a common enough name.

He drew a book from his messenger bag. *Good Morning, Midnight*. The last novel I'd delivered. I snatched it from him. "When?"

"A few weeks ago. I wanted to tell you —"

"Why didn't you say anything?" This was why the Professor hadn't been at home. No, it couldn't be. I started towards her apartment.

He followed. "Let me come with you."

"No."

"I'm sorry I didn't tell you," he said, grabbing my arm.

I pulled free and broke into a run. The wooden soles of my shoes hit the pavement and made a loud echoing sound. I passed the boarded-up butcher shop, the *chocolaterie* with no *chocolat*, the *boulangerie* where housewives hoped to buy bread, the *brasserie* where the Boches swilled their *bier*.

I leaped up the escargot stairs two at a time and pounded on the door. Someone stirred on the other side, probably the Professor preparing a pot of tea. She'd been out earlier, that's all. She was at home now. I heard the creak of the parquet, the tinny twist of the key in the lock. She's fine. It was a misunderstanding. I leaned against the wall and tried to catch my breath.

The door swung open. A blonde in a sleek blue dress said, "Yes?"

I straightened. "I'm here for Professor Cohen."

"Who?"

"Irène Cohen." Peeking past the woman, I saw the grandfather clock, its hands fixed at 3.17. The crystal vase was full of roses. The bookshelves now held a collection of beer *Steins*.

"You have the wrong address."

"This is the right address," I insisted.

"She doesn't live here any more. This is my apartment now."

"Do you know where she went?"

The woman slammed the door.

Who was that? Why was she in the Professor's home, among her things? Why did she say that the apartment was hers? Needing answers, I made my way to Paul's door at the hostel.

He gestured for me to enter, but I remained in the corridor.

"Why did you arrest Professor Cohen?"

"Her name was on the list of Jews."

"The list? There's a list?"

He nodded.

"Have you arrested others?"

"Yes."

I thought of the first abandoned apartment where Paul and I had trysted. Though I'd asked whose it was, I hadn't really cared. Now I understood who the apartments belonged to, why their treasures had been left behind. I covered my mouth in horror as I remembered how Paul and I romped in people's homes, how we cavorted in their sheets.

"Forgive me for not telling you sooner," he said. "I'll never hide anything from you again."

I looked at him, not sure what I saw. "How can I find her?"

"I'm a peon in the hierarchy. You know who you need to ask."

I left without a word. The foolish reference librarian. My job was to find facts; instead, I'd turned away from the truth. I should have asked questions instead of burying my head in the goose-down pillows of strangers.

At home, I realised that Paul was right — my father was the one to talk to. Once I explained everything to him, he would ensure that the Professor was released, perhaps within the hour.

The table was already set. Maman ladled the soup into our bowls. Grey noodles swam in water. "What I wouldn't give for a leek," she said.

Papa sipped from his spoon. "You do so much with so little."

"*Merci.*" For once she allowed herself to accept a sliver of praise.

"Papa, one of my friends has been arrested."

His spoon stilled. His eyes shifted nervously to Maman.

"Who is it, dear?" she asked.

"The Professor. I told you about her — she helped me get the job at the Library. Paul said he arrested her."

All atremble, Maman looked to Papa. "Why would he arrest some poor woman? Oh, this war."

"Now you've upset your mother," he told me.

I saw he wouldn't say anything more.

After breakfast, I set out for Papa's *commissariat*, composing arguments in my head. *I've never asked you for anything. Won't you at least try to help?* I passed the sleepy guard and hurried down the hall to his office. It was early; his secretary wasn't there to protect him. I pushed open the door.

He rose from his desk. "Is Maman all right?"

"She's fine."

"What are you doing here?"

Unsure of what to say, I glanced around. Dozens of envelopes were stacked around the perimeter. On the floor near the desk, letters pooled together, as if swept away by an angry fist.

I picked up a few. *Roger-Charles Meyer is a pure Jew, well, as pure as that race can be, and I will not* hide the fact that I would he delighted if he were taken away ... It is quite simply what this individual deserves. I would be ever so grateful if you could facilitate his fall.

I went on to the next. You aren't going to tell me that you approve of those dirty Jews. We've had more than enough. While our loved ones are getting killed or taken prisoner, the Jews run their businesses. We poor imbecile Frenchmen are dying of hunger. And it's not enough to die of hunger. When there are provisions, they're for the Jews.

And the next. I write to inform you about a case you should know about at 49 rue du Couédic, where a certain Maurice Reichmann, a Communist of Jewish origins, is living with a Frenchwoman. Often, we witness terrible scenes at their door. I think that you will deign to do what must be done, and, in advance, the businessmen of the street say merci.

The final one listed names with corresponding addresses and job titles, noting at the end, 74 gros Juifs: 74 important Jews.

"I don't understand." I threw the letters into the bin.

"Denunciations," Papa said reluctantly. "We call them 'crow letters'."

"Crow letters?"

"From black-hearted people who spy on neighbours, colleagues and friends. Even family members."

"Are they all like these?" I asked.

"Some are signed, but yes, most are anonymous, telling us about black-marketeers, Résistants, Jews, people who listen to English radio or say bad things about the Germans."

"How long has this been going on?"

"Since 1941, when Marshal Pétain went on the radio to say that holding back information is a crime. These 'crows' have convinced themselves they're doing their patriotic duty. It's my job to confirm the veracity of each letter."

"But Papa —"

"It's been made clear that if I find the work distasteful, there are dozens of men in line for my job."

"It's not right."

"Neither is letting you starve."

I'd assumed he spent his days helping people . . .

"This . . . is for me?"

"Everything Maman and I have done for the last two decades has been for you and your brother! His Latin tutor. Your English lessons. And that trousseau. Maman has nearly gone blind embroidering. By the time you marry, you'll have enough goods to fill a department store."

"But I never asked for anything."

"You've never had to."

The realisation hit me like a hammer blow. My entire life, I'd been proud, I'd never hesitated to rebel against Papa and to think for myself. I'd seen what happened to Aunt Caro, and I worked hard for my own independence. Now, with unsettling clarity, I understood that though I'd never asked for anything, I'd never needed to — my parents had laid clothes, opportunities and even suitors in front of me like a red carpet. I felt stunned. Paul wasn't who I thought he was. Papa wasn't who I thought he was. I wasn't who I thought I was.

My father fished the letters from the bin. "I'll do my duty and investigate each one."

"Duty?"

"My job is to uphold the law."

"But what if the law is wrong? What about the innocent men and women harmed by these accusations?" I heard my voice break, like it always did when I fought with my father. I reminded myself that I was here for a reason. "Papa, please, can we talk about Professor Cohen?"

"Every day, dozens of people ask for my help, searching for family members. I can't help them and I can't help you!" He gripped my arm and forced me out of the door. "I've told you before, I don't want you here. It's no place for a respectable young lady."

Outside, in the cold, I burrowed into my shawl. *How can I help the Professor?* I asked Rémy.

Inform the Countess, I heard him say. He was right. She had many high-ranking contacts. Surely, she could help. I rushed straight to her office.

At her desk, she stared into her teacup, her mouth a sad moue. "I've told the others and now I must tell you," she said shakily, "Our friend Irène Cohen was to be deported."

It wasn't too late. The Countess and Dr Fuchs could save her like they'd saved Boris.

"She was at Drancy."

A detention centre north of Paris. Wait. Was?

"Conditions there are deplorable. I could hardly believe my ears when my husband described it. We tried to intervene on Irène's behalf, but unfortunately . . ."

No. Not Professor Cohen, too. The floor beneath me swayed, and I reached out, palm flat against the wall, feeling that if I didn't hold on, everything would disintegrate.

"She tried to get a message to me, if only Paul had given me the book," I said. "My father . . . the letters . . . It's my fault."

"You mustn't blame yourself," the Countess said. "We learned Madame Simon's son and daughter-in-law moved into the Professor's apartment. One needn't be Sherlock Holmes to understand what happened. Apparently, madame and her son were in communication with several *commissariats* and even the Gestapo."

The scold with the tombstone teeth had written crow letters? We'd seen her nearly every day and only now discovered who she truly was? "She'd better never come back!"

"She won't, believe me. But I didn't finish. Irène has disappeared. My husband believes she might have smuggled herself out of the detention centre."

The Professor had endured the gruelling training of a prima ballerina and the almost impossible coursework at the Sorbonne. She'd taught there despite the odds and had outlived three husbands. If anyone could escape a prison, it was she. She couldn't return to her apartment, but she could stay with friends in the countryside . . . I needed to believe that she was safe, needed her to have a happy ending. I thought of a line

374

from *Good Morning, Midnight: I want a long, calm book about people with large incomes — a book like a flat green meadow and the sheep feeding in it ... I read most of the time and I am happy.*

CHAPTER
THIRTY-SEVEN

ODILE

Paris, November 1943

As I sat at my desk, pen in hand, I couldn't stop thinking about the crow letters. It was true that Parisians were aware of appearances, of how friends and strangers dressed. We admired a scarf worn the right way, the jaunty tilt of a hat, but now that appreciation transformed into criticism, even envy. Who does she think she is, flaunting that fur? Why does he have new shoes? What did Margaret do for that gold bracelet?

I wondered who would write such letters. I regarded the man in the moth-eaten suit. Did you write one? My gaze shifted to the woman in the blue beret. Or was it you? Everyone appeared normal. Or what had become normal — hungry and haggard.

Boris came to remind me that he had to leave early for a doctor's appointment. "You seem distracted."

"Just down," I said.

Those letters. There had to be a way to save others from Professor Cohen's fate. At the circulation desk, as Margaret and I stamped books for subscribers, I realised that if there were no crow letters, there would be no arrests.

I tugged at the collar of my blouse. How could it be so warm in November?

"You're flushed," she teased. "Thinking of Paul?"

I didn't *notice* the light tone and shook my head.

"Where is he, by the way? He hasn't been here in ages."

"I have to go out," I said, "just for an hour. Will you take care of things here?"

"But I'm only a volunteer . . ."

"Act as bossy as Boris. You'll be fine."

"But why must you leave? Are you feeling ill?"

"Yes," I said distractedly. "I'm just sick."

Speeding along the boulevard, I thought up explanations in case Papa's secretary stood guard: "I was in the neighbourhood . . ." In case he was working: "Maman wonders if you'll be home for dinner . . ." I hoped no one would be there, that I could get in and out and back before anyone but Margaret knew I'd gone.

In front of the *commissariat*, I hesitated. I was afraid of getting caught. When Papa was angry, his livid temper was frightening. Yet I was more afraid of the person I'd become if I didn't act. I thought of those letters, more arriving each day, and marched in. Avoiding the men in uniform milling about, I skirted the wall.

Papa's secretary was gone, and his door wasn't locked. I contemplated the mounds of letters on the desk, the cabinet, the sill, before shoving a fistful into my satchel. Fastening the flap, I peeked out. Men swarmed up and down the corridor. Clutching my satchel, I crept down the hall.

"You there, stop!" a guard shouted.

I held my head high and kept going.

"Halt!"

I was about to bolt when greasy fingers grasped the nape of my neck.

"What's the hurry?" the policeman asked, one hand on me, the other on the gun in his holster.

I'd fixated on Papa, and I hadn't considered there'd be danger from anyone else. I was so frightened I couldn't speak.

Men came out of their offices. Some looked stern, others apprehensive. A white-haired commander asked, "What's this disturbance?"

"I found her sneaking about, sir."

The commander frowned. "What do you think you're doing, mademoiselle?"

I didn't answer. I couldn't.

"Show me your ID," the guard ordered.

My *carte d'identité* was in my satchel. If I opened it, they'd see the letters.

The guard grabbed my bag, and instinctively, as if he were a hooligan in the Métro, I yanked it from his grasp.

Finally, I found my voice. "I'd hoped to see my papa, but he wasn't in." I pointed towards his office.

The commander's expression eased. "You must be Odile. Your father's right, you're the loveliest girl in

Paris. Sorry to have been gruff. We've doubled our security because of saboteurs."

"Saboteurs?" I said weakly. Was that what I was? Saboteurs received life sentences. At the Library, we'd recently learned that a subscriber had been condemned to hard labour for printing tracts for the Resistance.

"No need to be frightened," he said. "We'll keep your father safe."

I tried to say "thank you," but my mouth just quivered.

"You're a shy thing, aren't you? Don't worry your pretty little head. Run along home."

Hugging my satchel, I hurried back to the Library.

"Well?" Margaret said, trailing me to the hearth, "What was so bloody important?"

I threw the letters into the fire and watched them burn. "Something came up."

"Do you realise the risk you've run?"

Had she discovered what I'd done? "Wh — what do you mean?"

"Leaving the Library unattended is completely irresponsible! The Countess is exhausted — did you know she's so hell-bent on protecting this place that she spends the night in her office? Bitsi's practically a mute unless you're here. Boris shouldn't be working. We're counting on you."

From the courtyard, Paul stared at me through the window, his face full of sorrow. I shook my head. He left. Every few days, he tried again. He followed me through the stacks, through the streets, through the grey winter rain. He was with me even when he wasn't. I was angry he hadn't told me about the Professor right away. Angry at myself for being blind. Angry because, despite everything, I missed him.

I followed the pebbled path through the morning mist and was nearly at the Library when he caught up with me. "Can you forgive me?" he asked.

"Professor Cohen was sent to Drancy, you know."

"I didn't."

"No one knows what's become of her."

Head bowed, he walked away. I felt my shoulders sag. Seeing him reminded me of how I'd gladly closed my eyes and frolicked in the homes of the departed.

At lunchtime each day, I hurried to the *commissariat*, past the belligerent guard, to Papa's office, where I stuffed letters into my satchel. Back at the Library, I burned them. As weeks went by, I gained confidence. Instead of five, I grabbed a dozen. Hundreds remained and more arrived each day. Though I longed to destroy them all, I knew that would only bring scrutiny.

Nonetheless, I feared getting caught. On the way back to work, I glanced behind me. At home, I developed a twitch. Before Sunday Mass, I tied my scarf in the hall. Papa stopped to straighten his tie. Our eyes met in the mirror.

"Ça va?" he asked gently.

I nodded.

"I'm sorry I couldn't . . ."

"Couldn't what?" I said tersely.

He looked away.

When he went to get his suit jacket, Maman said, "You haven't been yourself these last weeks. What's wrong?"

"Nothing."

"You're positively . . . shifty. Why doesn't Paul come around any longer?"

"If we don't leave now, we'll be late."

She felt my forehead. "You must be coming down with something. Or you're . . ." She cast a horrified glance at my belly.

Flustered, I said, "It's not what you think."

"Stay at home. Rest."

After they left, I wrote in my journal. *Dear Rémy, I've been selfish and blind. I've let the Professor down, but I'm trying to make it right.*

The doorbell rang, and I answered, assuming Maman had forgotten her bag.

"I shouldn't have come," Paul said. "But they might find me at home."

Blood had dribbled and dried, caking around his nostrils.

"What on earth?" I gestured for him to enter.

He didn't budge. "I don't want your parents to see me like this."

"They're at church. What happened?" I asked as I sat him down.

"One of those Nazi bastards staggered down the street, dead drunk. I grabbed him from behind and started punching. I wanted to make him sorry he set foot here. He fought back, but I broke his nose for sure. Maybe cracked a few ribs. Then I ran for it. I don't regret what I did, but these days, you never know who's watching."

"You're safe now." I wiped his face with my handkerchief. I'd missed touching him, missed his touch. I was glad he'd come, though I wished we could go back to that day at the Gare du Nord, to a time when I only felt one thing for him — absolute love.

"Before, the biggest arrest I made was for disorderly conduct. When I — well, I never thought they'd keep an old lady like her."

"You couldn't have known." I remembered the books I should have delivered, "We all have regrets."

"I love you," he said. "Say you'll forgive me."

CHAPTER
THIRTY-EIGHT

ODILE

Paris, November 1943

In the Countess's office, I eyed the makeshift mattress where she slept each night in order to keep watch over the Library; she was seventy years old, yet ready to confront Nazi soldiers. A few books rested near her pillow, I leaned forward to see the titles, but Bitsi tugged at my sleeve, urging me towards the others who'd gathered at the desk. Meetings that had once teemed with staff had dwindled to the secretary, the caretaker, Bitsi, Boris, Margaret, me and Clara de Chambrun.

"Mr Pryce-Jones was arrested," the Countess began, "and sent to an internment camp."

No, not another friend lost, locked up for being an enemy alien.

"Monsieur de Nerciat has been fighting for his release," she continued.

"I've read distressing reports," Boris said. "They're not sending people to internment camps but to death camps."

"Propaganda," she said dismissively. "Think of the rumours we've heard."

"Was he denounced?" Bitsi asked.

"It's likely," Boris said.

This war was taking everyone I held dear. Everything — my country, my city, my friends — had been looted and betrayed, and I would put a stop to it the only way I knew how. I needed to destroy those letters. I no longer cared if I got into trouble. One thing was sure: something would burn. I ran out of the Library, Boris and Bitsi shouting after me.

"Come back!"

"You've had a shock."

At the *commissariat*, I sprinted to my father's office, closing the door behind me, I grabbed a letter and tore it in two, then another, then another. The rustle of paper being ripped had never sounded so satisfying. Realising Papa could enter at any moment, I stuffed a fistful of letters into my satchel, crumpling letters into ugly wads.

The doorknob clicked, and the door swung open. I stepped away from the desk, fumbling as I fastened the flap.

"My dutiful daughter," Papa said drily. "Here to pay me a visit?"

I didn't know how to act.

Offended? You suspect your own daughter?

Nonchalant? I'm here. Big deal.

Honest? Yes, I'm a thief.

"I've received letters asking why the police haven't followed up on information from earlier 'correspondence'. It was puzzling, since we investigated each accusation. I couldn't understand." He looked pointedly at the letters I'd torn apart. "Now I do."

My hand tightened on my satchel.

"You don't have anything to say for yourself?" he said.

I shook my head.

"I could be arrested," he said. "They sentence traitors to death."

"But surely you won't be blamed . . ."

"My God, how can you still be so naïve?" He placed his palms on his desk and bowed his head, almost in defeat.

"But Papa —"

"Anyone else I would arrest. Go home. And never come back."

I left with just a handful of letters. The most important thing I could do, and I'd failed.

CHAPTER
THIRTY-NINE

LILY

Froid, Montana, August 1987

Cornered in the closet, among the sweaters and secrets, I stared at Odile, still carrying her vanity case, elegant as always. The letters lay on the floor between us. *Why aren't you looking for undeclared Jews in hiding? My indications are exact, now it's up to you.*

"Who are you?" I asked.

Odile's mouth opened, then closed and became a taut line. Her chin rose, and just as I looked at her differently, she looked at me differently. Guarded, and with great sorrow. When she didn't say anything, I grabbed the letters and shoved them in her face. She didn't move.

"Why do you have these?" I demanded.

"I didn't burn them like the others . . . I meant to."

"I thought you were a heroine, that you hid Jews."

She sighed. "Alas, no. Only letters."

"From whom?"

"From my father."

"That's crazy. Wasn't he a cop?"

Her eyes were haunted, as if they'd seen a ghost. Silence filled the closet, the bedroom, our friendship.

There was only the lonely caw of a lost seagull, the garbage truck plodding down the alley, the pounding of my pitiful heart.

"At the beginning of the war," she said, "the police arrested Communists. During the Occupation, they rounded up Jews. People wrote to denounce neighbours. Some of the letters were sent to my father. I stole them, so he couldn't hunt down the innocent."

"You didn't write them?" Even as I asked the question, I knew that she hadn't.

Odile stared at the letters trembling in my hand. "I don't blame you for poking around my things because you're bored or curious." Her eyes grew cold until they were slits that regarded me like I was nothing. "But to believe I could write those words! What have I done to make you think I could be capable of such evil?"

She stared out the window, and I knew it was because she couldn't bear to look at me. I had no right to dig in her closet, to rifle through her past. To bring up things she'd buried for a reason. The war, the role her father played, maybe even the reason she left France.

"To think I came home early because I missed you." She sank on to the bed. She sat, not straight like in church, but with her back curled in sorrow.

"Go," she told me. "And don't come back."

"No, please." Shaking my head, I moved towards her. How could I have accused her of such a thing? I would make it up to her. I'd hoe her garden, mow her lawn, shovel all winter. I'd make her forget my foolish, impulsive question. "I'm sorry."

387

Odile rose and left the room. I heard the front door open. She'd walked out.

In the living room, I closed the door, then put her books back, hoping I got them in the right order. Watching for her, I sat straight as Sunday on the couch. Barely daring to move, I waited for an hour, then two. She didn't return.

Her tone had sounded final. That's what I said to Eleanor. I hoped she would yell, but she said, "Of course she's angry. Now you see why Dad and I told you not to snoop."

What I'd done was worse than snooping, but I was too ashamed to admit my real crime.

The next day, I knocked on Odile's door, but she didn't answer. That evening, I wrote a letter of apology and put it in her mailbox. When I left for school in the morning, I found it unopened on our doormat. At Mass, while some people prayed that we'd cream the Soviets before they creamed us, I got on my knees and begged for Odile's forgiveness. After the service, she and Father Maloney chatted in the vestibule. She glowed as she spoke about Chicago. When I walked over, she excused herself and headed home instead of to the hall. The following week, I sat in her pew, childishly hoping that after the "Our Father", when parishioners shook hands and said, "Peace be with you," she'd at least look at me. But Odile stopped attending Mass.

At the hall, the ladies gathered behind the buffet, serving juice and doughnuts. Odile had missed a month of Sundays.

"Has anyone seen Mrs Gustafson?" Mrs Ivers murmured.

"I tried to check on her," old Mrs Murdoch replied, "I could hear her moving around but she didn't come to the door."

"Like before."

"I wish we'd been kinder back then."

"So do I."

"Something terrible must have happened. Even when her son died, she never missed Mass."

Eleanor decided the silent treatment had gone on long enough and marched over to Odile's. "Lily knows she did wrong," she pleaded my case on the porch. "She's a young girl who made a mistake. A girl who loves and misses you."

Odile let Eleanor say her piece, then gently closed the door.

In need of divine intervention, I carried Joe to church and lit all the candles I could find. "We pway," he said.

I gave God two days. When He didn't respond, I tried a more direct approach. At the rectory, Father invited me into the kitchen. Without his robes, he resembled someone's grandpa. He scooted a plate of Oreos in my direction, but for once I wasn't hungry. Figuring that half-truths were better than no truth at all, I crafted a story, careful not to say anything about my accusations.

"That's all?" Iron-Collar asked sceptically.

For so long, I'd wanted to hold a secret close to my heart. Something that only I knew. Now I had one, but the secret wasn't exciting, it was pathetic.

"She caught me snooping. It's a pretty big deal."

"Enough for her to stop coming to church?"

"Why won't she let me say I'm sorry?"

"Sometimes, when people have gone through tough times, or been betrayed, the only way for them to survive is to cut off the person who hurt them."

She'd never gone back to France, never mentioned her parents or aunts and uncles or cousins. Odile had forsaken her whole family — it wouldn't be hard to leave me behind.

On Saturday afternoon, Iron-Collar's car pulled up to the kerb. I opened my window and ducked down so no one would see me spying. He and Odile spoke amiably on her porch about the food-pantry fundraiser. The minute he mentioned me, she backed into her house.

Life went on without Odile. I began my junior year without our French lessons. I hadn't suffered such a loss since my mother had died. But Mom hadn't had a choice. Odile chose to stay away. Trudging home from school, I passed her house. The curtains were closed. I knew if I tried the door it would be locked.

At lunchtime, Mary Louise and Keith made out under the bleachers, which left me alone in the cafeteria. Tiffany Ivers slithered over. "Bet your stepmother can't wait until you graduate and you're out of her hair."

Tiffany picked on John Brady because his father was the custodian; she got everyone to call Mary Matthews "Pepperoni Pizza" because of her acne. I was the only kid at school with a stepmom. Divorce was a big-city problem, and the death of a mother so young was thankfully rare. I wouldn't want anyone to go through what I had.

"Know how to say 'stepmom' in French?" I asked.

She stared at me, dull eyes half hidden by her foofy bangs. Why had I spent years comparing my luck to hers, my looks to hers? I remembered the sweater Mom had crocheted, how I'd cared more about Tiffany Ivers's opinion than I had about my mother's feelings.

"*Belle mère*," I said. "It means beautiful mother."

"Is that supposed to be French? Sounds like you have some kind of speech impediment."

A few years ago, this would have made me bawl. Now I knew that people who said cruel things should be cut from your life. I walked out. Away from her bitchy comments, from her narrow mind, I felt stronger.

Even in her silence, Odile taught me.

At 7.33 a,m. on Saturday, I awoke to the screech of *Scooby-Doo*. "People are trying to sleep," I yelled down the hall.

"Okey-dokey," Joe yelled back and lowered the volume half a notch.

Joe and Benjy, Benjy and Joe. I loved them, but they drove me crazy. Every time I sat down, Benjy grabbed at my waist and hoisted himself on to my lap. If our house had a chorus, it was "Joe, sweetie, will you get your finger out of your nose? Joe, take that finger out of your nose this minute. Get that finger out! Right now!" God, I missed Odile. There wasn't a moment that I wasn't aware of what I'd lost, what I'd thrown away by being reckless and selfish.

Eleanor peeked in my room. "Why don't you and I take a drive?" she said. "We'll put that learner's permit to use."

"What about the boys?" We never went anywhere without them. We never went anywhere, period.

"It won't kill your father to watch them. Just us girls today. We'll go to Good Hope."

I loved the feel of the steering wheel gripped in my hands, the purr of the car as I hit the gas, the long stretches of pasture, the cows that watched us fly by. I loved that as we approached the city there was more than one radio station. I loved getting away from school, from the boys, from how I'd hurt Odile.

Good Hope had 30,000 inhabitants. Right before we hit the city limits, I eased on to the shoulder so Eleanor could drive. We passed a Dairy Queen and a Best Western, chains that existed in the rest of the world. Froid had stop signs that no one stopped at; Good Hope had actual red lights. The sidewalks were twice as wide as ours, and drivers had to pay to park. We stopped right in front of the grandest department store in Montana, The Bon. That's French for "good". Five storeys of blond bricks glimmered in the sun. Even the doors were grand, brass and glass without a single smudge. Inside, we were met by the scent of Wind

392

Song. Islands of cosmetics beckoned. Eleanor guided me to the Clinique counter, where the saleswoman wore a long white jacket, like a doctor, like someone we could trust. She drew several shades of lipstick on her wrist. They resembled swatches of silk. The three of us considered them carefully, as if we were selecting drapes for the governor's mansion.

We settled on Perfect Peach, and Eleanor got out her cheque book.

"Aren't you going to get anything?" I asked.

"I don't think so."

"You deserve something nice."

"We'll see." She was embarrassed, but I couldn't understand why. She was a married lady. It was her money, too. Wasn't it?

I dug my heels in. "We drove all this way."

Eleanor let herself be convinced. She got a silver tube of Pale Poppies. And she looked radiant.

In the Mezzanine Bistro, which looked on to the ground floor, we chose a table next to the Plexiglas edge so we could people-watch as if we were in a Parisian café. After we ordered, I saw an elegant saleslady hitch up her stockings when she thought no one was looking.

When the waiter set down Eleanor's club sandwich and my French dip, she asked, "Are you having a good day?"

"*Mais oui*," I said, dipping my sandwich in the jus.

After lunch, Ellie and I washed our hands in the ladies' room. In front of the mirror, we puckered up and reapplied our lipsticks. It was the closest I'd ever felt to her. If we were French, this would be the moment I moved from the formal *vous* to the informal *tu*.

We got in the station wagon, and she drove us out of the city. The rock music on the radio disintegrated, and Ellie rolled the dial to our local country station. The Froid water tower, "water castle" *en français*, came on to *le horizon*.

Easing on to our street, we saw the fire truck. Hard to tell from five blocks away, but it appeared to be parked in front of our house. "The boys!" I gasped. Ellie sped up. The one day we were gone . . . Had Joe somehow found the matches in the drawer? *Please let them be okay*, I prayed.

The truck was at Odile's. Wisps of smoke wafted from her window. A fireman tugged a deflated hose away from her house. Ellie hit the brakes, and we jumped out. Neighbours gathered on the sidewalk, where we found Odile slumped on the kerb. Mrs Ivers wrapped a quilt around Odile, but she didn't seem to notice.

"What happened?" Ellie asked the fire chief.

"Kitchen fire," he replied. "Something left in the oven."

"Professor Cohen's biscuits," Odile said. "I think of her more and more. It was my fault."

"These things happen," Ellie soothed. We squatted down on either side of Odile.

"My fault," she insisted.

"You didn't mean to," I said.

Odile looked at me. I was so happy, I didn't even care that she stared, eyes wide like I was a stranger.

"I'm sorry," she said.

I swallowed. "No, I'm the one . . ." There were so many things I wanted to say. *I love you. Your forgiveness means everything to me. I'm still sorry.*

"Why don't you come to our place?" Ellie said.

I walked her to our house, to my room, where she lay down.

"Do you want me to go?" I asked.

"Sit down." She patted the bed. "I want you to know. There are things that happened during the war that no one talks about, not even today. Things so shameful that we buried them in a secret cemetery, then for ever abandoned the graves."

Her hand hugging mine, she introduced her cast of characters. Dear Maman and down-to-earth Eugénie. Blustery Papa. Rémy, the mischievous twin I would see every time I looked at Odile. His girl, Bitsi, the brave librarian. Paul, so handsome, I fell in love with him, too. Margaret, every bit as fun as Mary Louise. Miss Reeder, the Countess, and Boris, the heart and soul and life of the Library. People I would never know, would never forget. They'd lived in Odile's memory, and now they lived in mine.

By the time she finished, I felt the story was a book I'd read, a part of me for ever. When the Nazis entered the Library, I shuddered in the stacks. Delivering books to Professor Cohen, I tripped on the cobblestones, frightened that the Nazis would learn of my mission. As food grew scarce, my stomach rumbled and my temper

395

flared. I read those terrible letters and didn't know what to do.

"You were brave," I told Odile. "Keeping the Library open and making sure all people could check out books."

She sighed. "I merely did the minimum."

"*Le minimum?* What you did was amazing. You gave subscribers hope. You showed that during the worst of times, people were still good. You saved books and people. You risked your life to defy the fricking Nazis. That's huge."

"If I could go back, I would do more."

"You saved people by hiding those letters."

"If I'd destroyed all the crow letters the first time I saw them, more lives could have been saved. It took me too long to understand what needed to be done. I was too worried about being caught."

I wanted to keep arguing, but her eyes fluttered shut.

Over dinner, while Odile dozed, Ellie and Dad decided she would stay with us while her kitchen was remodelled, then went on to talk about this and that. I couldn't stop thinking about the crow letters. Though I liked to think I wouldn't have arrested innocent people, I'd proven that I was capable of believing blindly and lashing out. Watching Dad eat his beans, I noticed that his hair was turning grey. I wondered what worries kept him up at night, what he'd be willing to do in order to protect his family. I went through Odile's story again, feeling that something didn't add up.

Each summer, Grandma Jo and I had spent afternoons sipping lemonade on her screened porch. Her passion was jigsaw puzzles. Sprinkling the pieces on her table, we reconstructed blue skies over Bavarian castles. Since we were marooned in the middle of wheat fields, those fragmented photos were my first look at the outside world. Grandma's puzzle habit — two a week — got expensive, so Mom bought them secondhand. The pro: cheap. The con: hours spent on a puzzle only to find pieces were missing, lost long before the church rummage sale.

It had been a while since I'd felt the frustration of an incomplete puzzle, but I recognised the feeling now. An element of Odile's story was missing. A part of the frame or one of the corners. If Odile loved Paul, why had she married someone else?

CHAPTER
FORTY

ODILE

Paris, August 1944

The Allies are getting closer. The news rolled down the rue de Rennes, it lingered in side streets. It whispered along the paths of Père Lachaise and made it to the Moulin Rouge. *They're getting closer.* The news clambered up the steps of the Métro and bounced over the white pebbles of the courtyard to the circulation desk. We'd heard that the Allies had landed on the beaches of Normandy over two months ago, so where were they? The press — full of propaganda — was no help. We depended on word of mouth.

"The Allies must be getting closer," Boris told me as we loaned out books.

"I've seen Germans packing their vehicles in front of occupied hotels."

"Vacancy signs will soon be up!" Boris replied.

Mr Pryce-Jones, shaky from his time in the internment camp, leaned on a cane as he crossed the threshold. He'd been released three weeks ago; Monsieur de Nerciat followed close behind, hands held out, worried his friend would fall.

"I shouldn't be back in Paris," Mr Pryce-Jones muttered. "Not when others remain imprisoned. And did you have to use my age as a pretext to get me out?"

"No, my dear fellow, I could have told them you were feeble-minded."

I hid my smile behind *The Turn of the Screw*, 813. Some things hadn't changed.

"Where are the Allies?" Monsieur de Nerciat asked.

"They must be on their way," Boris said.

I couldn't wait to tell Margaret, who was returning after a week of nursing her daughter through a bout of the mumps. When Margaret arrived after lunch, I barely recognised her. The brim of a new white hat hid her eyes, and the matching silk dress was as snowy as a christening gown. *It's chic to he shabby*, I reminded myself as I ran a hand over my worn belt.

"That thing's more notches than leather," she said as she joined me at my desk. "Let me offer you an outfit."

"No," I said, more sharply than I intended. Everyone knew what clothes like Margaret's meant. Paul called the women who slept with *Soldaten* "stuffed mattresses". But perhaps I was being unfair. She'd always had beautiful clothing — I'd worn many of her things myself. The new ensemble wasn't necessarily from her lover.

"What did I miss?" she asked.

"They say the Allies will get here any day!"

I expected her to be thrilled like the rest of us, but she merely said, "Oh."

Bitsi came to say hello, my grandmother's pearly opal on her finger. When my parents had discussed giving the heirloom to Bitsi, I insisted. I wanted her to have it, to know we considered her family. I'd even showed her Rémy's and my secret place. Among the crumpled handkerchiefs and dust bunnies, we lay together, me clutching his toy soldier, she his favourite book, *Of Mice and Men*. I'd grown up believing that love lasted until a mistress tore a couple apart, but Bitsi had proven that not even death could destroy true love. In that dark womb, we sobbed, our tears welding us together as sisters more than any wedding ever could.

I'd received a letter from one of Rémy's friends and handed it to Bitsi to read.

Dear Odile,
We called your brother "Judge" because he's
the one we went to to settle our disputes. I
even fashioned him a gavel with a rock, twig
and a length of twine. Stuck here, far from
home, we're frustrated and angry. Bored
and hungry. Don't take much to set
someone off. "Judge," I'd say, "is your court
in session? Louis won't stop taking the
Lord's name in vain. It tears Jean-Charles
up, and he done tore into Louis." Our argu-
ments may seem petty, but Judge took each
one seriously and managed to soothe men
who'd reached the end of a frazzled rope.
We miss him.
    Faithfully yours,
    Marcel Danez

Seeing Bitsi's expression brighten as she read, I insisted that she keep the letter. Marcel's tribute meant the world to me, but she meant more. She held the scrap of paper to her heart and made her way to the children's room.

Watching her go, Margaret hissed, "That hair of hers resembles a crown of thorns! Little Bitsi will tire of the role of weepy widow, and take a beau."

Her insinuation — that Bitsi's grief for Rémy was an act — hit me like a fist. I couldn't bear the idea that Bitsi would forget my brother. My chest hurt so much I could barely breathe. I rushed from the room. If I'd slowed down, if I'd stopped to think, I would have remembered a time when Bitsi's virtue had made me feel tarnished, too; Margaret's scorn was less about Bitsi and more about her own shame.

When Boris saw me leave, he said, "Are you sure about leaving Margaret on her own in the reference room?"

"Believe me, she thinks she has all the answers!"

"She's been a good friend to you and the Library."

"Why are you taking her side?"

He winced. "Just go."

I needed to talk to someone who understood. At the precinct, Paul offered me his chair.

"You wouldn't believe what Margaret said."

"It's the war. We all say — and do — things we regret." He rarely referred to the past. My failure to deliver books that one time. His arrest of Professor Cohen. The way we'd romped in the sheets of the departed. It was the only way we could continue as a couple.

"I know."

"Life will go back to normal."

"We've said that for years. What if this is normal?"

"Nothing lasts for ever," he said, gently massaging my back.

"Last week, when I told Margaret that Maman went to the butcher's at dawn, and there were already ten housewives queuing, she said, 'Why doesn't she buy from the black market?' With what money, I'd like to know. Anyway, all her food comes from Fel —"

I stopped myself. *No, no, no, you always do this. Not this time. Keep your mouth shut!*

"What were you going to say?" he asked.

I exhaled. "Nothing."

"Margaret's a nice type," Paul said, "for an English girl, I mean."

"Nice? She insinuated that Bitsi was pretending to mourn."

"People speak without thinking. I'm sure she didn't mean any harm."

He wouldn't rush to defend her if he knew about her Nazi. Margaret had it easy. All she had to do was snap her bony fingers, and she had parties, couture, jewellery and trips to the seaside.

"She insinuated that Bitsi will take a lover."

"Of course, Bitsi will always love your brother, but maybe some day —"

"Maybe some day?" I said sharply. "She'll never forget Rémy. Never! Not everyone's a slut like Margaret."

Paul's hands stilled on my shoulders. "You don't mean that."

How could he believe the worst of Bitsi, but the best of Margaret?

"You don't mean that," he said again.

I turned to face him and took cruel pleasure in saying, "She has a German lover."

My claim floated in the air between us, the space of a breath.

Paul's lips curled in distaste. "Slut!"

With his echo of my word, I realised I'd let my temper get the better of me. I had to be more careful with my words and less judgemental.

"I shouldn't have said what I did. You were right, you always are. She's nice, so good to my family. Thanks to her, Rémy always had food. At the Library, I don't know what we'd do without her. She's there now, doing my job."

"Harlots like her will get what's coming to them."

"Please don't talk like that. Her husband's a cad. She deserves better. You're right, people speak without thinking, like I did just now. Please promise you won't tell."

Paul remained silent.

"You won't say anything, right?"

"Who would I tell?" He turned me around and continued to massage my shoulders, his fingers digging in harder this time.

CHAPTER
FORTY-ONE

ODILE

Paris, August 1944

In Paris, gas lines had been cut and almost no one had power, yet there was a certain electricity in the air. Posters pasted on the sides of buildings urged Parisians to "attack the enemy wherever he might be". The police went on strike, as did railway employees, nurses, postmen and steelworkers. Paul helped dig up cobblestones and create barricades, anything to trap and ambush the enemy.

Combat was something I'd read about, something that happened far away, but now I heard shots in nearby streets, and people were setting cars and tanks on fire. Rumours ricocheted like bullets. It was the Americans come to liberate us! No, it was de Gaulle! No, Parisians had had enough and were fighting back! The Germans were retreating! No, they weren't giving up without a fight!

Going to and from work, I crept along the sides of the buildings, scared of snipers, scared of bombs, scared nothing would change and we would live like this for ever.

On the evening of the 24th, as I tried to finish *Voyage in the Dark* before what was left of the candle flickered one last time and went out, the church bells in Paris rang. I rose and met my parents in the hall. In her dressing gown, Maman looked to the heavens, as if to marvel at God's miracle. Papa held out his arms, the way he used to when Rémy and I were little and we'd gallop towards him. I knew my parents and I were thinking the same thing: if only Rémy were here. Wordlessly, we embraced, knowing the Occupation was at an end.

Paris had been liberated. Mr Pryce-Jones limped through the Library, shouting, "The Germans have fled." Close on his heels, Monsieur de Nerciat exclaimed, "We're free!" After kissing me on the cheeks, the two men embraced, then quickly stepped apart. They were the only discreet ones. I hugged Bitsi, Boris and the Countess. Her servants brought over all the champagne left in her cellar. I drank more in one day than I had in my entire life.

"The war's not over," Mr Pryce-Jones warned.

"But it's the beginning of the end," the Countess said.

"I'll drink to that," Monsieur de Nerciat said.

"You'll drink to anything, old chap!"

On the scraggly lawn, staff and subscribers laughed and kissed and cried. The band — made up of six subscribers — swayed between "Stars and Stripes Forever" and "La Marseillaise". Paul and I danced all night long. It was as if I'd held my breath for months and could exhale. I'd lived in the present, almost fearing the future. But the fight to survive was over, and Paul and I could start making plans. I let myself dream about a home and children.

Despite city-wide festivities, Margaret was glum. Her Leutnant had been arrested, and she didn't know where he'd been taken. Worse, after a four-year absence, her husband had returned. Life with Lawrence stretched before her like a desolate country road. To take her mind off things, I invited her for a stroll in the Tuileries. Among the trees, in the dappled light, I watched her pick at her pearls. I wanted to console her, but didn't know what to say.

There was a ruckus coming from the other side of the fence, the pounding of a drum and Parisians shouting. Perhaps a parade to celebrate the Liberation, or even victory! Hoping it would cheer her, I coaxed Margaret through the gate.

On either side of the rue de Rivoli, hundreds of men, women and children clapped as a man thumping a bass drum passed. Next, an old man in a ragged suit dangled a plucked chicken, waving it in the air. Beneath the cadence of the beats, I thought I heard a wail.

"It can't be." Margaret pointed to the old man.

As he moved closer, I saw it wasn't a chicken but a naked baby that he held. At the sight of the sobbing infant, I felt myself go dumb with shock.

"The Krauts left a souvenir," he cried, swinging the babe by its legs.

"Bastard, bastard," chanted the crowd. "Son of a whore!"

Behind him, two men dragged a woman through the street. She was naked. And she was bald. Her feet were bloodied from being scraped along the cobblestones, her body white with fright. A dark patch of pubic hair stood vivid against her skin. She tried to break away, to reach her child, but the jailers jerked her back.

"Tramp!" a man in the crowd shouted. "Where's your lover now?"

I'd never seen a bare woman, and now felt naked and violated myself. I stepped forward to help her, but Margaret grabbed my arm.

"There's nothing we can do," she said.

She was right. This wasn't a parade, it was a mob. There was no stopping them. People were savages; I'd had years of proof. "Bastard, bastard," they chanted. "Son of a whore!" Tears rolled down my cheeks. Completely surrounded, Margaret and I tried to move on, through the sea of bony elbows and scornful finger-pointing.

"The Germans never would have permitted this," a middle-aged woman tsked.

"Do you see who's holding the young woman, there on the right?" another said. "Last week, he was serving beer and *saucisses* to the Fritz."

"Who cares about him!" a man said. "That slut broke the rules."

"You don't choose who you love," Margaret whispered.

"It isn't about love," he replied. "Only whores do what she did."

Margaret was shaking. Was she shocked by the condemnation of the crowd, or did she see herself in the young mother? I tucked her torso tight against mine and guided her home.

The day was not done. Four blocks away, on a makeshift scaffold in the middle of the square, a city official wearing a blue, white and red sash stood behind a woman and gripped her nape. Dressed in what appeared to be her Sunday best, she stared ahead while a barber shaved her head. Zip, zip, zip, as if it were the most natural thing in the world, as if he'd shaved dozens of women. As the clippers glided over her scalp, sandy tresses fell on to her shoulders. *Le barbier* tossed them to the ground like garbage. On the side of the stage, surrounded by men in uniform, *five françaises* watched what would become of them as the crowd jeered. There'd been no trial, only this unseemly sentence. Seeing the women, dry-eyed and dignified, I wiped away my tears.

Eating steak while they went hungry. Wearing a new dress while their women did without.

She wasn't a woman to them, not any more. They'd been beaten and humiliated. Now it was their turn to beat, to strike, to slash.

Paul fingered her pearls. "Who gave you these?"

"My mum."

"Liar!" He pulled them until they dug into her neck.

"They were my mum's."

"I bet they're from your lover." He jerked on the necklace, and the string broke. Pearls fell around her in a sad constellation.

"My mum's," she wailed as Philippe scooped them up and put them in his pocket.

"Shut up, or you'll be sorry." Ronan held out a knife to Paul. "Care to do the honours?"

She wanted to tell him, "We've eaten dinner together. You've been to my home. When Odile was unsure of you, I stood up for you," but her voice disappeared along with her courage.

Paul took the knife.

CHAPTER
FORTY-THREE

ODILE

Paris, August 1944

The forbidden room smelled of mothballs. It was perhaps the one place in Paris that hadn't changed during the war. The last time Maman had allowed me to enter. I was fifteen. With fantasies of the future floating in my head, I delighted in my trousseau, in the treasures the women in my family had crafted for my wedding. A wooden chest held a baby blanket crocheted by my grandmother. Soon, Paul and I would have a little one. I unfolded the flowing white nightgown that Maman had sewn. "For your honeymoon," she'd said shyly. I hadn't been with Paul since he told me about Professor Cohen, and we certainly hadn't sought a new trysting place. He and I sat primly on the divan while Maman chinwagged about chips in the china. A wedding would be a new beginning. I imagined walking down the aisle towards him. Engrossed in my daydream, I barely heard someone knocking at the front door. I made my way towards the insistent rapping, and found Paul on the landing, his face bathed in perspiration.

412

"What on earth?" I giggled. "You're like a little boy, pounding like that. Are you really so impatient?"

He grabbed my hands. "Lets get married."

It was as if he'd read my mind.

"We'll elope," he said. "Today. A civil service."

"Don't the banns have to be up? Maman will be devastated if we don't marry in the church. Besides, I'd like Margaret to be my maid of honour."

"Marriage is about the two of us, nobody else. Your parents will understand. Forget the banns, I have a special licence. I've carried it in my pocket for a long time now, hoping."

"A special licence?"

"Please say yes."

Paul always knew what I wanted. "*Embrasse-moi*," I said.

In my arms, he trembled. "I love you — I love you so much. We'll go away, we'll never come back."

Would my parents be disappointed if Paul and I eloped, or secretly relieved? There was no money for a bridal dress, much less a wedding feast. One thing was certain: after the long limbo of the Occupation, I wanted to be with Paul.

"Yes!"

"Leave a note for your parents. We'll go to my aunt's for our honeymoon. I need to get away! We need to get away."

"Are you all right? You don't seem like yourself. Maybe we should wait."

"Haven't we waited long enough? I want to marry you. I want a honeymoon."

Honeymoon, I thought dreamily, packing a few tattered dresses, the nightgown from my trousseau (almost sure Maman wouldn't mind), and dear Emily Dickinson for the train trip. Paul called the stationmaster and asked him to get word to his aunt. Scarcely out the door, my suitcase clasped in his hand, I said, "Hold on! I can't leave work."

"Tell them you need a week for our honeymoon. How can they say no to true love?"

As I penned a note for the neighbour's girl to deliver, I wondered if eloping was romantic or rash.

At the counter of the *mairie*, the secretary didn't look up from her paperwork. "Come back next week. The mayor has a full schedule."

I hadn't been so sure about eloping, but now that there was opposition . . . "Please," I said, "we're in love."

"Paris may have been liberated," Paul added, a twitch of hysteria in his tone, "but there's a war on. No one knows what the future holds. We're getting married, and you're going to help."

Taking in our tense expressions, she went to see if the mayor would perform a spur-of-the-moment ceremony. Paul paced; I sat on a scarred wooden chair. We should have done this years ago, but I'd wanted Rémy at my side. I touched the empty seat beside me.

"I wish he could be here, too," Paul said.

The secretary led us to the *salle des mariages* where wispy clouds covered the light blue paint of the ceiling. The mayor donned his blue, white and red sash and began the ceremony. Paul wiped the sweat from his brow with the back of his hand. He was so nervous that

414

when the time came to say, "I do," the mayor had to nudge him.

In the train compartment, Paul picked up the newspaper and read a line, then folded it hastily and set it on his lap. He crossed and uncrossed his legs. Each time he fidgeted, his knee jostled mine.

"What's wrong?" I asked, rubbing my leg.

"Nothing."

"No regrets?"

"Regrets?" He regarded me warily.

"About getting married."

He placed his clammy hand over mine. "I loved you from the first instant I saw you."

"You loved Maman's roast pork."

"What I wouldn't give for a huge slice now."

We'd taken so much for granted.

Paul's Aunt Pierrette met us at the station with the sway-back horse and wagon, "You're the one we've heard so much about! Pleasure to meet you." Her ruddy skin was like leather, but she looked healthier than most Parisians.

In the hearth, a pheasant roasted on the spit. Fat drizzled into the fire; flames jumped and sent up smoke. I hadn't smelled this rich aroma in years, and my mouth watered. On the table, steam rose from the mashed potatoes in a ceramic bowl. I wished I could dive right in.

"It isn't much of a wedding feast," Aunt Pierrette said. "But I didn't have much notice either." She pinched Paul, and he grinned bashfully.

"It's a feast to us," I said.

415

I tried to eat slowly, but dinner was too delicious — Paul and I wolfed it down. His aunt left us alone to enjoy dessert by the light of the fire. Paul fed me spoonfuls of flan. The cream slipped down my throat, dewy drops of happiness.

In our room, Paul worked a hand under my skirt while I closed the shutters. "Be patient! I have to put on my nightgown."

"I can't wait." He pushed me on to the bed. I kissed him softly. He unfastened his trousers and tugged my skirt up.

"Slow down," I murmured as he shoved my underthings aside. "We have our whole lives."

"I love you." He plunged inside me. "Promise you'll never leave me. No matter what."

"Of course, I promise."

The next morning, he harnessed the horse, and we rode the wagon to the village to buy a ring. In the display case at the jeweller's, dozens of *alliances*, wedding bands, gleamed, surely sold for a few francs by desperate people.

"It's not bad luck?" I asked Paul as he slipped one on my finger.

"A happy marriage doesn't depend on luck, but on intentions," the jeweller replied.

The gold band fitted perfectly. For the next seven days, I could barely stop grinning.

The train to Paris was delayed. When I fretted about being late for work, Paul insisted we could go to the

Library directly from the station. "You don't have to accompany me," I said.

"But I want to, Madame Martin. And you need someone to carry your suitcase."

"Won't you be late?"

"I'm on evenings this week."

In the reading room, on the table in front of the windows, I was stunned to see a wedding cake, chocolates, champagne and a samovar for tea.

"You planned this?" I asked him.

"They did." He gestured to our well-wishers. There was the Countess looking proud. Boris and Bitsi beaming. Monsieur de Nerciat and Mr Pryce-Jones bickering, "Told you they'd get married." "No, *I* told *you*." And Eugénie with my parents?

"I can see why you enjoy working here," my father said. "I wish I'd visited sooner."

"Oh, Papa! I'm glad you're here now."

"Congratulations, *ma fille*," Maman said as she and Eugénie embraced me.

I gushed over the sugary wedding cake (Oh, the rations everyone had donated! That meant more to me than anything!) and regaled them with Paul's passionate proposal. He then recounted the ceremony.

"Where's Margaret?" I asked Bitsi.

"She hasn't been in this week. We sent an invitation, but she didn't reply."

I frowned. Was she ill, or was Christina? I started towards the telephone, but a cork popped — the sign of celebration, my favourite sound in the whole world — and the Countess proffered a glass of champagne. Paul and I listened to tributes from family and friends as we stuffed our mouths with cake. I barely noticed when he kissed my cheek and slipped away to work.

Tipsy from the celebration, I tottered to Margaret's, along the gilded Alexandre III bridge where I caught a glimpse of the Eiffel Tower. "Hello, you beautiful iron lady!" I cried out to her.

At the door, Isa greeted me. A maid at the door? How peculiar. Perhaps the butler was ill, too. "Madame isn't here."

"When will she be back?"

Isa tried to shut the door. "She's not going anywhere in her condition."

I pushed my way in. "In her condition? Is she . . . with child?"

"I wish," Isa said tearfully.

"Is she ill? Is her husband here?"

"He's taken the little miss and gone to England."

"That doesn't make sense." The champagne had gone to my head, and I had trouble following what she was saying. "Hold on. You said she's not going anywhere. Is she home?"

"Madame doesn't want to see anyone."

"But I'm her best friend."

Isa hesitated. "She might be sleeping."

"If she is, I'll come right back."

I teetered down the hall, touching the wall now and again for balance. Of all the crazy things, of course Margaret would want to see me. A pity she'd missed the party. What a terrible time to come down with something. Only Margaret could be so unlucky.

At the threshold of the dim room, I watched her sleep and knew I should let her rest, but I couldn't contain my excitement and tiptoed closer. Tufts of hair clumped near her ear, and the rest was a few millimetres long. Her neck appeared to be bruised. I blinked. Clearly, I'd had too much to drink. *Mais non*, even after I rubbed my eyes, her hair was short and the bruises remained. Her wrist, wound with white gauze, rested on the coverlet. It appeared as though she'd had some kind of accident. No. She looked beaten and shorn like the young *maman* on the street. The thought sobered me.

Without opening her eyes, she asked, "Who was at the door, Isa?"

"Me."

Margaret sat up.

"What happened?" I asked.

"As if you don't know." Her voice was a hoarse whisper.

I stared at the grey bruises that pearled around Margaret's throat. "When?"

"A week ago."

I recalled Paul's edginess, his insistence that we go away. Something had been off. How could I not have seen?

"Why did you tell him about Felix and me?" she asked.

"I didn't . . ." I didn't mean to.

"*You're* the reason this happened!" She held a hand to her naked crown.

I began to tremble and grasped the headboard. "No."

"Then why did he do it?"

"I don't know."

"Liar!" Margaret said. "And I thought diplomatic circles could be vicious. Tell me, *friend*, what exactly did you say?"

"Nothing, really . . ."

"Yes, Felix gave me things. But I shared, believing you would do the same for me. You knew exactly who the presents came from."

"Yes, but I never would lower myself —"

"Lower yourself? You didn't have to, because I did it for you. And for Rémy."

"I didn't ask you for anything!"

"You didn't have to."

"This isn't my fault."

"Then whose fault is it?" she asked.

Her bald stare unnerved me. I looked to the window, to the dressing table, to the portrait of Christina.

"What's so wrong about wanting someone?" Margaret continued. "Being wanted? You were the one who said that I was in a foreign country, that I could do as I pleased."

"I meant learning to ride a bike, not taking up with a Nazi!"

Margaret reached up as if to touch her pearls, like she did when she was upset, but for once she wasn't wearing them.

She needed to know I hadn't meant to hurt her. "I didn't do this."

"Paul was the gun, but you pulled his trigger."

420

"What about *you?* What you said about Bitsi pretending to mourn —"

"Was unforgivable," Margaret said. "At least I can admit when I do wrong."

"I only told one person."

"How could you betray me?"

"I was envious —"

"Jealous of me, when you had the perfect job, a loving family and a devoted man?"

I never considered what I had, only what I wanted. "Surely it's not that bad. Your hair will grow out."

"You think the worst thing he did was to my hair? Because of you, I've lost everything," She held up her broken wrist. "See what they did to me? I can't dress myself, I can't write to my daughter. If you hated me so much, I wish you'd hired an assassin, because to my family I might as well be dead. The staff had a choice to remain with me or go to England with Lawrence and Christina. No one but Isa would stay in the flat with a harlot like me."

"I never meant for . . ."

Margaret threw back the coverlet and lifted the hem of her negligee, revealing the welts that peppered her legs. I squeezed my eyes shut, wishing I could take back my words, wishing I could undo the harm.

"Coward! If I can bare the scars, you can bear to look."

She bristled with anger. Her spirit had been bruised but not broken.

"Lawrence photographed me, you know. If I dare make a fuss, he'll use the pictures in court to prove I'm an unfit mother. Only sluts get their heads shaved, right? How am I ever going to get my little girl back?"

"I could telephone Lawrence, explain . . ."

"Telephone Lawrence, explain," Margaret scoffed. "You should go."

"I could stay and help. Make your meals, write to your family."

"I don't want any more of your 'help'. Please leave."

I moved towards the door.

"Wait!" she said.

I turned. I'd do anything for another chance. Surely, she'd forgive me. We'd been through so much together.

"There's a blue box on the shelf in the dressing room. Bring it to me."

I tried to give her the package, but she said, "For you. I asked Felix to find it. When you wear it, I hope you'll remember what you did, and realise what it means to be a true friend."

Inside was a red belt. The leather was buttery smooth, long and slim as a whip.

"How can I make it up to you? Please give me a chance."

Margaret turned her face to the wall. "Go. I never want to see you again."

CHAPTER
FORTY-FOUR

LILY

Froid, Montana, June 1988

"Dad's wife took away *Forever!*" I told Odile as I slammed into her kitchen. "She said Judy Blume writes 'smut'. Censorship is wrong!"

"So is throwing a fit instead of sitting down to have a conversation." Odile finished drying the last of her dishes. "You should ask Ellie what she fears."

"Huh?"

"Reading is dangerous."

"Dangerous?"

"Ellie's scared the book will put ideas in your head, scared you'll want to experiment with sex."

"I read *Out of Africa* and didn't establish a coffee plantation in Kenya!"

Odile smiled a little smile that meant she thought I said something silly. "Not many people do. Sex is a natural part of life. But it's a big step, and Ellie is worried."

"I've never been on a date," I said. "At this rate, I never will. Ellie's trying to ruin my life."

"You know that's not true."

"All she cares about are Dad and the boys."

"Aren't you tired of that refrain? Ellie does her best. Try to put yourself in her skin."

"Yuck!"

"In her *shoes*. Have you ever considered how Ellie feels? In all these years, she and your father have never bought a new couch or lamp. She cooks in your mom's pans, she eats off her plates. How strange must that feel? Are you certain that *you're* the outsider?"

She had a point.

"Love isn't rationed. Ellie can care about all of you. You should talk to her."

"What if —"

"Take the first step."

On my way home, I watched the boys run around the back yard. Joe waved a leaky water pistol at Benjy, who wore his baby blanket like a cape. They scampered towards me, and each one grabbed a leg.

"Mine," Benjy said.

"No," Joe argued, "she's mine."

"You're both mine." I hugged them.

Inside, I ran my hand over Mom's dining room table, the curtains she'd sewn, the pastel paintings of birds she'd chosen. Nothing here belonged to Ellie, the unpaid curator of the Brenda museum.

In the master bedroom, in my mother's rocking chair, Ellie darned my father's socks. "Finished with your hissy fit?" she asked.

"Sorry I ran off," I said, the fight gone out of me. "It wasn't very mature."

"Hon, I just want the best for you."

"I know." I went to her, and she hugged me.

To celebrate my driver's licence, Odile invited Ellie and me to the Husky House for a sundae. In the orange booth, Odile set a gift on the table. "Ordered from Chicago." Gently, I removed the velvet ribbon and opened the box. Inside was a beret, grey and downy like a dove.

"*J'adore!*" I lunged across the table to kiss her on either cheek. "I'll never take it off!"

She straightened the beret over my brows.

"You look French," Ellie said, the best possible compliment she could have paid me.

At home in my room, beret on my head, I took out the Josephine Baker record Odile had loaned me and ran my fingers along Josephine's face, jealous of her easy grin, her dewy skin, her confidence. I kicked off my shoes and yanked off my shirt and pants. In my white bra and panties, I stared at my scrawny reflection, wondering what it would be like to be a sex symbol in silk stockings. I grabbed a black marker and drew circles around my thighs, where I imagined the tops would reach. It wasn't enough. I wanted to draw myself a whole new life.

That summer before our senior year, Mary Louise and I worked at the O'Haire Motel. We vacuumed and made beds, cleaned toilets and scrubbed tubs. It paid better than baby-sitting, and Mrs Vandersloot gave us a Coke during our break.

The first week of August, the motel was full of custom cutters. The men worked from sunup to sundown and were old and grizzled for the most part, though we always hoped some would be young and good-looking. From Texas to the panhandle of Oklahoma, through South Dakota to us in Montana, they helped harvest America. The men weren't tied to a town, not like we were. They were free, and we envied them.

Their compliments made us blush. They looked at us like we were women. Last night, under a watchful crescent moon, Mary Louise snuck out to be with one. They guzzled booze and made out in the bed of his truck. She said Johnny knew what he was doing, more than her boyfriend Keith did.

The cutters were moving on today, taking their machinery and the promise of adventure with them. Hauling the vacuum down the hall, I ran smack dab into one. He grabbed the Hoover with one hand and steadied me with the other. I could smell the wheat on his worn cotton shirt. I straightened my beret and peered up at his face. Lord, he was handsome. Tanned from his time in the sun. Twenty-one or twenty-two years old. Eyes that had seen entire states, long stretches of road, and green lights, plenty of green lights. A man.

"What's a pretty girl like you luggin' this old thing around for? You work here?"

"Yes."

"Where should I put it?"

"Room four."

"No need to whisper, darlin'. We ain't in church."

I unlocked the door. He set the vacuum in front of the TV. The sheets were in a heap on the floor. Mary

426

Louise would have whistled and said, "People had fun in here last night!" But I wasn't Mary Louise.

"I like your little hat." He walked over, until we were an inch apart, I knew he could feel my heart pound. "You're as pretty as a doe."

My eyes closed with the shock of his lips on mine. Nothing had ever felt so good.

"Come on, Mike," a cutter hollered from the lobby.

We moved apart. I held my breath. His calloused hand caressed my cheek. "You okay?" he asked.

I nodded. He'd forget me the minute he hit the highway, but I would remember our kiss for ever. The rest of the morning, my fingers moved to my mouth.

After work, Mary Louise and I stopped by my house to fill Mom's hummingbird feeder. We continued on, past the Girl Scouts in the park. Right outside town limits, she and I lay on the prairie, its grass stiff like hay. A few feet away, a gopher poked his head out of a hole. It was hot and dry; it was always hot and dry. In the distance, we heard a combine grumbling over the field. I clasped my hands behind my head. Mary Louise sucked on a piece of grass. Clouds rolled past, never staying long. The rest of the world watched MTV while we lived reruns of *Little House on the Prairie*. School was a week away. I thought we would die from the peace and quiet.

"Promise we'll get out of here," she said.

On my last first day of school, I wore a skirt that matched my beret, and everyone gawked — in Froid, people who didn't wear jeans were mutants. Mary

Louise and I didn't have any of the same classes. Every time I caught a glimpse of her, she was down the hall with Keith, I waded through confused freshmen but never reached her. Robby and I had the same schedule. He was an aisle away, just like in church, just like always. Somewhere deep down. I knew he liked me. But I didn't trust deep down.

After school, chez Odile, I drank *café au lait* and contemplated her wedding photo. Would a man ever look at me the way Buck had looked at her? The way Keith ogled Mary Louise?

"I barely see Mary Louise any more," I said, hurt she'd dropped me as easily as AP Math.

"The thing about friendship is that you won't always be at the same place at the same time," Odile said. "Remember when you had your hands full with Ellie and the boys? It's Mary Louise's turn to be busy. First love is like that. It takes all your time."

"You make love sound like a leech."

She laughed, "Well, it is."

"No, it's not!" I said hotly.

"She'll be back. Give her time."

I thought of the way Mary Louise flushed when Keith slung his arm around her. When I drew near, he tugged at her waist and said, "Let's go." She followed because they wanted to be alone together. Mary Louise got everything first. First kiss. First base. First love.

"It's normal to be jealous," Odile said.

"I'm not!"

"It's normal," she repeated. "Only . . ."

"Only what?"

"Try to remember your day will come," she finished lamely.

Yeah, right.

At home, Ellie made my favourite dinner, steak and French fries served with a green salad. Everyone else had their salads first, but I ate mine last, followed by a piece of cheese like a *Parisienne*.

"Do you have to wear that hat all the time?" Dad asked.

"Its a beret. *C'est chic*."

"You haven't taken it off in months. Is it chic to stink?"

I ignored him. "*Le steak est délicieux!*"

"Can't you get her to speak English?" Dad asked Ellie.

She smiled. I think she liked it when I spoke French.

"Have you considered what I said about applying to college?" Dad asked.

"I told you, I'm going to be a writer."

"Writing isn't a profession," he said.

"Tell that to Danielle Steel," Ellie said, "She's richer than Jonas Ivers!"

"You'll study accounting," Dad said. "You need a back-up plan."

"A back-up plan? You think I'll fail? Anyway, it's none of your business what I study."

He poked his fork in my direction. "It is if I pay the tab."

"With you, everything comes down to money."

"One of the jobs of a banker," he said, "is making sure that everyone has a plan."

I had no idea how we'd gone from a nice dinner to a fight about college.

"I think," Ellie said, "your father's trying to say that he's seen people lose their homes, entrepreneurs lose their businesses, and he doesn't want you to suffer the way they have."

After dinner, I went to Odile's. "When you were my age, did you know what you wanted to be?"

"I loved books, so I became a librarian. You need to find your passion."

"Dad said I should learn a trade."

"He's not wrong. You need to feel alive, but you also have to pay the rent. It's important for a woman to have her own money. I worked as the church secretary, and appreciated the income. You want to have choices."

"I just wish he wouldn't lecture me."

"Dear Professor Cohen always said, 'Accept people for who they are, not for who you want them to be.'"

"What did she mean?"

"She was talking about my father. She said he had my best interests at heart, but I wouldn't believe her. You and your dad are different, but that doesn't mean he doesn't love and worry about you."

The day of the winter formal, I told myself it didn't matter that no one invited me to the dance. Boys in Froid didn't have any brains. I'd find my soulmate in New York; I had already applied to Columbia. With five million men, one of them was bound to like me. Simone de Beauvoir didn't find Sartre until she was twenty-one.

430

In the cafeteria, Mary Louise sidled up to me and invited me over after dinner to see her gown. For months, she'd forgotten I existed. Now she wanted to show off.

"Can't," I lied. "Too much homework."

"Please!"

Part of me wanted to be a good friend. A bigger part wanted Keith to dump her, so she'd be as miserable as me.

After dinner, I slumped in Odile's chair.

"Mary Louise abandoned me. Again."

"Didn't she invite you over to see her dress?"

I stared at the books on our 1955.34 shelf. *Bridge to Terabithia, Roots, My Antonia.* "I don't want to go."

"What if I come, too?" Odile asked.

I perked up. "It might help."

The whole way to Mary Louise's, she watched me. Like a hawk, Mom would have said. The minute we walked through the door, Mary Louise twirled for us. In the pastel gown, her neck and shoulders exposed, she appeared more delicate than ever.

Her body had changed almost overnight. Her breasts rose as bold as the Rockies, while mine stayed flat as the plains. Her hips curved like a bell, but my body, straight as a pencil, hadn't budged.

"What do you think?" She tugged at the bodice.

"Stunning," Odile said.

Crossing my arms over my stunted chest, I thought for a minute, until I found the compliment that would mean the most: "Prettier than Angel."

"No!" Mary Louise peered at the mirror beside the coat-rack. "Really?"

I nodded, not able to get any more words out. Jealousy welled like tears, and in that moment, the most beautiful she'd ever been, I could barely stand to look at her.

Keith arrived. He hovered near the door, and Sue Bob nudged him towards Mary Louise. The way he gazed at her made me feel hopeless. A sour bile rose in my throat; I swallowed again and again. Not sure I could last much longer, I inched towards the door. Mary Louise bounced over, and Sue Bob snapped a photo of the two of us. "Why should you be miserable and alone?" the bile said. "A real friend wouldn't have guilted you into coming over. She's gloating, can't you see that? Tell the pimply jockstrap what she said — that the custom cutter she made out with kissed better, did everything better."

With Mary Louise's arm wrapped around my waist, I said, "Keith . . ."

Odile frowned.

"You should know —" I continued.

"Don't," Odile whispered. "It only takes a word. I can see the crows circling in your head."

CHAPTER
FORTY-FIVE

ODILE

Paris, September 1944

How could you betray me? Margaret's question echoed in my head as I drifted along the pavement, towards the river, towards home. Though the magnificent Alexandre III bridge loomed before me, I only saw Margaret's stubbled scalp. I wanted to hide in my room, or confess to Maman and Eugénie. But both would be horrified by the way I'd put my dearest friend in harm's way. In Paul's way. No, I was too ashamed to face Maman. I couldn't go home. And I couldn't go to the Library, where everyone loved Margaret. She had made it clear that she never wanted to see me again. This meant she wouldn't return to the Library if I still worked there, and she'd lose her friends and her calling.

Not long ago, I'd cast suspicious glances at subscribers and wondered what kind of person would write a crow letter. Now I knew: someone like me. *Monsieur l'Inspecteur, Margaret Saint James — a British subject — dared to fall in love with a German soldier.* I'd even delivered my complaint to a policeman.

I started across the Seine, belt buckle in hand, the leather swaying like a switch. Leaning over the railing, I watched the water. I was a brute, every bit as much as Paul. I tugged at my wedding ring and hurled it into the river. There. He was no longer my husband. We'd divorce, and never speak again. Divorce. A divorcee was lower than a fallen woman. "What will the neighbours think?" Maman would ask. My mother wouldn't care *why* I was divorcing. She would cast me out, just like Aunt Caro.

An hour earlier, I'd celebrated my future. Now there was only darkness. I didn't know what to do with myself. I ambled up the Champs-Élysées, past couples dining at an outdoor café, around a line of cinema-goers, and continued on, not knowing where I was going until I arrived at the American Hospital. As I passed by the ambulance in the drive, a nurse said, "Glad you're back. We could use the help."

Margaret didn't want anything to do with me, but I could care for the wounded here. I'd stay at the hospital — staff and volunteers slept on cots — like I had at the beginning of the war. I wouldn't have to face my family and friends, and Paul would never find me. Relieved, I slumped on to the cement stoop by the back entrance.

Margaret had been right. I'd never admitted how angry it made me when she insulted soldiers like Rémy or when she insinuated that Bitsi's mourning was a charade. I'd never admitted I'd been jealous of her glamorous life, I'd bottled up my resentment, and like a magnum of champagne that someone had shaken, sticky emotions came bursting out. In the moment, I'd

434

wanted to punish her, and a moment was enough to ruin a life — Margaret's and her daughter's.

An American soldier on crutches hobbled over. "Hello, little gal."

I sniffled, and he tendered a handkerchief.

"What's wrong?"

I bit my lip, afraid to open my mouth, afraid the whole story would rush out.

He sat beside me. "What's wrong?"

"I've done something terrible."

"Well, that's something that most people can understand."

His gaze was so intense that I had to deflect his attention. "Which state are you from?"

"Montana."

"What's it like?"

"Heaven."

Subscribers from Kentucky had said the same thing, so had soldiers from Kent and Saskatchewan. "You'll have to convince me."

"Montana's the prettiest place on earth, and that's saying something, sitting where we are, in gay Paree. I wanted to get away from my hick town, but if I'm lucky enough to go back, I swear I'll never leave. The people there are decent. Honest. I used to think that was boring."

"Boring might be nice for a change."

"How come you speak English so good?"

"I learned at the American Library when I was a child."

"There's an American Hospital *and* an American Library?"

"Don't forget the American Radiator Company and the American Church! Monsieur de Nerciat, one of our subscribers, used to joke that Americans had colonised Paris without telling anyone."

He laughed. "What subscribers?"

"I'm a librarian. Well, I used to be."

"I'd love to see your Library. Maybe you could take me."

I frowned.

"You're right." He rubbed his thigh. "With this bum leg, I should stay put. But I'd like to spend more time with you."

The following afternoon, we picnicked on the stoop. He traded his cigarette rations for ham and a baguette. He told me that fields in Montana resembled a patchwork quilt. He told me there wasn't a cloud in the big sky. He told me I needed to taste his mother's beef stew. Two days later, he asked me to marry him.

I wanted to go away without seeing anyone I knew ever again. To start over and become someone else, someone better. I'd miss my parents, but they were better off without me. I'd miss my colleagues and my habitués, but in my absence, Margaret could remain. *I love the Library, but I love you more*, she'd told me. I loved the Library, but Margaret meant even more to me, and I would prove it to her.

"Little gal?" Buck gazed at me with such understanding, I felt I could tell him everything. Yet somehow, I sensed he already knew.

436

"Of course, I'll marry you."

He pulled me close. I felt the warmth of his chest, the soft cotton of his shirt. I felt safe.

The day I'd come back from Brittany, I'd taken my suitcase to the Library. At dawn, when no one but the caretaker was about, I retrieved it along with the last batch of crow letters I had stolen. At Bitsi's desk, which was covered with children's drawings, sticky pens and her favourite teacup, which no one else wanted because it was chipped, I wrote:

> *Dearest Bitsi,*
> *Please take tender care of Margaret. Tell*
> *Maman and Papa I'm fine, tell them I'm*
> *sorry. Look after the Professor's manuscript.*
> *I love you like a sister, like a twin.*
>   *Yours,*
>   *Odile*

I meandered through the Library to say goodbye. First to the periodical room, where it all began. To the reference room, where I'd learned as much as subscribers. To the Afterlife, where I ran my hand along the spines of the books to let them know they wouldn't be forgotten. And I left the Library for the last time.

CHAPTER
FORTY-SIX

LILY

Froid, Montana, January 1989

On the way home from Mary Louise's, Odile asked what I'd almost said to Keith.

"Nothing."

"Lily," she chided.

"She cheated on him with a custom cutter."

"That's none of your business. Why would you tell?"

"I don't know!"

"Well, think about it."

"I wanted her to myself again."

"Is it possible that you're angry with her?" Odile asked.

"Maybe."

"What's her real crime?"

"I don't want to talk about it."

"Tough!"

I knew she wouldn't let it go. "I don't have a boyfriend, but she does. These last months, she completely forgot me."

"I understand," Odile said.

It felt so good to hear those words. The sour bile dissipated.

438

"If Mary Louise has done something to hurt you, tell her," she continued. "Don't bottle it up, and don't think her being unhappy will make you feel better. Mary Louise has a big heart — there's room for you and Keith."

As we moved on to Odile's driveway, she said, "You'll have boyfriends, too."

"Yeah, right."

"Believe me." Under the stars, I could see her solemn expression. "Love will come and go and come again. But if you're lucky to have one true friend, treasure her. Don't let her go."

She was right, I needed to treasure Mary Louise. But if I was ever to confess to Mary Louise what I'd almost done, I was sure she'd never talk to me again.

Odile unlocked the front door and we sank on to her couch.

"I want to run away."

"Don't run," Odile said.

"Why shouldn't I?"

"I'll tell you why. Because I ran away."

"What?"

"Like you, I felt ashamed. I ran away from my parents. My job. And my husband."

"You left Buck?"

"No, my first husband. My French husband."

I was confused.

"You're not the only one who was jealous of your dearest friend," Odile admitted.

"You?"

"I betrayed her." She touched her tarnished belt buckle. "Margaret said she never wanted to see me again. She and I shared the same social circle, and we both adored the Library. But for her, it was a labour of love — she'd volunteered selflessly, giving without getting a centime in return."

"How could you leave?"

"If I'd stayed, she would have lost everything, most especially the place she called home. I loved the Library, but I loved Margaret more. Too ashamed to tell friends and family the truth, too afraid of the consequences, I married Buck, and left France without saying farewell. I've never seen my brother's grave and hope my parents were able to claim his body," She took a deep breath. "I ran. And until you, I've never told anyone."

I threw my arms around her, but she didn't hug me back.

"I can never forgive myself," she whispered.

"For what you did to Margaret?"

"For abandoning her."

"She told you to go."

"Sometimes that's when you should stay."

"But . . . you always know the right thing to say."

"Because I've said so many wrong things."

Stunned by what she'd said, I surveyed the ferns near the window, the tidy stack of records, the shelf of our favourite books. After the tornado of revelations, I almost expected to find that these things had crashed to the floor.

"Are you really a bigamist?"

440

"Buck's dead. So not any longer."

We chuckled, though it wasn't funny. But it kind of was.

"What did you do? Was it so bad?"

When Odile finished telling the tale of Margaret and her lover, and how Paul and his cronies had attacked her, the missing pieces snapped into place and I could see the whole picture.

"Even if what you say is true —"

"It's true," she said sharply. "They shattered her wrist."

"It wasn't your fault. You didn't break any bones."

"I might as well have. I told."

"Each person is responsible for their actions."

"Generally, I'd agree," she said, "but not in this case. The stakes were too high. I put Margaret in danger. I never breathed a word of this to anyone, not even Buck." She looked me straight in the eye. "But I'm telling you because I don't want you to make the same mistake. Control your jealousy, or it will control you."

I wished I could convince Odile of what I felt to be true, that she would never hurt anyone.

"Do you ever wonder what happened to Margaret? Do you think she went to England for her daughter? Did you ever try to contact her, to see if she's okay?"

Odile opened a drawer and took out a newspaper clipping from June 1980 of the *Herald*, and I scanned the profile of Margaret Saint James:

We'd lost lovers, family, friends, our livelihoods. Many of us were picking up the pieces of our lives, though some pieces were lost forever. We had to recreate ourselves.

I had an acquaintance who dealt with this loss by destroying things. The crashing of plates hitting the floor was her solace. Perhaps she wanted to break things before they broke her, but the destruction bothered me.

Those were lean years in Paris; rationing continued well after the war. We were hungry and tired. I asked her maid to give me the shards, thinking that I could mend them, but they were beyond repair. I put fragments together to brighten my daughter's worn clothing. Library subscribers admired the brooches. I started selling them, and Parisiennes wore my work. What is fashionable in Paris is soon worn the world over.

I was thrilled to glimpse Margaret, alive and well, and a real artist. "Are you sure she lost custody of her daughter?"

"She was certain she would . . ."

"According to the article, her daughter lived with her."

Odile studied the news clipping. "I never interpreted it like that."

"Maybe things didn't end so badly for Margaret. There's the address of her boutique in Paris." I pointed to the page. "You should write."

"She might not want me to."

"You should try."

"I want to respect her feelings."

"You're afraid she won't write back."

"That, too."

"Write to her!" Maybe this was how I was like my mother, a guerrilla optimist. I felt there could be a happy ending for Odile and Margaret, I felt it with my whole heart. *Love will come and go and come again. Treasure your best friend. Don't let her go.*

"I'll think about it."

We'd gone down a dark road, fraught with ugly feelings, but she'd seen me at my worst, and still loved me. I kissed her on both cheeks and said goodnight. Once again, Odile had saved me.

CHAPTER
FORTY-SEVEN

ODILE

Froid, Montana, September 1983

I spent another birthday alone, with track and field on the television, because Buck and Marc had liked sports. I remembered how we three had watched together on the couch, how Buck had hit the mute button ("Damn announcers never say anything good, anyway"), so I could listen to Bach on the stereo.

Perhaps I lived too much in the past. It was easy, when many memories were sweet. I savoured my wedding night with Buck, somewhat surprised to have found pleasure again. *Love is like the sea. It's a moving thing, but still and all, it takes shape from the shore it meets, and it's different with every shore. 813, Their Eyes Were Watching God.*

Of course, there were trying times. Meeting Buck's parents, at their home, on what felt like their terms. "Ma, Pop, this is the surprise I was telling you about. Here's my little gal, Odile," Buck had said proudly and pulled me to his side.

"It's a pleasure to meet you," I said, enunciating clearly like the Countess.

"A deal?" his father said.

"Ordeal," his mother corrected.

"*Oh-deal* and I got hitched in France," Buck said.

His father regarded me warily. His mother's vague smile became a bitter pucker, "How can you be married if we weren't there?" she asked.

"What about Jenny?" Mr Gustafson said.

"She's like a daughter to us," Mrs Gustafson said. "While you were . . . away, we spent the holidays together."

Away? Buck wasn't taking the waters in Europe, he was in combat.

"Everyone assumed you and Jenny had an understanding," she continued.

I looked to Buck. "She was my high-school sweetheart," he explained. "I never asked her to wait. I'm not a kid any more. The war . . . She'll never understand like you do. Of everybody, you're the only one who knows."

It was true, Buck and I had the war — his mother couldn't even bring herself to say the word. But time moved forward, and he and I had so much more: a home and a son and happiness.

My in-laws never warmed to me, but Father Maloney was kind. He hired me as the church secretary, and I enjoyed writing the newsletter and assembling a small library in the vestibule. It took time for the locals to forgive me for "stealing" Buck from his high-school girlfriend, but the tarter the towns-people, the sweeter he was. When I showed Buck a photo of the ALP courtyard, he planted a border of petunias like the

445

Library's. Through an army friend back east, he found books in French, and my shelves were covered with Professor Cohen's novels, set in Egypt after the war. Though the manuscript she'd entrusted to me had never been published, I liked to think that it was safe in the Library. Buck never complained about the expense of my subscription to the Paris edition of the *Herald*, never pointed out that the news came a week late. "Some women want jewels, you need paper," he said. "I knew that when I married you."

I read each "ALP News" column, which is how I knew that Miss Reeder had resumed work at the Library of Congress; Miss Wedd had been released from the internment camp and gone back to keeping the Library's books; Bitsi had been promoted to Assistant Director; the Countess had published her memoir and Boris had retired. It was a satisfaction to know that the Library continued. Over the years, I'd seen my father interviewed about the rise of drugs in the city, and Margaret featured in a profile piece. I missed them, especially Margaret.

Now, I wandered about the house, a ghost with no one to haunt. I ate alone. I slept alone. I was sick of being alone. In the wardrobe, I stared up at my jewellery box, where I'd stashed the letters I couldn't bring myself to burn, I'd made mistakes. I'd learned, but never fast enough. If my life had been a novel, full of chapters both dull and exciting, painful and funny, tragic and romantic, it was now time to reflect on the final page. I was lonely. If only my story would end. If only I were brave enough to close the book once and for all.

Buck's rifle was propped in the corner. Dust had gathered on the scope. I wondered if the gun was loaded. Knowing Buck, it was. *You were the gun, Paul was the trigger.* No, that's not what Margaret said. *Paul was the gun, but you pulled his trigger.* You pull the trigger. Hold up the gun and pull the trigger. I picked it up.

The doorbell rang. I didn't care. The doorbell rang. My finger inched towards the trigger. Someone walked in and said, "Hello?" I recognised the voice. It was the girl who lived next door, I shoved the rifle back into place.

"Anyone home?"

Dazed, I walked to the living room.

"What do you want?" I asked.

"I'm writing a report on you. I mean, on your country," the girl said. "Maybe you could come over so I can interview you."

It was strange to see someone else in my living room.

"It looks like a library in here," she added.

The last time had been four years ago, when the undertaker took Buck's body.

The girl turned to go.

"When?" I asked.

She looked back. "How about now?"

It seemed that life had offered me an epilogue.

CHAPTER
FORTY-EIGHT

LILY

Froid, Montana, May 1989

"College will be a new chapter in your life," Odile told me as we exited Mass, "Up to you to make it an exciting one." It would be, I'd been accepted at Columbia, Mary Louise at the New York Institute of Art. Thank God, because I couldn't imagine life without her. Keith had enrolled at the Vo-tech in Butte but promised to write to her. Robby was staying put. Tiffany was headed to Northwestern, or maybe Northeastern. I felt an unexpected nostalgia for my classmates, even the ones I didn't like.

In the hall, each table had been specially decorated with baskets of flowers in the senior class colours, red and white. At the percolator, the men talked about wily President Reagan, in Moscow for a summit. We women waited in line for pastries.

"You must be so proud of Lily," Mrs Ivers told Odile.

"I suppose she'll go off to college and come back smarter than the rest of us," old Mrs Murdoch said.

"She's already smarter than some," Odile replied, looking pointedly at the other ladies, who scurried off.

448

I remembered the phrase *envoyer balader*, which literally means to send someone for a walk, but really means to blow them off. "They always try to talk to you," I told Odile.

"Who?"

"Those ladies. They say, 'Nice weather,' or 'Lovely sermon,' and you send them packing."

"They were mean to me."

The petulant tone surprised me. It surprised her, too — I saw a dawning in her eyes.

"They've tried to make up for it," I said. "Isn't it time you gave them a chance?"

Odile regarded the ladies who were pouring themselves some coffee. She joined them at the percolator and picked up the pitcher of cream.

"Invigorating sermon today," she told them.

Smiling tremulously, Mrs Ivers said, "Indeed it was."

"Father was inspired," Mrs Murdoch added, holding out her cup.

Odile poured the cream.

On the morning of graduation, I put on my beret and Gunne Sax dress, grabbed my speech, and went to Odile's. On the lawn, robins were pecking at the ground. *You were almost a Robin. Be brave.* Oh, Mom, I've tried . . .

Odile was as excited as I was for graduation. She'd even replaced her tatty red belt with a stylish black one.

"*Très belle*", I said.

She blushed. "Read me your speech."

449

I pretended to be on the stage. "People say that teens don't listen. Well, we do. We hear what you say and what you don't. Sometimes we need advice, but not always. Don't listen when someone tells you not to bother a person — reach out to make a friend. People don't always know what to do or say. Try not to hold that against them, you never know what's in their heart. Don't be afraid to be different. Stand your ground. During bad times, remember that nothing lasts for ever. Accept people for who they are, not for who you want them to be. Try to put yourself in their shoes. Or, as my friend Odile would say, 'in their skin'."

She beamed at me. "You hold so many people in your heart."

I hugged her. She felt little, like a hummingbird.

Ellie came with the camera, and Odile insisted on reapplying lipstick before posing with me. Then it was time. The boys wanted Odile to sit in the "way-back" of the station wagon with them. Ellie and Grandma Pearl sat in the middle. Dad let me drive. He didn't even offer his usual advice à la *Don't run over the kids playing on the sidewalk*.

At school, Mary Louise, already in her gown and mortarboard, put a black tassel on my beret. In the gym, our class of fifty was seated in the front rows. Like heavy heads of wheat whispering to each other right before harvest, our murmurs rippled. I glanced back, to friends and family who'd come to support us. The town was always behind us. They were already behind us. This was goodbye. This was hello. I was done, I could leave. This was what I had wanted for years: out. And yet.

When I gave my speech, my voice trembled. Scanning the audience, I saw Dad's proud expression, and added, "Finally, some advice from a banker's daughter: find your passion, but make sure you have a job that pays the bills." Everyone laughed. The band played "Only the Young" by Journey. One by one, each student's name was called out, and we collected our diplomas at the podium. Afterward, with a roar of excitement, we threw our mortarboards into the air. Mary Louise and I hugged. A door had been thrown wide open.

At home, Joe, Benjy and I tumbled out of the car, and the adults followed. Friends arrived for my party, and Ellie herded them into the house. "Sue Bob made the cake, chocolate of course, you know Lily!"

I looked at Odile. "A French lesson?"

"A quick one."

At her kitchen table, I was glad to have Odile to myself, just like always. She handed me an envelope. Inside was a plane ticket to Paris and a black and white postcard. I hugged her. "I can't believe it!" I examined the ticket. There was only one.

"Where's yours?" I asked. "Aren't you coming?"

"Not this time."

I read the card. "To Lily, for your summer, with all my love," Paris. It didn't seem possible. Where would I stay? With my dorm room and orientation session, New York was simple in comparison. But Paris? I didn't know anyone. Where would I meet people?

When I turned over the card and saw the picture, the answer became clear. In front of a majestic old mansion, there was a pebbled path bordered by pansies or maybe petunias. Standing inside, looking out the window, was a woman in white whose face was hidden by the sweeping brim of her hat. Underneath were the words: "American Library in Paris, Open Daily".

Author's Note

In 2010, when I worked as the programs manager at the American Library in Paris, my colleagues Naida Kendrick Culshaw and Simon Gallo told me the story of the courageous staff who kept the ALP open during the Second World War. Naida curated an exhibit about the Library during and after the war, consulting with librarians as far away as Boise, Idaho. She is brilliant, and I think of her as my Miss Reeder. Simon has been with the Library for fifty years and knows everything about the ALP. In addition to sharing his knowledge, he went over all the Dewey Decimal numbers in this book. The numbers are the ones used today, not in 1939. He explained that each library has its own way of classifying books.

I am amazed by the bravery and dedication of the librarians at the ALP during the Second World War. Traits that continue in the staff today. Researching the novel took several years. During this time, Director Audrey Chapuis and Assistant Director Abigail Altaian were extremely supportive, sharing stories, documents and contacts. I met Boris Netchaeff's children, Hélène and Oleg. From them, I learned of Boris's experience in the military as well as information about his family. Boris's wife Anna was a countess, Comtesse (*née*) Grabbé; Boris did not hold a title but his ancestors were all titled princes or counts. When Anna and Boris left Russia, they left everything behind. Hélène was mentioned in the *The Paris Library* — she was in the apartment when the Gestapo burst in and shot her father. She wrote: "During my childhood I spent many days at the American Library . . . I was only a few months old when Papa carried me to the library . . . I still remember the sound of the beautiful parquet that creaked or crunched when someone walked fast, or the smell of books, and other details such as closed rooms where I was not allowed to go. I wondered why, and I still think that there might be people who were hidden." The Library used every available square inch of space, so Hélène's comment made me wonder if the librarians hid Jewish subscribers during the war.

Boris worked at the Library until the age of sixty-five. He died in 1982 at the age of eighty. Hélène said he was "*increvable*" (relentless or puncture-proof), despite being shot in the lung three times by the Gestapo and inhaling a pack of Gitanes per day.

When Miss Dorothy Reeder returned to the States, she raised money and awareness for the Red Cross in Florida. She then worked at the Biblioteca Nacional in Bogotá, Colombia, before rejoining the staff at the Library of Congress. Thanks to the American Library Association Archives, Miss Reeder's top-secret report on life in Paris during the war is available online. I am grateful to Cara Bertram and Lydia Tang at the ALA

Archives for their support. It was a pleasure to read Miss Reeder's correspondence and to share it with you in this book. My favourite letter was to her colleague Helen Fickweiler.

> One of the hardest things I have ever had to do is ask you and Peter to leave the Library and go back home. I know, however, it is the only right and just decision and both my head and heart will function much easier the day I know you are safe and sound in New York.
> Words cannot express my deep gratitude for your loyalty and devotion in staying with us through such difficult and trying times. Your work has always been excellent, and without your knowledge and efficiency, I doubt if we would be in a position to carry on.

Miss Reeder mentions the money that Helen should receive from the Library fund in New York when she arrives — $ 100, the equivalent of a month's salary — and the letter of recommendation she will receive. The Directress closes her letter with: "As for you, if ever I have a personnel, no matter where I am, you shall be first on my list of co-workers, dear Helen, how can I ever thank you, or tell you what I feel."

Helen Fickweiler and Peter Oustinoff got married when they returned to the States. Kate Wells of the Providence Public Library shared an article from the

19 June 1941 edition of the *Evening Bulletin*. "Miss Fickweiler lost 12 pounds during her stay in Nazi-occupied Paris and she says she doesn't want to look at another turnip as long as she lives after being forced to consume the vegetable in so many different guises." Helen and Peter's granddaughter Alexis wrote: "Helen had been working with the resistance movement in Paris and met Peter there. He was also with the Allied forces and went on to work with the US, French and Russian forces. Helen was a librarian in New York at the Chemists Club and later at the University of Vermont."

The bookkeeper Miss Wedd returned from the internment camp and worked at the Library until her retirement. I have a lovely photo of her at her retirement party. Her face is radiant and she is wearing a corsage. Evangeline Turnbull and her daughter both worked at the Library until war was declared. As Canadians, and thus part of the Commonwealth, they were considered British subjects and enemy aliens. They returned to Canada in June 1940.

Dr Hermann Fuchs, the Bibliotheksschutz or "Library Protector" in charge of the intellectual activity in Occupied France, Belgium and the Netherlands, returned to Berlin after the war and remained a librarian. It was not Fuchs but Dr Weiss and Dr Leibrandt, the latter a specialist on Eastern Europe, who organised the pillaging of Slavic libraries in Paris. Martine Poulain, an expert on French libraries, writes: "The exact role that Fuchs played remains difficult to determine. Considered with goodwill [*bienveillance*] by his French colleagues before, during and after the war, he was without a doubt more involved in the Nazi wrongdoings than the collective memory will allow." Dr Fuchs left Paris with German troops on 14 August 1944. He wrote to a French colleague: "I leave as I came, a friend of French libraries and of certain French librarians . . . First under the orders of Mr Wermke, then as head of the service of libraries, I did my best to not let the ties that unite us break. I did not always succeed in what I wanted to do, and I could not help all those who asked. Often, circumstances were stronger than I was; often, military necessities forced me to give up on actions that I'd begun. It is up to you French to judge my conduct."

In her memoir *Shadows Lengthen* (Scribner, 1949), Clara de Chambrun wrote that Dr Fuchs warned the ALP staff to be careful because the Gestapo was laying traps, and that she was later summoned by him to explain why the Library collection contained anti-German material. The Countess also described the time a subscriber threatened to denounce the Library. Denunciation letters were rampant at this time. One source claims three to five million such letters were sent, another claims 150,000 to 500,000. I created the denunciation letters about the Library; however, they were modelled on letters in the archives of the Mémorial de la Shoah, France's Holocaust Museum. The letters that Odile finds in her father's office are real. These letters, filled with such hate and anger, are hard to read. Many letters are violent and irrational. Most are anonymous and criticise family members, friends and co-workers. In addition to denouncing

Jewish people, accusations range from listening to the BBC to saying negative things about the Germans, to the infidelity of wives whose husbands were POWs, to people who bought or sold goods on the black market.

The events of the book are based on actual people and events, but I did change some elements. In real life, it was the secretary Miss Frikart who accompanied the Countess to the Nazi headquarters to answer to Dr Fuchs. It was Miss Reeder who said about books that "No other thing possesses that mystical faculty to make people see with other people's eyes. The Library is a bridge of books between cultures," when she publicised the Soldiers' Service. Also, I condensed time after Miss Reeder's first encounter with Dr Fuchs. The Countess was away at her country home. Her meeting with Miss Reeder and the staff took place a few months later.

My goal in writing the book was to share this little-known chapter of Second World War history and to capture the voices of the courageous librarians who defied the Nazis in order to help subscribers and to share a love of literature. I wanted to explore the relationships that make us who we are, as well as how we help and hinder each other. Language is a gate that we can open and close on people. The words we use shape perception as do the books we read, the stories we tell each other and the stories we tell ourselves. The foreign staff and subscribers of the Library were considered enemy aliens and several were interned. Jewish subscribers were not allowed to enter the Library, and many were later killed in concentration camps. A friend said she believes that in reading stories set in the Second World War, people like to ask themselves what they would have done. I think a better question to ask is what can we do now to ensure that libraries and learning are accessible to all and that we treat people with dignity and compassion.

The American Library in Paris:
A History

The foundations of the American Library in Paris were laid in 1917, when the American Library Association's Library War Service shipped over two million books donated by libraries and individuals to US soldiers serving abroad. These wartime donations formed the original core collection of the American Library in Paris, which was officially incorporated as an independent non-profit institution on 20 May 1920 at 10, rue de l'Elysée.

The Library revolutionised the role of libraries and librarians in France, introducing an open shelves system — which, unlike more traditional libraries, allowed readers and members to browse at leisure — and the popular Story Hour, much beloved by younger patrons. Throughout the 1920s, the Library was also a favourite haunt of the famous Lost Generation, counting among its habitués Ernest Hemingway, Gertrude Stein, Henry Miller and Edith Wharton.

With the outbreak of the Second World War, the Library — based at 9, rue de Téhéran since 1936 —

readied itself: doors and windows were reinforced, gas masks gathered, the Soldiers' Service launched to provide books to Allied troops. For Directress Dorothy Reeder, and for her staff, "There was never a thought we should close". When Paris fell to the Nazis in 1940, they refused to be cowed by the Occupation, instead risking their lives by hand-delivering books to Jewish subscribers who were deemed no longer "desirable", in the Library or anywhere else. Their courage ensured the Library remained "an open window on the free world" throughout the war.

Today, the American Library in Paris can be found at 10, rue du Général Camou. It is the largest English-language lending library on the continent, and regular host to world-famous authors. Its core values — a celebration of the written word, of language and literature, culture and community — remain unchanged. And inside each book in the collection, an ex libris, bearing the original motto: "After the darkness of war, the light of books".

Acknowledgements

Un grand merci to agent *extraordinaire* Heather Jackson for her kindness and for finding the perfect house as a home for *The Paris Library*, and her co-agent Linda Kaplan for bringing the book to the attention of agents and editors all over the world.

Tremendous thanks to the team at Atria, from my editor Trish Todd who convinced me with her first words, 'You had me at the Dewey Decimal System,' to Libby McGuire, Lindsay Sagnette, Suzanne Donahue, Leah Hays, Mark LaFlaur, Ana Perez, Kristin Fassler, Lisa Sciambra, Wendy Sheanin, Stuart Smith, Isabel DaSilva, Dana Trocker for their support and enthusiasm. Heartfelt thanks to Lisa Highton and Katherine Burdon and the team at Two Roads in the UK. A round of applause to copy editors Tricia Callahan and Morag Lyall for their attention to all my details.

Gratitude to my husband, sister, and parents, as well as to friends and colleagues who read drafts and whose encouragement sustained me: Laurel Zuckerman, Diane Vadino, Chris Vanier, Wendy Salter, Mary Sun de Nerciat, Adélaïde Pralon, Anna Polonyi, Maggie Phillips, Emily Monaco, Jade Maître, Anca Metiu, Alannah Moore,

Lizzy Kremer, Kaaren Kitchell, Rachel Kesselman, Marie Howzelle, Odile Hellier, Clydette and Charles de Groot, Jim Grady, Susan Jane Gilman, Andrea Delumea, Maddalena Cavaciuti, Amanda Bestor-Siegal, and Melissa Amster.

I grew up loving libraries and bookshops. We need such spaces more than ever, and I thank the dedicated, hard-working booksellers and librarians who create these literary havens.